THE STARS OF

MOUNT QUIXX

S.M. BEIKO

Published by ECW Press
665 Gerrard Street East
Toronto, Ontario, Canada M4M 1Y2
416-694-3348 / info@ecwpress.com

Editor for the Press: Jen R. Albert
Substantive Editor: Jennifer Hale
Cover design: Lisa Marie Pompilio

LIBRARY AND ARCHIVES CANADA CATALOGUING
IN PUBLICATION

Title: Stars of Mount Quixx / S.M. Beiko.

Names: Beiko, S. M., author.

Description: Series statement: The Brindlewatch quintet ; book one

Identifiers: Canadiana (print) 20220430926 | Canadiana (ebook) 20220430950

ISBN 978-1-77041-695-6 (softcover)
ISBN 978-1-77852-121-8 (PDF)
ISBN 978-1-77852-122-5 (Kindle)
ISBN 978-1-77852-120-1 (ePub)

Classification: LCC PS8603.E428444 S73 2023 | DDC C813/.6—dc23

This book is funded in part by the Government of Canada. *Ce livre est financé en partie par le gouvernement du Canada.* We acknowledge the support of the Canada Council for the Arts. *Nous remercions le Conseil des arts du Canada de son soutien.* We acknowledge the funding support of the Ontario Arts Council (OAC), an agency of the Government of Ontario. We also acknowledge the support of the Government of Ontario through the Ontario Book Publishing Tax Credit, and through Ontario Creates.

ONTARIO ARTS COUNCIL
CONSEIL DES ARTS DE L'ONTARIO
an Ontario government agency
un organisme du gouvernement de l'Ontario

Canada Council
for the Arts
Conseil des arts
du Canada

PRINTED AND BOUND IN CANADA

PRINTING: FRIESENS   5 4 3 2 1

MIX
Paper from
responsible sources
FSC® C016245
www.fsc.org

For Peter, first, who believed in Quixx before he saw it on the page. And for all of you who look up at the stars with wonder, and dream.

PROLOGUE

I can handle whatever Mount Quixx throws at me, Klaus had joked, before work had swallowed the weeks and she'd left him that last time. He was always so sure of himself. And Camille had been sure of him, too.

But the smoke peeling off the mountain now was thick and cruel — the best evidence that there had been an explosion, save the dull ringing in her head. So many flares of sharp, jaundiced light that shook the world, still there when Camille closed her eyes. Neighbours screamed, running down the street in their nighties. The night was alive with fear.

But will we *survive what Mount Quixx has thrown at* us?

Camille tightened her fist around her scarf, her heart keeping time with the hallway's carriage clock. She should've hidden beneath the kitchen table throughout the blasts, but her body wouldn't allow it. She'd watched it all, silent as stone. The house had been sturdily built and wasn't about to be knocked down. Neither was Camille. What it came down to was this: Klaus was on that mountain, which had just been haloed in celestial bombs. Camille was sturdy, but not sturdy enough to lose him.

She counted the seconds between the aftershocks, held firm to the counter as broken china littered the parquet.

The house was still. She'd waited long enough. Pushing her spectacles up her nose, she was a flurry out the front door.

The hackled mountain next to where Camille had grown up was practically on the doorstep, which is why this arrangement had been so perfect for her and Klaus. Except now her doorstep was ringed in fire and doubt. The house was located across from a clearing, and then the mountain, but now there was a crater where the clearing had been, a quarter mile wide and charred. Camille barely pulled her spectator shoes from the edge in time, arms spiralling as she landed on the road behind her. She'd already waited for the worst of the blazes to subside, yet still the air scorched her skin. She pulled her legs back under her anyway and got up, shaking. She tried to peer down the street to see if there was a better way. But smoke — no, fog? — seemed to rise from the crater, rise and spread, its fingers greedy, swallowing Camille's neighbourhood before her eyes.

She looked up at the bent spire, up and up to the place where she knew the observatory was, hidden now by fog and maybe a little bit of doubt. She knew if she went directly down this new slope the crater had made, it would be the most direct route to Klaus. The fastest. Never mind that it was all crackling brimstone; this had to be just another of the mountain's many tricks.

That is, *if* the observatory was still there.

Camille shut her eyes. Tried to listen. *Tell me what I should do*, she begged the night air, searching for the voice that had always guided her. *Please tell me that he's all right.*

No answer. Just the wind. Just the fog. The barest sense of a great pain. So she scrambled into the chasm as fast as she could — she had to get up the mountain, and to Klaus, whatever the cost.

It was taking much too long to reach the bottom of the crater, too many throat-scorching gasps, Camille splaying out her arms and teetering blindly. She hadn't even tried to find the launcher in the chaos — *that* would have been the most direct route — but with all the fog and the possible damage to the landing zone, who knew where she'd end up. More questions shot through her: *What if I'm too late? What if the telescope caved in on top of him while he was scribbling in his damned notebook? What if the sky has fallen and all of them are* . . .

She shook her head, catching a dangling root in her outstretched hand and hanging there. *Keep going.* She put her feet back down. Soon she was at the bottom of the crater, the mountain ahead and up. Red embers and burning brush showed her the way to the steep mountain pass, and though every step was peril, Camille knew it was time to forget everything. Forget everything and let the mountain take her where she needed to go.

To keep her steady, she imagined Klaus's brogue, as clear as if he were whispering directly into her throbbing skull: *Physics are useless here*, he joked. The scarf on Camille's shoulders floated around her head as she turned a corner. Her feet slipped off the ground as she entered a familiar pocket of geographic anti-gravity. *The mountain has its own rules.* That, she'd always known. And she'd learned them well. But she expected that all to change after tonight. Camille grabbed for anything she could on the rock face and pulled herself upward.

You can do anything if you're foolish enough. That proverb had been hers. As she climbed higher and higher, her body half-floating as if it were a bit of dandelion, making progress around the dark trees that bearded the slate. The stench of smoke became enough to lead the way. All she had to do was keep going up.

But Camille's panic finally caught up with her body. Her skin prickled as the hot wind chomped her heels. She couldn't spare a hand to find the next hold. The tears were a surprise, the air searing her light-starved eyes. Camille never had patience for tears. She needed to take another step. Yet when she tried, she lost purchase and slipped, hand and foot, the upside-down momentum sending her flying upward and out of control.

The mountain caught her like a cradle, with a slab of rock at her back. As the air came back to her lungs, she tried to look ahead, above. There was no sky, but the mountain was a bleak burnt temple blending with the dark. Her body pressed into the rock and she heard the mountain. *Pain*, it echoed. *My pain. And yours.*

Camille permitted one sob to bubble up, burying her face in the scarf as she thought of the small, strange family she had built on this mountain — a mountain that was hurting but which had betrayed her all the same. Her tears floated up past her head. The fabric still smelled like Klaus: resin and spilled ink and bergamot tea and country air. She held on to that. She knew with terrible certainty that she'd never smell him again.

"Please," came a voice almost as miserable as her thoughts. "Please don't cry."

Camille stiffened, her head turning wildly as she adjusted her glasses, her eyes, and tried to see what she didn't want to see, but what she must.

"Where are you?" she croaked, trying to find relief. "Are you hurt? Is he—"

"I wasn't brave enough."

Camille held fast to the outcrop of rock so that she wouldn't float away, turning towards the broken voice.

"It's all right," she said into the dark. It was very much *not* all right, but she needed to be strong. Strong for both their sakes. She held an arm out. "I'm here now."

Camille couldn't shrink from the whimper, from the sharp arrowhead pain it sent through her as the figure clarified. There was nowhere for her to go. The whimper fell into an aching sob.

"I *didn't know* — I tried. I — I was . . ."

Camille would be surprised at herself later, that she had no reaction save numb silence as she stared at Klaus's body held close in four shaking indigo arms. Even in this night of shadow and fog and long-extinguished fire, the white of his tight curls still shone, brilliant, as he had been. Brilliant as a *star,* one that would no longer shine, save in memories.

The mountain had nothing direct to say about it. Not now. But Camille swore she heard the faintest offering — *We can one day heal from this. Just not yet.*

1

THE BELL'S FOR THE BIRDS

She'd let her mind wander for just that one second. *I'm dancing, as always. I know the dance well. But somehow I've lost the steps. The music is still playing — but what comes next? The air is filled with smoke and fire and butterflies . . .*

"What's this now?"

Ivory broke the silence in the car as it came down the patchy hills and valleys outside of Ferren City.

"What?" Constance broke out of her daydream like a ship's figurehead through a storm. This was her first time driving outside of the City, alone no less. Her eyes didn't leave the road, but her mind had. She was definitely *not* a daydreamer. Where had that come from?

Ivory unstuck her face from the window. "Are you blind, Connie? The light's fading and there're no clouds out."

Her sister was right, even with the barb. Constance checked the dashboard clock. The sun should be bright in the morning sky, but it was slowly choked out by a soupy haze. As they went deeper into the valley, it only seemed to get darker.

Constance shook her head. "Maybe there's a fire. At a farm, or something." *Smoke and fire and butterflies . . .* She tried to refocus her mind on driving.

"We'd be able to smell it," Ivory countered, rolling down the window of their parents' brand new car and inhaling grossly.

Constance sighed, unwilling to get into another match of Who's the Better Detective this early.

"I'm sure it's nothing that won't clear up by the end of the day." But Ivory, as usual, wasn't about to let up.

"Maybe it's coming from Quixx," she guessed. "Maybe the whole town's on fire and we'll have to turn around and go home, and Mother and Father will give up trying to send us away for the summer."

"Ivory!" Constance snapped. "Stop wishing for disasters. One day they'll come true." Constance swallowed the retort: *Mother or Father could send us to the other side of Brindlewatch, but the split continent wouldn't be a big enough distance between us and them.*

The younger sister rolled her eyes. "Oh, Constance. Always so proper. Don't pretend you're remotely invested in this trip. A disaster would be more likely than any of this working out."

Constance pressed her mouth into a tight line. She wasn't about to admit anything to her fourteen-year-old sister. Now wasn't the time. She *needed* this trip to be a success. She would not succumb to a bitter back-and-forth when they hadn't even reached their destination. Constance would keep her mind open.

"A summer getaway?" her father had repeated after Constance had made the suggestion, barely looking up from the documents on his desk or turning to face his daughter from his wingback chair. It was just before the end of term, and Constance was . . . more than desperate. "What for?"

He'd sounded amused, as if she were a child again, tugging on his pant leg and asking for another pair of dancing shoes.

But she was eighteen now, almost graduated, and her needs were not as frivolous. She was trapped aboard a freight train hurtling towards a blown-out bridge, and she had been sitting calmly in coach sipping tea for far too long.

She'd found her own voice just long enough to stammer, "Wouldn't it be nice? All of us, together? Like . . . old times! Before I go away for good, to college and . . ." A wilted hand gesture, signifying whatever came after that, and a weak smile to seal it. "Well, Father?"

A creak of leather and cherrywood. Her father's pen laid flat but still a threat. Constance was less surprised that he said *fine*, and more that she had orchestrated all of this on her own: one last attempt. A weak S.O.S. to be saved by summer's end, before college, before everything changed forever, one shot to convince Mother and Father, before—

"In all my reading," Ivory went on, her leonine face buried in the crinkled brochure, "I've never heard of Quixx. And it's so close to Ferren. 'A gentle valley hamlet hemmed in by hills and forests at the foot of a stately mountain.' Sounds like pastoral propaganda to me."

"And you'd be the expert," Constance said, plucking the broadsheet away and sliding it into the glove compartment. "You've read that thing end to end. Leave something to be surprised by."

Ivory made a show of throwing herself backward into her seat. "I'm trying to take a leaf out of your book, little Miss Girl Scout. Always be prepared."

And Constance was prepared. Usually. She swallowed the rising panic, unsure what was getting her worked up this time. *Just focus on the road.*

"A seaside resort would've been more diverting," Ivory said, digging around in the extremely large army bag at her feet. "The time I spent gathering and reading marine life periodicals from the school library could have me on the faculty by next term."

"*Gathering*," Constance snorted. "You mean stealing. You'd better return those books by next—"

"And anyway, we both know they chose this place with the same amount of thought they do everything. Father must have shut his eyes and determined *Quixx is the place* depending on where his cigar ashes fell." A snort, then a meek glance out the window. "Though there must be *something* interesting here. Maybe something to do with Father's business. Or Mother's socialite-ing. Otherwise, they wouldn't be joining us at all . . ."

Constance's jaw worked, her fingers tightening on the steering wheel. To say their parents had been absent most of their lives might be an understatement, but the only one who'd say it was Ivory. Constance took a different tack. "At least it's a vacation, out of the City. And when was the last time we all went away as a family? I think it will be a perfectly splendid experience." This attempt at a silver lining was met with a pink tongue.

"*If* they actually come," Ivory countered. "It could also be a neat scheme to send us even farther away. Out of sight, out of mind. More so than usual."

That time, Constance did take her eyes off the road, regarding her little sister slumped and staring out the window at the ever-fogging landscape. She seemed like she belonged out there in the smoke and the smudge — all scrawny knees, mud-stained stockings, snarly hair, and dark-circled violet eyes. Though this trip wasn't so far away from their daily lives as she'd wanted, at least Constance would get some time alone with Ivory. The last school year had been harder than ever. Children were cruel to those who didn't conform, and Ivory had been drifting further and further into a world of her own making.

And that was both the problem and perhaps the solution.

Ivory always had some kind of plan for her future. Even if it changed constantly, at least she was determined. Any time Constance tried to imagine life beyond the path set out for her, there was only darkness, a fog thicker than the one before them now. And though the elder sister was as ever the embodiment of What Was Proper, the younger was the absolute inverse — all mess and chaos and "freedom." It had Constance more than worried. Rules were all that kept her upright. Without them, she would crumble; she was convinced that rules were the only thing keeping her together, even now.

And Ivory was on a dangerous path; she'd been shirking the rules all her life, and her own future was now as uncertain as Constance's — though Ivory didn't yet realize it. It didn't matter. Constance could be just as determined. She would spend the summer steering Ivory towards the right course. She had to.

"A summer getaway." That was when her father had swivelled in his chair to face Constance at last. "A getaway can sometimes mean an escape. You haven't changed your mind, have you?"

Ivory perked up and Constance was thrust back into the present as a very decayed hand-painted sign came suddenly into view, barely distinguishable through the creeping tendrils of fog and scraggly overgrowth. Constance couldn't believe she was flicking the headlights on.

"'Mount Quixx, five miles,'" Ivory read, craning against her seatbelt to keep it in sight as long as possible. "That sign looked a thousand years old. I wonder if I could try carbon dating it."

"Sit back, Ivory," Constance snipped. Ivory huffed, crossing her arms.

"I don't think I'd know what to do on a vacation with Mother and Father," she went on, gnawing on her fingernail. Constance flicked her hand without turning her head. "Being raised by nannies and tutors my entire life hasn't exactly resulted in a strong parental bond."

Constance couldn't help her ensuing smirk. "You might have bonded with the nannies and tutors, if you weren't so hellbent on sabotaging them."

Ivory shared the grin. She'd revelled in a naughty streak as much as Constance took pride in avoiding it.

She knew Ivory wanted to bond, but she couldn't help defending their parents again. "Mother and Father invested a lot of money for our educations and upbringing." She took the next corner with maybe too much care. "We should be grateful for all the opportunities life, and their sacrifices, have afforded us."

"Grateful." The word came out bitter, and Ivory was back to staring out the window through her black tangles. "Soon I will thank them thoroughly by running away and making many exciting discoveries, with treasure enough to fund my endless adventures. Besides, all the money in the world never made either of our parents very happy."

Constance didn't know what else to say. She could lead the debate team or organize the glee club or sew a nice flag for the charm and etiquette society, but talking about feelings wasn't what made her class president four years running.

Constance almost jumped when an ornate sign flashed into view:

Welcome to Quixx, the Township Extraordinary!
Melodious Mountain Majesty!
Population ~~709 652 503~~ 112

Ivory ripped open the glove box and tented the sunny brochure in her bony hands again, comparing reality to the faded photos.

"You're *sure* this is the place?"

Constance chewed her lip, a habit she'd had her own wrist slapped for more than once. The car bumped the sisters out of their seats as the road went from paved to cobblestones. When they drove under a wrought-iron archway that spelled out *QUIXX* in rusted cursive, Constance slowed. The mist hung around like it *owned* the place.

Constance wanted to see the bright side, but in the grim, nothing bright could survive. The electric lampposts were already lit. The grand elms adorning the blocks were black skeletons snagging lopsided brick buildings. After taking a wrong turn around a rusted fountain whose angel statue was woefully decapitated, the sisters figured they'd landed on the wrong side of *Melodious Mountain Majesty*.

Until the mountain broke the grey.

"Stop for a second, Connie?" Ivory asked.

Though she'd already put the brake on, Constance hesitated to get out. "I think we should just find the boarding house before we—"

But Ivory was already outside, studying the brochure carefully with the sickly mountain silhouetting her wiry body. Constance shook the cobwebs out of her head, getting out to join Ivory when she realized how much her hands ached from clenching the steering wheel.

She shut the door behind her and took in what she could. The houses seemed waterlogged, rooftops sagging and iron fences poking paranoid out of the dirt. The air itself was damp and chill as it stirred vapour curls around her ankles, despite it being summer. Constance pulled her hunter green jacket closer over her blouse, smoothing the wrinkles of stiff hours from her tartan skirt. Was the town deserted?

"I just don't understand all this *fog*," Constance said, trying to break the silence with something that could take her mind off the dark mass looming in front of them. A strange inkling was teasing her heart, like a jagged fork testing a steak.

Twitter-tweet. Constance spun, but saw no birds.

"'Mount Quixx is a wonder to behold,'" Ivory read in her best nasal drawl, dismissing the noise. "'It is the highest mountain in Old Kiplington to boast a near-vertical ascent from base to peak. It has rarely been scaled, though this mountain, and the range behind it, boasted the century's finest lumber for miles around . . .'"

As Ivory went on, Constance couldn't help but walk ahead, searching for clarity in the mountain's mist-obscured face. She could make out the shapes of trees, jutting horizontally like broken teeth. The peak was hidden entirely, its curve a broken finger accusing the sky.

"'. . . flora and fauna surrounding the mountain have yet to be catalogued by a botanical authority . . .'" Ivory's voice faded in and out as Constance drew closer to Mount Quixx. There was something hypnotizing in the way the fog peeled away or clutched it close. Shapes, questions. A fluttering collection of malformed sounds. She listened hard, something coming through the winding canals of her ear—

"*Connie!*"

Constance woke from her trance a half step from a vast trench. She wheeled back, heart in her throat, and Ivory took a hold of her sister's arm before she could topple.

"Jolting Jordana," Constance breathed. She looked down. The trench curved at the edges like a crater. The slide down was at least twenty feet, and what would be met at the bottom was just as mysterious as the rest of the mountain. And likely as dangerous.

Ivory didn't waste any time. She got down on her knees right at that edge. "Nifty!" she crooned. "The brochure doesn't mention a crater at the mountain base like this. Do you think there's a way down?"

Constance pulled her sister back up. "I don't think we should be here," she urged. "Let's find the boarding house. This place gives me the unaccountable shivers."

"*Everything* gives you the shivers." Ivory rolled her eyes, rubbing the dirt deeper into the darts of her shorts. "I think it's Coolsville."

Constance nudged Ivory ahead, turning away. "Slang is sloppy," she muttered, her eyes hooked on the leering outcrop behind her. The mist was still purling and shifting. She suddenly longed for the crowded chaos of Ferren City to trample the eerie silence carving a hollow in her heart.

"Hello, my dears!"

Constance jumped. A shadow emerged from the fog, echoed by the same birdsong she'd sworn she'd heard earlier. Constance held fast to Ivory's arm as the figure approached.

"Ow, Connie, geez!" Ivory yanked away, rubbing her shoulder.

From the knotted fume strolled a hunched, thick-set brown woman, a basket filled with persimmons and bread on the crook of her sweatered arm. It was not only the vivid colours of the fruit that caught Constance's eye but the bullfinch twirling around the lady's white coif before it nested there, satisfied.

"Um, ma'am . . ." Ivory began, about to point out the bird, but Constance pushed her hand down. The woman peered inquisitively from a pair of giant, round glasses that magnified her eyes tenfold.

"You're lost, aren't you?" The woman's voice had the sing-songy pitch of her avian companion. "No wonder Frederic was making a fuss all the way from Farrowmarket."

The finch puffed its red chest out like it understood the woman.

Constance winced, attempted a smile. "Not surprising in this fog." She stepped forward and offered her hand, glad that Quixx wasn't a ghost town after all. "I'm Constance Ivyweather, and this is my sister, Ivory."

"I can't say I see a great deal anyway, fog or no!" the lady chuckled, and only when her hand completely offshot Constance's did she realize she was extremely nearsighted. But Constance had no time to backpedal, for the lady found Constance's hand quickly, clasping it tightly.

"I've been expecting you little Ivyweathers!" she sang, jostling Constance's arm in tendon-ripping excitement. "Come, dears, I'll take you to the Happy Bell straight away!"

The eldest Ivyweather pitched forward when the landlady let go of her, mid-drag, but she managed an uncertain squawk. "You must be Ms. Pomegranate?"

The lady chuckled. "Oh, that was *last week*, dearest. I've decided to go with something a little more subdued. I'm Ms. Bougainvillea, now. Come, come, we have to settle you!"

Ivory didn't bother stifling her grin when Constance wrenched free.

"We'll have to move our car," Constance cut in, patting the landlady's knotted shoulder. "You can ride along with us and tell us the way."

"Don't be silly, dear," she said, her face an elegant kaleidoscope of wrinkles as she grinned. "You're already here."

With a skillful wrist-flick, Ms. Bougainvillea undid the latch on the gate beside her. The fog pulled back like a curtain in the wind's fingertips to reveal a large manor, unkempt and thickly overgrown with stunted Almonia creeper. A shingle hanging on a broken chain over the front steps, equally rotting, proudly boasted *The Happy Bell Boarding House*.

"Oh," Constance said.

"Good thing we stopped," Ivory piped up, making a triumphant beeline for the car.

The fine hairs on Constance's neck prickled. She took a look over her shoulder at the shadow of Mount Quixx behind Ivory struggling in the trunk. How was she going to sleep with something like *that* across the road, appraising her as if it were a thing alive?

But Ivory was too excited to take in the scenery. She'd nabbed both their suitcases and her giant army bag, hustling into the badly kept yard like a sherpa.

"The vacation may not be lost yet, Connie!" she bellowed. "We're so close to the mountain, *which means* we can explore it later and uncover all of its dastardly secrets! And the bird-brained landlady — literally! This is going in my memoir."

Ivory pressed past and up behind Ms. Bougainvillea, who was having a tough time at the stairs. Constance sprang out of her reverie.

"Let me help you with that!" Constance took the basket on the crook of her own arm and linked the other with Ms. Bougainvillea's.

"My, how gallant of you! It's these old bones slowing me down, that's all."

Ms. Bougainvillea sighed with the effort of the last step, and with a deep breath and her palms at the swell of her back, she stopped altogether. Ivory and Constance waited, exchanging glances.

"Gah!" Ms. Bougainvillea exclaimed, causing the sisters to jump only slightly. "The key. Now where did I—"

Constance noticed the bullfinch, Frederic, had disappeared from the landlady's hair, only to return with two much larger starlings. One of the starlings dropped a huge iron key deftly into Ms. Bougainvillea's outstretched palm, then fluttered off.

"There we are!" she sighed, patting down the wood panelling until she found the lock, fitting the key inside. With a grunt, she thrust open the double doors, throwing a proud arm to give a panorama of the foyer.

"Welcome to the Happy Bell, my dears!" she cried, nearly whacking Ivory in the face as she spread her hands wide. "'This place is your home as long as you're here, ring the bell twice — let your woes disappear.' Oh I have *missed* our motto!"

Constance's well of questions was dammed at the sheer size of the house. Given the landlady, she didn't have trouble guessing why the place had fallen from what may have been some kind of glory days. But the air of old grandeur still hung like familiar gossip in every inch of faded mahogany and peeling crown moulding.

"Come, come! We'll get tea started, and you can settle in. Your room is up the stairs and to your right, first door in the hall. You two will be in the Butterfly Room. Our other rooms are, ah, indisposed. As in . . . inhospitable."

Meaning our room likely isn't far behind, Constance groaned inwardly.

"We have to *share* a room?" Ivory cried. Constance took her suitcase and motioned Ivory to zip it.

"If you need a hand," Ms. Bougainvillea went on, steadying the furniture she bumped into, "I'm sure Bernard could make himself useful." A goose, which had been dozing in the corner, honked, insulted, before it wandered off.

Ms. Bougainvillea turned with a sudden afterthought, making the sisters flinch. "Do be careful going up the stairs, though, girls. There's a creak in the middle I'm sure is about to give."

They nodded and started forward. In the middle of rearranging her silvery tresses, Ms. Bougainvillea squawked. They jumped.

"And if you hear a scurrying, don't be alarmed. The walls are thin, the mice are populous, but they're part of the birds of prey benefits package, so there's not much we can do but bear it."

Whatever that means. Constance felt her eye twitch. The Ivyweathers smiled sheepishly at Ms. Bougainvillea's blank expression, thinking that was the last of it. They turned to go, Ms. Bougainvillea let out a yowl, and the girls shrieked in surprise, but when they turned back to assess what was the matter (if anything), the landlady just smiled serenely.

Constance desperately wanted to sit down. "Tea, Ms. Bougainvillea?"

"Yes, yes, of course! Can't get along without, now can we?" Ms. Bougainvillea finally pressed the front doors shut and scurried away to the kitchen, bumping into an end table and nearly knocking over a gigantic Icanian vase.

As soon as the landlady had gone, Ivory burst out laughing at last. Constance groaned.

"But your *face*," Ivory pointed.

"It's not funny, Ivory. She's very old and obviously confused."

"At least she's *interesting*. I hope I'm that looney when I'm a hundred."

"You're looney enough *now*."

Constance felt a sharp draft snag her hair. She went to close the nearby window, but she struggled against it. They were all nailed open.

Then Ivory cried, "*Duck!*"

Constance pivoted and saw a massive black shape swooping down on her and careening towards the window. She managed to leap out of the way before being impaled on the open beak.

"Was it a duck?" Constance shouted, trying to see where the bird had flown off to. The question was underscored by the rattle of crockery shattering in the kitchen.

"Close enough," Ivory muttered, awestruck and pointing at the banisters lining the immense staircase that rose and split the foyer. Though she didn't see a duck, there was a gathering of birds, large and small, perched on the woodwork or cutting a figure on the balustrade.

The patrons of the indoor aviary were uninterested in the new visitors, instead fluttering in and out of either the house proper or the various rooms within. It seemed like the seeing-eye birds of the Happy Bell all had important tasks to do, and mucking about with introductions was a waste of valuable time.

An oriole came to Ivory's shoulder and nipped at her tangles, clucking notes of disapproval. Constance decided to take the encroaching weirdness in stride, for now. "Maybe they'll get you to comb your hair, at least." She shooed the bird off, still vigilant about communicable diseases.

Ivory turned her nose up, grinned, and dashed for the stairs.

"Wait, don't!" Constance fumbled and took off after her.

"Live a little, Connie!" Ivory called, her tongue out, as her foot struck a stair and went right through. The fall was so sudden that Constance, following close, tripped right over Ivory and landed in a heap on top of her. Their bags exploded, unmentionables everywhere. A chorus of chattering — laughing? — birds lit out from the hall.

It seemed Ms. Bougainvillea had more success than them, appearing with two trays in her hands and everything effectively arrayed.

"Unpacked already? So quickly, too!"

"Expedient," Constance grunted, rearranging her pleated skirt as she got up.

Ms. Bougainvillea was oblivious, which seemed to be her custom. "Tea, girls! Very important!"

Constance hauled Ivory out of the hole and to her feet, uninjured. They stared at the sprawling hole in the stair. Constance exhaled. "We'll just . . . patch it up later."

"Going out on a limb" — Ivory shrugged — "but I think we can leave it for the birds."

They were seated in a grand parlour that Ms. Bougainvillea referred to as the solarium. The room faced south, built, likely, to profit from the striking effect of daylight. The huge eight-foot banks of glass, of course, did not afford any light at all, caked in years of grime, and any sunlight was choked by Quixx's natural haze.

Ms. Bougainvillea didn't seem to mind, though, for she smiled, radiantly proud of the room, calling it the *crown jewel* of her estate. Without a word to the contrary, Constance quietly turned on the lights so they could at least see their tea.

"This house is very sought-after, you know." Ms. Bougainvillea nodded gravely. "They think I can't keep it up! But all of my guests have sung its praises from Ferren to Connaught. It's almost an historic landmark. Just a few more years!" She patted a nearby wall affectionately. A crack splintered up the plaster. Constance cringed.

"Are we sharing a room because of the other guests?" Ivory blurted past her fourth sugary tart. Delicious butter-filled treats were not allowed in the Ivyweather household, and despite her earlier gloom, Ivory took to their offering with the stamina of a heavyweight champ.

When Ms. Bougainvillea finally stoppered her laughter with a snort, she fanned herself. "Oh, Miss Ivory, you are a pear."

Constance frowned into her tea. She wasn't used to this kind of company, to say the least. "So no other guests, then."

Ms. Bougainvillea wiped away a tear. "My darlings, you are my first guests in decades. Not for lack of trying, mind you. But there are so many thrills in the Far Cities that no one comes out to the valley anymore. I was surprised to discover the phone still worked when your houseman made the reservation!"

Ivory pulled the folded brochure out from her plaid pocket, scanning for any clues. She thrust the paper under Constance's nose and pointed. It was dated over fifty years ago.

"People have been trickling out of here for a long time," the old lady went on, Frederic taking sneaky nips at her untouched muffin. "But there are some for whom Quixx is a fixed mark in their lives. The Stannishes have been here since the Kembran Clock of town hall started counting backward, and that was before my time. And the Motts — a proud pair, the husband off flying in the war and the wife minding the schoolhouse here with her own ideas for expansion. And of course, there're the Dannens . . ."

Constance suddenly realized she had been looking out the window, and that, despite the grime, she could still see the bent backbone of Mount Quixx, stark and sudden. She realized she was holding her teacup so tightly she was about to take off the handle.

She found herself blurting, "The mountain—" Ivory looked up at her, surprised.

"What about it, my dear?" Ms. Bougainvillea reached for her muffin, and thinking it her cup, took a sip.

Constance lost the words. Swallowed, tried again. "What I mean to ask is . . ."—she composed herself—"well, it's a very strange mountain, isn't it?"

Ms. Bougainvillea's smile deepened. "Certainly. But isn't it lovely? And so unique in its strangeosity! Why, people came to the Happy Bell simply because it's the closest boarding house to the slopes. And people have come far and wide for that mountain, let me tell you. Even a world-famous astronomer!"

"Astronomer?" Ivory perked, wide-eyed at the mention of one of her most precious fields of interest.

"Yes, and what a silly man! He came here to get away from the glare of the Far City lights and to study our stars. What a well-intentioned ninny he was." Her breath hitched and she shook her head. "But our mountain. Oh, the treasures and tragedies it has given us all!"

Ivory's chair scraped across the parquet as she sidled closer to Ms. Bougainvillea. Constance knew Ivory's sleuthing mind had been flicked on for keeps.

"What *kind* of tragedies?" Ivory asked, hands knotted under her pointed chin. She knew she should stop Ivory, but a curious thrill fluttered in Constance's chest, building momentum with each passing second.

Ms. Bougainvillea blinked. "The usual kind." She shrugged. "I'm sure much more interesting things happen in Ferren City, what with all its industry and fast living. When I was born, Quixx was a logging town! The wood from the valley and the surrounding mountains was the best in the territory, but when the forests were all but used, investors turned to the trees on Mount Quixx. It was the finest lumber anyone had yet to see on the market! But when people find a good thing, they become greedy for it."

Ivory seemed to be editing out the superfluous bits of Ms. Bougainvillea's story. "Mm-hmm, yes, yes, but the *tragedies*. Were there accidents? Mutilations? Decapitations? Political and economic collusion gone horribly awry in a torrent of bloodshed and gin?"

Constance winced. "Ivory."

Ms. Bougainvillea nodded. "Of course there were. But the real bit of trouble came when they disturbed the *inhabitants* of the mountain."

Ivory's eyes danced as she leaned in closer. "There were . . . *are* . . . people living on the mountain?"

"No, my dear, don't be silly!" Ms. Bougainvillea tried to take a bite out of her teacup. "Not people. Just the monsters."

Charged, delicious silence.

Ivory tapped her fingernails excitedly against the tabletop. "Monsters? Monsters. What does that mean? What do you mean, Miss Bee?"

She cocked her head. "Come now. You *must* have monsters in the Cities."

"In bedtime stories," Constance muttered, folding her arms. She was startled when she saw Ms. Bougainvillea's glassy, blind eyes fix precisely on her.

"You are a long way from home, Miss Constance," she warned through a cheerless smile, all evidence of vapid exuberance gone. "Do take care to remember that."

The same chill that, in the presence of Mount Quixx, had tattled its way up Constance's good nerves haunted her again. Ivory's fingernails stopped abruptly as she and her elder sister shared a quick look.

Ms. Bougainvillea waved their confusion away. "But alas, that was long ago. And that was the Happy Bell's finest hour! Attending the needs of business tycoons and lumbermen alike by the hundreds every season! So many stories to entertain every night in the dining hall. But they all should have had more sense to know what they were getting into."

She groaned to her rickety feet. Constance bolted up, propriety interrupting her cynical wonder.

"Never mind," Ms. Bougainvillea huffed. "Come, I will show you the house properly!"

Frederic trilled with concern around his mistress's ear before settling on her shoulder, head tilted. Ms. Bougainvillea sighed, groping for Constance's arm.

"He's being very overbearing today," she snorted. Constance just smiled, grateful for the distraction.

The three ladies took to the foyer, Ivory leading the way as the old innkeeper rattled on about the rusted bell that was set into the wall above the doorway. A gift, she said, from a Captain Fairway and his freighter *Le Belle Joyeux* over seventy years ago.

"I'm sure many interesting people have passed through that door." Constance tried to change the subject as they took to the stairs, careful to avoid the gaping hole covered temporarily with an old blouse.

"And they all left their mark on Quixx, one way or another," affirmed Ms. Bougainvillea.

Ivory stopped at the mid-landing, staring up into a portrait that hung there above an empty urn. With a passing glance, Constance took in the portrait's imposing figure, with white curling hair, set against a starry sky. Someone had rubbed away the paint on the part of the canvas where the face once was.

"And what about that astronomer?" Ivory asked. "Did he find his stars when he went up the mountain?"

"Heaven only knows." Ms. Bougainvillea blinked her rheumy eyes. "He went up the mountain and died there. Doomed. Just like everybody else."

2

SLANNER DANNEN AND THE KADAVER'S SOIREE

I t was the fluttering that got to her. Relentless, insistent. She couldn't turn her uneasy dreams away from the sound. A thousand sighs in perfect cadence, a zephyr with a message. It pointed her to a black backbone and burning lights. She reached.

The fluttering was louder, the wings crushing out the light. All around, whispering, singing, telling her, warning her: *Please go. Please hurry.*

Constance shifted on her stiff mattress, the sheets crinkling around her ankles as she gave a brief shudder. Disappointed curiosities hung in the corners of her bleary eyes, but they evaporated as she put a hand to her sore scalp full of pins and crooked brush rollers.

Her heart seized. She squinted around the strange room, trying to get her bearings. Silhouettes of unfamiliar, ancient furniture. The limp skins of clothes over chairs. And another presence. Breathing. *Loud* breathing.

Ah, yes. The recognition that she was not at home in her own bed, her own lonely room, eddied like mercury across marble, and Constance rubbed the worry away. She groped for the lamp on her bedside table.

Something furry, warm, and *much bigger than expected* woke her up entirely when her hand made contact. Constance bounded over to the other side of the bed, sending the lamp crashing to the floor as she shot onto Ivory's mattress. Her sister barely stirred.

"Five more minutes," Ivory mumbled, turning over. "I thought we were on holiday."

It was the younger sibling's turn to be startled awake as Constance mountaineered over her prone body, reaching for the other bedside light. It took a knee to Ivory's spleen to wake her into battle mode.

"I said *no*, you horrible snipe!" Ivory grappled with the light. "If you want to get up and swan about I'll have no part in it!"

Constance was more than willing to let madness take over, the two thrashing and swiping to get their way. It ended with the light flickering on, Constance diving behind Ivory, using her as a shield from the towering figure in the corner.

Ivory forgot her fury the minute she spotted the creature. "*Pisaura mirabilis!*" She crowed in a tone that suggested lovers reunited.

"Of course, you know what it is," Constance finally croaked, "but I bet you can't identify it once it's *dead.*"

She made a hawk swoop for the overused atlas that Ivory had been leafing through the night before, but Ivory snatched it from her mid-pitch.

"I won't bear witness to atrocity this early in the morning," she huffed, taking the book with her as she crawled under the bed in search of her suitcase. "Science before murder, please. We are *ladies*."

From what had already seemed an overpacked mess in her suitcase, Ivory produced an empty terrarium. "*Pisaura mirabilis*, an umbrella term for fishing and rat spiders, but most commonly, and in this case, the nursery spider."

Constance felt the nerves at the surface of her skin barb-sharp. The bedside light was strong and illuminated every copper hair on the eight legs scrunched in the room's corner. The spider had frozen there, weighing its failed escape and mirroring the elder Ivyweather with a bit more class.

"No, *no*," Constance seethed through hardened teeth. "This is not another one of your pets!"

Ivory pressed on, undeterred, glass tank in hand. "They resemble wolf spiders, but they carry their egg sacs with their jaws. Many species are able to walk on the surface of still bodies of water, and can even jump a distance of five or six inches to escape predators."

The thought chilled Constance through every inch of her eyelet nightgown. But Ivory crouched and stepped away from the spider. It seemed to be shivering. Or winding up.

"Sometimes, the female spider will attempt to eat the male after mating." At that the spider sprang up, jumping the predicted distance, and with a sweep, directly into Ivory's terrarium.

"Smart girl. Don't let yourself be pushed around, least of all by *men*." She locked the lid and deposited it on her sister's night table.

"Put it somewhere else, Ivory. Like the garbage. I don't want to look at it." She wrapped herself up in Ivory's sheets and turned away.

"How about here?" Ivory offered, placing the terrarium directly in Constance's face. She shrieked and bucked to the floor. "You know, from her perspective, you're the monster. I mean you *are* a thousand times larger, after all."

"Thanks for that." Constance rallied to her feet, smoothing her nightgown thoughtfully over her belly.

Ivory rolled her eyes. "There is nothing wrong with being fat, Connie. With a bust like that, you won't need to eat your inevitable scores of suitors. But you should." She spoke to the spider then: "She's being very clutchy, today, isn't she?"

"Clutchy indeed." Constance huffed back to her own side of the room. "If it had bitten me I'd have swollen up and drowned in my own fluids, but oh, poor sweet venomous so-and-so."

Ivory snorted. "Constance Ivyweather, blue-ribbon dancing champion, head debate coach, senior editor of every school periodical there ever was, afraid of nothing save for impropriety, foul grades, and insects one-sixtieth her size. I can't wait for the day when *people* are put in exhibitions, and I may volunteer you as the main attraction."

From behind the glass, the spider tapped its forefeet against the barrier. Ivory's face softened. "I will name her Arabella."

Constance, at this point, had regained some gall and taken to the window, refusing to be drawn into Ivory's monologue. She threw back the heavy drapes, her fervour curtailed by a plume of dust and a darker shade of day.

The fog, the clouds, the gloom. None of it would relent. It had been morning upon morning without sun since they'd arrived, and the dark-lit days were chipping away at her already-eroded optimism. Ms. Bougainvillea said they'd get used to it eventually. *By the time we do, I hope we'll be long gone.*

She started undoing her hair, yellow curls bouncing down her cheeks as she stowed each pin. "What shall we do today, then?"

They'd already seen the small square called Farrowmarket with "Miss Bee," shopping for limp vegetables and scrawny chickens. Then they'd taken in town hall and its backward-reeling clock. Walked around the headless, very much dredged fountain. Tried idly to identify, as well as sidestep, the plethora of birds in the house. Met a few curious, withdrawn locals.

But Constance knew the one burning thing her sister still desired, and she shrank away from it as it approached.

"*You* may do as you like," Ivory replied testily. "But *I* am going to have a closer look at the mountain, once and for all."

Constance didn't even turn. "You're a very broken record," she said dryly. "But I'm the one in charge of you, and I'm not about to let you get into mischief on some bizarrely shaped haunted triangle in the middle of nowhere."

Ivory had been deciding between her best pairs of explorer socks when she turned an eye that was three tablespoons perspicacity and one cup derision on her sister.

"I know what it is." She tried burning a hole in Constance's back with her keen stare. "I know why you won't look at that mountain, why you won't even acknowledge it with the awe it deserves! It's the *monsters*, isn't it?"

Constance pinched the bridge of her nose.

"There are raging fascinating beasties just on our doorstep, and Gloria forbid you fuss up your tresses on an adventure in search of one." Ivory continued to dress herself in the most unladylike way possible (wool leggings, khaki shorts, and a button-up Oxford). "I respect that you're afraid of what you don't understand, but it's my choice to delve into this delectable mystery. Dead astronomers, dark mountains, dangerous creatures. We're lucky to be here when it's all happening!"

Constance rolled her eyes. "Nothing is happening. It's happened already. Decades ago. There's nothing else to discover." Since the house's pipes creaked and groaned too much for her liking, Constance fetched the water for their toilette basins and poured, the sigh on the ceramic matching hers. "Try to be sensible," she went on. "There's no mystery. Anything these daffy townspeople feed you about that mountain is a direct result of boredom and superstition." Two good synonyms for backwoods ignorance.

Though she hated the sanctimonious tone her voice took on, Constance railroaded on with each roller she removed; she had a mission this summer, after all. "It's time to put away all those childish things. There's so much expected of you, and fairy tales will only get you so far. The real world may not be as exciting, but you'll have to live in it with the rest of us one day. Best make it bearable."

As Constance finished her hair, she looked at Ivory on her unmade bed, knobby knees at her chin as she stared into Arabella's terrarium. It was bad enough the other girls in their suburb refused to invite the youngest Ivyweather to their fine houses for Spring Fling teas or Etiquette Evenings. They weren't too keen on her preference to wear mechanic's overalls and crawl around the mud looking for interesting invertebrates, either. Ivory would enter Ferren Academy's Upper School in a few short weeks, where Constance knew her endless quirks and queries would not be tolerated. A terrible fate awaited her. She remembered her father, in his study, and his warning.

Constance shook her head, mentally sidestepping any reliving of that interaction. She wanted the best for her sister, and Ivory had to learn what it meant to fit in or fall out. The latter was not an option for an Ivyweather.

Ivory suddenly got to her feet, stomped into her scrummy boots, and snatched up the terrarium. When she came closer, Constance realized her sister looked worried. "Live your life for once, Connie," she warned ominously, "before it's too late."

Constance, unblinking, watched Ivory clomp out the door with her head held high. Rolling her eyes, she patted her shining hair in the vanity and got dressed. Her own clothes were well-made and perfectly tailored to her bigger figure, which Ivory had pointed out with her usual envy. Blouses and skirts and shining shoes and everything in its place. Constance maintained tight control of every aspect of her outward appearance. She always had to look perfect. Even if she felt that all her careful control had been slipping.

Constance took one last look at the Butterfly Room, an apt name given the walls covered in numerous butterfly specimens pinned behind tarnished glass. Trapped forever, in the middle of a flight to nowhere.

She needed to get out of her own head.

She went to follow the path her tangle-headed sister had blazed out the door but was stopped in the hallway by the now-familiar goose, Bernard, pecking at her shin.

Its *hornk* was muffled by the envelopes in its beak. Constance cleared her throat and held out her hand. "Thank you." She took the mail quickly and scrutinized the goose as it waddled away down the corridor. Alone, she shuffled through the three envelopes. Finally, some news. Whether it was good or not remained to be seen.

Constance hustled down the stairs and skirted the patched-up hole, making for the solarium, where they routinely took breakfast. "We have two wires!"

Ivory snatched one while Constance tore open the envelope of the other. They had only been in Quixx for a week — the slowest week of their young lives — and they had thought the proximity to the City would allow for efficient telegraph service. This assumption was wholly incorrect. They'd been anxious to know when their parents would join them, considering they'd promised to be only a few days behind.

"'Dearest daughters, *stop*,'" Ivory began, but she trailed off as she read the short message to herself in under ten seconds. The paper, and her violet eyes, dropped to her lap. "They're not coming for another two weeks."

Constance's brow wrinkled. "When's yours dated?"

"A few days after we arrived."

Constance handed over the second. "This one's from yesterday."

Ivory read it out loud. "'Dearest daughters, *stop*. We regret to inform you that our calendars have been overbooked, *stop*. We will not be able to join you at least until next quarter, *stop*. We apologize for any inconvenience this may cause you, *stop*. Yours sincerely, Your Parents, *stop*.'"

"Magazine subscription cancelled, dearies?" Ms. Bougainvillea chirped as she brought in the scones.

"Sure sounds like it, Miss Bee." Ivory slouched, shoving the toxic yellow telegrams into her pockets.

Constance only shrugged. She had expected this, yet the disappointment was a sharp shard to swallow. But swallow it she would, for Ivory's sake.

"They're busy people . . . and I'm sure things will work out and they'll join us eventually." *They promised*, she thought. Surely they would keep it this time, with what Constance had promised in return. Straight-backed, she made sure to stare into her cup, deeply focused on stirring her tea, lest she meet Ivory's eyes and give herself away.

"Sure, they'll join us. When we're both *dead*." Ivory furiously slathered jam onto her scone. "Busy, yes, certainly. Busy forgetting that they had two daughters somewhere in between a charity ball and eyeing the stock ticker." She shoved the sticky mass into her fuming face and said no more. Constance was glad of it. She was beginning to agree with Ivory, and that was never a promising thing.

"Never fear," Ms. Bougainvillea comforted. "They'll soon realize there's a very large hole where you used to be. Why, when my mother ran the Happy Bell, she barely knew I was there until the tenants gave their compliments on my fig and veal stew. She always meant well, but Mumsie was a scatterbrain. Lucky I didn't inherit *that*." Frederic stirred in her hair with a sarcastic trill before going back to sleep.

Ivory dug her fist into her cheek. "And who's the third one from?" She jutted her chin at the red stationery. "Probably Old Kiplington Child Services asking for an Absentee Parent Tax."

Constance had forgotten all about the third envelope. She lifted it closer to her face and was assaulted with a potent aftershave. Constance coughed. "Someone by the name of . . . Slanner Dannen?"

The seeing-eye birds that had been taking a break from their early morning shift suddenly lit awake and cast fervent glances at each other. A ripple charged through the room, and everyone shuddered.

"You poor things." Ms. Bougainvillea held a gnarled hand to her cheek, shaking her head. "You're on his radar now."

Constance lifted an eyebrow as she delicately tore the envelope open. Ivory had already climbed out of her funk (as well as her chair) to have a closer look. "I take it he's a well-known figure in Quixx."

"There's no other way to know Slanner Dannen." Ms. Bougainvillea's usual airiness turned dry and unimpressed. "He's the local entertainment."

"A *crooner*!" Ivory cried. "Like the blues? Jazz? Rock 'n' roll?"

"Whichever." Ms. Bougainvillea waved her off. "His band had a very popular record years ago. Brought quite a few hotheads from the Cities to gawp and canoodle and make him even more insufferable than when I'd had to babysit him years earlier. But when the next big fad came around, he was yesterday's wire."

The Ivyweathers blinked. Ms. Bougainvillea sounded as if she knew what she was talking about.

As if to correct this incongruence, she stood up abruptly and sent every bird within three metres scattering. "Shoo!" she cried irritably, shuffling to the sideboard to pour (spill) some more tea. "You two are pretty girls from the Cities, which makes you *very* easy targets." She sipped from her empty cup. "Still, it will do you some good to be social, Miss Constance. Far be it from me to say that any clever girl *needs* a counterpoint, but a little attention wouldn't hurt your confidence."

Constance coloured and ignored her sister's snickering, trying to focus on the letter in front of her.

Salutations Little Ladies,

I bid you welcome to my humble (and I mean humble) town. This town isn't much on the enter-taining, but there is one show that ought not be missed while you fine fillies are about. Won't you join me at my Expansive Manse in North Quixx for a jilty good time and a taste of what put this town on the map?

See you soon at noon at number 6 Bune,

Slanner D. Dannen

"Wow, so much jive talk, even in writing," Ivory swooned, already seduced.

Constance warbled through her nose. "I suppose we can stop by for a *bit* . . ." She tried to ignore Ivory's victory whooping as she looked up at Ms. Bougainvillea. "Is it safe for us to go without an escort?"

The old woman waved her hand, softening. "Slanner means well. Just like everybody else here. But be careful not to give him *too* much attention, or you'll never shake him." She looked at the general area Ivory was celebrating in. "I have a feeling your sister could take him if he got out of hand, anyway."

Constance tilted her head, then looked down at the address: number 6 Bune. That wasn't far from Farrowmarket, which suited her fine, especially if things went badly . . . She pushed the usual anxiety as far back as she could before it started creeping to the forefront again, Ivory's words haunting her now more than the mountain. *Live your life, before it's too late.*

"How do we RSVP?"

"You don't RSVP to Slanner Dannen," replied Ms. Bougainvillea. "You show up, or he shows you."

"Hurry up slow-bjorn! It's nearly noon!"

Ivory was making a ridiculous pace up the hill, despite clutching Arabella and her terrarium. Excitement glistened at the tip of her nose where the mist coalesced.

Constance tripped for the third time, certain her shoes would be ruined by the time they got back to Ferren City. "These crooners are never what you hope they'll be," she warned, as if she'd ever met a crooner before. "Prepare to be disappointed."

A furious groan welled up from Ivory's deepest depths. "You always ruin everything before it has a chance to be ruined."

Thankfully they'd reached the top of the hill, and as Ivory raced ahead, Constance turned around. She could see the

Happy Bell beyond Farrowmarket below, or the shape of it at least, being pawed at by the fog. The light was on in the Butterfly Room, even though Constance didn't remember leaving it on.

And beyond the boarding house, there was the mountain, ungainly and huge and pinning Constance in place. She could see, from up here, that the Happy Bell was the only active house near the great trench. There were no lights elsewhere in the rumpled bungalows nearby. Around the majority of the rim, a tall wrought-iron fence had been set, but it, too, was crumbling and in need of repair. A frequency of super-stition and fear of Ms. Bougainvillea's monsters had felled whatever life there could be at the base of Mount Quixx. Yet the Happy Bell held on.

"Wouldn't be a good idea to use the car, my dears," Ms. Bougainvillea had said, handing them a basket of scones to take with them. "There's an auto thief in our midst. Best to leave it where I can keep an eye on it."

So they'd walked, and though the cool air crept close to the bone, Constance was sweating in places she'd rather not think about.

She vaguely heard Ivory call her again, but she found she couldn't look away from the Happy Bell as the light in their room flickered off. And the mountain seemed to demand her attention more than she liked. Since she'd arrived in Quixx, in fact, she'd felt something insistent growing underneath her rib cage, curling around her bones like butterflies itching to migrate. Even now on the hill, it took a particular strength to force her eyes away, to press on with the mountain, the Happy Bell, and all their secrets at her back.

"Slow, slow, so very slow." Ivory was leaning against a gate, tapping her foot. "You're doing this on purpose."

"I'm right here, hold your horses," Constance muttered, checking her watch. Five minutes to. "We're early."

"Ooh maybe he'll give us a signed vinyl for being punctual!" Ivory capered up to the door.

Constance rolled her eyes, shifting the basket of scones to the other arm as she absorbed the gaudy shape in front of them. The entire two-storey house was orange, a mass of odd angles, and very narrow for what was considered either "expansive" or a "manse." The facade was razored with rose bushes and vines, devoid of flowers but abundant in barbs that wended illicitly around the brickwork.

When Constance reached the tapered door and its guitar-shaped knocker, she couldn't help but feel a twinge of excitement beyond the usual nausea. Ivory was right — they *were* on vacation. There was the quickest twitch at a nearby window, and Constance knew there was no turning back. She took a deep breath—

The door flew open. The Ivyweather sisters yelped backward as the entrance glittered and a voice, deep inside the shimmering shadows, hummed, "*Come in, come in, it's about to begin . . .*" The shadows smelled like the rude aftershave soaking their invitation, mixed with coffee grounds and bad cigars.

Ivory dove, but Constance caught her by the waistband of her khakis. "*Hey!*" She struggled, but Constance was stern in her sister's face.

"No matter what happens, stay close to me, and curtsey at least *once*. And if he offers you anything that smells strange, nod and throw it away. If anything goes wrong, pinch. Understood?"

Ivory wriggled from her grasp. "Stop making it weird," she hissed, straightening herself and tucking Arabella under her arm. Constance fluffed her blond curls and swiped her brow, leading the way. They were swallowed by the shadows and the smells, the door clicking shut in their wake.

One beat, two. Then the dark was pierced by a spotlight jolted directly on the sisters. Constance shielded her eyes, briefly distracted from the bass beat scaling slowly up the walls. Hands from an unseen stranger shot from the shadows at their shoulders, nabbed the basket of goodies, and pushed the two girls down a ramp. The spotlight followed, and a harmonized humming took up between faint piano tinkling.

"Salutations and good-noon, gentleladies," crooned a voice an octave higher than the hum.

"Good after—" Constance tried, until the ground underneath them shifted. Hollow creaking and whirring started up, unseen fixtures rattling while the guts of the house churned. Constance threw herself forward to grab Ivory as a seam opened up in the floor.

"Don't be alarmed, little girls, though it's sweet of you to be. The Expansive Manse just needs some room to breathe."

The spotlight revealed that the floor, and the room, was indeed expanding. So much so that suddenly they were banked by rows and rows of seats, flipping upright as, at their front, an entire stage unfolded. With a final *ding*, the room assumed its upright position, leaving the Ivyweathers perplexed but in one piece.

"Take your seats now, you're just in time, the overture's spent and so are we!" The follow-spot returned and stopped at a pair of seats at the front into which Ivory yanked Constance. Already shaken enough, she unbuttoned her collar for whatever came next, and the watching voice mistook her queasiness for anticipation.

"I know!" it cried. "Front row, dead centre. You're the luckiest cats alive. It's a full house tonight, boys! What say we light 'er up?"

What sounded like a sea of finger-snapping brought up a new tempo, the harmony rising and joining full-stop. The trumpets blazed. The stage came alive. And the crimson-zoot-suited promised crooner spun his alto into a suspended microphone.

It's good, it's grand, oh, isn't it great? (Yeah!)
Gonna bring fast jive, make you sal-i-vate — (Oh!)
Fast times, live, they're comin' on hot
(Sssss) And oh baby gonna hit the spot
Can't stop me now — (Oh wee, oh whoa)
Gonna rock, and how — (Oh no, oh no)
Put out all the stops and man alive, ain't no cadaver
gonna stunt my jive

Slanner Dannen slid his Cosmocaster over his shoulder, slithering out the chord and winding up the note until there was nothing left. He was flanked by another guitarist, all languid energy like a human lava lamp; a tall tenor sax player with a hard, throaty blaze; a piano-man trying to keep up; a drummer letting loose on the snare; a short keytarist clamouring to keep up; and a bassist who took it home. Slanner sweated into the mic with his voice, tossing his close-cut rooster hair with the precision of a python — until it all reached the top. The houselights came up to the sound of Ivory clapping with wrist-breaking fury, and Constance felt surprised at how much she was enjoying herself.

Their two-woman standing ovation broke Slanner's smirking face. "I'm Slanner Dannen, that's the Kadaver's Soiree, and we are done. Good night!"

Their applause stopped abruptly as the curtain dropped.

"Uh." Constance blinked. "Mr. Dannen?"

"Slanner, baby," he said, suddenly in the seat behind them, reclining like he'd been there the whole time, watching the show rather than performing it. "Mr. Dannen is my pops, wherever he went."

Constance tried to ignore her prickling at *baby*, putting on a wincing smile as she stuck out her hand. "I'm very glad to meet—"

He was on his feet, snatching her hand and twirling her before she could react. As he pressed her in close, his smile waxy and wide, she noticed how his red suit — which had seemed so regal in the stage light — was really moth-eaten. The aftershave was even worse close-up. She flinched out of his proximity.

"No need for intros. I've got my spies, little Miss Con. Ain't nothing new passing through this town that escapes my attention!" His teeth shone in the post-concert afterglow. "'Specially a pretty little thing like you, from the City and all."

"Ah . . . yes." Constance edged away in a single stride, desperately willing the redness climbing her neck to recede. She thrust Ivory forward like a sacrifice. "My sister, Ivory."

The younger curtseyed — just to get it out of the way — and shot her hand out. "It's an honour, Mr. Dannen! Really, your show—"

"Yeah, I know." He grinned, thrumming his fingernails against his lapel. "I'm definitely gonna feel that one tomorrow, let me tell you."

Constance had no idea how a crooner should act, but his sharkish teeth aimed straight at her put her on edge. And though he was all primed to take the praise, Slanner faltered at the sight of his bandmates filtering from the stage and into their midst. He rolled his eyes. "Here comes the entourage."

He placated them with a quick introduction that guaranteed their names would be forgotten. "The Kadaver's Soiree — Bartek, Sluggo, Vatos, Hatch, Avila, and Leal . . . on bass."

Five hands shook theirs and left them in that waiting room of nervous laughter and curious expectation. The one named Leal, who must have been on good terms with Slanner to have had his instrument mentioned, strode forward to shake last. His smile was distracted and sweet, his two-tone black and white outfit at least taken care of, thin charcoal tie inoffensive — the ducktail hairstyle could be forgiven in light of his gangly grace.

"Leal Synodite." His smile creased into his eyes as he took Constance's hand in both of his. "Did you like the show?"

Constance rosied up, pleased that some air of courtesy had been remembered in Slanner's wake. "I've never heard anything like it!" And she hadn't. Years of studying with symphony records in the background never offered the chance to hear another side of music. And beyond her better judgment, she liked it.

Leal looked genuinely happy. "It's a real pleasure to've played for you, honest. We don't get much chance to perform these da—"

The air went out of the bassist when Slanner elbowed him, either to cut him off or to cut in on the lovefest. "What he means is we don't have such a varied audience." His cobalt sneer snatched Constance's earlier praise away. "We're a prize act, you know. Not many stars let regular folks into their humble abodes to catch a glimpse of the magic. Or offer them a tour. *If* you please."

He practically dragged Constance from the theatre into a modest foyer, hemmed in by overgrown plants and several waterlogged, unopened boxes marked *Merchandise*.

"To the galleria!" Slanner cried.

Metal and wood groaned, and the stage folded itself up as neatly as it had opened. Constance was glad she wasn't in the middle of it this time. Where it once stood were French doors that Slanner led them through, and they went down halls whose wallpaper had more stains than damask left, to what was probably the best room in the house.

Posters and glamour shots lined the walls, Slanner's sparkling smirk and tossed fire-engine-red hair glossed behind immaculate frames. As in real life, it seemed the rest of the band was an afterthought that didn't think it safe to step forward. Half-museum, half-studio, with a dimmed-down elevator track of the song they'd heard moments earlier, the room — alongside Slanner's vanity — was mesmerizing.

Constance was thrust out of her wonder and mashed inches away from a glittering case at the back of the room, tucked close under Slanner's arm as he pointed.

"There it is," he whispered, like the record behind the glass might stir if they were too noisy. "The *Platinum*."

The 33-format vinyl, suspended in its crystal cabinet, was unaware it was the single glory around which the entire house orbited. Sluggo, the impossibly tall saxophonist, wiped away a tear. The album title shone silver: *Slanner Dannen and the Kadaver's Soiree: Night at the End of the Tunnel.*

Constance didn't really understand what she was looking at. Ivory whispered, "It means they sold *a lot* of records."

"Oh," Constance replied, suddenly further out of her element than she'd expected. To Slanner: "You must have been very famous back then."

There was an audible record scratch as the music stopped and the Kadaver's Soiree winced collectively. Slanner's grip was tightening on her arm, but Leal safely extracted her before detonation.

"*Are*," he cut in quickly, putting his long bony hands on Slanner's shaking shoulders. "Are very famous. Always have been. Always will be. We're Platinum, after all." His voice pronounced the word soothingly. "*Platinum*."

Slanner's pin-dot pupils expanded as he sighed. "Platinum," he repeated, harshly smacking Leal away and adjusting his jacket as though nothing had happened. "Always will be."

The elevator music started up again. Even Ivory looked skeptical at this point.

"So, ladies," Slanner said, bringing both hands in an admiral's stance as he rocked in his saddle shoes. "We've been at this biz fifteen years now. But we need a way to bust out of the old and into the now. Point being: we ain't been to the Cities in a while. Tell us what's on the in-trend."

"The what?" Constance asked.

"You know, the up and coming, the what's-in, the who's-got-the-beat. Give it to me, sister, I'm sure you *know*."

Constance's throat constricted. Not only did she ignore popular music, but in her social circle, jazz was frowned upon . . . but the expectant, glowing eyes of the band, and the harsh, chiselled cheekbones of its master, were difficult to escape.

"First of all, rockabilly still has its in." Ivory stepped up. "And though jazz is still on shaky legs, it's taking the reins as bigger labels experiment and pick it up. Labels are looking for a fast track to an edge, and you've got it in spades."

Constance stared at Ivory as her pulsing heart settled. *I've got your back*, the younger's eyes twinkled, and Constance was thankful in that moment that Ivory was who she was.

The band chattered, shyly coming forward to ask Ivory more questions. Slanner stroked his chin, but he wasn't looking at Ivory. He strode into Constance's bubble before she could stop him.

"Your li'l sis knows a thing or two," he oozed, charm missing its mark. "But you're old enough to soak it up first-hand at the gin joints proper. I bet you're a real firecracker despite the preppy duds. Blondies usually are."

Constance blushed again, patting down her hair as she wormed out of his sticky grip. "No time for gin joints." Her discomfort at an all-time high, Constance nabbed Ivory from the circle of conferring musicians, pinching her.

"Ow!" She jumped. "What now?"

Slanner bolted between them, a cataract to their confidence. "Say, little Miss Con, you don't mind if I call you that, do you?" He was herding her away. "We could use a bit of your City charm around the ol' abode. Stay for a nosh while we gab and get to know each other better?"

"We really must be going, though," Constance peeped, yet her protests were drowned out as a small cheer rose up and the band moved out of the galleria.

But Constance couldn't escape the feeling of splinters in her pores. *Oh no. Not now.* She knew it was the anxiety, and she tried to reason it away, but it devoured logic. It always did. She clawed her brain for an excuse, for anything that might get her back outside and out of the suffocating ring of attention as panic gripped her stomach and squeezed.

"*Post!*" her lungs managed to push out, with feeling, while holding off the oncoming panic attack.

"Where?" Avila, the small keytarist, shrieked and ducked.

Constance tripped out of Slanner's hands and yanked Ivory beside her. "I meant. The post . . . office. We need to go there." She turned to her sister, speaking through her teeth and holding back tears. "Ivory, please go and fetch your things."

Ivory looked more worried than upset, so she obeyed. She headed back to the theatre's former entrance to grab Arabella and the terrarium she'd left behind.

"So soon?" It was Leal who sounded the most disap-pointed.

The edge of the ensuing panic attack ebbed away, and Constance clamoured, "We um . . . we've got to send a wire to our parents. Tell them that we've met the Kadaver's Soiree. I'm sure they'll be, you know, a'flutter."

Leal brightened, but Slanner shouldered in again. "Have it your way, m'lady," he drawled, "but it's no trouble for Leal and I to escort you there and back to the Happy Bell."

Constance tried to stay even. "I don't think that's—"

"Hope Batty Bougie ain't gotcha down yet. Feisty old nutbar." Slanner held out his arms as Vatos and Hatch helped him slide on a yellow-and-black checkerboard overcoat.

"Changes her name as quickly as her old birds flap off. Won't sell me her dopey old house, either . . ."

Slanner was trying to buy the Happy Bell? For what ends, Constance didn't ask. All she could do was button up her jacket as Ivory's pinching fingers caught the small of her back.

"What?" Constance mouthed, but the complexion that perfectly matched Ivory's name had gone a shade pastier. She held up the empty terrarium and Constance's nausea thunderclapped back.

"Shall we?" Slanner held out his arm, interrupting Constance's terror. She swallowed, teeth out and ready to conceal everything as she took his offer. He grinned. "Maybe a jaunty walk with the ol' Slanner-Danner-doo will help ya change your mind about the luncheon."

He winked to his crew, who gave him a well-meaning thumbs-up as the four set off into the dog-eared afternoon.

Constance wanted to survive the day, but she had to micromanage. Living through the trip to the Post and Telegraph was the priority, so she had no time to worry about the spider's whereabouts. She was keen to be rid of it and inwardly promised to keep scolding Ivory about it to a minimum.

This was only half the hardship. Slanner grilled Constance with questions at every turn. He wanted to know their connections, people he could invite to Quixx and schmooze with. She kept it civil and tried not to feel as anxious as she had in the Manse. After all, Leal was there with them. He seemed like the lightning rod of Slanner's eccentricities, absorbing it all in stride on everyone's behalf. Even his tendency to mildly abuse his bandmates.

Constance changed the subject as they entered Farrowmarket. "Have you two lived in Quixx all your lives?"

Slanner had already broken away from them, signing autographs for people who hadn't asked. "Most of the band has," Leal answered, "Slanner included. But I came here from Oiros when I was a kid. My dad played the accordion and my mom was a music teacher. They got tired of how fast everything was closing in around them, so they came to the valley for some peace."

Oiros City was the largest of the growing Far City Network, even bigger than Ferren, known for its aeronautic travel developments — and much bigger than Quixx, by far. "But I didn't mind coming out here," Leal explained. "I like it. It's quiet. Like me."

Constance smiled in spite of herself, and Ivory chirped in before Constance could stop her. "Leal, how are you so normal?"

Leal blinked, making sure they were out of earshot before he shrugged. "It's just his way," he replied. But why he'd thrown his lot in with a character like Slanner Dannen grew clearer as Leal watched him across the square, his eyes glittering with a mischievous smile. "Slanner and I were neighbours growing up. He liked me 'cause I was from the City, so we started a band. Seemed like a good idea at the time."

"Oh," was all Constance could say, before Slanner swept back over.

"Onward!" he cried, marching them into the Post and Telegraph with as much fanfare as he could kick up. He barged through, whirling like a Dervish, cutting in front of a mannequin of a man in a golf cap. Leal let out a sigh that rattled through his whole body and dove in to subdue the oncoming damage.

In the meantime, while Constance stood in line for the telegraph, Ivory sulked against the wall with the empty terrarium.

"It's just a spider," Constance said.

Ivory ignored her. "I don't get it. I would have set her free somewhere more conducive to her environmental requirements."

Constance couldn't help feeling guilty; Ivory *had* helped her out back at the Manse. "I don't think spiders can decipher good intentions." She smiled, admiring her younger sister's absolute altruism, even to arachnids.

Ivory looked up. "Are you feeling better?"

"Fine," Constance lied quickly — it came out almost a bark. "Just needed some air, that's all."

Ivory knew better and said no more. Constance's anxiety couldn't bear being discussed in a public venue. The panic attacks had come more frequently since graduation day when she'd realized the path she'd walked since birth frightened her more than abandoning it. She swallowed the thought as far down as it would go.

When it was Constance's turn in line, she kept the message to their parents short. Anything more detailed might make her expect a heartfelt reply, and she refused to be disappointed again. She made sure Ivory was elsewhere, browsing a near-empty postcard rack. "Remember our bargain, stop." *I'll keep my promise if you keep yours.*

"Excuse me," came a voice behind Constance, and when she turned she was face-to-face with the biggest, brightest blouse bow she had ever seen. When she looked farther up, a face with defined cheekbones and rich umber skin was glowering down at her from behind gold horn-rimmed spectacles.

Constance swallowed. "Yes?"

"It's all right, Mother, I can get it," piped up a second person, who slid in front of the elegantly tall woman, an earnest smile perking up her warm dimples. The girl wore elegant French braids in natural hair. "If you'd just move two steps to the left, miss."

Constance automatically shifted, and the girl, dressed in a bright pink ballet skirt with matching slippers, pliéd on her square toes and snagged a blank telegraph from the rack that Constance had been blocking.

"Thank you." The girl smiled again, curtseying. "You're the girls from the Cities, aren't you?"

She turned with every grace to Ivory nearby and for the first time, Constance noticed her sister had stiffened like she had a steel rod for a spine.

"Ferren City," Ivory added, visibly trying to keep her cool as she came forward, eyeing the mother and daughter pair. "I'm Ivory Ivyweather. And this is my sister, Constance."

The girl's grin grew. "Madeline Mott. My mother—"

"You may call me Mx. Mott, if you please. I am the principal at Cardinal Quixx Hall." She clicked back into their periphery. Mx. Mott was a wonder in purple trimmed with acid green, and she must have been six-foot-three *without* the shining patent mules. Her tweed handbag swung from a slender forearm, bedecked in bangles. She was stylish, gorgeous, and more than formidable.

"That's the school here," Madeline offered, since the sisters were clearly at a loss. "It really is the best in the county."

"But it could be better," Mx. Mott waved airily. "We're central. We offer a peace and tranquility that the Cities can no longer boast. I've designs to build a university, but naturally, I've come up against a few roadblocks."

"Like the total lack of people and the fact there are universities in the Cities?" Ivory quipped, and Constance shot her a glare.

Mx. Mott's eyes narrowed, and Madeline's darted. "There's always room for more, I think," Madeline said, trying to steer the conversation elsewhere. "Look, Mother, it's Mr. Dannen."

Constance's jaw tightened as the crooner sidled up to their little gathering, almost having forgotten him. "Motty," he greeted icily.

"Mr. Dannen," she nodded, nose in the air. "My worst student who gave up his education to pursue a *musical career*." She lifted her spectacles from her long nose and let them rest on their gold chain at the breast of her blazer. "I can't imagine there's much of a market for you, what with a *war* going on?" Mx. Mott tipped her head to puncture Leal with her critical stare. "Surely you must have at least some influence on him, Mr. Synodite?" Leal had no time to reply before Mx. Mott sniffed at Constance. "My *brightest* student. Shame about the rabble he associates with."

There was something obviously simmering here, but Constance had little time to guess before Ivory was yanking on her sleeve and pointing with a gasp.

Constance stiffened. She dropped the fountain pen she'd still been holding, which splattered ink between her, the Motts, and Slanner when she stumbled backward. He jerked and Mx. Mott dodged sideways.

"Ah, watch it, girlie, these zoot suits ain't meant to get inked!"

"Not ink, Mr. Dannen." Constance brought a shaking finger up. "*Pisaura mirabilis*."

Arabella was perched very innocuously on Slanner's shoulder before he glanced up and screamed. Both he and the spider barely had time to evade Mx. Mott's well-aimed handbag as it flew judiciously through the air. "Someone get me a rolled-up *Quixx Quarterly*!" she cried. The Post and Telegraph erupted in chaos.

"No! Arabella!" Ivory cried, lunging with the prowess of the famed naturalist Caden Morbatten, wending around bloated and knobby ankles that stomped and scattered as Mx. Mott shouted directions and Slanner leapt onto the post wicket. Arabella darted behind a pair of ballet shoes, though, and Ivory froze.

"It's all right." Madeline turned, bent gracefully, and cupped the spider safely in her hands in one smooth movement. "You're among friends now, but it's time to go home, I think." And with one last smile to Ivory, she delicately placed the shivering spider back where she belonged in Ivory's outstretched terrarium. From the corner she'd pressed herself into, Constance relaxed the hand at her chest as she watched Madeline help Ivory stand, dusting off her sister's rumpled shirt — Constance was shocked that Ivory let her do so.

"Heinous little beastie!" Mx. Mott hissed in Ivory (and Arabella)'s direction as she grabbed Madeline and guided her away. "You intentionally brought vermin into a public place?"

Slanner, still slapping the phantom bugs from his suit, blustered towards the door. "One thing we can agree on, Motty." He then mumbled something about having to go home and un-harsh his mellow. He shoved Leal out ahead of him, thankfully forgetting all about Constance's lunch invite.

Mx. Mott gave Ivory a long, piercing glare while picking careful fingers through her afro. "Perhaps summer school might keep you better occupied than bizarre insect collecting, Miss Ivyweather."

Ivory's mouth opened, but nothing came out, which was just as well, since Mx. Mott had already made two long strides to the door. Her mouth clamped shut as Madeline followed, still smiling beatifically.

"I think Arabella is lucky to have a friend like you," Madeline said, eyes only for Ivory. And then they were gone, but that didn't stop Ivory from watching the tutu fade into the mist. Constance took her back to the Happy Bell on a cloud.

"A daring rescue indeed," Constance later said in the Butterfly Room, referring to the creature in the terrarium. "Saved from the *grabby* hands of Slanner Dannen by the *scuttly* hands of a nursery spider."

"I don't know why he liked *you* so much," Ivory teased. "You who has no concept of cool."

"I know plenty!" Constance said, hairbrush in hand, even if Ivory was right. She put the brush down after the hundredth stroke, making a decision. "Anyway, come over here. I'm going to attempt to oppress that hair of yours."

Ivory groaned out from under the heavy tome she'd been studying, schlumping over to Constance's vanity stool. Usually she wouldn't be so accommodating, but after meeting Madeline Mott, Ivory seemed willing to make the attempt. She sat in front of the tarnished mirror with Constance at her back.

"Don't slouch, you're not eighty." She tapped the curve of Ivory's back. "And don't sulk, you look like a pigeon."

"*Columba livia,*" Ivory added. "And what if I want to look like one? At least I could fly away to anywhere I wish."

"And you'd be swimming with disease and probably missing a foot," Constance added, trying first to pick through Ivory's black tangles with her fingers. "Are you *trying* to build a nest in here?"

Ivory smiled. "Miss Bee seems content with having one."

Constance tried the brush, disentangling the strands as gently as she could. "You always used to comb your hair like me," she said.

She did not say *but that was before Mother and Father began to really ignore us.* Ivory just shrugged, wincing at the tugs to her scalp.

"Are you really jealous that Mr. Dannen paid attention to me?" Constance asked.

Again the shrug. "No. But it would be nice to be noticed for something other than looks. You're a full-figured beauty, dear sister, but you're head's as thick as a stupa."

This only made Constance comb harder. "It's difficult to be noticed for your brains when they're tied up under this mess."

Ivory flinched. "Connie, that hurts."

Constance faltered. She pulled the brush away, seeing something she didn't like in the reflection of the vanity — Estella Ivyweather, standing over a much younger Constance, with a comb, and her expectations, poised to strike. And even though her parents weren't here, were *never* there, their judgment hung over their daughters, and Constance, for a moment, forgot whose side she was on.

She handed Ivory the brush, though she was still intent that she understand. "Looking the part is the first step to playing it properly."

Ivory's violet eyes sparkled and sharpened. "I don't want to play the part someone else is picking out for me."

Constance's jaw set. "You were self-conscious when you met Madeline Mott. I noticed straight away, because it mattered to you. Look." She turned Ivory to face their reflections in the mirror. "You are so bright and have so much potential. But no one can see that past all of your . . . your *quirks.* Mr. Dannen flounces around expecting accolades when he's just a ridicule magnet. I just don't want the same thing to happen to you!"

"At least he's *himself*," Ivory countered. "Didn't it feel awful for him to be all over you because of where you're from? Don't pretend he was interested in who you are inside."

"That's not the point," she snapped. "You're too young to understand. I won't let you sabotage yourself." She grasped the brush and thrust it at Ivory. "Now come on!"

Ivory smacked the brush away, getting to her feet and sending the vanity stool tumbling. "Mind your own hair and leave mine out of it!"

Constance gasped, feeling the heat of her aggravation at the top of her head like a lightning strike. She moved to try to brush Ivory's hair herself, but Ivory was quick, and grabbed at the brush, the two of them grappling for supremacy. It didn't matter that this wasn't at all about Ivory's hair; Constance *had* to make her see. If Ivory could only comb out her tangles she'd look in the mirror and see how much something small could change her, make her see that the future wasn't so—

Ivory finally won, snapped the brush over her knee, and threw the pieces at Constance's astonished feet.

"I don't want what any of you want!" she screamed, taking the bristled head and pitching it across the room. It hit the wall by Arabella's tank with a *BANG* that made the spider scurry.

"I don't . . ." Ivory said, "want to be like you. I want to be *me*."

Constance was still clutching the handle tight to her chest, as though it could protect her from the horrible, violent shock of Ivory's pain.

"I just want to help you," Constance said quietly.

Ivory was already thrusting her boots on and throwing her heavy wool coat over her pyjamas. "You just want to help yourself," she seethed, only half missing the mark, leaving Constance in stunned silence. "I bet you're excited to see me off to Ferren Academy, just so they can turn me into another stuck-up *drone* ready to forget everything I ever dreamed of. One less thing for you to worry about, in my little box, doing Mother and Father's job for them!"

She snatched the terrarium into her arms and stomped out. Constance leapt up, wanting to explain, but too angry to admit she was wrong. "Where are you going? It's the middle of the night!"

"To sleep in the car," Ivory spat back, already in the hall and making good on her escape. "I can't be in the same house as someone who has such vile machinations towards me."

Constance followed her to the top of the stairs and tried to nab her by the cuff of her sweater but missed. She dared not go any farther, in case she woke the birds or the landlady. "Get back here!" she hissed, clutching the banister. "I'm warning you, Ivory!"

But Ivory spun on her heel, injury still playing on her face. "You're my sister, Connie." The nickname plunged into Constance's heart like a blade. "I thought you were supposed to like me no matter what."

Ivory turned the foyer doorknob and was out in a flicker, leaving Constance at the top of the stairs, judged by the faceless gaze of the astronomer's painting.

Despite the complete and utter dark, comfort was impossible. Ivory tossed and turned on the backseat, cold for having forgotten a blanket and resigned to staring into Arabella's terrarium. She could barely see into it by the light of the lamppost shining through the open driver's-side window. But the spider still offered companionship with her tiny presence. Her front legs clicked against the glass. Ivory pressed her forehead to it.

She was exhausted and miserable, but she wouldn't go back inside. Not for the world. She knew it was what Constance expected, and that made the protest all the more precious. Ivory mustn't give in; she couldn't. She needed to show her parents that she was her own person; now, sadly, she needed to show the same to her sister, whom she'd imagined, maybe with spending more time together this summer, could become a kindred spirit. After that display upstairs, though? Ivory felt like Constance was no different from her parents. After a fitful hour, Ivory finally fell asleep.

But something crept out of the darkness and past Ivory's restless dreams. Silver threads spun through the driver's-side open window, which Ivory had forgotten to shut. The threads wound deftly around the parking break and, with a slow push down, disengaged it. More gauzy threads wrapped around the body, the chassis. With calculated strength, they worked in concert to turn the car and edge it carefully to the rim of the Mount Quixx crater.

Slowly, precisely, whatever was at the other end of the threads pulled it down into the cavernous maw of the fissure, and both the car, and Ivory in it, vanished into the dark.

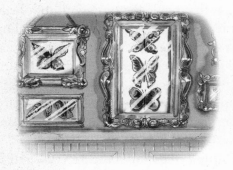

3

THE MOUNTAIN WITH
A MIND OF ITS OWN

"No, Klaus!" the high voice giggled, somewhere on the edge of Constance's recognition.

"Shh," came the laughing reply. "No one will hear us up here."

"Maybe not, but the butterflies will give us away!"

Who is in my room? Constance felt her face screw up but she couldn't open her eyes. *And why are they being so inappropriate?*

Yet their laughter was so happy, so ridiculously free. Something spooled out of her heart like throbbing thread, and Constance suddenly felt sad. She had never laughed like that with anyone in her life.

But the laughter was fading into a diminished tinkling, like a broken bell, and it was then she opened her eyes. Her heart lurched when she caught a flicker, a reflection in the butterflies' glass cases: a white-haired man lifting a dark-haired woman in his arms, twirling her like she was the world, and he was her axis.

Constance bolted, fumbling for the bedside light. The room was awash in orange. And she was alone.

A dream, she reassured herself, trying to disentangle her slow-moving, waking mind. Her eyes raked across the butterflies surrounding her, but they gave no comfort or answer. And neither did Ivory's empty bed.

So she'd stayed out in the car all night. *Typical tenacity.* Constance sighed back into her starchy pillow. Just thinking about last night made her heart creep up her throat. Apologies *were* in order, but she still wished she could explain, or even show Ivory why her crusade was so important. She wouldn't have to compromise herself forever. Just long enough to make it through school in peace. After that, Ivory could be whoever she pleased. Or at least *marry* whoever she pleased. That's how it was going to go, right?

But after all her social grandstanding, that last option made Constance the sickest — marriage — in a way far worse than any examination or school presentation ever had. Wasn't there more to life, after all her sacrifices, her hard work . . . couldn't she do more than settle just as her life was beginning? But she couldn't avoid reality forever. She wasn't prepared to face the consequences of disappointing her parents. Or her school friends, who were all on the same track. These were the people whose opinion Constance valued. Still, she wanted to keep who she was intact. But she didn't know who that was anymore.

Constance got out of bed and tied her robe neatly at her waist. She would extricate Ivory from the car before breakfast, at least, to try to start the day off properly.

The seeing-eye birds coming off the night shift swept in as she went downstairs, pecking their shift mates out of the roost so the house might wake up. Mourning doves and nuthatches pulled back the draperies while the mail goose, Bernard, snoozed on the porch, his head tucked under his wing. Constance tiptoed around them all, still avoiding the queasy thought of animals changing her linens.

The fog, now no longer much of a surprise, was stirring like a marvellously hearty soup today, and Constance could barely see past the gate. No matter; she knew the car was parked just across the street beside the mountain crater. She stopped at the curb, squinting for a sign of headlights of other cars, before remembering the tail-end of another strange thing Ms. Bougainvillea had said. Something about cars. Something about thieves . . .

Constance shook it off, her hands stretched out as she crossed the street, waiting for them to connect with the smooth steel of her parents' car.

Suddenly a wind took up and, like an airy solvent, worked the fog away. Constance hissed sharply when she realized how close she had come again to the lip of the cliff that curved down into who-knew-what.

She backed up, carefully looked again at her surroundings. Houses stood in rows like a crowd of drooping mourners, close-shouldered and miserable. A dog let out a warning bark somewhere and promptly fell silent. A large black crow divided the clouds curling around the mountain and entered the open kitchen window of the Happy Bell.

The car was gone.

Constance ran back into the house, panting and scattering the birds that had come home to sleep. "Ms. Bougainvillea!" she shouted.

She found her in the kitchen, tapping something into the crow's mouth before it flew back out the window. "Did you fall into the stairs again, dear?"

Frederic twittered around Constance's head as if scolding her for being so loud. She swatted him away.

"I'm sorry, Ms. Bougainvillea, but I . . ." Constance caught the reflection of herself in the landlady's ridiculously huge glasses. Panic-stricken, hair askew. She decided to breathe. "Have you seen Ivory this morning?"

Ms. Bougainvillea and Frederic tilted their heads as one.

"I mean. Did you . . . hear her? Around?"

"Not yet, dear," she replied. "It's early, and she's young. Let her sleep in a little before she wakes up looking like me!"

Constance paled. She didn't want to get into the curdling details of the previous night. "Yes, well . . . she isn't in bed. Might you have seen— I mean—" Deep sigh, hand to forehead. "Our car, Ms. Bougainvillea. It's—"

The landlady's cup clanked on her saucer. "Is it gone?"

"It . . . yes," Constance rattled, trying desperately to sound nonchalant as her molars ground to a fine paste. "Wait a moment!" She whirled for the foyer, for the little bowl on the stand by the door where she'd left the car keys. Ivory was brazen, but at least a fourteen-year-old behind the wheel was easily spotted.

The keys, however, were still in the bowl. Which meant—

"Oh no." Ms. Bougainvillea sucked on her teeth at Constance's shoulder.

"What?" Constance didn't like that look.

"I'm so very sorry, dear, but I don't think you're going to see your car again. Whoever's been stealing cars has been hiding them curiously well."

Constance cleared her throat and pushed back the oncoming panic attack, trying to move forward. "Is there anywhere I might file a report?"

"Mm." Ms. Bougainvillea groaned, leaning against the rickety hall table and looking as if she hadn't slept in days. Frederic clucked but she shooed him off. "Constable Derraugh has been filing any complaints, I think, though I'm not sure where. The police station has been quite useless for the last few years, but luckily he lives a few roads away. Best to tell him all about it."

Constance shot up the stairs and was halfway out of her robe before Ms. Bougainvillea called after her. "And don't fret about your sister. I'm sure she's just playing a trick. Sisters do like to torture each other."

Constance paused at the Butterfly Room's doorway, shaking off her remorse and relief at the statement. Maybe Ivory *was* just trying to make her worry. And Constance felt, deep down in her heart, that she deserved it.

Constable Derraugh's door may have been the first, but it wasn't the only one Constance knocked on. In fact, she was introduced to the bulk of Quixx's citizens by the middle of the afternoon, and her knuckles, as well as her usual string of pleasantries, were worn out.

"Yes, thank you, I'll be sure to give these to her . . ." Constance quickly retreated from Mrs. Calabash's front stoop, a box of cinnamon pastries under her arm. She juggled it with the other assorted prizes she'd been given to take back to the Happy Bell.

"An' best stay away from the mountain, lass!" the rakish housewife called from the door. "Don't want to be stirrin' any ghoulies up, hope your sister didn't try the same!"

Constance nodded and nearly fell onto the sidewalk as she tried to renegotiate her packages. And her jaded skepticism.

Even though it was eighteen households, four hours, and ten hand-outs later, Constance really had nothing to show for it. The pastries were kind, but everyone seemed keen on wringing their hands about the impossible — if Ivory disappeared and happened to go to the mountain (the place she'd been determined to go since they arrived), she was a lost cause. Monsters being what they were and all. *Best not try a rescue attempt.*

The constable, as well as most everyone else, had shown up at the door wearing a robe over his tattered cotton pyjamas and had not been as helpful as she'd hoped. With a pipe in the crook of one gnarled fist and the other scratching the globe of his ponch, his droopy eyes barely appraised her.

"Constable Derraugh?" Constance asked dubiously.

"Of the First Quixx Division, yes'm," he replied through grey whiskers, sounding dozy and less proud than he might have once been. "What seems to be the trouble?"

Constance raised an eyebrow at his lack of uniform. "I wouldn't want to bother you if you're not on duty . . ."

"Don't be daft, love, the First is always on duty. We can scrabble with the best of 'em, even in our unsundries."

"Right." *Best get down to brass tacks.* "It's about my car—"

She gave him a detailed description, when last she'd seen it, and tried to ignore how the constable wrote it all down on the palm of his hand with a pen fished out of his bathrobe.

"Mm-hmm," he sniffed, his sagging blue eyes as ineffectual as his sideburns. "I'll be sure to file it with the rest of them, love, and no mistake."

With a resounding lack of confidence, she managed an ill smile. "Thank you. I don't suppose I could file a missing persons report while I'm here, too?"

He blinked at her very slowly, then looked at his other hand. "Maybe a brief description, or else I'll have to write it on me leg."

Her last request had been to see the constable's illustrious "file" on the other citizens who had lost their vehicles lately, and after rifling around in some old hat boxes in the spare room, he produced a very neat (to her surprise) file complete with names and addresses. This had, of course, led to all of the pastries and the monster warnings, and she was no better off as she went back to the Happy Bell.

As she considered it, there were only two possible outcomes that could arise from the car being taken, and neither one was really so dire as Ivory's disappearance.

One: if the car was gone for good, Constance would simply telegraph her parents, who would now be completely obliged to drive up to Quixx and join them, or at least come and pick them up. Then they could have some time alone, to talk, to get everything out in the open and deal with it, and Constance wouldn't feel so trapped the upcoming year. Maybe they could even strike up a different compromise than the one she'd given prior to summer's start.

Two: her parents would be angry. Which would still mean she would get to speak to them, in trouble or otherwise. Not so bad. She imagined a third avenue, too, but knew it was better to laugh off than entertain: she and Ivory would be stuck in Quixx forever, forgotten by their parents until they grew as blind and bird-brained as Miss Bee. *Though Ivory would probably feel right at home*, Constance thought.

As noble as her quest may have been, knocking on the doors of all the car-theft victims proved as useless as going to Constable Derraugh in the first place. One of the addresses was Mx. Mott's. Constance stood before the enormous duplex, conservative and tidy, and remembering their first encounter and the principal's sharp frown, had felt the urgent desire to walk briskly in the other direction. Yet this wasn't about her, not at this moment. She'd gathered up the courage, knocked, and received no answer. As she left, she made a note to try the school, in case Mx. Mott was there, doing schoolmaster-type things . . . she would have enough courage restored after teatime, surely.

It was past one by the time she returned to the Happy Bell, unloading all of her parcels with the help of a pair of overzealous pelicans and Bernard (a slow day for the post, apparently). She was far too dejected to announce herself as she flopped onto the stiff sofa in the solarium, kicking up dust and sneezing it away. *I'll bet Ivory somehow hotwired the car and is on a tear hundreds of miles away by now,* Constance clucked. *I wouldn't blame her.*

Ms. Bougainvillea shambled in, watering can in hand and Frederic on her finger, tapping with his beak when they came near a plant pot. Constance watched her for a while. How did this woman *really* manage around such a massive house, alone, with only birds to guide her? Had she been a miss her entire life, always managing without a husband and surviving on wits alone (if she'd ever had any)?

But then again, as Constance had learned today, encountering house husbands and stolid working mothers and overlapping family networks, as brash as they were bucolic, there were plenty of people in Quixx who got along on the periphery of "normal." Surely Constance could, too . . . but towards what end, she couldn't even dream up. That was Ivory's specialty. How much longer could Ms. Bougainvillea survive on her own, anyway? And could Constance even be brave enough to imagine such a life?

"What did you discover, pet?" Ms. Bougainvillea chirped, her back to Constance as she poured water into a dieffenbachia.

Constance sat up primly. "Only that you are very popular with your neighbours, Ms. Bougainvillea." *And everyone thinks Ivory, and the car, were eaten by monsters.*

She laughed, a grating rusted-gear churn in the back of her throat. "It's a small town. You either grow up with everyone or help raise their children."

"Or both," Constance remarked, getting up to take the watering can to finish feeding the plants. Ms. Bougainvillea held on to Constance's arm as they made the rounds.

"I bet your sister could tell you where all of these green things came from," she said. "That Ivory is so much sharper about the world than me, and she's lived in it less."

Constance sighed. "She is very bright for her age. But she can be too headstrong for her own good."

"She values her dreams. You must tell her to take care of them." Ms. Bougainvillea smoothed the leaves of a brome-liad. "I had dreams once, but I've forgotten where I put them."

Constance tried to smile, but it was no use. "Did you ever have a sister, Ms. Bougainvillea?" It took a moment for the landlady's face to change, and Constance backpedalled. "I don't mean to pry, of course . . ."

"It's all right." Constance helped Ms. Bougainvillea sigh her rickety bulk into a chair at the tea table. "I was just thinking how different things may have been, to have a sister."

Constance was taken aback as she sat down. "What do you mean?"

"To grow up with another woman, to share everything with. To have someone who accepted you while still knowing what a fury you could be. It's a very special bond . . . I imagine."

Constance's chest tightened, but she pressed past it, trying to defend herself. "I'm just worried about Ivory, that's all," she said. "She doesn't know what's best for her at times."

"And do you?" Ms. Bougainvillea tilted her head.

"Well, *yes*." Constance straightened, incredulous that she was being painted into a corner by a blind octogenarian and her avian employees. "I'd like to think I've done most of her raising, after all. That I've worked hard to give her an example of what's proper and good. And I don't want to see her getting hurt because she's stubborn about the way things are and what is expected of her."

"Mm." Ms. Bougainvillea shut her milky eyes and gave a single nod. "But you can't protect her forever, my dear. The world will find its way under such high fences."

Constance suddenly realized she had never spoken so openly to an adult before, about Ivory or about anything. It was horribly cathartic, but she didn't want to go too far.

"We had an argument," she blurted.

"Mm."

"And now I don't know where she's gone." Constance bristled. "If she's doing it to torture me, it's working."

Ms. Bougainvillea looked surprised. "Come now," she said, "you know your sister best out of anyone. There has to be somewhere she would go, knowing you wouldn't dare follow her."

And then, the feeling again. It prickled in gathered patches up her spine and encouraged the knot in her ribs to cotton up tighter. Constance looked over her shoulder at the oppressive shape beyond the solarium window, taunting her with its crooked curve. Something tingled in her inner ear, like a chord that refused to resolve.

She swallowed, barely whispered. "She wanted to go. But I told her she couldn't."

Frederic let out a sharp chirp and fluttered out of the room. Ms. Bougainvillea's flashing eyes spoke of a sudden waking from a long coma. "The mountain?"

"Yes," Constance answered, her body gone numb as her heart pumped jaggedly. Ms. Bougainvillea straightened to her aching feet, face hardened.

"Mount Quixx is not a place to be ignored, as I'm sure you know," she said. Constance wanted to sidestep her meaning, but she nodded anyway. "Ivory won't have gotten far, but she can't come back on her own." She came round the table and took Constance's hand. "You have to find her before something else does."

Constance felt both chilled and heated by those dead eyes, and the clammy, shrunken hand that had captured hers. She tilted away. "Isn't there anyone who can—"

"No." Ms. Bougainvillea's hard face suddenly softened. "It has to be you. No one has gone up that mountain in many years. And once you get there, you'll know why."

Constance pulled away, but she refused to entertain what she'd heard all afternoon. "The 'monsters,' you mean? You can't expect me to—"

"It doesn't matter if you believe me or not." Ms. Bougainvillea turned, extending her hand as Frederic led a sparrow hawk clutching a very faded scarf into the room. She grasped it and handed it to Constance. "You must find her before dark. And you must have your wits about you."

Constance took the scarf, feeling more eclipsed by this nonsense as the minutes passed. She grimaced, forgetting the tender moment she'd just shared with this obviously batty old woman as she moved to leave. "You've been really helpful, Ms. Bougainvillea, but I think I can manage without a scarf."

The same clammy grip now snatched at Constance's wrist, precise and holding on with a demon strength. "Take care, my love," she warned. "Cynicism won't save you. But the scarf just may."

Suddenly the room was clotted with birds. Constance hadn't noticed them fly in, and never before had she been so struck by all of them looking down at her. Even Frederic seemed to have a new menace in his tiny black eyes. Constance backed out of the room.

"Ah," she cleared her throat, skin rippling. "I'm sure she'll be fine. I'm sure I'll be fine. Thank you. It's . . . a lovely scarf."

The birds collectively fluffed their guard feathers out, their discordant squawks following Constance out the front door. She didn't dare turn around until she was safely out of eyeshot, and into the road.

The way down the crater at the base of the mountain wasn't as difficult as it had at first looked. Though she had spent nearly half an hour pacing around, undecided, Constance finally willed her knees into obedience and sat on the crater's edge. It grew darker the longer she hesitated.

It has to be you. This was stupid. All of this. But it was the only place Ivory would go. And she'd do it just so Constance would have to go after her.

So with a scowling groan, Constance turned over, placing one leather-shod foot, and then the other, into a bare foothold in the rock a shin's depth down. Then she found another one, until she had managed a good few feet in. All the while, she stared straight ahead, gaining purchase by feel alone. She refused to look down. She refused to look up. *No. I can't do this.* She started climbing back out. *There has to be someone who—*

The breeze plastered her long kilt against her legs and teased her hair out of the confines of Ms. Bougainvillea's "magical" scarf. Where was the Constance of old? The one who weighed every decision carefully? Who would never have dreamed of clinging to the side of a cliff at the bottom of a mountain that everyone feared was infested with murderous beasties?

While trying to hoist herself out of the crater, she made the mistake of looking down. Beneath her the mist had the consistency of quicksilver, weaving deceptively around what seemed to be antler bracken, maybe trees. The curling grey shapes looked to be opening their arms to her. Feverish to snatch.

Something — someone — caught the corner of her eye. Close to the Happy Bell, standing at the edge of the crater. The figure of a slight woman. She, too, wore a scarf about her head and stared defiantly at the mountain. Maybe this was some kind of sick ritual. Constance ducked her head, not wanting to be caught out — then peeked back up, realizing she may have been seen anyway. She called, "Hello?"

No reply. Before Constance could fumble an explanation for what she was doing, the woman dove down the crater edge and vanished into the mist. The movement was a flash, like a seal slipping into the sea. As quickly as the woman had disappeared, Constance slipped. And tumbled.

Down, down, down, indeed. Fortunately, she twisted herself over so the curved dirt wall of the crater was at her back instead of coming down in a free fall. She toppled and screamed, and she couldn't stop for what seemed like her entire life, until she crashed through the black branches and came to a stop at the bottom.

Ripped skirt, torn jacket, and twig-filled hair aside, the damage wasn't severe, she realized, as she lay still in the crumbling leaves. She was, admittedly, made of sterner stuff, but her muscles, including her behind, ached something fierce. When she looked up, she couldn't see at all where she'd come from, for the tight grip of the dead-black trees interlocked and crushed out the sky. She sat up and touched her head. The scarf was still there. Of course it was.

But she was not alone in the pit. Sinister, hungry shapes loomed all around her, giant jaws wide open in soundless, insatiable sleep. She scrambled back, throwing herself to the ground and shielding her head. She tightened, waiting for the blow.

And kept waiting.

Constance peered out from under her arm. The shapes hadn't moved. Steeling herself, she got shakily to her feet, picked up a discarded bough, and advanced.

She threw the stick and leapt back when it rebounded with a *clang*. One of the beasts was within reach, and finally impulse won out over logic, and she put her hand out.

Smooth. Cold. What she had thought a jaw was a hood. She spun around. Cars. Maybe twenty or more huddled around her, all perfectly unmarked, except for the fact that their engines, tires, and parts had been stripped. Whoever had been taking them had done a good job of keeping it quiet and hiding the evidence.

Which meant . . . Constance darted from car to car, only able to tell the makes or models when she was inches away. Then she found it, untouched — her parents' car! She practically dove through the driver's-side window.

"Ivory?" she said, despite herself. Aside from a heavy wool jacket, the backseat was empty, and so was the terrarium underneath it.

Suddenly the notion that Ivory was here of her own accord vanished with the speed of Slanner Dannen's fame. Someone, or something, had brought her down here. And it may not be far away.

Constance remembered the woman from moments earlier. "Hello?" she cried weakly into the darkness. She heard nothing, not the sound of crunching undergrowth, of human breath, of fear. The silence was opalescent, somehow shimmering. She was truly alone.

The panic was a claw under her chin, but she had to focus. Constance looked for clues instead. She cursed herself for not bringing a flashlight, until she realized that the path underneath her carried fresh, familiar boot treads. Bent over and scuttling, Constance followed them with renewed vigour, hair and clothes and even the scarf being yanked at by insistent bracken. One caught her by the skirt, and as she wrestled with it, she stumbled backward into a wall.

Not a wall. The mountain itself. Constance looked about and realized, from here, that the bracken started growing upward and sideways, lifting off the ground and rooting horizontally. And hidden amongst the trunks of the mutilated trees and shrubs was a path. It was rough, and it had probably taken years to hew into the rock, but it was wide enough to climb up by, even if the way was so steep. It made more of a ladder than anything else, but luckily there were two ropes on either side, allowing her to get a grip and lift herself up each step.

Constance did not recall ever having to do something that took so much out of her as that climb did. Even her marrow felt raw. How could Ivory have made such an effort, or her captor, for that matter? The exertion was inhuman, and she was happy there wasn't anyone around who could hear her grunting savagely or witness her ripping her skirt angrily just to get better range of motion.

Suddenly the ascent changed. It felt more like Constance was crawling forward than clawing up. Her arms felt light. Her whole body. She looked down. But she was looking more backward than down. How . . . ? Then her ankles lifted off the ground, and everything went upside down.

Constance didn't have time to scream before she scrabbled at the black rock beneath her — beside her, over her. Anti-gravity pulled her end-over-top, her tailspin gathering momentum the higher she floated up. She grabbed an exposed root, her fingers slipping, until a hard wind buffeted her, slamming her back-first into the mountain, throwing her up and up—

Until she stopped.

Constance shut her eyes hard, her head whirling, counting backward. When she opened them, she squirmed, twisted her neck. She was stuck in a close-knit clot of trees whose spindly arms jutted from the mountain and now sheltered her. The mist blew away as she kicked her legs up, and beneath her torn stockings and ruined shoes, Constance could see down into Quixx. She had fallen higher up than she wanted to think about.

The scream sounded so much like her own that, for a moment, Constance thought it was an echo. But it rattled into her skull a second time, and she knew exactly who it belonged to.

The trees trapping Constance grew in tightly set layers, and she clawed through the resin-soaked needles to the next tree above. The more branches she pulled down, the more light broke through, and eventually so did she. She hoisted herself into the open air, limbs shaking, seeing another clump of trees maybe ten feet above. Crouched in the centre of them, and still in her pyjamas—

"Ivory!" Constance bellowed.

Her sister whipped her ashen face towards her voice, purple eyes lit with terror. "Connie!"

Constance didn't falter this time. "Just hold on!"

But Constance wasn't going anywhere, either. Her shoe was lodged in a tight cranny between a whorled root and the rock face of the mountain behind it. Her entire body went cold when she realized she was stuck, and then straight to jelly when she saw Ivory wasn't looking at her anymore.

It was scaling down the trees and rocks with abrupt movements on four sinewy legs, just above Ivory's platform. It was the colour of bloated fish flesh, with a flat plane where its eyes should have been. Horrible muscles rippled under the thin scales, and even though it had no eyes, Constance knew it was watching them. It opened its mouth, and a shattered-glass rattle faltered out.

Constance was so close to losing herself to the oncoming panic attack, the edges of her vision going black, but she only saw Ivory. "I'm stuck," Constance whimpered, shaking her head as the stars prickled in her eyes. "You're going to have to come down to me!"

The creature scuttled down in a pulse-beat, and Constance realized it was not four legs but four *arms*, inverted and splayed with slick spikes sticking out of the skin. Its head made a terrible creaking sound, cracked, then swivelled a full one-eighty. It edged closer to Ivory.

"No!" Constance screamed, both at the monster and her own body betraying her. The beast leapt towards her, landing on the narrow canopy as Ivory dove out of the way. Constance could see tears on Ivory's cheeks, but the younger Ivyweather was trying to stay focused and climb down.

The creaking rattle came again, but it sounded more vicious as the spine-arms chopped away the trees with a swoop. Full branches came plummeting past Ivory and into Constance's face. Ivory was caught at the edge of the trees when the creature leapt into the air, aiming directly for her.

Crash. Rip. A guttural moan raked up and down the mountainside. Something larger and fiercer, a flash of orange and indigo, had taken hold of the beast and thrown it face-first into the obsidian rock. When the spine-armed thing tried to retaliate, the greater creature threw the smaller one aside, then scuttled after it in such a flash that neither Constance nor Ivory could tell what it was. The mist drew tighter.

"Ivory!" Constance screamed again, losing sight of her, almost losing herself entirely as a wave of icy dread numbed her hands. Then she heard a horrible crack and smash that ended the fight, and she saw the eyeless beast tumbling towards her.

Constance flattened inside the trees and crouched around her confined ankle, narrowly missing the blow of the body ripping through the trees around her. They fell away like flotsam, following the screaming creature down into the crater beyond.

"Connie?" came her sister's voice out of the impenetrable grey.

"I'm all right!" she called back, panting and almost laughing in her survivor's disbelief. "I'm—"

Creeeeeak. Crack. Crack *CRACK.* The roots she clung to her were pulling out of the mountain under her weight, and she still couldn't rip her foot free.

"Ivory," she whimpered. "Ivory!"

But her foot *did* come free. Followed by her entire body. Time went thick. It tore off Constance's best intentions with the sinews still attached. And then there were the final visions playing keen in her dying sight — a giant spider falling towards her, too many arms and legs outstretched — before her heart choked her panicked brain into oblivion.

Ivory did not look away as the creature split the mist in front of her. In its steady arms, Constance seemed oddly at peace. The creature extended two more empty hands towards Ivory.

She only hesitated a moment, long enough to straighten her torn pyjamas and wipe her nose. Then she went into the hands, and they climbed up the mountain together.

4

TEA WITH THE
ARACHNASTRONOMER

There were old paths, old ways, the mountain whispered. *Those who lived on me knew how to navigate them best, knew how to master the crags and jetties, the atmosphere, and they were grateful for this place and its wonders.*

But there is a scar. I feel it teased by the wind, a gash on my face. It still burns. The sky betrayed me, dropped something unforgivable. And the sky murmurs, sometimes, promising that it will fall again, and my body won't be enough to protect those below.

A balance will be set. Even the best intentions can bring down a mountain. There were old paths, old ways . . . please walk them one last time.

Constance could feel her forehead crease, as it often did in the lecture halls at Ferren Academy. Trying to tease out the teacher's answer.

But all she could think was, *Why are you telling me? What can I do? Will this be on the exam?* And then with a pinch of terror, she realized she hadn't studied for the exam, and that she would fail, and that'd be the end of everything, and—

A crow's call cracked the air like lake ice, dragging Constance into waking. She would have sprung up, were she not stuck fast to the surface on which she'd been sleeping.

Sticky. It took her more strength than plausible to wrest her cheek from the pillow — *Was it a pillow?* — and lift her head into the light. *Light.* Strange. She blinked. There was a gleam coming in through the doorway, something resembling the sun, which she hadn't seen in weeks. The light stung her eyes, illuminating ruined stonework, as well as the shimmering webs that held it together.

Sticky. Webs. *Oh, Jolting Jordana, NO.*

Constance ripped herself from her nest, which used to be an old brass four-poster bed, half caved in and fluffed up with thick white bands of the sticky stuff that kept the building surrounding her from coming down. She held her arms close, her eyes squinting to discern, in the strange light, what kind of nightmare she'd woken up into.

Suddenly lightheaded from her few exploratory steps, Constance caught herself in the charred doorway of her chambers. *No, stay upright*, came her next thought. *Ivory.* Yes. That was why she'd come out here, wasn't it? Here . . . the mountain. But this couldn't possibly be on the mountain, this house? Manor? Thing? Perhaps she was back in Quixx. Or even better, Ferren City. *I'm in a house of horrors, either way.*

She needed to calm down. She inhaled sharply, exhaled slowly, turning and shielding her maladjusted eyes from what had to be the setting sun, casting colour and dusky shadows into the room, and for a moment Constance thought she hadn't seen a sunset in years.

Wherever her current location, she was in an old stone cottage with high, beamed ceilings, with a thick floor dug into the very rock of the mountain, but something had torn through a good chunk of the far wall, rending stone and woodwork like it was paper, leaving it to rot. And rot it had, save for the patch job, anyway. Constance reached out and tapped the unassuming white stuff. It was light, silky, and cool. It only felt sticky the longer she left her finger there to warm it. When she tried to pull away, she found it snared like a Silanese finger trap.

Whatever it was, it was tough. And supple — she had slept on a bed of it, after all, and nothing ached in her body except her ribs, which her heart was sledgehammering against. Impressive stuff but picturing the legion of scuttlies that made it made her skin crawl. She didn't have Ivory's curiosity.

Ivory. Back to basics.

Constance crept out of the room into a barren hall. The huge doorless front entry led outside and into the air, and on the opposite side of the hall, a giant stone staircase whirled up into a tower. Constance quailed at the idea of more climbing, but she had come this far (somehow), so she took to the stairs.

Constance ran out of breath more quickly than usual, and despite the circumstances, couldn't for the life of her attribute it to fear. The air simply felt thinner. She picked her way to the landing and passed by more empty rooms, until she came to a wooden stepladder, the top rungs busted, that led to a trap door above her head.

It's now or never. She went as high as she could, took a deep breath, raised her arms, and pushed.

Inch by inch the heavy hatch rose until it slammed open with a crash. Constance would have fallen down the stepladder at her heels but for clinging to the opening she'd burst into.

The light pierced her eyes again, and the breeze coming in from the open roof snagged her hair, which was no longer protected by the scarf. Oh. *The scarf . . .* Constance had only half a second to remember that it was important, still not really understanding why, before she caught a glimpse of her sister perched on a high stool across the room, a giant book in her lap, safe as houses.

Ivory couldn't help but smile, shaking her head. "Even without style and timing, you always make an entrance, Connie."

"Ivory!" Constance cried, lifting a leg to clamber into the room.

"You always were the frail one, though," Ivory admonished, rushing to help Constance into the open attic, whose roof, it seemed, had been partially ripped off by whatever had ravaged the rest of the place. Constance sprang into worry mode faster than Ivory could reply.

"You're not hurt, are you?" She patted Ivory down, her only reply a bemused head shaking before Constance snatched her hands angrily. "How could you go off on your own like that? And the car! Mother and Father are going to stuff and hang me. How am I going to get it out of that trench? And how are *we* going to get out of that trench? I'm getting ahead of myself. We'll figure something out. Come on."

After adjusting the skewed flannel collar under Ivory's chin, Constance tried to tactfully drag her to the hatch. But Ivory resisted.

"Don't just stand there!" Constance's worry meter was hovering over hysteria. "It's nearly dark, and I'm not about to stick around and wait until the older sibling of that *thing* on the mountainside comes for us!"

Ivory folded her arms, looking more bored than anything. "You're overreacting."

"*Isth thar sumfig tha mattah?*" asked a muffled voice behind them.

Constance whirled, nerves tight as a primed bayonet, and realized what had eclipsed the evening light behind them.

It was a horse. With eight legs. Eight legs that were at least ten feet long, tapered into pincers, suspending the thing from a roof beam on an impossibly thin thread. *Thread.* Oh, Dinah. Not a horse, no, not a horse at all.

A giant . . .

Spider.

Constance tore backward into a large bookcase, sending herself and the shelf's bric-a-brac flying . . . but she didn't hit the ground. And neither did the shelf. She was suspended in the air, defying gravity as she had when she'd floated up the mountain, but in a less violent way than before. She could feel herself being carefully righted on to her feet. The glare of the setting sun caught the threads wrapped around her wrists and midsection, and the others attached to the bookcase and its contents.

The light cast the huge body — *thorax* — of the beast into crisp relief, its horrible legs working akimbo as it pulled itself down the length of the thread, and Constance felt her blood calcify as the creature turned over and landed in front of her.

Yes, her inner voice said, wry and snide, *this is what a heart attack feels like.* She couldn't do more than shrink into the shelf at her back, staring — for the monster had eight legs, oh yes, but there were arms, too, four of them, spindly and just as narrow, and they reached out and . . . and . . .

. . . went about repairing the huge rip in her skirt with precise stitches until it looked good as new.

"*Em dredall urra out tha!*" the stifled voice made a comeback.

Constance's throat, she was sure, had seized up, but her precious courtesies clung to life. "Pardon?" she squeaked.

She twitched as she felt the threads that were holding her up disentangle and fall about her scuffed shoes. One hand, as there were four, reached up and lifted the welding mask from the face of its owner.

"Phew. Sorry, forgot I had this thing on." The voice was softer and more jovial now, and the mask and gloves were discarded on the shelf. "I'd said I'm dreadfully sorry. The scare, I mean. I was so distracted up there that I hadn't even heard you come . . ."

Her pulse fell. *It speaks.* And its diction, so crisp and refined — what was happening? Constance stared into the four bright amber eyes above her, and she could feel her heart pumping. *Those monstrous eyes,* came her next thought. *They're as bright as sun-caught maple syrup.* Reason slammed back into place, and she closed her mouth. The eyes were suddenly expectant. She'd been tuning out the conversation.

"I said *it's lovely to meet you,*" the creature enunciated louder, their words creeping from a long, thin mouth, producing an elegant accent and an assured smile.

The exceptional manners threw Constance off. She suddenly pictured one of the many books she'd had to study (and balance on her head) on the careful art of conversation. She flipped madly through the pages, searching for the current scenario. *Spider-creature thing is trying to bounce polite candour off you. Spider-creature may be basting you in a delectable sauce with its mind. The correct course of action, despite your imminent death, is—*

"Constance Ivyweather," she choked, her brain telling her to curtsey. It came out more like a faltering jig.

"Constance." They seemed to be searching for something inside their own head, tapping a temple with a slender finger. "Ah yes. 'Assured. A fixed mark, steadfast.' Like the North Star, our only fixed mark in the heavens."

She couldn't stop staring. Mesmerized. Like at the scene of a crime. The creature's welcoming countenance changed. "Are you sure you're all right, Miss Constance?"

Slow blink. *Spider-creature asks how you are — is really asking how do you taste?*

"I don't . . . know," she finally replied. Ivory shot her a look, which was piercing enough to make Constance wobble on her weak ankles and nearly topple over again. The beautiful hands caught her.

"How about we sit you down? Don't want you landing on something we can't fix." The thorax twitched and turned — one moment a thread shot deftly from a spinneret, and the next it had pulled a chair from across the room and under Constance's failing body.

"Tea?" the creature asked Constance. Ivory pulled up her stool.

"Tea would be lovely. Isn't that right, Connie?"

Numb, she looked at her hands. *I guess I would go well with tea.*

"Please." Ivory rolled her eyes. The creature moved off to a workbench behind them, leaving the two to their own confidence.

Ivory thrust her sister's chin up in her very serious hand. "Listen to me, Constance Ivyweather. I know what you're thinking, and I know what you're like." Constance's eyes were swimming back into focus, and her mouth floundered around a hundred different pleas. Ivory pinched her lips closed.

"Right now, we are guests in the home of the person who saved our lives. Nod, please." Constance nodded. "And we don't whimper or stare at our hosts when we are guests in their home, do we?"

Paralyzed, Constance shook her head slowly. "Very good. We drink our tea, and we keep our heads, and we act normal. Remember, being normal is *so* important to you."

She released her sister's face, the last few words ringing with callous revenge as Ivory smoothed the dirt-stained lap of her also-patched pyjama pants. With everything that had happened, Constance had forgotten about last night. About the shame she'd subjected Ivory to, and how it had brought them both here in the first place. She was at everyone's mercy, it seemed.

The sound of the tea trolley pulling up beside them rattled Constance's nerves and put her into a temporary state of lucidity. *Fine.* She would play Ivory's horrible game of *tea-time-from-the-netherworld.* And maybe they'd have a chance at surviving the next few minutes.

Constance sat up stiffly, her ankles tucked under her chair while her blood surged, tiny spines of fear bursting under her flesh. The only thing that gave her away was how tightly she clenched her recently repaired skirt, her eyes trained on the three-fingered hands moving gracefully from the teapot to the sugar tongs. She didn't want to look at them, at *it,* Good Godot, but she couldn't stop herself. The double-jointed, round body was bright orange, striated with black, yet the creature's main body was smartly dressed in a crimson necktie, olive waistcoat, and black overcoat. The cuffs were gold-buttoned and crisp.

"Three lumps just as you like it, Miss Ivory," rung that soothing voice again. It passed her sister a cup with a third hand, since the first pair was occupied with the pouring. The fourth hand picked up the next cup, presumably Constance's.

Ivory smiled back. "Thank you, Derrek." She glanced at her elder sister, and realizing she was still staring dead and sidelong at the tea trolley, she kicked her.

"Ow!" Constance rubbed her shin, and found the creature was blinking down at her again.

"And yourself?"

I will probably be fine at medium-rare.

"Black," Constance peeped.

The creature — Derrek — poured the tea with the skill of a Havanese shrine maiden, reaching over and placing the cup and saucer directly into Constance's shaking hands. She coloured, spilling half of it onto her kilt.

"I'm sorry! Allow me—"

A huge, hairy leg swept a napkin over the spill site, and Constance braced herself to pass out. *Stop! Stay awake, damn you!*

"*Hurk*— I— all right, that— that's fine, th-thank you— Derrek," she stumbled dumbly, trying not to leap out of her chair, let alone her own skin. The furry appendage was inadvertently tickling her. Ivory seemed to be enjoying herself mightily.

Derrek flushed hard, his powdery blue complexion turning dark lapis as he snatched the napkin back. "Oh no. I didn't introduce myself at all, did I? Forgive me — I haven't had visitors in so long."

The creature pressed all four hands together, bowing over them. Constance cringed, her throat clamping. "My name is Derrek." They — or he, perhaps? — spread an unbelievably charming smile as he straightened one hand out. "I'm so glad to have you in my home."

"Thank you," Constance found herself squeaking. Then she cleared her throat and filled the space with nervous laughter, Derrek's outstretched hand jerking away. Cats within a ten-mile radius shrank into the shadows.

Ivory seethed. "How about a *thanks for saving our lives*, sister dearest?"

Derrek leapt up, cheered and oblivious. "You don't need to thank me for that." He beamed, taking his teacup in his upper set of hands and handling the pot with his lower set. Constance's gorge at the back of her tonsils greeted her like an old loyal dog.

"That was Arnold you met out there. Just having a bit of fun. I knocked them for a loop, but they'll recover. I think." He played with the pin in his stock. "Mount Quixx is not a place to underestimate, as you've seen," Derrek continued, "and I'm sorry that your first impression of it was so . . . exciting. But that's the charm of it, I always say."

Constance pretended to sip what was left of her tea as she scouted out emergency exits. The brew tasted earthy and unrefined, and it warmed her marrow against her will. *Forget the bloody tea*, she thought. She took stock: charts and tomes scattered everywhere. Notes, maps, a great chalkboard, workbenches, a gigantic machine prominent on the far side, enormous, and taking up half the room (*probably a human blender*).

"You have quite . . . a home," Constance blurted. *Nest? Trap? Lair?*

Derrek crossed the room to wind a wilted Cordova music player, a jaunty tune popping out of the massive sound horn when he turned aside. The shrug was self-deprecating but almost charming. "I'm not much of a homemaker, as you can tell. Housekeeping has been quite remiss. Must speak to the union about that one."

"I think it's *lovely*," Ivory said.

Constance was so beyond hysteria that she couldn't tell if her smile was out of genuine amusement or germinating insanity. Her warped inner monologue had become too conversational. *What a splendid day*, it chirped. *At tea with bedraggled sister — previously missing, later found trapped in a tree by something hideous and hungry — and now hosted by our illustrious saviour, owner of a great but poorly appointed home we are sure to be devoured in. I wonder how much blood is in the human body, Constance. Answer: more than enough to make pudding.*

She zoned back in so fast she almost suffered whiplash. Ivory had pulled another book into her lap, and she was pointing out a section that Derrek had asked her to find. They'd completely forgotten Constance was even there.

The pang of exclusion washing over her was among the last things she'd expected to feel. She abandoned her teacup with a clatter.

"Well!" She clapped, bolting to her feet with scarecrow rigidity. "Lovely to meet you, but we'd best be on our way!"

Ivory looked like she might leap across the room and go for her sister's eyes, using her own to say *you capital ruiner.*

"I have to advise against that," Derrek said before either of them might react.

Constance prickled, her skin losing all feeling under visions of suffocating in that beautiful, gauzy thread.

"And why is that?" she replied bravely, masking the grotesquery churning in her head.

He sighed. "Because, as you've already seen, the creatures of the mountain don't take as kindly to strangers as I do."

Constance was desperate. "Then escort us back to Quixx yourself." At least then they'd have a chance to get away if he'd point them in the right direction.

"Another snag in that." Derrek rubbed the flat plane intersecting his four downcast eyes, rising to his full height and adjusting his well-tailored coat. "The sun is nearly set, and you won't get back to Quixx before it does. The others come out in full force at night, and there is only one of me to protect you from their pranks. I wouldn't see you hurt. Today was a close enough call as it is."

He'd said *protect* as though he actually cared for their safety. Constance tried to shake the possibility of his good intentions before they broke her steely resolve. She froze as Derrek glided past her, looking absently up at the exposed rafter beams.

Constance turned helplessly to her sister. "Please," she tried one more time, so overwhelmed she was tearful.

Ivory slammed her book shut. "I like it here," she replied icily. "And Derrek is *exactly* my kind of people. Who's to say I want to leave at all? Especially with *you.*"

Even though they'd recently locked eyes during an attack that surely should have killed them both, their last argument still hung suspended, cavernous between them. But there wasn't time.

"Be rational for once in your life!" Constance railed. "I don't know how hard you hit your head, but that, over there, is not peo—"

There was a thud that made Constance jump and whirl. Derrek had leapt onto the wall, the full weight of him springing nimbly onto the sparse roof. He scurried off and disappeared, but Ivory was over to where he'd gone quicker than sparks.

"What happened?" she called. Derrek had vanished so swiftly that Constance was sure they were alone. She grabbed Ivory. "We're going. Now." But Ivory struggled. "I know you hate me, but I'll make it up to you by not having you watch as my succulent juices are made into a fine gazpacho."

Before Ivory could spitfire ridicule, Derrek landed with a soft tap in the space beside them. Constance screeched out of her skin.

"Didn't mean to run off in the middle of the conversation." His hands were cupped gently at his chest. "She was stuck, you see."

He unfurled them, a furry brown mass coiled in his palm. "Arabella!"

One point Derrek; Constance minus ten.

The nursery spider's front legs reached out experimentally, making a tapping motion against the air. Ivory held out her hands, even though Constance made a protest in her throat.

"It's all right, it's quite safe," Derrek reassured. "She followed you here, Miss Ivory. She was dreadfully worried about you."

Ivory's eyes were alight with wonder. Constance had not realized how much she missed seeing that expression.

"Really? She told you that?"

Derrek folded all of his arms, each long enough that he may have folded them twice. "She's a mother. She worries."

Arabella made a strange kind of mewling noise as she slowly mountaineered to Ivory's shoulder. "Wow, my very own familiar."

Constance, more than disbelieving at this point, scoffed loudly, and Ivory scowled back. "If we can protect you from the almighty cynic over there, Arabella, we'll be in business."

"Cynic?" Derrek blinked each eye a second apart, and they burned holes of shame into Constance's better judgment.

"Constance doesn't think we should stay, Derrek. She's dreadfully opposed to having a *good time*, with anybody." Ivory's every word was a savage stab.

Constance flushed, fear overtaken by a tidal wave of humiliation. "That's not it at all!" she protested. "Truly, we've — uh, it's been a wonderful time, very nice, and we don't want to overstay our welcome, and, but, well . . ." She deflated under the expectant eyes. "What *are* you?"

The hand Constance slapped over her mouth was too late to prevent what had already spilled out. Either now she'd insulted him enough he'd just kill them outright, or he'd simply be mortified into silence — at this point, she couldn't tell which she'd prefer.

Ivory was horror-stricken. "What's the matter with you?!" she cried, but they were both surprised when Derrek clapped.

"This is a perfect opportunity!" he exclaimed. "Come, let me show you!" He glided past both of them to the unseen curve of the room, beckoning with one of his four outstretched hands.

Ivory moved coolly past her sister. "I wish all of your tight-faced lady friends could see you making such an idiot of yourself."

She went ahead without another word while Arabella turned and made a hissing sound surely aimed at Constance. She reeled, but what else could she do? Maybe this would finally be the end of it all . . . well, she'd predicted it incorrectly so many times now she was starting to get annoyed. So she followed.

Derrek stopped and pivoted, arms open like a showman as he stood before a massive shape obscured by the shadows — the one Constance had assumed was some kind of killing machine. He tapped a switch. "Ladies, may I present to you, my invaluable partner in a long, soon-to-be-illustrious career." Flick. *Shunk*. Lamplight flooded the dark work area.

It was a telescope, and it was massive. It was housed in a circular enclave, flanked by more workbenches, charts, and open books. It was the only part of the tower where the roof was entirely sealed, the best-kept thing Constance had seen in the house so far. It gleamed pearlescent in the deepening dusk.

"Beautiful!" Ivory swooned, reaching out to touch the scope above them reverently.

Constance looked from the telescope to Derrek, uncomprehending, but something tickled in the back of her brain. The painting in the great foyer of the Happy Bell, its face rubbed out and haloed by the stars . . .

Derrek beamed but tried to maintain his humility. "To answer your question, Miss Constance — I'm an astronomer."

Constance's mouth parted. "That's not what I—"

"I grew up here, on the peak of Mount Quixx, transfixed by the stars and the heavens," he went on, "and I grew so entranced that I knew, one day, I must learn more about them. So I came here, to study them. The movement of the moon through the houses. The advancing of the planets in our earthly scope. Stars that went from yellow, to white, to red, to nothing." His excitement turned wistful, suddenly, something painful intercepting his speech. "At any rate, that's how I keep busy these days."

He started moving back to the open part of the tower, and Constance shuddered. So the monster was a creature of science. Would that make him less inclined to eat them? Or would it inspire him to slice them thin as paper, in cross-section? He hadn't done either, and she didn't know what he was waiting for . . . unless his intentions were as good as Ivory believed them to be.

Her younger sister was filling the air with a barrage of questions, to which Derrek merely smiled. Why couldn't Constance do like Ivory and just let go of every anxiety that prickled her?

She followed them out of the room but stopped closer to the edge of the tower where the wall and roof had once met, but were now sheared off into oblivion.

And she looked down. And indeed, oblivion was all she saw.

"We're on the peak of Mount Quixx?" she said to no one in particular, staring deeper. The light outside was nearly gone, but she could see masses of trees jutting out from the rock face, and beyond them, shadowy nothing. They must have been hundreds of feet above anything, even the fog. The air was clear and shining, and she realized there were more mountains beyond Quixx. Mountains and sunset and sky, precious sky.

Derrek turned to her, still smiling. "Close to it! The air is too thin up there, though, even for me." But when he saw Constance precariously bend over the exposed wall, he was at her side in a flash.

"Careful now." He steered her away from the edge; his hands were a gentle pressure on her shoulders, and her stomach flipped. "You've toppled over quite a bit today, let's keep that to a minimum."

"Oh," she said. Then Derrek drew her unexpectedly into confidence.

"I truly am sorry I can't take you back tonight," he said. "I know how much you must worry about your sister to have come here, and so far, by yourself. It was very brave."

Constance blinked, surprised, but warmed, too, that her struggle had at last been acknowledged. She cleared her throat and adjusted her blouse's neck bow, still unnerved enough to back away a step. "My parents would have a fit and a half if I let anything happen. To either of us."

Ivory audibly rolled her eyes. "I highly doubt that."

Derrek quirked an invisible eyebrow as he moved back to their improvised common area. "What do you mean, Miss Ivory?"

She scoffed. "I'm just often shocked that our parents remember our names, let alone worry about how we're doing."

"They were supposed to come to Quixx with us," Constance tried to level Ivory, and the conversation, into silence, but she didn't take the hint.

"But they couldn't *condescend* to. They think small towns are beneath their City Sensibilities, even for a vacation." She flipped through her book absently.

"Ah, so you're from one of the Great Cities!" Derrek clapped. "That must be dreadfully exciting. What with the bustling industry, the daily advances in science and culture!"

Ivory let out a sardonic *feh*. "Dreadfully exciting if your greatest concerns are pennies and petticoats."

Constance took her seat, suddenly exhausted despite being unconscious for most of the day. "We didn't always live in Ferren City," she found herself saying. That may have been the first time that day that Ivory had truly looked at, and seen, her. "We came from a lake town called Knockum. After Ivory was born, Father's business took off. He felt moving to the Cities would be a new adventure for us. Better educational and job opportunities. There was a mermaid statue just at the edge of town in Knockum, by the water. People used to believe they lived in the lake . . . it was an odd statue, though. A mermaid but not quite . . ."

Constance's eyes shone, as though she were still there. She was four when they'd left, but she could still remember riding her father's shoulders along the craggy beach, gathering snail shells as tiny gifts for baby Ivory. Her parents had been different people away from the Cities. Everything had been different.

She realized suddenly that the room had gone quiet. She hadn't thought about Knockum and the odd mermaid since they left. She hadn't talked about it at all, either. Why would she remember all that now?

Ivory was stock-still. "I didn't know any of that."

"Didn't know what?" Constance felt peculiarly dazed.

"About Knockum. I thought we'd always lived in Ferren."

Constance frowned. "Of course you knew. Mother and Father must have told you about it. Or one of the nannies, surely." *Or did the nannies even know?*

"No." Ivory looked like she was carved out of stone. "No one told me."

Pictures. Hadn't there been any? If Constance had felt guilty before, she didn't know what this dark feeling coiling up inside her stomach was. How could she forget part of her life?

Derrek cleared his throat.

"If it's any consolation," he said, "I haven't seen Knockum, nor the Great Cities, nor even Quixx. Not really. Far too busy to travel."

That seemed to distract Ivory. "You haven't seen *Quixx?*"

Of course he hasn't. Constance's reliable internal monologue made a cameo. *He's the most monstrous monster the town could conjure.*

94

"No, but its reputation precedes it," Derrek replied, tidying up their tea as he talked. "The baking of Mrs. Dindlehorn? The storytelling prowess of Constable Derraugh? I hear there's a famous crooner in town, too. And a little birdie told me you're staying with Ms. Bougainvillea at the Happy Bell!" All his eyes seemed to dazzle.

Constance grew wary. How could he know all that? If he went down there, he'd be likely to have his head on a pike and the rest of him sold to the world of science he so highly regarded. She looked away. *I'm sure he'd forget the charms of Quixx once they greeted him with the hospitality of a lynch mob.*

"I think Quixx is lovely, too, in its way," Ivory said behind a yawn. "But Constance doesn't agree. She's like our parents. Small towns bore her."

"That's not true!" Constance started. Is that what Ivory really thought of her? The corner of her eyes prickled suddenly to be compared to her parents, of all people.

"Now, now." Derrek waved a long finger at Ivory. "You really must give your sister credit. Quixx takes getting used to. Sometimes its charms are slow to show themselves, that's all."

Like yours? Was on the tip of Constance's tongue, but she clamped her lips.

She realized, as she watched Derrek remove their teacups and the cart with an elegant stride in all eight legs and four deft hands, that she felt much calmer than earlier. And such calm had stirred in her memories of a simpler time, and even though it was painful that Ivory hadn't known anything about Knockum and their life there, that it still lived in her heart put Constance at ease.

It made her forget the fact that they were in a place few people knew of, or had seen, and that it would be a perfect place to go missing . . . *enough of that now.* She was still on edge, but for now, she enjoyed just sitting and not fretting so much.

Ivory's yawns had become more frequent, and she curled herself around the giant book. Even Arabella, on her shoulder, seemed to be winding down. In that moment, Ivory's face forgot to be angry and defiant, and she looked like a smaller child than her fourteen years would suggest. Constance wondered where her little sister had gone. She put a hand on her knee.

"What?" Ivory jerked up, suspicious.

"I think it's time to go to bed, Ivy," Constance said quietly.

Ivory softened. "You haven't called me that in a long time."

Constance bit her lip a little. "It's for special occasions. Just like you only call me *Constance* when you're murderously mad."

Ivory looked at her feet. "I'm not mad. I'm just . . ."

"Bedtime?" Derrek returned, hands on his hips — err . . . thorax? Constance wasn't sure how long he'd been there. She pulled away, smiling awkwardly.

"It's been a long day."

"It certainly has," Derrek agreed. "I'm glad you're here tonight instead of out there. The accommodations may not live up to the Happy Bell, but you'll be tucked up safe and sound."

Constance remembered the springy, webby bed that awaited her down below, and suddenly felt glad of it despite how very easily she could be rolled up in it for a midnight snack. She wondered just how much sleep she would get tonight.

Ivory yawned a *thank you* as she and Arabella made for the door in the floor.

Constance went to follow her but stopped. She physically made herself turn, her legs stiff as iron bars rooted in the floor. She faced the arachnastronomer alone, but she was determined to keep her resolve.

"Derrek?" she tried, focusing on his gentle eyes instead of his enormous, lanky body. He turned, surprised.

Her fists were like coiled, throbbing hearts at her sides, but she forced the words out. "Thank you for helping us. Without you, I don't want to think where we'd be. And Ivory hasn't seemed so comfortable in someone's home in such a long while. So . . . yes, thank you." She swallowed. Despite the terror, she meant it from her core, whatever happened.

Derrek smiled and moved in. He was so close that his forelegs surrounded her on either side, the top joints coming all the way up to Constance's shoulders, the curved claws at the tips settling into the floorboards. If this was the moment he stabbed her with a venomous stinger and wrapped her up for feasting, there was none better. At least she'd been polite.

Without warning or precedent, Derrek took her hand and bowed. "I am grateful for the chance to protect you, Miss Constance. That's all the thanks I need."

Constance felt the blood creep back into her cheeks. He seemed to finally notice how close they were, and in an awkward rush, pulled back, letting go her hand.

"I hope you can get some rest," he managed, smoothing his inky-coloured hair that was fastidiously clubbed at the nape of his long, cerulean neck. He really did have the air of a blue blood, skin and all.

Still, Constance drew away, escaping the claustrophobia of his huge spider body next to hers. She turned and followed after Ivory, relieved, too, to be out of the scrutiny of those amber eyes swallowing her up.

As she made to pull the hatch closed, Constance watched Derrek turn, his dignified hands clasped behind his back as he gazed into the starry distance beyond the ruined roof.

His furry legs made barely a whisper against the floor as they bore him farther into the shadows and out of sight.

Constance looked down at her hand, flexing it. It was still warm. A shudder crawled on eight legs up her spine as she closed the door.

5

A Gift of Sky

Ivory rolled her eyes. "Do you want to get back to Batty Bougainvillea's or not?"

Constance fidgeted with her hands, feebly trying to wring a solution out of the sharp morning air. "Isn't there a path? Something we can all walk down together?"

Derrek held out his hand again, insisting. "Really, Miss Constance, it's best if you just ride along. I don't mind, honestly."

Ivory was perched comfortably on Derrek's . . . well, on the precarious space between what would be the thorax and the abdomen, the carapace shifting back and forth like a tectonic plate every time Derrek tilted from leg to leg to leg. Constance took an experimental peek over the sheared edge Derrek was proposing to take them down and felt her last nerve fray.

Getting up here had been fine. Granted, the hardest leg had happened while Constance had been in a convenient coma. Now, totally arrested in the light of morning, she realized that, short of using a flying machine, there was no possible way they were getting off this peak in one piece without another miracle.

And now he was telling her the easiest way to get to the bottom was to take a *ride on his back*. Aside from it being completely inappropriate, the idea of riding a giant spider down an unpredictable mountain was less palatable than never leaving the mountain at all.

"But it's just . . . it's a straight drop and — I mean, how did anyone get up here to build *that*." She gestured wildly at the observatory. "And I'm so much heavier than Ivory . . . I'm just— I'm sorry but—"

Constance had little time to squeal as Derrek scooped her into the crook of his finely boned arm and slipped her neatly onto his back in front of Ivory. He swivelled to face her as well as he could — holy Dinah, he could turn 180 on his spine — and patted her hand kindly.

"I've made this journey many times, and there's a bit of a trick to it. Trust me, Miss Constance. It's much safer than you imagine."

He didn't give her much room to protest, bringing her hands around his waist and holding them there as he picked the first few steps down the rock. Constance felt her lungs lurch as they neared the wending fog, the weight of Ivory at her back and Derrek at her front offering little reassurance.

"Just leave it to me," he said. They were headed down a direct vertical drop, relying entirely on Derrek's feet to cling neatly to the black rocks beneath them. Constance shut her eyes and envisioned level ground to combat Ivory's constant *oohs* and *ahhs* while her stomach jolted as if filled with a lurching load of bricks.

"Wow, Connie, look at that!"

"I'd rather not," she moaned.

They hit a bump, and with the force of it, Constance's eyes flashed open. The world was clear and crisp, nothing like it had been in town. Then suddenly they were in free fall, hurtling through a fog bank and whatever emptiness beneath.

Constance let out a squawk, then buried her face into the tailored back of their captor-cum-hero, clinging for dear life.

"Connie, you are an embarrassment," Ivory trilled, laughing to beat a hyena as they continued falling.

"It's quite all right, Miss Constance," Derrek croaked. "But you are choking the life out of me."

Constance opened her eyes, realizing they weren't exactly falling at a clip anymore — almost floating now, really, as Derrek clasped swaying cliff-suspended vines. She quickly loosened her grip. "Sorry."

She took a quick peer around his back, trying to cease shuddering as his long, powerful claw legs swept past her own, eight digits moving in delicate concert across the mountain face they'd reached again with efficient calculation.

"I take this route often," Derrek was saying, swinging the girls and his body with a sudden dexterous leap he didn't bother warning them about. "I'm not sure if you've heard the local colloquialism yet in town, but the mountain has a mind of its own. It likes to play games. With physics."

Constance continued to shiver, the faint recollection of strange dreams itching the corner of her mind. "You talk like the mountain is a person—" When she looked back, one of Derrek's four eyes, set in the corner of his brow, took her measure independent of the others. She jolted.

"I think it's romantic," Ivory cut in. She surveyed the scenery with the collected grace of someone eyeing up their destiny. Constance envied her, not for the first time. "How long have you lived here, Derrek? And who built your observatory? And what about the other monsters you warned us about? Are they like you? Educated and genteel and stylish, I mean."

Constance was about to twist around and admonish Ivory for the battery of questions, but Derrek laughed, and the sound was so full of joy that her scolding dried up.

"It *is* good to have company." Derrek shook his head, happiness radiant on his strange, azure face. "I have lived on this mountain my entire life. Time here is a bit different. I wasn't really aware of the world beyond until fifty years ago—"

"Fifty years!" Ivory cried. "You really don't look your age. Must be the mountain air."

They stopped suddenly, and Derrek's body reared up, arms and first four legs gripping the rock while the rest of him shot under, sending a rope of silk before them like a cable into the fog.

"What are you—"

"Forgive me, Miss Constance, but now's the time to hang on tightly." And quick as that, Derrek dropped down the cord like a zip line, through misshapen trees and mist, Constance's screams echoing off the granite.

Leal stood in the doorway of the master bedroom, surveying with a sigh. He picked his way across the shag carpet through scattered clothes, disorganized vinyl records, and a photo book left open, facedown. He bent to scoop it up, and though he'd come in to drag his off-his-rock-and-roller bandleader out of bed, he softened.

It was their high school yearbook, when the pair of them had started their first band, performing for the seniors at a dance Leal would never forget. The night they'd made their pact to play together forever, on any stage they could find, united in their dreams to make the kind of music that would last long after them.

A snort, a shifting of the mountain of bedsheets in the bed behind Leal, and the bassist groaned to stand. That was a long time ago. And every time he thought he was close to convincing Slanner they should leave Quixx and chase that dream . . .

But it would be different, this time. Now that the Ivyweathers were here.

"Slanner?" Leal gave his semi-snoring shoulder a tentative shake, getting only a grunt and a lip smack for his trouble. He tried again, much harder, and Slanner simply pinwheeled an arm, which Leal neatly dodged. Slanner tucked deeper into the pillow like it was a liferaft in a boiling sea.

Not like this was anything new. Leal rolled his eyes. "You're really going to make me do this? Again?" And he put a gentle hand on Slanner's ribs under his arm, fingers plucking like the bones were the strings on his bass. "Wakey!"

It had its desired effect, but once Slanner kicked free he walloped Leal with a face full of pillow and, that time, he went down.

"What do you—" Slanner ripped off his eye mask, which was embroidered with a piercing neon set of made-up lady eyes. "My beauty sleep, man! You know it's precious!"

Leal spat out a feather. "Remember when you made me promise to give you a heads-up when an opportunity to shine arose? Whatever it took?" He raised his ridiculously thick eyebrows.

Slanner collapsed back onto the bed beside Leal. "The dream I was having." His lip pouted, and he slapped Leal's leg with much less force, his voice a low growl. "You didn't have to *tickle* me. What if the guys saw? My *rep*."

"Desperate times," Leal sighed, managing one last poke before getting to his feet.

"Not desperate enough." Slanner took one look out the dreary window and threw the sleeping mask at it.

"Well, what if I told you a certain pair of visiting City-sisters have gone missing?" Leal eased his awkward broad height into the bedroom doorway, adjusting his skewed necktie. "And what if there was a way a certain despondent crooner could, I don't know, rise to the occasion and show everyone the hero I know's in there?"

Slanner's head was a slow, blank marionette's when his eyes met Leal's. They had been bandmates — *more than that* — for too long for Leal not to know what it took to get Slanner going. Sure, Leal was maybe taking slight advantage, but his intentions were good. He'd taken a real shine to the Ivyweathers, and he wanted to help them. But he couldn't do that without Slanner, and Slanner had been a mess since the skirmish with Mx. Mott, questioning himself, sleeping the days away, throwing his temper around when he wasn't shutting himself in. He needed a pick-me-up, and the girls could be in danger. So why not save two birds with one—

Slanner leapt to his feet, ripping his pyjamas clean off to reveal a silk lounge suit underneath. "Assemble the band! Take me to my public!" he howled, eyes wide, practically bowling Leal over as he dragged him out of the Manse. "Hatch! Avila! You lazy so-and-sos! It's time to earn those brownie points!"

"Brownies? Where?" Sluggo popped out of a broom closet, his sax slung over his back. Leal didn't bother asking what he was doing in there.

"Never mind," Leal patted him forward as Slanner yanked levers and pushed buttons, beating the walls down and out of his way. "At least he's up."

It wasn't Ivory's loud sigh that eventually did it, but the stabbing finger prod into Constance's ribs. "You can open your eyes now, Connie."

Constance jerked, but Ivory was clean away across the crunching leafy ground before she could retaliate. *The ground.*

"Oh." Constance gawped, realizing as she took stock of her surroundings that they were back at the base of the mountain where she'd first come down — the bracken-twisted canyon, peppered with derelict cars.

Her hands were stiff talons, which she plucked from Derrek's middle, sliding awkwardly off his back and landing in a heap in the leaves.

"Are you all right?" Derrek bent over to examine her, placing a hand on her forehead. Constance's neck ached when she tilted her head up to look at him. She flinched away, tripping to her feet and shaking out her skirt.

"Don't fuss, Derrek. It only makes her stronger." Ivory waved, sticking her face under the hood of a car.

"I do apologize again, Miss Constance," he went on, a hand rubbing the back of his neck, another adjusting his necktie, and the other two rearranging the waistcoat that had gone wrinkled from Constance clutching it so tightly. "The heights, the speed. I figured you wanted to get down as quickly as possible. I never intended to frighten you."

"It's fine." Constance's desperation for propriety overrode the sensations vibrating between her shoulders as she watched all of Derrek's digital machinations, unable to keep up with them. "We're safe, and we are that much closer to—"

"Wow, a '32 Comet!" Ivory crooned, fingers brushing the rusted steel before darting to the next. "And . . . I can't believe this. A Model-F? Some of these cars are decades old! Where did they come from?"

Derrek joined her, hands in thoughtful repose at his back. "You've a good eye, Miss Ivory! You know about cars and machines?"

Constance raised a finger, but she had nothing to interject with. A different sensation, apart from the gnawing desperation to get back to their own little world, clutched her insides. She'd felt it earlier, too wound up by her own terror to have been grateful, let alone join in the civil conversation.

She felt *left out*.

". . . just what I've read. I read a lot, you know. Helps to pass the time. And not just what I'm given in school. Education curriculum these days is woefully behind. I have to substitute it with something invigorating or I'll go mad."

"You're not far from it," Constance muttered, but well enough in earshot for Ivory to bristle. "And in any case, if you hadn't noticed" — her fervent eyes darted between them accusingly — "these cars have been stripped of parts. Remember the auto thief? It seems we've finally met them." She folded her arms, desperate to be involved, even if it meant pointing the finger.

Ivory was, as usual, mortified by her sister. "Connie!"

"No, no." Derrek held up two palms, the other two wringing at his waist. "She's right. However, I'd distinguish between *stealing* and *borrowing*. I have every intention of returning the vehicles once I'm done with the parts! Or, once I've found suitable replacement parts, anyway . . ."

Constance kicked the tire of the Model-F, its body having sunk into the crater's floor and become a part of it. "I doubt the owners will be expecting these to be returned. If they're still alive."

"What are you using the parts for?" Ivory asked, ignoring Constance. "Is it for your observatory?"

Constance waited for the answer and found Derrek's face had taken on a certain panic. He tented his twelve fingers. "It's a bit difficult to explain." His eyes met Constance's, then quickly looked away.

"Please!" Derrek staggered when Ivory leapt on him, tugging at the edge of his coat. "I'm *dying* for some scintillating intrigue, or tales of discovery, or literally to be read the phone book. We aren't in any rush, are we, Connie?"

Constance had been standing by their own car, pulling out Ivory's wool coat through the open window. She bumped her head when she jerked it out. Could another few minutes really hurt? Both Ivory and Derrek seemed to be waiting for her approval, and her heart sank when she met Derrek's gaze again and heard, clear as a bell, *it is good to have company*.

"I suppose not . . ." Constance muttered, handing Ivory her jacket.

Derrek cleared his throat. "I'm sure you've noticed the fog?"

Ivory waved her hand in front of her for emphasis. "Sort of impossible not to. Does it ever clear?"

Derrek had moved to their parents' car, deftly popping the hood and cracking his knuckles like he'd cut his teeth in the oiliest garages this side of Luxe. "You saw the clearest skies at my observatory, near the mountain's summit. The town has been choked by gloom for too long now. It's not like any fog you'd likely have seen before, either." He bent down, rifling around and bracing himself on his long, graceful legs. "As I said earlier, this mountain . . . it is unique. As you can tell from going up and down it. Rare and exceptional creatures are born on it. And long ago there was . . . an incident. The one that made the crater we are standing in. Since then, the fog has remained, never clearing. Even I'm stumped as to why it stays, or where it came from. It has its own rules, too, that defy logic." He stared off wistfully, and though Constance couldn't see what he saw, he shook it off before she could ask. "The past itself is difficult to escape. As is the fog. Not much for the Quixxians to do about any of it."

"They could leave," Ivory scoffed, but her usual haughty tone was met with a look of challenge from Derrek, which surprised both sisters.

"People do leave. But it's not the fault of the people of Quixx who stay," Derrek admonished, and Ivory had the grace to look abashed. "This is their home. All they can do is try to live their lives in spite of the fog. And they've tried, believe me. Certainly, it's only fog. But it blocks out the light; how long it's been since Quixx has seen a sunset! Nothing can grow, not properly. The fog weighs on everyone's hearts, the gloom. And folk must leave. I understand. But this town is nothing if not resilient. Especially in these uncertain times. Not to mention that there's a war that just seems to go on and on overseas! Yet we must fight our own battles at home."

He went back to considering what lay under the hood, and Ivory rushed to his side, a toolbox she'd swiped from another scavenged car in tow. Arabella had even popped out of Ivory's pocket to observe.

"Thank you." Derrek stuck a hand in, rummaged, and nabbed a wrench, diving back into the car. "This should do it."

Constance quailed. "What are you — wait, don't!" She surged forward, but something clicked and snapped free, and Derrek, with a slight grunt and a grease smudge on his cheek, came out clutching the prize — the engine's motor fan.

Now Constance was worse than dead.

"Resilience can only get you so far, though." Derrek grinned. "And this is going to change all that." The spider astronomer-inventor-whatever was all twinkling eyes as he admired the little fan. When he looked back at Ivory's and Constance's blank expressions, his face fell.

"I'm going to change the residents of Quixx's *lives*," he impressed, spinning the fan. "I'm going to get rid of this terrible fog plaguing the town once and for all!"

"With that?" Ivory pointed.

Derrek swept his four arms out. "I've been busy." He winked, then he tucked the fan into his jacket, despite Constance's noise of protest.

"I've built a machine," he went on, adjusting his lapels, "a wind machine! Capable, I hope, of not only blasting this damnable fog to kingdom come, but of giving Quixx back something it's not seen in fifty years."

He was looking straight up now — not much to see, since the canyon was vaulted by the twisted briars and rampant bracken.

Constance frowned. "You mean . . . the sky?"

When Derrek looked back down at her, his own daze clearing, it was as if he was seeing her with new eyes. His smile was slow and tender.

"Not just any sky," he said, and Constance couldn't look away this time. "The *night* sky. The stars!"

Ivory let out a protracted *ohhhh*. "That explains the observatory! Sort of." She rubbed her chin. "You study the stars, you said. What's that got to do with changing people's lives?"

Derrek's grin widened, and for the first time, Constance caught sight of what lay beneath those thin lips — teeth, of a sort, puckered in the corners like single pincers. She would have lost her legs beneath her if it weren't so oddly charming.

"You've an inquiring mind, Miss Ivory. Imagine it like a chain reaction." Derrek began pacing, gesticulating wildly with every hand. "This town has been derelict for too long. People simply stopped visiting it as the fog worsened. And no one would come here to settle down and make lives of their own. It's like the fog itself *erased* Quixx off every map. But Quixx has something the Far Cities will never have — an unparalleled view of the night sky. From the mountain, that is."

Constance considered this. In Derrek's observatory, terrified as she'd been, there had been sun, and clear air, and a view unlike anything she'd ever seen. It truly was another world, and it had lifted her spirits — when she forgot she was keeping company with a monster, of course.

"My observatory offers, in itself, an escape, a wholly unprecedented experience from the modern laboratories that many modern scientists are stuck in today! And I would be more than willing to share the observatory. And update it. But we have to get people back here first. And to do that, I must remove the fog, and once that's done, the people will remember that Quixx is here, and they will come in droves, and those already here can benefit from a renewed sense of purpose. Of local pride, you could say. The Kadaver's Soiree would find new audiences. Mx. Mott could expand her curriculum. Think of it! Who doesn't look up at the stars and dream of more?

"And so," and he shut the hood of their parents' new, very expensive car, still smiling, still very sure of himself, "that is why I'm not so concerned about *borrowing* some of the necessary parts to make my machine a reality. In fact, the people of Quixx will be thanking me before too long, overjoyed that they were a part of such ecstatic transformation."

In the silence that followed, Constance didn't have much to offer. Sometimes, when the boys she'd been forced to entertain at parties or dances went off on their interests, all Constance was trained to do was smile and nod, but this was different. She was making up the protocol on these interactions as she went along. What do you do when you really *are* engaged?

"Ecstatic transformation!" Ivory crowed, catching Derrek in a laugh with her wide lilac eyes. "Derrek! It's an ingenious idea! How far are you from completing it?"

Now Derrek faltered. "Close. Perhaps not as close as I'd like. It has been slow going. Not very many cars forthcoming with the parts I need. And eight legs and four hands are better than none, but there is only one of me and limited resources . . ."

Constance knew where this was going. "Ivory—"

"I'll help you! I've mechanical knowledge, and a good eye, you said it yourself. It could be like a bona fide internship! I'm sure I could find the parts you need in town, or improvise. We could co-author a paper on this, have it published in all the periodicals—" She was a frantic dervish of energy. "The anthropological study alone! It would be the most divine of opportunities—"

But when she spun, Constance was in her path, hands on her hips.

Ivory's eyebrow twitched. "Now Connie, don't be so—"

"That's very generous of you, Miss Ivory," Derrek intervened in what was clearly the brink of a screaming match. "I'm sure you two will be quite busy on your visit here—"

"Busy, my left eye!" Ivory stomped, eyes blazing. "Connie, don't you think it's only fair that we repay Derrek's kindness for *saving our lives* by lending a hand? Wouldn't that be the *polite* thing to do?"

Now Constance felt a crack in her defences, fingers biting into her elbows. "Ivory, we can't—"

But Ivory, all bony fierceness in her adolescent body, had stalked right up to her big sister, jabbing her in the stomach. "You don't want to appear *ungrateful*, do you? After we've imposed so much upon our host? After you rode on his very back to safety? After you pushed me down here in the first place?"

"Err . . ." This time, Derrek backed away.

"We are *not* getting into this now," Constance retaliated. "I said I was sorry. But I *did* come all the way here to see you safely back, and we *both* nearly died, no less, and now that we are where this started, taking you back is what I'm going to do." Her entire body was shaking, and tears were welling up in her eyes, and as the anxiety climbed, there was nothing more she wanted to do than shut herself up in her closet at home and bury her face in her Fandango gown like she had on graduation night . . .

Ivory deflated. "Oh, just forget it." And throwing up her hands, she trekked away to the edge of the canyon.

"Ivory, wait!" Constance tried, but she didn't go after her. "I think I've made things worse."

Constance flinched, but the thing that brushed her cheek was a handkerchief that Derrek was offering. A moment's hesitation, but she took it, turned, and daintily blew her nose.

"I'm sorry you had to witness that." Constance tried to laugh it off, momentarily forgetting who she was talking to. "In any case . . . I think we ought to . . . be getting back." She almost handed the cloth back, before realizing she'd well soiled it. "Um. I'll . . . clean this, and—" But returning it meant she'd have to *see* Derrek again, and—

"Keep it," Derrek blurted, seeming to read this. "You need it more than I do. No tear ducts." His chuckle was punctuated by a sharp throat clearing.

Constance felt herself smile. "Thank you," she said, and the two started off in the direction Ivory went.

"I don't have sisters — or any real siblings, come to think of it," Derrek said after a tense pause, "but behaviourally speaking, most worries come from a place of sincere concern. They wouldn't crop up if the issue wasn't important." Ivory was leaning against the rock wall, picking her nails, staring at the ground.

"Right," Constance said, startled when Derrek turned around and reared, spinning and shooting deft tethers of webbing until after much flurry, there was a basket and a pulley, one end grasped firmly in Derrek's hands.

"In any case" — he shrugged — "neither one of you would be upset if your intentions didn't mean so much to you. Both of you." He smiled, a hand open and beckoning Constance to step into the basket.

She took it, because manners demanded she do so, but this time she didn't shiver or feel the need to wipe her palm on her skirt. Instead, her fingers tingled, but the feeling was short-lived. Ivory brushed past her.

"It was really the best of pleasures to meet you, Derrek." Ivory shook his hand firmly, stepping in behind Constance. "I wish you luck in your scientific endeavours. I won't be far if my *chaperone* loosens her iron grip."

"And what a privilege it has been to hear your opinion on my little project." Derrek saluted, his face comically stern. He and Constance surveyed each other one last time, until his eight legs backpedalled, and he began pulling the cord, and the two of them, up the canyon wall.

"Wait!" Two feet off the ground he stalled them, a hand darting into his waistcoat. He reached back up to Constance with the bundle. To her surprise, it was the purple scarf that Ms. Bougainvillea had given her.

"Best you keep this handy," Derrek said, and Constance pressed the scarf close as the basket rose again.

"Why?" she blurted, Derrek and the foggy brambles fading with each strong pull of his arms.

It was that last grin that undid her. "Because purple goes well with your hair," he said, and Constance was glad they were well out of view so the monster who had saved them couldn't see her blush.

Slanner wasn't really surprised that he'd roused so many townsfolk this early in the morning. If there was one thing the people of Quixx thrived on, it was gossip.

"Now, when we get to the crater, people, remember who got this mob up in the first place!" Slanner yanked the bespectacled dork who ran *Quixx Quarterly* over, peering at what he'd scrawled on his reporter's notepad. "Front page, right, champ?" Slanner shook the boy, his glasses coming off an ear.

"And what are you gonna do when you get to the crater?" Leal nabbed Slanner back in kind, rubbing a smudge off his scowling cheek with a licked thumb. "I thought you were just, you know, going to help the police. We aren't putting on a show, are we?"

"Relax!" Slanner smacked Leal so hard on the back he nearly swallowed his gold tooth. "*Life's* a show! I'm improvising. You know that's my strong suit."

"On a guitar solo, not a rescue mission," Leal muttered, and before they knew it, they were across the street from the Happy Bell, and bug-eyed Bougainvillea herself was tottering towards them, a massive crow clutching for purchase on her knobby shoulder.

"Inspiring speech time." Slanner smirked, shoving his way not only around Leal but to the front of the crowd, hands up. "People, people! Before we go any further, let me just say, that none of this could have happened without me—"

"Ah," came a voice, and the crowd of well-meaning nosy neighbours parted, revealing the yellow- and black-haired sisters they'd been roused from their tea to find, safe and sound.

"My dears!" squealed Ms. Bougainvillea, slamming into the both of them with the force of an ocean liner as she gathered them into her arms. "I feel torn clothing and bruised egos!"

The blond shied from the crow flapping its wings and taking off, and Slanner tried to move around the dispersing, muttering crowd. "Wait! My speech! Don't I get a medal for *trying*? I should get more than a medal! I knew where they were! I should get all the *credit*!" But as usual, Slanner's bellowing went over everyone's heads, and he whirled on the not-so-missing sisters.

"Ladies!" He beamed, switching tacks so fast Leal felt his

ears whistle. "Aren't you a sight for sore whatever? Heard you got into a little mishap. Is there anything I—"

"Thank you, Mr. Dannen." The firecracker — Constance? — lifted her hands, backing quickly across the street as she was towed by Batty Miss Bee. "Really, you shouldn't have."

Slanner stopped short of the boarding house's gate, the huge double doors slamming closed once the girls had been dragged inside to be mollycoddled. Missed his glory by a few minutes, tops.

Slanner slapped the air right out of Leal as he drew up beside him, patting him hard to the back. "Couldn't have woken me up sooner, huh?"

Leal sighed. "I'll try to be a better alarm clock next time."

"Feh. They'll come around." He took a cautious survey behind them, hands on his hips, the rest of the Kadaver's Soiree lingering at the edge of the mountain's crater. Slanner hadn't been this close to it except on a dare when they were kids, and the damn sight was as nasty as ever.

"If I had my way," he snarked, "I'd blast the thing to kingdom come. You know what would look better there? A billboard. Or condos. Or a *real* theatre venue. Mountain's more trouble than it's worth . . ." And he stalked off, back to the Manse, Leal and the band following close without a second glance back. Those sisters were wily — since they'd arrived, there'd been an unprecedented amount of excitement, and no one had come back alive and kicking from that mountain in fifty years.

All the more reason to dog them harder now. City girls. They had all the answers, didn't they?

Bedtime in actual beds was a well-earned victory after a day of Ms. Bougainvillea's peculiar brand of comfort. Constance had expected her to prod them more for information, but she merely expressed her gratitude that they were safe and meandered about the Happy Bell twittering as if they'd never been missing at all. Even the town gawkers had only milled about the front gate for a short while before dispersing, as if their curious disappearance and re-emergence wasn't really any of their business. Leal managed to finally drag Slanner away when they refused to answer the door the third time, and for the most part, the sisters were allowed to recover in peace, stuffed with tea and cakes and mindlessly watching the birds come and go. Constance felt mildly disappointed that there wasn't more of a fuss. It made her question if any of it had really happened at all.

Through the day, Constance found herself glancing out the window from time to time, unable to stop herself. She looked to the mountain, so close by, yet so remote and strange. She squinted, trying to see the place where the observatory was, to convince herself their adventure had been real. But the fog wouldn't allow it, as if intentionally preventing her from making absolutely certain.

And she'd seen, forbidding as ever, Mx. Mott standing at the Happy Bell's gate, manicured fingers poised to push her way in as she, too, stared at the mountain, then turned her head quickly to look towards the boarding house. Constance had hid behind the curtains, heart pounding, and when she looked again, the schoolmistress was gone.

Why did Constance feel like Mx. Mott had already discovered their secret?

Now, bedtime achieved, Ivory fluffed her pillows, building herself a nest just the way she always had since she'd got a bed of her own.

"I didn't really mind the web bed, though," she went on to Arabella, perched happily at her shoulder before scuttling to her own resting place in a newer terrarium on the nightstand.

"It was comfy. And so silky, too! Could you imagine the thread count on the sheets?"

Constance made a noise of agreement from her own bed, though she wasn't quite sure what she was agreeing to. She was too busy staring at her hands, which clutched the handkerchief, and she smoothed it with the pads of her thumb. It really *was* silky, a fine linen. Could it have been spun from the same thread she'd seen in the strange observatory, patching holes or making a bed or cabling them down a mountainside . . . ?

She turned it over. Stitched neatly into the corner were the cursive initials DB. As if it was a real token, like from a medieval tale of chivalry—

"What's that?"

"Nothing!" Constance jumped, crumpling the square in her fist when she whipped back up to Ivory's pointed nose. She yanked the covers up under her chin, settling back into the lumpy mattress and staring at the pinioned butterflies on the wall and ceiling above her.

"I do say," Ivory went on, unfettered, "that it was truly a diverting adventure. Exactly what I needed."

"Was it?" Constance said. Ivory had barely spoken a word to her since they'd arrived back at Ms. Bougainvillea's, but she seemed to be buzzing now. "I suppose I'll try to ruin your life more often then."

"Silver linings, etcetera." Ivory leapt into her bed, sprawled and kicking the sheets, her socks almost at her knobby knees. "Even you have to admit it was thrilling, Connie. The nick-of-time rescue, the daring descent down the mountain." She rolled onto her side, head on her fist. "Just imagine! We're the first people to see what Mount Quixx is hiding in *fifty years*. Not since that astronomer, anyway, the one from the painting. Do you think there's any connection to Derrek there? And the *monsters*, Connie! I told you they were real! What I'd give to meet more of them."

"You'll do no such thing," Constance muttered, shutting her eyes, trying to will away the throbbing at the back of her skull. Thrilling wasn't the word for it. Constance wondered if she was just suffering from post-traumatic nightmare encounter syndrome. Why was she still fiddling with that stupid handkerchief underneath the sheet? Why was she suddenly feeling like the mountain wasn't just watching her anymore, as Mx. Mott had been, but that it was asking her a question, begging a favour . . .

"Connie?"

Her eyes flew open, fingers stilled, when she sat up to look at Ivory across the room. The plea in her sister's eyes was genuine.

"Ivory, please don't ask me again," Constance begged. "It may have all been just a joyride to you, but there was a moment where" — she swallowed — "I thought I'd lost you. And I know I haven't been the best of sisters in your eyes sometimes, but if anything had happened to you, I would've flung myself off Mount Quixx there and then."

Ivory's eyes were wide. "Oh," she said, her turn to be speechless. "Um. Thanks, I guess, for coming to save me . . ." She scratched her snarl-ball coif. "But I was going to ask you something else."

"What?"

"It's silly." Ivory fell back into her pillows after shutting out her light, the room taking on its eerie darkness, not even a moon to light its finer shadows. "Only . . . I wondered if you could tell me more about Knockum. About the place where you and Mother and Father were happy."

Shutting out the light had certainly been strategic. Constance settled into her own bed and gave up trying to see Ivory's face. "I don't have much more to tell," she admitted. "I hadn't thought of it in years. So much has happened since. So much has changed." Living in the City seemed to have blocked out much of those serene days in the town by the lake. Days that were now bubbling back to the surface the longer they were in Quixx, a simpler town like the one from Constance's past, but this one trapped by time and fog.

"It was nice," Ivory said after a while, "to see the stars from Derrek's observatory."

"Yes," Constance whispered, tipping her head to look out the window as a breeze wafted in. She imagined — somewhere above the gloom — the moon, and the stars, things that, even in the City, she could barely see for the light pollution. And when she shut her eyes, her mind travelled like one of the Happy Bell's birds, past the crater canyon and straight through the cloud bank, climbing higher and higher to the mountain's stark face, where there was a great observatory hidden, and inside was a monster who was a scholar, alarming and charming, looking down on them even now, and dreaming of the sky he'd take back for them all.

Constance smiled, and let sleep take her at last.

6

THE VOLUNTEER STAR BRIGADE

Ms. Bougainvillea sat in the solarium by the sky-reaching windows, staring straight ahead. Her eyesight wasn't the best, true, but it wasn't what was in front of her she was most concerned with. Just the things behind her. Memory. Precious and pure. She shut her eyes and heard the ghost of laughter and wings shivering. Time was a series of chipped tiles, bouncing with an earthquake, the pieces out of place. *Then* could just as easily have been *now*. She hummed brightly at the back of her throat, keeping time with the mountain's whisper.

Then, wings nearer at hand — heavy black ones, a featherweight dropping to the table in front of her.

"Mind the china, Mathias." She cracked an eye with a sniff, reaching for the note tied deftly to the crow's ankle with silvery thread.

She put her glasses down, rubbing her brow. Her eyes were so weak she could barely read anymore, certainly not without a great effort. At least his letter was in plain, large cursive.

"Hmm," she hummed around her dentures. "So they refused to help, did they? That won't do."

He hadn't asked directly — he never did. But a mother has a way of knowing.

She ran a finger down Mathias's oily chest, and the crow trilled. She passed him a Fentish delight from the crystal bowl. The clattering on the second floor meant the girls would be up soon. A new day.

"No message back this time." Ms. Bougainvillea nodded to herself. "Best to keep some things a surprise, don't you agree?"

But Mathias had already fluttered off, past an awestruck Constance, who dodged affably.

"Were you saying something, Ms. Bougainvillea?"

"Just figuring out the day, my dear. It's going to be an eventful one, don't you think?"

Constance sighed, a placating smile in her words. "Just like every day, Ms. Bougainvillea," and, Lavish love her, she moved off to start the tea.

Ms. Bougainvillea grinned, rolling up the message and tucking it into her hair, Frederic filing it away with the others. Just like every day, indeed.

"To market, to market," Ivory sang, swinging the giant empty basket and twirling. Constance chose, instead, to focus on the list in her hand, tucking the purple scarf under her chin with a jaw twitch.

"*Ohhh, purple goes so well with your hair!*" Ivory trilled. Constance felt her *face* turn purple.

"Knock it off and help me," she fumed. "These ingredients Ms. Bougainvillea wants . . . I doubt we're going to find them at the Quixx Grocer." Essence of Disdain? Log

Driver's Waltz Hardtack? And what in Gilda's name were Flintabattey Flonatin Turnovers?

And please, the bottom of the shopping list pointedly ordered, *Make a stop in at the junk shop*. For what, the note didn't specify. But what else were the Ivyweathers doing, anyway?

"Leave it to Miss Bee to liven things up around here," Ivory sighed, gravely surveying the market square when they finally reached it. "And bless her for trying."

Constance finally looked up and stopped short. The square outside of Farrowmarket was drab, like the rest of Quixx. A handful of shops were built around the decapitated fountain statue, which, despite being headless, seemed to watch the sisters as they rounded the cobbled street. The flower shop's *CLOSED* sign looked like it didn't have an *OPEN* side, but the junk shop was the opposite, with regular customers coming and going. In fact, it was the busiest place Constance had seen since they'd arrived, which meant a constant stream of curious stares as they passed, enough to make her clench her fists. She muttered *good days* and *pardon mes*, the whispers seeming to grow louder, the eyes wider. It was nothing compared to the crowd that had been waiting for them when they'd climbed out of the trench yesterday, but word had travelled fast, obviously.

It wasn't the market's fault. The crowd wasn't the only thing unsettling Constance. She kept checking over her shoulder, thinking she heard . . . but no, there was no way. Because each time she looked, it was just the massive bent pose of Mount Quixx at her back. The whispers she'd heard were from people in the crowd, surely, but it had long dispersed, and the sound was a rustling in burnt leaves, humming an unfamiliar melody . . .

She hadn't slept well. That must be it. All the strange dreams. Waking with the creepy crawlies. She would've thought their adventure on the mountain had been part of her tossing and turning, but Ivory made sure to go on and on about it from the second they'd woken up. Her sister, at least, would not allow Derrek and his stars to fade into doubt.

Constance spotted the post office near the grocer's. "I'll have to send that telegram once we're done."

Ivory chewed the ends of her hair. "You could put it off another day, surely? How likely is it we'll get a holiday after this if Mother and Father come and get us?" She scowled. "I mean 'send' for us."

Constance screwed her face up but didn't reply as Ivory pushed her way into the tinkling doorway of the grocer. The car was irretrievable now at the bottom of a pit — and picked for scraps. They had no way of getting home unless Constance telegrammed her parents and had them send a car to bear them back. But what was waiting for Constance there? Punishment for being careless? A summer surrounded by her not-so-friendly friends all preening for college and demanding to know her plans, which she didn't have a clue about? Or just a cold shoulder from her parents, who'd had *expectations* for her on this trip, in the first place—

"Miss Ivyweather!"

Constance woke as quickly as one does before stepping into oncoming traffic, or in this case, bumping into the force that was Mx. Mott.

"Have a care where you're going," the principal admonished, two bulging butcher paper bags in each arm. Suddenly her mouth pursed like she'd bitten into a lime when she saw Ivory. "I do hope you've left your entomology project at the Happy Bell."

Constance could see Ivory fighting to keep her grin down. "Arabella is taking a much-needed sabbatical from social frivolity."

A prominent vein popped out on Mx. Mott's forehead, her mouth tightening. "Indeed. Madeline, the door."

Madeline Mott stepped gracefully from behind her mother, carrying a large jar of pickled beets. Ivory noticeably tensed, but Madeline smiled at her. "I'm glad you're all right, Ivory."

Ivory blinked.

Madeline jerked her chin towards the mountain. "You know? The mountain? You were . . . missing?"

Ivory cleared her throat. "Yes. All fine." She raised a finger. "Your . . . err, braids are perfectly symmetrical today, Madeline."

Her face lit up as she held the door open for Mx. Mott. "I could show you how to do it sometime, if you like." Though when she took in the full extent of Ivory's tangled hair, she smiled again.

"Come along, Madeline. It's time for your ten-string vaux lesson," Mx. Mott was calling from the sidewalk, and with one last meaningful look between the two girls, Madeline was obediently gone.

Ivory was going patchily red up her neck, thrusting a hand into her black hair. "Wretched . . ."

"I don't want to say I told you so," Constance mewled, marshalling her sister back into the store towards the produce.

"*Maybe* I'll allow you to help me fix it. If you're less barbaric this time."

Constance shook her head, reaching for a fresh pear, but someone else's shopping basket bumped her in passing, and when she recovered and turned around again, she shrieked and snapped her hand back from the face in the fruit bin.

"My," she said, her heart in her throat as she clutched her frilly collar. "I, err — Vatos, was it?"

"*He's* Vatos," the face asserted as it drew up to its owner's massive height, thumbing at the drummer, a wider man with the pompadour hairdo climbing out of a carefully constructed soup tower. "I'm Sluggo." He pulled up a crate full of apples and peaches.

"Leal!" Ivory cried, and Constance whirled in time to see Ivory and Leal exchanging some kind of jazzy secret handshake. "Is the whole Kadaver's Soiree here?"

Constance stiffened, eyes darting for their slick-toothed bandleader. "Slanner's out at the post office." Leal grinned, his sharp cheekbones lighting up. "We all work here part-time. Being famous doesn't seem to pay the bills like it used to." He leaned on a broom, pouting, but it didn't seem to wreck his chipper mood.

Bartek, the lead guitarist, stepped out of a walk-in freezer, dusting ice crystals from his shoulder. Avila, the keytar player, popped up from behind the deli counter, butcher knife slamming to the block. And Hatch, the piano player, came down a ladder after replacing a light bulb (though it still flickered when he reached the floor).

"There's nothing wrong with working a steady job outside of your passions," Constance said, noticing for the first time they were all wearing white shirts, black bow ties, and aprons — a much different look from their hectic loungewear. "Does Mr. Dannen work here, too?"

The band exchanged a look and cackled.

Ivory snarked. "Guess being a diva's a full-time job."

"But don't let Slanner hear you say that," Leal said, eyes crinkling. "How have you ladies been? Must have been an awful tangle getting lost on Mount Quixx. And being the first to live to tell the tale."

"We weren't lo—" Constance hip-checked Ivory into silence before she could say anything further.

"Awful, yes." She thrust Ms. Bougainvillea's list into Ivory's hand, then shooed her away. "But we're fine. Just took a . . . wrong turn, that's all."

"Down a cliff, through a canyon, up a mountain, and so on," Bartek cut in as he loaded the freezer. He wasn't as tall as Sluggo, but he was all gangly arms, and his brown hair was a cumulus cloud on his head.

"Did you see any monsters?" Avila stepped up to them with his hands clasped under his chin.

Constance felt the blood leaving her face. "Well, I—"

"Fellas, fellas." Leal stepped in, hands up. "I know we don't get out much, but let the lady breathe."

Constance blinked up at Leal smiling down at her, and she coloured again. "Thanks."

He grinned. "We *are* about due for a break, though." Out from behind a rack of dusty greeting cards, Leal pulled a tiny stringed guitar — a ukulele — and began tuning it with nimble fingers. "You don't happen to sing, do you? You seem the type. Alto?"

"She does!" Ivory whirled back in, the brimming basket swinging on her arm as she dumped it at Constance's feet. "You should try it, Connie, really, it might help."

"Help with what?" Sluggo quirked, polishing a kazoo with his shirttails.

Constance shook her head, her mouth a hard line. "Nothing." Then she glanced around. "Are you sure you're—"

But Leal was already strumming and humming. Vatos began percussing a gentle beat on the soup tower, and while Sluggo pinched out a few notes on the kazoo, the others sang, harmonizing perfectly.

You saw her in the kirkyard
While the moon arose,
She had a shovel in her hand and
Nobody rightly knows
How in all this bare wee town,
In this yawning big old world

There's none like her so tender
The dead could never render
Our corpsely dear mad mender,
The Bonnie Body Girl

I've seen her out cavorting
With the lads just down the way
The ones in their fine coffins
With nothing left to say
She dresses them so dearly
And whispers them so sweet
While gravestones and old augurs
Dance at crossroads 'neath her feet

Constance went still, her fingers tingling. She felt the corner of her lip twitch, her foot tapping. When she looked around again, the bent and rumpled customers were all smiling, too, straightening like flowers in a rare sunbeam. Leal was all the charm that Slanner thought he had, and it wasn't any wonder. It seemed, however impossibly, that the clouds of Quixx parted when the Kadaver's Soiree had the breathing room to shine, and Constance realized in those few minutes what Platinum really meant.

Didn't Charlie O'Brien
Look so damn near fine?
At his wake last Sunday
We all stood in the line —
But at the back of church
Young Bonnie did she grin
For yes she loved 'em all
With her joyful pale and pall
We'd come to if she'd call —
The Bonnie Body Girl!

When the last chord was plucked, Constance found herself clapping almost as fervently as Ivory.

"That was lovely, really," she said, and Leal bowed so low he was nearly doubled over.

"Lovely as a bleached spat in June," oozed a voice, and Leal jumped up so fast he bowled into his bandmates, who dominoed through produce. Leal pulled his collar, a rangy scarecrow once more as a Slanner-shaped cloud passed over him, shoving a heavy box into his waiting arms.

Constance and Ivory stepped back in the silence, Slanner adjusting Leal's bow tie over a bobbing Adam's apple. "Am I going as loco as these chickies," he snarled, "or did I hear a little ditty floating through here that wasn't over the intercom and also wasn't on our last album?"

Leal straightened. "We were just on our break, Slanner—"

"I've got another *break* for you — a break *up*." Then he clapped his hands smartly on Leal's paling brown cheeks and spun on his heel for Constance, only to have Ivory block his way.

"Small fry." He arched a ginger brow, yanking on his magenta lapels.

Ivory peered around him. "What's in the box?" She pointed, reading aloud: "'Demos' and 'Return to Sender'—"

He swept Ivory aside with a snip-snap of his fingers, gliding on his own oil slick. "Say, there was another vocal I heard just as I was about to crash your little sock hop. An alto. Which one of you was it?"

It seemed all eyes were on Constance again, but she blinked in genuine surprise. "It wasn't—"

Ivory elbowed her. When she looked up again, she realized it was the band's turn to be surprised. How tired was she that she couldn't recall singing in public or not? She lifted a shaking hand to her mouth. "But I didn't!"

Slanner was too close for comfort and Constance yelped and hopped backward. "You holdin' out on me, little darlin'? You have a sweet sound, could use a little tuning for the crooning. What say you come by later and we *jam*?"

Constance's throat was so thick she was sure it was an allergic reaction to the sleaze. "Have to go!" She snapped up Ivory's wrist and the basket, which emptied its contents at their feet, and took off as her lungs filled with imagined fibreglass.

They only stopped on the other side of the headless fountain, when Constance realized there were tiny stars in front of her, and she wasn't really choking, but the scarf had wound itself around her neck too tightly. Ivory freed it while she counted.

"One one thousand. Two one thousand. Breathe, Connie." Constance held on to her sister's words. Her *younger* sister, so much more put together than Constance ever would be, and here she was, having panic attacks still, at her age, and being coaxed back to the dizzying surface by Ivory at *her* age . . .

"There." Constance rubbed her eyes, and the lead in her chest seemed lighter as Ivory pulled the scarf back up over Constance's hair. "You really shouldn't let Slanner get to you like that. Men may be after one thing, but they're nothing to be afraid of."

Constance's crossness recovered before her dignity. "I wasn't — he didn't — and anyway, he was in my space." Constance stood, surveying their empty basket and their failed mission. "But I suppose we'll have to go back in there now, after all that."

"Let's take a detour first. It's on the list, after all," Ivory offered, and this time she was pulling Constance willingly along to the junk shop.

Mercifully it was much quieter inside now. The woman behind the counter smiled wanly while juggling triplet toddlers and pulling them away from the towering aisles of breakables.

"I wonder where all this stuff came from," Ivory said, tipping backward to take in crystal chandeliers, full sets of encyclopedias, and a bicycle with a front wheel as big as herself.

Constance shrugged. "Mx. Mott said it herself. So did Ms. Bougainvillea: people are leaving Quixx in droves. Better to leave the stuff behind and start over." She reached out and swiped a layer of grime from a bell jar over a carriage clock, stiff and still and keeping nothing but memory.

"You really were singing along, you know," Ivory whispered when they'd marvelled all the way to the back of the shop, a collection of chipped porcelain dolls surveying them from creaking shelves. "Did you really not notice, or were you just . . ."

Constance shook her head. "I don't know what's the matter with me. Maybe I haven't been sleeping well." But it was only in the Happy Bell she wasn't sleeping. She'd slept so perfectly once before, in a bed made of spun silk. She flinched at the memory, at the four golden eyes crinkling down at her from a face as blue as the sky she hadn't seen in days. She was desperate to change the subject. "They really are good musicians. However strange that is to admit of a jazz outfit."

"Too bad about the lead singer." Ivory shrugged, then she squealed and darted forward. "Connie, look!"

She stiffened. "Of course . . ."

It was a fan — massive, the kind used in big factories or warehouses, as wide as Constance's arm span.

She glanced at Ivory's gaping mouth, her face clearly showing a plan and a plea forming.

"No."

Ivory's mouth clapped shut, eyes all glistening innocence. "No what?"

"You're going to suggest we buy this eyesore as a gift." Constance folded her arms over her bosom. "And that we deliver it to your imaginary friend as a token of our gratitude, just to get you back to a place neither one of us can speak of, ever again, to anyone."

Ivory threw up her arms. "But that's the fun of it! A secret, Connie. Just for us. And a last hurrah for you?" Ivory switched tacks. "Besides, *I* didn't say anything. Something is clearly on your mind. Hmm, I seem to have a sniffle. Do you have a *handkerchief* I might borrow?"

As Ivory strolled away, Constance gritted her teeth, refusing to play into her sister's prodding. Couldn't Constance have anything to herself? But she turned back to the fan, her reflection warped in the polished metal. *A gift?* She guiltily thought about the handkerchief, tucked away in her pocket, the gesture with which it was freely given. And what had Ivory meant by a last hurrah, anyway? Constance stepped back, her fists tight. No. There was no way. Neither one of them needed the excitement. But Ivory *had* helped Constance through yet another anxiety attack . . . No! Besides, how would they—

The triplet-juggling clerk sighed loudly as the kids scampered past, breaking Constance out of her spiral. "Sorry about them, miss."

"Oh, it's . . . no trouble." Constance smiled weakly, leaning against the glass counter, actually relieved for the distraction from her endless internal debate. "They have so much energy!"

At that, the clerk clucked. "Oh yes. And I'm glad of it. The fog and this town, it seems to drain the spark from some of us. But with the young, there's always hope."

Constance didn't look to Ivory, though the sentiment made her think of her sister. Instead, she looked out the window. "It's tenacious, for sure." Derrek said that it had risen, and remained, after an "incident" he hadn't elaborated on. Constance glanced warily at the clerk. "Do you know why—"

Constance jumped as the mother made a sharp warding sign with her fingers, before she adjusted her heavily beaded sweater and gesticulated dramatically. "It came from the mountain," she intoned, as if the register were a bonfire, and she was suddenly a prophet. "A great calamity, fifty years ago! No one saw what caused the sound, like a bomb dropping. That's what they say it was! Perhaps that famous astronomer, who set his sights on the mountain, brought the heavens down on our heads and on his own! Ah yes, some say he caused it all. None can say, or none *would* say, had they seen it! Yet when all was said and done, or said was none, there was the crater, and there was the fog, and Quixx itself seems to have disappeared."

Constance admitted to feeling a slight chill, but it could've been the breeze from the open window. "Quite a story, Ms. . . ." She quirked her eyebrow at the name badge on the thick, festooned knit: "Ms. Letitia Cord." And the woman dropped her arms, shook herself, and was a tired mother of three once more.

"Happened before I was born." She shrugged. "Point is that since the fog came, it's almost been impossible for Quixxians to dream. Many leave to find new prospects. They don't come back. Don't blame 'em. And those that stay, for nostalgia's sake or family, work on cockamamie projects to try to get people to come back. Or to keep people's hopes up." She thrust her nose at the fan Ivory was still eyeing. "That for the Manse?"

At that, Constance *did* feel a chill. "Heavens, no." Then she tilted her head. "Why would it be?"

Letitia seemed to be enjoying telling stories to someone other than her offspring. When she grinned, she flashed a silver incisor that mesmerized Constance instantly.

"The Manse was built as, how you call it, a tourist attraction. By Damocles Dannen. Now *that* was in my lifetime. Another attempt to bring folk back here. And it worked to keep locals' spirits up, his kid performing there for many years. But Damocles kept adding on to the house, and it kept breaking down. Folks'll say he's trapped in the walls or something, but," and she leaned in conspiratorially, "he just drives round the farms trying to find parts to fix it up. Comes in here every month or so seeing if I've got anything he needs. At least he keeps busy."

"Mm," Constance said, but kept her thoughts to herself. The triplets came swirling back in, and Ivory was already at the back shelves near that Gilda-forsaken fan, trying to figure out the best way to pull the whole thing down. Constance let the clerk's words fall over her like a gentle shroud, like the fog had done to the townsfolk. *Cockamamie projects to keep people coming back or to keep their hopes up.* Derrek belonged here more than he knew. And just because it was a small town, did it make the dreams of those remaining any less important?

Ivory grunted as she struggled, and Constance groaned. *With the young, there's always hope.*

Letitia was more than happy to get rid of the fan for a pittance, and wrap it in paper and string, no less, in exchange for them hauling it out of her overcrowded shop. Constance didn't know who was more surprised — herself or Ivory.

"This doesn't mean we're going to go back to that miserable mountain," Constance warned again, for the tenth time.

"Okay already!" Ivory grunted, having taken it upon herself to carry the package despite how it eclipsed her entire body. "Just point me towards the trench — hey!"

Ivory yelped as the load was snapped out of her grip, Constance stumbling under it before regaining her balance.

"I'll do it," Constance snorted, and found she could manage, with her height and weight, just fine. She was too used to boys trying to carry her schoolbooks for her without her consent — she'd forgotten she was strong.

"I can just see it now," she said, feeling the sweat and fog beading at her temples as she managed down the road. "You careening down that canyon, using this as a sledge, fast-tracking to more peril that I'll have to get you out of."

"You really should have considered professional weight-lifting," Ivory appraised, ignoring the rhetoric.

"I'll suggest that for the next career fair, shall I?" Constance peeked around the edge of the bundle, squinting into the shifting gloom. "Now, I suppose we can just go back to the Happy Bell . . . the trench *is* just across the road . . . then we throw it down with the cars, and that's that. I don't want to hear any more about — well, you know. Afterwards, I'll send that telegram. Perhaps it would be best to just have a home holiday. That would be much less . . . eventful." Even if it put a dent in Constance's plans that both her and Ivory's futures depended upon.

Ivory chipped a stone across their path with her shoe. "Yes, that's *exactly* what we both need."

Something flashed in the corner of Constance's eye, preventing her from pursuing any further melancholy about either of their prospects. Had that . . . ? Constance blinked hard, shook her head. But she *had* seen that same shape before — not just a shape, but a person, a woman, taking off at a clip just to the right of the path. Constance turned sharply, not knowing why, feeling an itch behind her ear, below her jaw. A nagging impulse, a flare.

A melody.

"Where are you going?"

Ivory's voice was far away, especially when Constance caught sight of the woman again, or maybe just the corner of her scarf. Because it *was* the woman Constance had seen days ago, when she'd gone after Ivory, the one diving into the trench with a determined look in her eye. Constance blinked hard, feeling a glittering flash behind her eyelids. The snatch of the scarf. The flutter of butterfly wings—

"Connie, stop!"

Ivory's gripping hand on Constance's arm was like a dog bite. Constance jerked and pivoted, wheeling off-balance until her own hands slipped and let the fan go as a means of self-preservation — but instead of falling into the trench as Constance nearly had, the fan careened and clanged to a sudden halt in the soupy fog a few feet away.

Constance panted, pulling the edge of her jacket down in shaking relief as Ivory went to investigate. "Well that was—"

"Eventful?" Ivory retorted, and when Constance caught up with her, they both stared in awe at the contraption that had brought the fan to a comfortable stop.

Ivory rubbed her finely boned hand over a sign — hand-painted and faded, but still legible in the dark paint. "'The Volunteer Star Brigade'?" she read aloud. "What's that?" Then, before Constance could stop her, Ivory was clearing away thick brambles and dried-husk brush by the fistful, revealing rusted metal, springs, and a platform, down a slight incline in a passable crevice in the canyon lip.

Constance reached for the sign, accidentally pulling away a sticker in the shape of a star that she'd imagined to be painted on.

"Curiouser and curiouser," Ivory mused, fiddling with a lever and what looked like a round crank.

"Don't play with that." Constance yanked Ivory's wrist away. "Whatever this is, it's been long-hidden for a reason. You have no idea what it is — or what it does."

Ivory's face was a well-curated gallery of distaste. "I think I have more knowledge than you on engineering, dear sister." Ivory pulled away, flourishing a hand. "You see this? It's some kind of pumping mechanism. Most likely for generating a charge, though from what power source I can't readily see. Everything is so rusty and croggled . . ." She tapped what could have once been a console. "This would provide a reading for the charge. Perhaps pneumatic, since hydraulic wouldn't make much sense. It's not a weapon, I don't think, but its main mechanism requires propulsion. Or creates it." She began experimentally turning the crank again. "But I can't tell if it's registering the action or not. A component may be broken—"

"Ivory, stop it!" Constance reached out and tried to wrest the crank out of Ivory's hand, but instead the mechanism made them crank backward at a speed that didn't allow Constance to release.

"Clever!" Ivory cried. "It moves widdershins!"

"Widderwhat?" Constance bleated, and they both brought the crank to a jerking stop when they heard something loud and rusty click into place.

"What was that?" Constance had one last chance to ask, before something else released beneath them, and Constance, Ivory, and the package containing the enormous fan were catapulted into the fog and the bloody unknown.

Each breath was a scream as the fog cut around Constance's face and pinwheeling arms, the face of Mount Quixx itself speeding ever blunter towards her, until she slammed into . . .

the open air? Her arms still akimbo, stopped but suspended in glittering mid-air, her screams continued.

"Connie, *please*, my eardrums."

Constance gathered herself enough to look below. How was she just hanging there? Beneath her were trees growing sideways, at right angles to the ground, the canyon farther below in the mist-shrouded dark. Constance looked aside, and there was Ivory, blinking owlishly.

Since Constance hadn't yet pulled herself out of single-syllable babbling, Ivory sighed. "The machine was projectile-based. I could tell you were dying to know.

As usual, Ivory seemed much less out of sorts than her older sister — after all, rollercoasters on the midway were elementary to her — and she peered around, taking in the sights, ignoring the fact they were suspended miles above nothingness in a hostile, monster-populated environment. Again.

She plucked the nearest sticky string she could reach. "We appear to be in a web of some kind." Then her face brightened, even as a shadow fell over it. "Which means—"

"Miss Ivory! Miss Constance!"

Constance tipped her head up slowly, her jaw slackened in desperate hope she wasn't about to see a giant spider in a cravat descending on them.

Alas.

Derrek drew himself astride the sisters on a slender thread, four amber eyes blinking as the same number of hands plucked her from the only thing keeping her upright. "You really are the most perplexing girls I've ever met. Though we all know I haven't met many."

Unable to help herself, Constance kicked wildly, then gripped tightly to Derrek as the second the web came sucking away from her clothes, and he, too, let out a cry of surprise as she flinched into him, the panic too much to bear.

"There, there, it's all right. I've— I've got you."

With a grunt, Ivory had pulled herself out of her own jacket, and thus the web, scaling deftly up and beside Derrek.

"Connie," Ivory said in a neutral voice, putting her hand on her sister's shaking shoulder. "Just breathe, all right? Count! One one thousand, two one thousand—"

"I am *fine*, thank you very much," Constance snapped, her teeth gritted, eyes shut painfully tight. "Just please can we discuss this nonsense when we get to level ground?"

Constance *felt* Derrek's laugh through his lithe, strange body more than heard it. "We already are."

In the silence that followed, Constance dared to peek, then flexed the toes of her shoe on the wide, even ledge before them.

"I . . . ahem." She pushed away, but his grip was still tender and sure, seeming to wait until she found her footing. This time, when Constance looked up at his frankly concerned face, she was glad it was there.

"Derrek!" Ivory blustered between them, and Derrek, for all his limbs and surety, jumped back, a bit frazzled himself as he released Constance prematurely. "How capital it is to see you again!"

"And you as well," he snorted, shaking her proffered hand. "This is somewhat of a . . . surprise." He raised his brow at what Constance now saw as a massive, intricate web set between two rocky plinths. "Not to mention the means you used to get here."

"While I do like taking the credit, it was Constance's fault this time. She found the launcher contraption — *and* figured out how to use it properly. The most surprising part, I think."

When Derrek appraised her again, Constance turned away, rubbing her shoulder. "Just lucky, I guess."

But Derrek's focus had gone back to the web, and what was still stuck in it. "And what's this?" He plucked it free like it was just another fly.

"That's a gift! For you!" Ivory preened. "Also Constance's idea. Well . . . *she* was going to just push it into the trench, but, direct delivery is a better guarantee."

"A gift?"

Derrek's eyes were wide, shining. Constance surprised herself by responding.

"You could open it now. If you like. Here." All of Derrek's hands were gently searching for a seam in the paper, but Constance reached out and yanked on one of the twine loops, and in one swish the paper, and string, fluttered away, swallowed by the fog below.

"My word," Derrek said, holding the huge fan away from his body, making it seem almost small in comparison. "It . . . it's *perfect*!"

Suddenly Constance was swept back up in those four hands like she weighed less than a fresh batch of cotton candy, the fan leaning against the rock face as she and the world twirled, and when she screamed this time, there was at least an undertone of delight.

Derrek put her down quickly, picking up the fan again, running his fingers over the blunted blades. "This is exactly what I need to do a test run! Would you like to see? Oh please, it's the least I can do, and you're both a part of the miracle. My very first intentional benefactors!"

Constance looked down again, realizing they'd have to prevail on Derrek's hospitality either way if they were to get back to Quixx safely. She was still wobbly from the "flight" over. "I'm sure Ivory would like that but — I can just wait here."

In a spray and a whirl, the fan was cocooned and fastened around Derrek's front on a harness of his own deft design.

But his eyes were disappointed. "Really, Miss Constance? I would very much like—"

Ivory, in the meantime, vaulted onto Derrek's broad carapace with ease, cutting off his plea.

"Ivory!" Constance paled. "You can't just keep climbing onto a gentleman's—" Wracking her brain for the correct anatomical arachnid term, she clapped her mouth shut.

"It's no trouble, really." Derrek smiled. "Besides, I'm not sure if *gentleman* is the proper term. I consider myself gender fluid, or certainly non-binary, as are many of my compatriots on the mountain. Though I've decided that the fixed gender pronouns are all right. He, him, they, them. It's quite a challenge when one is a class of one's own."

"You can say that again!" Ivory said, never missing a beat. "I don't believe science or society has caught up to your modern sensibilities, Derrek." She looked, then, to Constance, eyebrow raised. "Don't be a stick in the mud, Connie. It won't kill you to experience a scientific marvel firsthand."

Constance's mouth opened and closed, but she had no retort, especially not to Derrek's expectant look. Pressure mounting, the last thing she wanted was to suffer the indignity of riding along with Ivory, let alone going at all.

"I— I mean, it does sound . . . interesting. But I think—" She just needed a moment to herself, and at the very least to get them to stop staring, so she unbuttoned her jacket and tied it around her waist. "I'll go up myself, and meet you there."

Ivory snorted, seeing right through Constance's feint but letting her have it. Chin in the air, Constance strode past and made to awkwardly step up onto a series of rocks that looked like a set of passable steps, trying to make a good show of it. "You two just, you know, go on ahead. Don't wait for me."

"To use one of Ivory's fascinating expressions: 'capital!'" Derrek chirped, certainly buying into the act. "I admire your indefatigability!" And not missing a beat, he hopped to another ledge nearby, as Constance stoically broke a nail on the next rock she gripped. Just when she decided to focus on finding a foothold, she felt Derrek very close and nearly jumped out of her skin.

"Just a step to the right," he said, his voice soft and resonating in her ear, but when Constance turned to reply, she misstepped, and with a yelp let go of the rock. Instead of falling backward, she was suddenly tumbling upward in a pocket of air as she had on her first sojourn.

Her skirt billowing around her waist as she modestly fought to keep it where it belonged, it didn't take long to catch up to Derrek and Ivory — the former of which was making a good show of pretending he hadn't seen her skirt fly up. The airstream this time seemed much less fickle and more on the playful side.

Derrek bit his lip, unsure if he should laugh or not. "Do you need—"

"I'm still quite fine, thank you," Constance said, pushing her hair out of her face with one hand and clenching her skirt in the other. Trying to get over the fact she'd been somewhat bamboozled into following, she glared at Ivory, who was snickering behind Derrek.

And though he'd given her space, Derrek met her eyes again and openly demonstrated how a little nudge from the rock here and there with an elbow or a light touch could make them drift quicker and more directly, and with burgeoning courage, Constance awkwardly emulated him with good results. Then Derrek stretched out a hand again, and Constance, beyond her better judgment, took it.

Her mind whirled as the long blue fingers clasped gently about hers, thoughts finding footing. Gender fluid, he'd said? Non-binary? The three of them went up in companionable silence, marvelling at the mountain and the raw sky as they broke the fog. Constance could barely process that this was all happening, *again*, as rock and tree and crag streaked by with the balletic precision of the eight shifting legs by her side. But however confusing Derrek's speech about himself had been, Constance supposed he knew better about his own identity than she would, and her confusion left her embarrassed.

"I'm . . ." She cleared her throat. "I'm sorry."

"Hm?" Derrek said as the upward current ran its course, helping her to land less awkwardly on the level ledge.

"About . . . if I . . . misgendered you." She was staring at her shoes but turned her chin up when Derrek laughed.

"Communication is usually key. Thank you for allowing me to explain."

Constance felt her lip quirk, cheeks warming.

"Beauty!" Ivory cried, and Constance broke away as her sister clamoured up beside her.

"Isn't it?" Derrek smiled. Both of them were talking about the machine jutting as precariously off the side of the mountain as they were, the harsh wind whipping Constance's hair into her stinging eyes.

On an elaborate setup of trees, stilts, and all manner of pulleys, gear, and silvery thread, were countless fans. Fan heads and blades of varying sizes and metals, whispering as the mountain air streaked past, tinkling faintly like a symphonic chime. They were all attached to a tangled body of tubes and wires, surely the device's great brain.

"And here we are, the viewing base." Derrek directed them down to a much more civilized platform, complete with a balcony surround, that didn't move an inch for the powerful blasts of air buffeting it at this altitude. Constance didn't bother asking how it was attached, since she frankly didn't want to know as it creaked under her feet.

With Derrek and his reassuring grip gone, Constance could only clasp tightly to Ivory, pressing into the mountainside. "Here!" Ivory shouted, passing Constance a pair of goggles that had been tucked inside a case belted to the platform.

Her eyes no longer stinging, Constance watched from behind foggy green lenses as Derrek pulled the fan up from his front, swiftly undid its bindings, and picked his way carefully over each smaller fan, until he was hanging upside down from the outermost outcrop. Constance felt her stomach flip in sympathetic panic. The machine and its blades hung at least ten metres off the mountainside, and while Derrek had repurposed his harness to be attached to a web cable, she wanted to scream *be careful!* Though over this wind, she doubted he would hear her.

Then Derrek disappeared from sight, and all they could hear was a faint clanging and whirring.

Utterly numb and stiffening her entire body against the wind, Constance tried to eke out a better view, but the air caught her skirt and turned her aside. Ivory's small hand just barely missed grabbing a handful of Constance's blouse to stop her from tripping, until the banging abruptly stopped.

"There," came Derrek from behind, pulling Constance back from the brink once more. "I think you'll be more comfortable over here, Miss Constance," he said, before wrapping her, too, in a silky-threaded harness, fastening her lifeline to the balcony edge as he'd already done with Ivory seconds earlier.

She felt the air go out of her lungs as the harness tightened, counted the spots as they rose in front of her eyes. Derrek noticed her plucking at the harness's lines and loosened them.

"Is that better? I know it's uncomfortable, but I don't want to see you blown away."

Constance swallowed and forced herself to nod, grateful for Derrek's understanding and concern. She was glad for the goggles, too, so that neither he nor Ivory could see her eyes welling up. Why had she come up here at all?

Then her hands were bundled up in two of his, and Ivory's, too. "Are you ready to make history, my friends?"

Friends? Constance's heart skipped.

"History!" Ivory screamed over the wind, and Constance's face twitched into what felt like a smile, but she couldn't be sure. She had never done anything like this before, and her chest was shuddering, either in excitement or sheer terror.

Then in a flourish and a flash of his own double goggles, Derrek leapt up, eight great legs clinging to the viewing ledge as he reached for a giant lever in the rock above, and with all his meticulous might, pulled down.

Silence.

Constance blinked and lifted a shaking, stiff hand to her goggles to make sure she was seeing clearly. Derrek's body slackened, shoulders dropped. He looked back at them, helpless.

"That's not—"

An explosion rocked the mountainside and the viewing ledge, and Constance's ears popped and rang before the world went black.

"I said *I hope your eardrums are intact*," Derrek shouted again, and Constance shied away, her hearing coming back in a sudden wince of her jaw.

"Sorry," Derrek coughed meekly, recoiling, maybe his thirtieth apology by now. "I was quite certain . . . but perhaps it wasn't secured . . . and experimentation, being what it is—"

"I thought it was thrilling," Ivory cut in charitably. As Constance's focus swung back in, she inwardly thanked Ivory for her experience culling nervous babbling — which Derrek was doing in spades, presently.

"Thrilling is the word for it," Constance sighed, springing up and nabbing the rattling teapot that Derrek just about dropped. They were all a bit shaken up. He ran a finger about his throat and under his necktie.

"Frightfully—!" His voice faltered. "Ahem. Yes, well. Embarrassing, also, is a word one might use." He moved away from the impromptu parlour they'd settled in. They had not gone to the attic as before; Constance had only blacked out for the moment and knew she'd come back here partially on her own steam, but she had been in a daze when they returned to the observatory to calm down and wait for their ears to stop ringing, and she wasn't about to climb those stairs. Even Derrek, so graceful and careful, seemed to be shaking on every leg.

Constance snorted, knocking back the black, bitter tea. "I suppose failure is a vital part of the scientific method." But when she glanced at Derrek, who smiled but ultimately looked defeated, she immediately regretted her words, and so she picked up the tray and looked round the room for a serviceable sink to make herself useful.

"I can—" Derrek stumbled up, but Constance leapt back defensively, still not sure on her own feet, and when they crashed into each other at least Ivory was up and snatching the tray away from them both.

"Criminy — sit down, you two!" the youngest Ivyweather admonished. "You've got four hands, Derrek, but they're of no use to anyone right now."

In point of fact, every single one of them was holding tight to Constance, but he quickly released her. "I admit I'm not myself," he muttered, plucking at his coat. "My mind's as much of a mess as this place."

He wasn't wrong. If there were surfaces like shelves or tables or serviceable chairs, it was difficult to find them in this downstairs hall. The walls were hewn rock and charred, the floors crumbling and creaking and dusty, and Constance went to a mound of mystery items, absently picking things up.

"What happened here?" she asked, floundering as she knocked a pile of parchment askew, wrapping her arms around it before it scattered to the wind coming through the paneless windows.

"This and that," Derrek sighed, finally resigning to sitting still in one place — however much a creature like him could sit, resting low on his arachnid haunches. He clasped his cheek with one hand, pinched an elbow with another, gaze turning inward.

"We're all okay, Derrek." Ivory patted him on the shoulder. "See? All one piece and fit as a fiddle. And after all, you can always go and see what the problem was when the smoke clears and try again tomorrow, can't you? Surely you didn't lose *all* of your work because of one malfunctioning fan."

Derrek's faraway look seemed to resolve, and he smiled meekly at her. "Before we evacuated, everything looked relatively intact. I must have blown a breaker somewhere. Everything is wind- and water-powered, even the electrical. I was just a bit too excited, I suppose." And with that he got up smartly, smacking a fist into an open palm. "Right! Tomorrow is another day! And thanks to you two there *will* be a tomorrow. Perhaps if I came up with a remote start, instead . . ." From a pocket he produced a worse-for-wear remote with a bright red button, bringing it close to a corner eye.

"Connie?" Ivory peeped, and Constance spun, her heart in her throat. Derrek's eyes were wide.

"My word," he said, marvelling at how, in just the few moments he'd been distracted, the corner Constance had found herself in had become relatively . . . tidy.

"Erm," she said, hands sheepishly behind her back. "I, ah, cleaning clears my head. Sometimes I don't notice I'm doing it, really." She ran a hand through her hair, realizing how untidy it, too, must be. "I don't have a mind for science or mechanics like you two. But I could achieve a Ph.D. in organizing, probably." Her hand absently went along a shelf, and she bit her lip, but her fingers stopped on something that, when the grime rubbed away, shone in the afternoon light. Without thinking, she picked it up.

"I'm sure you have many talents, Miss Constance." A large shadow fell across the object in her hand as Derrek joined her side, gingerly removing what was, really, a gilded picture frame. Constance took note of how tenderly he rubbed the dust away on the edge of his frayed coat, finally placing the picture upright on the shelf where she'd found it.

"Who are they?" Ivory asked, standing on her tiptoes. "The white hair! Connie, do you think this is Ms. Bougainvillea's long-lost astronomer?"

The frazzled gears in Constance's mind clicked, and she felt a tingling beneath her skin, seeing suddenly a flash of the faceless painting in the Happy Bell's hall, a snatch of half-remembered laughter. She swallowed and looked at Derrek. His usually jovial mouth was a thin line, forehead wrinkled.

"Yes, that's him," he confirmed flatly. "Professor Klaus Bedouin." Derrek moved away without providing further details.

When Constance looked back at the photo, she took in the man standing at Derrek's side, arms folded lightly, mouth breaking into a laugh, crinkling keen, bright eyes beneath white curls over a dark forehead. Derrek, in the photo, seemed unsure of himself, but he was smiling regardless, pulling on the wide bow tie at his throat as if it were a novelty. The observatory behind them looked freshly minted.

And on Derrek's other side, a woman, with black flowing hair, golden spectacles, and a scarf about her brown shoulders. They all looked so happy. What a beautiful portrait of three friends . . . *or family*, she whispered, inwardly jealous, for never having taken such a picture with her parents, or Ivory, all together, where they looked remotely as happy as this group.

Constance suddenly, desperately, needed to know who this woman in the photo was, but Ivory was taking up the remaining oxygen in the room with a thousand fire-spat questions: ". . . in the town, they say the astronomer disappeared fifty years ago, right? And *you* said you've been here all that time, and of course this *proves* you knew him, and must know what happened to—!"

This time it was Constance's turn to snatch Ivory by the sleeve, stoppering the tidal wave of her curiosity, which sometimes lacked tact. She snapped up at Constance, first with teenage outrage, but it softened when Constance jutted her chin at Derrek, who was standing by the rickety stairs to the attic, four hands folded tightly at his back.

"There was a fire," he said, turning finally. He did not look upset or melancholic or angry — merely tired, somehow still smiling through whatever memories were churning deep in those flashing amber eyes. "This observatory was Klaus's finest achievement, and I was privileged enough to know him and be a part of it." He looked about the damaged room wistfully. "It was his final wish to deliver the stars of this mountain back to the world, and I have been trying to fulfill it ever since. A silly dream, perhaps. And a protracted one.

"But Klaus showed me a world — an entire cosmos — beyond this mountain, and I would like to be a part of that world in the way he taught me to be. Despite appearances, this was once a fine house of scholarly research. And perhaps, to you, I seem like I don't know what I'm doing. But I am trying my best. Klaus used to say my best was enough when challenges arose, which they seem to be doing quite a lot lately. I've wondered many times if Klaus may have said that just to be kind."

Constance was moving underwater, his words echoing sentiments she thought could only be her own. The lack of certainty. The self-doubt. Constance's feet took the steps of their own accord, and she only managed to stop them a respectable breath away from Derrek, her chest tight as he blinked at her in surprise. Her words, though, were far more surprising.

"Ivory will help you."

Derrek's mouth fell open, but he didn't have time to respond as Ivory was leaping up and crying out. "Really, Connie? You mean it?" She'd danced over and grabbed Constance's hands, twirling her about the room. "We should blow things up more often if it will change that intractable mind of yours!"

"Miss Constance, I . . ." Derrek's hands were in the air, unsure, themselves, of what to do. Constance watched his cheeks visibly purple as he caught her eye and looked away. "The offer is very kind, but your safety—"

"Psh, safety!" Ivory quipped, wrapping an arm around Constance's waist and yanking her close in an embrace. "Constance is the most anxious person I know, and she not only survived being catapulted here half a mile, but she went up onto a rickety platform on the side of a gusty precipice and survived a shelling! Obviously, the mountain air is doing her some good."

Wasn't this trip geared towards changing Ivory? Maybe the shock had erased the nonstop thrills now that they were in a civilized sitting room, but when Ivory leapfrogged away, Constance collapsed onto a settee with little ceremony. *Is the mountain really changing me?*

"Ah yes, the catapult!" Derrek grinned, hiding a look of fond remembrance behind his hand. "Klaus's wife built that when she got tired of climbing to deliver us our tea. And once she did build it, she learned much more about herself and her abilities. In the end, *she* was the mechanical one, while Klaus was the theoretical component. She facilitated quite a lot of the building of the observatory, in fact. Later, she called us the Volunteer Star Brigade."

"What a perfect name for our outfit! Don't you agree, Connie?"

Constance released her fistful of skirt, and when she turned her hand over she saw the star sticker still firmly pasted there. She couldn't help it. Despite everything that had happened, despite the implausibility of the moment, looking up into not only her sister's violet eyes filled with wonder and excitement, but Derrek's four amber ones, in a charred room crowded with papers and books and burning ghosts, despite every anxiety and the whispering unknown tickling beneath her skin, she felt, at long last that she could . . .

Her father, in his study. *You haven't changed your mind, have you? Then I'll make you a deal—*

"Ivory is keen enough for the both of us, so I'm all right with her spending time here, as long as she's careful, though it's not her strong suit. As for me" — Constance swallowed the growing lump in her throat, standing — "I would just slow you down."

Ivory turned suddenly. "What do you mean, Connie?" And Constance glanced quickly between their crestfallen faces, then away. "You can't mean you'll just wile away the summer cooped up in Batty Bee's place while we have all the fun?"

Constance backed up a step, her head seeming to swell. "It's just that . . ." She bit the inside of her cheek. "I don't have much to offer in the way of help. I'm not clever like you two. Really, I'm good for little other than fainting and nagging and falling off things. I wouldn't be very much fun. Don't worry about me."

The silence was more painful than anything else, and all Constance wanted was to go to a dark room and shut the door, because what was worse was that she wanted, very much, to be a part of this, but she had never been as brave as her little sister, as she'd been reminded more than once. And bravery just seemed to get them both into trouble.

"I'd like you to come."

The sisters turned. Derrek blinked between them, colouring. "Err. I don't want to make you uncomfortable, Miss Constance," Derrek ventured, his jaw noticeably stiff. "But I have very much enjoyed your company. You may think you don't have much to offer, but your support — and your astute project management and organization — well, it has been important to . . . me." He folded all four hands at his waist. "It would feel wrong if you weren't here with us."

Now Constance really was going to cry.

"Besides!" Ivory threw her hands up, clapping Constance on the back and preventing the spill-over. "This workspace is atrocious! We need someone tending home base if we're going to get anything done! And parts! We'll need a parts hunter! You can be our production manager!"

A warm spot was growing in Constance's chest, a pinprick of purpose and belonging in a loony situation. "I suppose I *can* do a bit of managing . . ."

"It's your choice," said Derrek, unable to keep the excitement out of his voice. "But I would feel very sad if you didn't join us, Miss Constance, and I don't mind admitting it."

"There, it's settled." Ivory grinned, looping arms with Constance and stretching her hand to Derrek. "But let's shake on it officially before Constance comes to her senses and changes her mind."

Derrek took Ivory's small, bird-thin hand and shook it firmly. She whirled off, boasting out loud of the plans for the next day, thrilling with each imagined adventure that lay before them.

Watching her, Constance sighed. "At least it'll keep her busy for the summer. What did she call it? An internship?" She swallowed and looked up at Derrek, his spider legs holding him tall and proud now, his slightly singed waistcoat and shirt swelling with each delighted breath. *A class of one's own*, he'd said earlier. He wasn't wrong.

She held out her hand to him, trying to keep it from trembling, and Derrek stared at it a bit too long.

Then, as he had when they'd said good night that first time, he gripped it warmly. "You won't regret this," he said. He looked like he would've said more, but Ivory bustled back into their periphery, promising Derrek they would search Quixx for more parts he needed, and that they would have to come up with a communication system between the Happy Bell and the peak.

"Detalia Dots and Dashes with signal lamps, maybe?" Ivory babbled and, shaking her head, Constance steered her towards the door.

They made their way to the bottom trench through meandering jetties and downward currents, and arrived back at his improvised basket-and-pulley system.

"Tomorrow, then?" Derrek asked breathlessly.

"Tomorrow," Constance and Ivory said together, and as they rose back through the brambles to Quixx's foggy, lamplit street, Constance couldn't help but look forward to it.

7

THE FUTURE FANDANGO

"I."

Bang!

"Have."

Bang!

"*Had it.*"

Crash!

Leal sighed, lifting his fingers away from the bull fiddle's strings and propping it against a wide-mouthed island carving set piece. He went to the drums in two strides and righted the high-hat Slanner had kicked over.

"Are you hungry, boss man?" Hatch asked, cowering slightly behind his upright piano but still true to his concern.

"Hungry for *action*," Slanner seethed, cracking his knuckles. "I can't stand it one more minute." And with that he whirled out — out of their practice space, out of the Manse, likely out of his mind.

At times like these, the band looked to Leal for guidance, as they did now, literally, across their instruments. Should they follow Slanner? Should they stay behind? Should they continue this song and dance forever? Leal had to make the calls and keep his head too many times, too often. And the outbursts didn't happen without reason — Leal could tell, as he sighed and gestured, the band filing out of the house to follow Slanner down the road, that this particular tantrum was going to be about—

"Little Miss Con thinks she can ignore me?" Slanner was grinding his teeth, like he did in his sleep, and Leal took a breath as the rest came, as expected. "How many notes did I send to Batty Bee's? Probably all buried in bird scat! You know what I have to offer?"

"A lot," Leal finished.

"A lot!" Slanner cried. "I'm Platinum! That's still worth something! She thinks she's *better* than me?"

Leal tried a different tack today as they whipped up fog in their great march down the hill, towards the boarding house. "And what exactly do you think you're gonna get out of Constance Ivyweather?"

Slanner's mouth, hanging open mid-tirade, clamped shut, his glare turning innocent. He pulled on his lapels. "My intentions are pure," he admonished, throwing an arm around Leal's shoulder, shaking him. Leal swallowed, trying to keep it cool. "A little banter. A little ego rubbing. Maybe a few Big City contacts! Appreciation. That's all I'm after."

"Right." Leal broke away, and for the first time, Slanner looked dismayed. Leal knew a thing or two about seeking appreciation that never came. "And what will you *do* with Big City contacts, my main man?" He shot Slanner as withering a look as he could conjure, making sure to act as annoyed as he felt. "Will you finally consider moving to said Big City, so we can, I don't know, play music for an actual audience?"

The rest of the band stopped in their tracks. Avila clapped a hand over his mouth and Bartek shrank as if expecting an oncoming slap. Leal, towering over Slanner by a head, folded his arms. "Well?"

Slanner glanced from Leal to the rest of the Soiree, then down the fog-crusted road.

"We're *Platinum*," Slanner repeated, though quieter now, less sure. "We'll go to the Big City when we're Big City material. Can't do that without connections, right? And if I gotta do that all on my lonesome, then so be it." And he started off again, as if he'd won.

Leal's stomach tightened like he'd been sucker-punched. After all they'd been through? He couldn't tell if it was Hatch or Sluggo who'd let out a tiny gasp. The band wasn't stupid — they knew Slanner was cooking something up, and whatever it was, it probably wasn't above-board. But they were loyal to a fault. So was Leal. Always had been. And Slanner had taken advantage of it for too long.

Leal was about to blow his stack, but someone new was waiting for them on the path ahead. The path to the Happy Bell, the one they'd taken every day to see what the Ivyweathers were up to, only to be told they were busy.

Slanner winged his arms out, and the band stopped abruptly behind him as if he was a shield. "Mottie."

"Dannen." Mx. Mott raked her sparkling eyes up Slanner, from his scuffed saddle shoes to his fiery mop, leaning askance to take in the entire motley crew. "Entourage."

"Afternoon, Mx. Mott." Leal stepped up, trying for affability. "You're looking lovely today."

Mx. Mott flicked her towering afro. "Thank you, Mr. Synodite. At least one of you has grown into a fine young man since you were in my charge."

Slanner grumbled, and her eyes sharpened, so he grinned. "And what brings you to Batty Bee's Bell today?"

Mx. Mott glanced up at the house, its crumbling architecture, and let loose her grip on the gate as she closed it. "I could ask you the same, but I won't bother with the pretense that I care. I've made the landlady an offer. She refused. Again."

Leal sucked in a breath and looked at Slanner, whose expression had gone slack. "You're still trying to buy it?"

Mx. Mott's jaw tightened. "What of it?" Then she swept her hand out to the mountain beside them, watching the entire exchange with its usual guarded silence. "It has the best views in all of Quixx. It would make a better university than a boarding house." Then her anger redirected from Slanner to Ms. Bougainvillea. "But she won't see sense. Just clings to the past in this rambling, dust-choked estate."

"She's so old, though," Sluggo whispered to Hatch. "She must be on her way to . . . you know . . ." He made a choking sound.

Leal spun, horrified. "Sluggo!"

But what horrified him more was Mx. Mott's demure smile behind her well-manicured hand. "What a thing to say." Then she eyed Slanner, approaching like a hungry python, and Leal almost stepped in front of Slanner to protect him. He didn't like the look in Mx. Mott's eye.

"I hear you've made her an offer, too. Tell me." She was still a tall, imposing woman, same as she was back when they all were confined to Cardinal Quixx Hall before they'd dropped out to pursue the fame they'd all been sure of. "What would an overgrown boy blowhard who fell asleep in every class he was in, with his own, albeit crumbling, circus tent up the hill, want with the Happy Bell?"

Leal watched Slanner's Adam's apple bob. Even Leal didn't really know what Slanner wanted. He'd been trying to buy the Happy Bell for a while and wouldn't say why. But Leal doubted Slanner really knew, either, and he was getting as red as his hair. He threw up his hands. "I just *do*, okay, lay off!"

Mx. Mott clucked. "You never did have much vision, did you?" She slid her horn-rimmed glasses up her nose and shifted her handbag. "Higher education, Mr. Dannen. Then perhaps you'd find your way. Best stay out of mine."

She stalked past, and Slanner looked like a boiler about to burst when Mx. Mott turned one last time. "And best stay out of the way of those girls. They're trouble, and they'll be back where they came by season's end, and you'll be as forgotten in their minds as you are in everyone else's."

Leal hadn't expected that blow. He heard a whimper and clamoured to Avila's side, gathering their smallest member into a hug. "She didn't mean it," he lied, rubbing his friend's shoulder. He looked to Slanner, who was standing at the Happy Bell's rotting gate, staring hard up at the grimy windows like he was casting a spell.

"I'll show her," he snarled, tone electric. "I'll show them *all*. No matter what it takes . . . I'll do something they won't be able to ignore."

Then he turned heel and headed back up the hill, and all Leal and the band could do was exchange worried looks and follow.

"Are they gone? Did they see you?"

"Curiouser and curiouser," Ivory said, drawing away from the window when the coast was clear. Constance peeped over her sister's tangled head, watching the Kadaver's Soiree slumping back up the hill, with Mx. Mott devoured by the fog in the other direction.

"I hate it when you say that," Constance scoffed. "What are they all up to? Slanner's intentions for coming around here — those are obvious." She rolled her eyes. "But Mx.

Mott can't be serious about buying the Happy Bell for a . . ." Just saying it sounded ridiculous. "A university? In *Quixx*?"

Ivory zipped up her canvas backpack, securing the belt firmly across her chest and waist and pushing her handcrafted goggles up onto her head. "Stranger things have happened." She looked Constance up and down. "Like those trousers. I didn't know you had anything other than skirts and ball gowns!"

Constance blinked, looking down. "There was that one retreat the student council went on. Hiking and . . . such." The pants were less about utility and more about style. They hadn't done much hiking on that trip over all the gossiping. The pants, though, were high-waisted, tartan-patterned (her favourite) but with deep pockets and ankle kick-pleats. The tennis shoes she'd borrowed from a dusty cupboard down the hall. These were the least mud-caked. And anything would be an improvement over climbing a mountain in a skirt.

"I wonder if Derrek will have a conniption when he sees you." Ivory waggled her eyebrows then she bounded for the bedroom door. Constance pushed her sister lightly and she nearly toppled under the weight of her bag.

"Maybe you should wear that get-up when you see Madeline Mott next," Constance countered, which shut Ivory up — not an easy task.

Ms. Bougainvillea greeted them at the door. Two runt cassowaries stood with twin packages in their bills. Constance had become used to snatching these by now and was rewarded with a *quork* for her effort.

"Your tea for later, dearies," Ms. Bougainvillaea said. Her placid face was bright, but she looked somewhat deflated. Frederic was in his usual spot in her bouffant, but he, too, looked tired.

"Don't let the Man get you down, Ms. Bee," Ivory said, stomping onto the porch with a fist in the air.

Constance paused. Even though they hadn't been forth-right with where they went every day, Ms. Bougainvillea still happily made sure they were fed and looked after. If this had been home, their nannies would have grilled them and provided sharp curfews. Constance hadn't realized how nice it was to be independent and also so supported.

She rested a hand on the landlady's shoulder. "Are you all right?"

Ms. Bougainvillea blinked. "Fit as a fandance, my love!" She patted Constance's cheek. "I've got the butterflies to keep my thoughts in line. Never fear."

Once again, Constance didn't bother asking what that meant. Ms. Bougainvillea's riddle-speak would probably always be beyond her, but with each passing day, her statements seemed more tangled than the last.

Constance shook her head. "Be back for supper," she promised, and she skipped after Ivory, once they'd made sure the coast on the walkway was clear.

The routine was rote now, though they'd only been at it a week. Ivory preferred the launcher, which Constance escorted her to, before doubling back to the pulley basket that Derrek had rigged to be self-serving, like a dumbwaiter. It was easier than sliding down a canyon, and though it was not as direct, Constance valued the time to herself. When the basket passed through the bracken, she caught a glimpse of Ivory's epic flight, tucking and rolling, until she was blocked out by the mountain's gaping back. Constance shook her head, smiling.

Once in the auto-wreck graveyard, she wondered why she'd ever been afraid of the place. Sure, the fog still clung to everything like gauzy paper, but the place was as familiar now as her garden in Ferren City. She passed the derelict cars, sinking rusting and heavy into the ground, having made the sacrifice for the work that would take up Derrek and Ivory's day.

But Constance was still troubled. Her ear twitched at the strange sounds and the pockets of silence as she went up to make the first current. The hum resolved and disappeared, and she cast her attention to the recent past, to what she'd overhead Mx. Mott saying as she'd crept down the stairs, crouching by the empty urn beneath the faceless astronomer painting.

"What a shame that this once-great house has fallen so far," Mx. Mott sighed. "You have put so many years into this place. Wouldn't you like to retire? To have a rest?"

Even recalling Ms. Bougainvillea's response sent a chill up Constance's back: "I'll rest soon enough, and the Happy Bell will still be in my family long after I am gone."

Constance cried out as she grasped a root for purchase after stepping out of the pulley basket, but a blue hand caught her by the wrist and shuttled her to sure footing.

"An improved time every day." Derrek smiled, letting go of her arm and tucking his pocket watch away. "But Miss Ivory is always quicker. She's gone up ahead."

"Of course," Constance said, and holding out her arms, she let Derrek fasten her a harness, so she could climb with a bit more security beside him. "Soon you'll be out of work if she gets to the airfield first."

He grinned. "I do feel rather lazy these days."

A crackling sounded and Derrek dug around in his coat for the radio Ivory had given him: "Check one-two Professor Web Leader, do you have Spaghetti-Squash-Head? Over," Ivory's voice rasped through the tinny speaker.

Constance snatched the radio from Derrek's hand, mashing the button. "Spaghetti-Squash-Head can hear you, Tangle Face, over."

"Roger that. Tangle Face over and out," Ivory snickered, and the channel switched off. Sucking on her teeth, Constance slapped the radio back into Derrek's waiting hand.

They broke the cloud cover, and for a moment, Derrek stopped climbing, holding securely to Constance's line as the wind skated past them. Constance held her hand to her eyes, her sight readjusting to the brightness. She looked to Derrek to see why he'd stopped, but he was merely staring out into the distance, to the crystal and majestic sight of the mountain range beyond Mount Quixx, stretching wide and ancient like a giant's teeth. For a blessed moment, Constance imagined soaring free over those mountains as the Happy Bell's falcons might, and the vision was so clear that her breath hitched.

"I haven't travelled far," Derrek said, and Constance hung on the words beyond the wind, "but there can't be anywhere else on Earth with the same splendour as Mount Quixx."

His gaze was far — farther than the mountain range, farther than the stars hidden by daylight. Had he even been speaking to Constance? But his mouth lifted, and he fixed the top corner eye on her and the rest followed until they were all resting on her face. She had to look away when the wind came back up, and the moment was lost to it.

"I'm sure everyone thinks the same thing," she croaked, as Derrek hauled them the rest of the way to the path to the observatory. "About their home, I mean."

He dipped his head, conceding, though they'd had similar conversations. "Do you feel the same way about Ferren City?"

Constance looked back down the mountain behind them, realizing, suddenly, she hadn't felt a sense of home, in any place, for a long time. "I suppose not."

But her shoulder twitched, like someone had tapped it, and when she turned she caught sight of something on the peak face, under the observatory. Something black.

Something terrible. *Like a scar*, the thought skittered, and she pointed.

"Do you see that?" she asked, looking from Derrek to the evil smudge on the rock, and she knew he'd seen exactly what she meant when he looked away just as quickly, his brow pale.

"Here we are," he replied instead, undoing Constance's harness in a hurry and winding the silk between his two lower forearms. Unlike every other time, he didn't help her to the path, instead going ahead without her.

Constance wrung her hands, caught between following and glancing behind her, her skin prickling with that mindless hum again, which must have just been the wind, the lonely air, beneath them both.

She dashed up the path and through the doorway when she could have sworn that she'd heard the wind asking her to stay.

If anything could be said for Constance, it was that stress made a machine of her.

She worked in a daze, her weapons of choice a duster in her back pocket and a handwritten list she whipped out after tackling each item, striking them off like victims on the battlefield. Derrek had gone, as he always had, to join Ivory on the east side of the mountain — the airfield, they called it — where the wind hit sharpest and where the fan-brain needed the most work. Each day, Constance would dive back into where she'd left off the day before in her organizing. She was upset with herself today, angry that she was incapable of asking Derrek what was bothering him, for letting him go without showing any concern.

This certainly wasn't the first time her tongue became heavy as granite, the words plummeting down the abandoned well of her throat. *Don't get too familiar*, she'd warned herself after she'd agreed to join this escapade. *Don't get too close*, emotionally or physically; after all, Derrek may have all the manners of *Lady Avalon's Absolute Etiquette*, but he still was what he was: not human. He was graceful and lovely and gentle — she would be the first to admit that, but the long spindle legs and the quartet of eyes and hands were things she could never get away with explaining to her not-so-friendly friends in society. And this whole strange waking dream had to end sometime. She didn't imagine she'd be coming back to Quixx once she sent that telegram to her parents, the one she'd been putting off, the one that would see them sent back to Ferren City and the doom that surely awaited Constance there.

But thoughts like these just fed the fire, made Constance's heels kick up like she was a cursed princess wearing shoes of hot lead, pirouetting from pile to nook to cranny, stirring dust dervishes. She toiled faster, harder, as if it was some penance for all the things she wanted to say but couldn't: *Thank you for wanting me here, Derrek. I really do like helping. I'm sorry I can't stop staring at you. I should properly ask you what's on your mind. I'm glad Ivory is enjoying herself. I'm worried about Ms. Bougainvillea. I feel like I'm being torn apart inside. I wish society wasn't so awful, so I could tell everyone about you. I wish I knew what I was doing. I wish I knew what I really wanted. I wish— I wish—*

She was humming. This time, unlike in the grocery shop, she knew it was really her because her mouth was numb with trying to hum louder, to sing above the noise in her head and in her hectic heart, her voice desperate and wanting . . . she scarcely knew what. She carried the notes like precious cargo pressed into her chest, higher and higher, not caring where they came from, or where they took her . . .

"A summer getaway," her father had repeated in her memory. "You haven't changed your mind, have you?"

Back then, Constance had felt the blood leave her face, leave her entire body. She imagined she was not flesh at all, just a doll. Fragile. Easily broken. "About what?"

He waved his hand, noncommittal, as if she were some employee he'd never known the name of, not his eighteen-year-old daughter. "College. The plan. Matching you up with one of the firm's sons or daughters. You know. Your future."

If you could call it that. All of her rigorous studying, the dance lessons, the etiquette and rule-keeping — she realized now, much too late, that she was being primed all these years for an auction block. If only she'd really thought about it before, instead of being so intent on pleasing her parents. Now she'd changed her mind. But what she'd do now, she had no idea. Diverting from the plan, was not *in the plan*.

"It . . . it's not that—"

"Use the summer to stall all you like," Father had said, "but a plan is a plan. You won't change either of our minds, Constance." He'd stood, then, stuffed his newspaper under his arm, and passed her perfunctorily as he headed for the door.

"But— it's not . . . what I want!" She had scarcely raised her voice, but it had worked to stop him.

A slow blink — a family trait. "You have some other notion, then? You don't seem the type." That stung her further into silence. Then a sigh. "Fine, then. What about a compromise?"

She'd shifted from foot to foot, a different sort of dance than the one she was doing now, remembering this exchange. "What kind of compromise?"

"Your sister," he sniffed, as if his second daughter was also less than an afterthought. "Do something about her over the summer, won't you? I'm tired of her antics and paying to keep their consequences mum. Have her shape up, and show her that there's a comfort to conformity. Then, perhaps, I'll hear you out about your plans. At any rate, your mother and I know what's best for both of you. So, when in doubt, remember that." He was already walking away, as if this weren't about the entire rest of her life, as if it were a comfort and not a calamity.

Constance had spun on him as the world did, but even in the memory, burning up like a cinder in her mind, he was out of reach and through with listening. "Father, wait!"

"Geez, Connie, any louder and you'll bring down today's work with the vibrato."

Constance startled from the window she'd been wiping, hair in her face. Derrek stood in the doorway behind Ivory, carrying as many lines of cable in his four hands as Ivory had in her two. He looked flushed, eyes wide, and she tidied her hair.

"What's, um," Constance sniffed, stuffing the rag into her back pocket as she pointed at the wires, trying to come back fully to reality, "all that?"

Derrek blinked as if he hadn't heard her, then looked down at his double armload. "Well—"

"We're re-wiring *everything*," Ivory broke in, throwing herself into a stiff wingback chair after dumping her cargo. "It just makes the most sense. And once we're through it'll not only be a self-perpetuating energy system using the wind, but we're going to make it remote-operated! No more malfunctioning cranks or burst generators. So we are starting from scratch. Won't take us that long, though, between us!" She undid her goggles, the patch of white around her eyes an inverted raccoon mask against the dirt smudges on her cheeks.

"Not without its growing pains," Derrek remarked, collecting his wiring with Ivory's into an empty crate by the stairs. "Miss Ivory isn't a stranger to combustibles."

Constance handed Ivory a fresh dust rag to wipe her face. "I'm not even going to ask what you were combusting up there."

Ivory stood and moved to clean herself up in the reflection of the steaming kettle.

"You have . . . quite a beautiful voice," Derrek said, catching Constance off guard, as usual.

"Hearing Connie sing is like seeing Hackleton's Aurora, Professor — count yourself blessed." Ivory presented herself for inspection between them, and Constance barely nodded before she did a double-take, quirking an eyebrow.

"'Professor?'"

Derrek chuckled. "I'm not sure I'm worthy of the nickname; I've been out-scholared all day."

"Besides, you think her *voice* is good?" Ivory went on, biscuit tin in one hand, greedy hand digging. "You're looking at Constance Ivyweather, blue-ribbon winner of the Ferren City Multi-Partner Fandango Championship."

"No," Constance said, prying the empty tin out of Ivory's hands and replacing it with the full one they'd brought up from the Happy Bell. "Do *not* go there."

"The Fandango!" Derrek said. "That's a difficult dance to master!"

Constance scratched her cheek. "You know it?"

"I can't dance it, of course — four left feet, you know — but I've certainly read about it!" Derrek rushed to the row of shelves. Constance fully expected him to pull out a dancing manual like the ones she'd carefully studied in all the lessons her parents had forced on her. But instead, he brandished half a dozen dog-eared paperbacks with lurid covers, his face absolutely serious.

"The Fandango is a complex hybrid of intricate steps, dependent on the sharp skills of improvisation and training . . . spelling doom or destiny for those who dance it."

Constance and Ivory blanched.

"Derrek," Ivory started, visibly failing to contain her laughter as she pointed at the books. "What do you think those are?"

Derrek's face fell, and he turned the covers over to inspect them closely. "Well these are . . . accounts of—"

"No wonder you're in such a terrible mood!" Ivory cried, snatching the books away to judge them up close. "You think romance novels are non-fiction!?" She checked the spines, which were thoroughly cracked. "You sure do read a lot of them. And *often*."

Derrek went from surprised to confused to embarrassed in four blinks, scrambling to snatch the books back and clutch them closely. "That's—"

"Why are you in a terrible mood, Derrek?" Constance wanted to drag them all out of the mire of what she was witnessing.

"I'm not!" Derrek countered, but Ivory flapped her hand.

"Distracted, then. I'm sure it's just work stress. Everyone experiences it." Ivory began shifting the chairs and the steamer trunk they used for a table. "But why don't you show us your moves, anyway, Connie, as a bit of a distraction? Please? For Derrek and his romantical obsessions?"

Constance stiffened, her tongue swelling again as Ivory made space on the pine board floor.

"*Obsession* is taking it a bit too far," Derrek demurred, looking slightly wounded as he undid his tie, which had oil spots on it. "But I wouldn't say no to a demonstration, if you're willing, Miss Constance."

Something stirred in Constance's chest when she realized Derrek was making a fine show of keeping his shoulders from drooping. She *wanted* to cheer him up — oh, Dinah — and she was still wound up from the long afternoon.

"All right," she said, with fresh determination, and taking her place in the centre of the floor, she nodded at Ivory to keep time, as she had done whenever Constance needed to practise for a competition.

Ivory pounded out the rhythm with her workboots, and Constance stepped to. The first steps had to be light and conscientious — this was so the audience could be misled into thinking it was a meek performance of swaying hips, so they'd be wowed by the frantic double- and triple-time that the dancer took up steps later. There were deep strides and turns and spins, too, complicated ones that could fell anyone with a slight vestibular sensitivity. But not Constance, not now — true, she could be clumsy, but when she danced, that faded. Each performance was a battle, but the flourish worked best with a partner.

She spun and clapped by her own ears to Ivory's beat. Her eyes flicked to Derrek, who himself had stiffened, his front-facing eyes never blinking, while the top corner ones flickered in a daze. Her arms swung and she semi-fouettéd, which would have been difficult for a dancer half Constance's size, but her weight always offered a strength to the move, and she suddenly nabbed Ivory by the hands and spun her right along, laughing despite herself, and when she released her staggering little sister, she bowed low.

"There," she panted, hands on her hips. "One thing I can manage that you can't."

Ivory had always been envious of Constance's talents, and after being bested in the brave scientific pursuits of the last week, Constance needed the sibling rivalry victory. Ivory narrowed her eyes, even though she'd dared Constance to dance in the first place.

For all of Derrek's hands, his clapping could have been the applause of the Ferren Academy Dance Hall. Constance remembered the feeling of dancing for an audience. But she also remembered why she'd stopped dancing. Why she didn't sing anymore except to herself. And when she stood up straight she was dizzy, less with vertigo and more with memories better pushed down deep. *What is the point of dancing and singing when I'm about to be fettered and silenced forever?*

"On my word, Miss Constance." Derrek was all breathless delight above her. "I bet people came from miles around to see you! Why, Brindlewatch is at your feet with such talents."

Constance could feel her smile faltering. "Well—"

"You're so well-rounded! An achieving graduate. A deep-feeling community organizer. You could be anything!" He counted off the possibilities on his twelve fingers, each suggestion a hammer on Constance's nerves: "A great chanteuse, an adroit dancer! A local politician, a charity engager, a teacher of anything your heart desires. Maybe even an entrepreneur. You have your pick of any opportunity!"

The applause in the dance hall galleria was growing louder, harsher in Constance's memories. *You're so talented. But you're not going to do anything with it, are you?*

"Don't bother, Derrek, she's had every path offered her and scholarships out the wazoo. But she's yet to pick one." Ivory folded her arms. "Anyway, it doesn't matter what college or course she takes. It'll be short-lived. Constance is out to make a match, like all other eligible ladies her age. Which she'll do easy enough."

Derrek seemed confused at that. "Oh?"

The room began to spin again, even though Constance was standing still. "I—"

"The future isn't her strong suit." Ivory shook her head, as if it was a consolation and not a bitter dig of her own. "But the sun will rise and set anyway, and she'll have to face the future sooner or later. That's why—"

"And it's all well for you!" Constance shouted, and Ivory's run-of-the-mouth teasing dried up. "You, with your, your . . . weirdness. Your quirks. You're so sure the world will encourage you in all your cockamamie adventures and mischief? You're so sure of everything, aren't you? Well! Well you don't know *anything*."

And feeling like spreading the fury evenly, Constance spun on Derrek. "And you! You've got your science projects and experiments and you think it's a straight line to success, do you? That it's *easy*? That it's a matter of reading something in a book or learning some steps and the world is your oyster? You're both so . . . childish!"

And with that bitter speech, Constance spun on her tennis shoes and threw herself out the observatory door, heading down the path dotted with horizontal trees and blinded by hot tears. She didn't hear what Derrek called after her as she went down on her rear end and shuffled into what she thought was certainly an air current she'd taken down before — she didn't need his help! She didn't need *anyone's* help!

But there was no air current. Just a drop so sudden down the face of the mountain that Constance didn't have time to scream.

She crashed through brambles and conifers, needles tearing through her blouse and snagging her hair into sappy tendrils. When she did land, the air went out of her, and she grasped her head. She was in a bare clearing where the trees dipped inward like a huge looming claw over her.

And in the trees were eyes. Too many eyes.

Constance shook her head, assuming she'd hit it harder than she thought, but she wasn't seeing double. And the eyes were red, glowing in the mist, for she'd gone back through the fog bank.

She turned her head slowly towards the crackling throat-noise of something just above her shoulder. Something with more than one mouth. Constance tried to scream for help, but only one note came out of her. An unpracticed one — not a scream, but a chord.

The red glowing eyes all blinked, and that's when Constance realized that it wasn't many monsters, but one huge one — and that it wasn't trees at all above her, but the curling tendrils of the monster's undulating body, hundreds of them. The thing slithering towards her shoulder was a much smaller version of the great beast clinging to the trees.

At least the fall down here tenderized their ensuing meal, she managed to think as the baby tangle of eyes and tentacles crawled down her shaking arm, resting there, blinking up at her.

Then a tentacle rose up and wiped away the tears that were still fresh on Constance's cheeks.

The giant monster surveying the scene above them let out a comforted purr, rose out of the trees, and floated away, trailing a tendril that the little monster grabbed hold of affectionately, floating behind its parent like an errant balloon and waving its tentacle goodbye at Constance as they disappeared into the mist.

She stared at the space the monsters had inhabited for a long time, just breathing, her mind blank. All of her usual hectic, panicked worries seemed to float away with her strange visitors, and she didn't come out of that fragile peace until she felt a pair of hands underneath her arms and another pair on her waist as she was lifted back to her feet.

"Are you all right?" Derrek held her tight, almost frantic. Constance stared up into his worried face and shook her head slowly. Then they both looked back to the space where the creatures had been, for a clicking call echoed across the cliff, and Derrek took Constance to it to look out.

Beneath them, the tangle-creatures floated and frolicked with others like them, but there were even more monsters of too many stripes to catalogue cavorting in the trees and the rocks. If they noticed Derrek or Constance there, they gave no sign of agitation. She stiffened, though, when she saw a familiar shape — a creature with a blank face, spines protruding from its arms . . . the creature Derrek had saved her and Ivory from.

He squeezed her shoulder, as he held on to her, keeping her upright. "I know you remember Arnold," he reassured her. "Harmless, really." They both winced when Arnold cuffed another monster clean off the mountain. Derrek backed them from the cliff and manoeuvred Constance away. "Err, mostly."

Constance still hadn't spoken. It seemed the mountain had woven a spell around her, and she was the charm. She didn't want to break it. But when Derrek let her go, she kept walking, staring at the ground.

Derrek slowed their pace until they stopped. "I'm sorry," he said.

They seemed to trade too many apologies in their interactions, and Constance was coming back to herself. "For what?"

"I presumed too much," he said quickly, eyes darting away. "I didn't mean to pry about your, well, future. And . . . you're right. I am a bit naive. The romance novels don't help."

Constance sighed. "No. You were just trying to be nice. I know that. Sometimes I . . ." She looked back the way they'd come, leaning against the glittering black rock they'd arrived at. "I'm jealous of you. And Ivory. Your plans. I'm embarrassed that I don't have a plan. I should know what I want. But I get scared. I'm very sorry, Derrek. It has nothing to do with you and I didn't mean what I said. I'm trying to . . . get myself under control."

Derrek folded his hands but nodded. "You didn't seem scared just then, though. With Maurice and the little one, I mean."

Constance twitched a smile. "Do you name them all?"

Derrek's replying smile was sad. "Not me. Someone else who had a way with them, like you seem to. But you weren't scared, that's for certain."

Constance shut her eyes, remembering the rare peace and her quieted mind in the presence of creatures she should by all rights be terrified of. By the creature standing before her who should inspire the same but instead seemed to make her heart expand with his open empathy. "The future is far more frightening than any monster, sometimes."

Derrek held out his hand. "It doesn't have to be," he said, and they went back up to the observatory together and said no more, since nothing more needed to be said.

8

An Old Fire Still Burns

"And what have you been up to, my dears?"

Constance had been staring out the huge solarium windows, her tea getting progressively colder, as she watched Mount Quixx sway in and out of view through swirling fog and pouring rain. She turned, slowly, to Ms. Bougainvillea, who was stuffing a whole trout into Bernard's bill, but for all this still keenly appraising of the silent sisters.

Constance and Ivory exchanged a glance — the most they'd exchanged since yesterday — and Ivory took point. "Many grand scientific explorations, Miss Bee." And she pulled out a chair that Miss Bee groaned into, rubbing her knees through her moth-eaten wool dress and shooing Frederic, who had a thermometer clutched in his beak.

"Feeling under the weather?" Constance steered the conversation artfully back, pouring the landlady a fresh cup. Frederic cheeped up at her, almost helplessly.

"In this weather, everyone is under it!" Ms. Bougainvillea cried, her arms pinwheeling so suddenly Ivory had to duck.

"Frederic is the grandest worrywart in all Brindlewatch, heavens." She tapped his crimson head, not unkindly. "I'm a braw lassie, and always will be."

Ms. Bougainvillea's brown cheeks seemed slightly sunken, her body creaking the merciful chair beneath her. But Constance didn't pry, instead retrieving a letter from under Ms. Bougainvillea's saucer. "You have a note here, Ivory," she said. It was snatched away quickly.

"Just came in with Emmett," Ms. Bougainvillea said, referring to the mottled little owl who was apprenticing with Bernard, the mail goose. Her blind eyes danced. "I believe it's from a certain schoolmistress's daughter. Can't mistake the scent of chalk dust and hyacinth of Mx. Mott's greenhouse."

Constance glanced at Ivory. She was crushing the small envelope in her pointed fingers, staring like she was trying out newly minted S-ray vision goggles — but she wouldn't open it.

"Mx. Mott seems to have a lot of plans for Quixx." Constance switched tactics, leaving Ivory to herself. "I suppose she's lived here—"

"All her life." Ms. Bougainvillea nodded, battiness letting up. "Like most Quixxians. Folks mistook Victoria for a boy when she was born, but she knew right away it was a clerical error and corrected it. Luckily she found Victor, a man who immediately saw the diamond sparkling beyond Victoria's rougher edges." She shook her head sadly. "But he's been fighting in the war for years now, has Captain Mott. A daring pilot. And Victoria has much on her mind — raising her daughter on her own and using that sharp mind to over-tutor the little ingenue who desperately needs her own life. Mx. Mott has Quixx's best at heart, but she isn't practised at showing it."

When Constance looked back at Ivory, she'd gently placed the unopened, if slightly crinkled, letter by the vase of desiccated flowers, shouldering her backpack. "No time for social frivolity," Ivory sniffed, self-consciously touching her messy hair. "A scientist's work is never done." She took one look at Constance and spun, blustering through a flock of pigeons that scattered out of her way.

Constance hurried after her, smacking her hip on the doorframe as she stumbled and grabbed the note. "Ivory! Wait!"

She met her outside the gate and Ivory stopped and turned suddenly, her violet glare piercing. "What?"

Constance stretched the letter between them. "You forgot this."

"I have work to do, as you well know." Ivory stared off towards Mount Quixx, seemingly not caring a jot for the rain that pattered on her steely face or canvas gear.

"I know you're mad at me, as usual," Constance started, "but I—"

"I'm not mad!" Ivory snapped, then looked away again. "It's just . . . everything has always been so easy for you. The parties. The social climbing. Mother and Father prefer your gentile manner to my mischief. And I get it. I'm difficult. I'm *different*." She scuffed her boot on the cobblestones. "The problem," she continued, "is that we both think we are living in each other's shadow. You can make any match you want, and I envy you for a lot of things. I'm not what Madeline Mott wants. Certainly not what *Mx. Mott* wants. I am trouble. So I best continue developing my brain. That's what I'm good for."

If anyone had asked, Constance would have blamed her stinging, tearstruck eyes on the mist and the rain. She straightened. "Ivory Eleanor Ivyweather," she said in her most commanding voice, "today you are going to take a day off from science and follow your heart."

Ivory looked suddenly cornered, eyes darting. "What do you—"

"Madeline Mott wouldn't have wasted the ink and the paper if she didn't want to see you! And she *has* seen you, if you recall. She seems like a kind, intuitive girl who knows exactly what she's getting into. Besides, you'd probably be a welcome distraction from her mother's machinations." Without warning, Constance tore into the envelope, and Ivory leapt forward, but Constance, being taller and stouter, held it out of reach as she skimmed. "You see? Mx. Mott is out today, even. It would be just the two of you! Aren't you always telling me to live a little?"

Once Constance had given it up, Ivory curled herself around the paper as she read the note at breakneck speed. She was blushing by the time she stuffed the moistened paper into her pocket. "Well I . . . it is a nice gesture and . . . but what about you?" She seemed to be looking at Constance with new eyes. Suspicious eyes. "And what about Derrek?"

Constance huffed, holding her arms above her nearly soaked hair. "Derrek could probably use a break, too, from his overly enthusiastic intern," she mused. "I'll go visit him and let him know. You have a nice time with Madeline and maybe use some of the manners I so desperately tried to teach you."

Ivory yanked up her rainsuit's hood, unable to help her crooked grin. "Thanks, Connie." She took off, presumably in the direction of the Motts' house, sloshing through every puddle she passed.

Constance shook her head and went back inside to get a raincoat herself — but she stopped dead in her tracks as a familiar hum wove through the Happy Bell.

The song was quite clear — rising and falling like a comforting lullaby. The birds, all at their own perches on shelves, banisters, side tables, and mottled wicker chairs, dozed peacefully. It was a melody Constance herself had sung, only yesterday, without thinking, wordless and clear in the observatory. It was an enchantment, a spell. And as she tiptoed her way to the solarium, she peeked round the doorway to find Ms. Bougainvillea sitting by the window, face turned towards the mountain, the song coming from her.

Her huge spectacles shimmered despite the rainy afternoon and Quixx's usual dark. "*And I will come home to dark lonely peaks, to the place that I know is mine,*" she sang. "*And when I return, my darling, my dear, all our fears will sparkle and shine.*"

In her lap was Frederic, who she stroked with two gnarled fingers, gentle and kind, until he, too, rested.

Constance moved away back to the foyer, heart shivering, as she glanced up at the portrait of the faceless astronomer then went out to the mountain that haunted them all.

The Motts' house was unlike any that Ivory had seen in Quixx. And this, too, was a part of Quixx Ivory hadn't yet been to — the east side of the valley, a crest of houses with a view to the border of the town, and much farther from the mountain than the Happy Bell.

Still the fog slithered about fences and overgrown shrubbery, and on the way there Ivory had passed the school everyone had been talking about — Cardinal Quixx Hall. Mx. Mott's kingdom of faded brick and, because it was summer, abandoned classrooms. It looked like it could have been haunted, and Ivory walked quickly past it — not that she was scared! Of course not! But a canny scientist never ignores the feeling in their gut, and she was glad when it was behind her. She checked the address again on Madeline's note and entered the cul-de-sac that was her destination.

The house was not grand, of course, like the houses on Ivory's block in Carrigan Park, massive estates that bore names like Skye House or Grenfell Gardens and seemed more like museums than homes. The Motts' house was a modest two-storey, but the paint was fresh and bright red, the trim white, the roof in good shape. Because of the damp weather and lack of sun, they'd taken out any gardens and meticulously arranged rocks and cedar chips in the beds, which still looked tidy and smart. Given Mx. Mott's icy disposition, knowing she wasn't at home put Ivory at ease more than the crisp paint.

The stairs going up to it were hewn into the small hill the house was built on. She took each one preciously, a sudden anxiety springing up that reminded her Constance. *What if it's a prank, like with the girls back home? What if you've been invited here as a joke, and the door will open to laughter and they send you away?* She didn't want to imagine Madeline was cruel like that, but sadly Ivory had taught herself to be ready for anything. This sterile approach galvanized her for the world Constance was always trying to protect her from — but as she raised her hand to knock, she still very much considered running in the other direction, back to the mountain that felt more like home than anywhere in the world. To Ivory, that was the logical option.

The door opened before she got the chance, and Madeline's serene smile pinned Ivory in place. "I saw you coming up the steps!" she said, taking Ivory's hand, which had dropped to her side. "We can visit better inside than on the stoop, though."

Ivory cleared her throat as she went in willingly, Madeline shutting the door behind them. *What does Connie always say when she gets invited places?*

"Thank you such a beautiful home for having me," she said robotically, then choked when she played the words back in her head. "I mean—"

When Madeline laughed, Ivory felt right away it was not directed *at* her. It was meant to be comforting.

"Don't worry. I got the gist." She looked Ivory up and down, blinking at her feet. "You're soaked through! Maybe let's start by putting that sherpa pack down and hanging up your coat."

Ivory jerked in surprise, having already forgotten herself. "Right. Yes. I'm— I'm sorry." She dropped the pack and took off her jacket, and unsure what else to do, opened the door and flung the offending garment out.

"Gads! You didn't—" But Madeline cut herself off when she tried to lift Ivory's bag and nearly fell over with the effort. "What do you have in here? A body?"

Ivory scrambled forward and grabbed the bag. "Err. Not exactly." She undid the buckles and flipped the top over, sliding out the terrarium and its sleepy inhabitant. "Arabella likes to travel in comfort."

"Hello again!" Madeline leaned in, pressing a delicate finger to the glass. Arabella stirred and tapped her forelegs against it. "You're such a clever girl, aren't you?"

Though Madeline must, surely, be speaking to the spider, Ivory blushed all the same. "I was on my way out with Arabella when I got your note. I hope she isn't a bother. I know your mother . . ."

"Mother is at the school and will be occupied there for some time, so no need to worry." She clasped Ivory's hand again and led her farther into the house. "But there's something I wanted to show you! Both of you."

She led them past the staircase, the wall bordering it covered in family photos, past a sideboard with more than that — trophies in both Madeline's and her mother's names, and perhaps her father's . . . blue ribbons for a Victor Denza dotted the shelves for dance and ballet.

Ivory smiled, unable to help herself from pointing. "That's

such a neat coincidence," she said, running her finger along a label underneath one photo. "Victor. Victoria. They really were destined for one another."

Madeline grinned. "They were. But they chose their own names, later in life. That they're similar was by chance . . . probably destiny though, you're right."

Ivory, uncomprehending, squinted at the photo in question; Madeline's parents, smiling at one another, almost mid-laugh, holding armfuls of flowers and greenery, and wearing formal gown and suit.

"Is this their wedding photo?" Ivory tilted her head, and Madeline sighed dreamily.

"Sort of. This is long before that, when they were still in high school. My parents were made for each other." She shook her head. "When my mother was born, they thought she was a boy, and they thought my father was a girl. They chose to become the people they were truly meant to be, and so they picked new names to represent that. This was their New Naming ceremony, except they wanted to surprise one another with their selections . . . it was the perfect reveal. They really think alike."

Ivory nodded, taking this in stride. So both of Madeline's parents were transgender! This put Ivory in mind of Derrek's explanation of his identity, but she stopped herself smartly before spilling the beans about her secret mentor. Instead, she said, "That's wonderful. You must take after your father, then, with the ballet and all."

"I can throw a mean shotput, too." She winked, flexing, and continued leading them through the kitchen, snagging a fresh scone, which she tossed to Ivory, who caught it in the hand that wasn't holding Arabella's terrarium.

"And your father . . . he's fighting in the war, right?" Ivory had always been abrim with curiosities about that far-flung conflict across the Sorrento Sea, which seemed worlds away from Ferren City and the privilege the people there enjoyed.

"He's a pilot. The most daring of them all." Madeline always gave off a bright aura of joy, but it was solid pride she radiated now. "Two years. We get wires, though not often. We aren't sure where he is, most of the time, but I am sure he is being very brave, wherever he's ended up." Her eyes shone when she turned, but she still smiled and took Ivory's hand once she'd popped the scone in her mouth. "Through here."

She opened a white door with a crystal knob, and Ivory nearly swallowed the scone whole for what she saw.

This, certainly, explained the smell Ms. Bougainvillea had so keenly picked up on Madeline's letter. They stepped through a wall of moist heat, and Madeline shut the door quickly behind them lest it escape. The greenhouse within was a sprawling beauty, specimens that had no right to be thriving in such poor conditions as Quixx's, yet here and there bright lights shone at precise angles, and vines and shrubs and orchids that would have been more at home in the Grand Swamp of Destine nestled comfortably under Madeline's benevolent grin.

"Alphanumeric," Ivory breathed, placing Arabella carefully down on a ledge, so she, too, could take in the view.

Madeline picked up two spray bottles, passing one to Ivory. "Would you mind? They do need an awful lot of misting."

"Do you collect the mist from outside? That could be Quixx's chief export." Now Ivory was getting giddy, but she didn't mind allowing it to spill over in Madeline's presence.

"That would make sense, you're right." Madeline sprayed a violet affectionately. "I spend a lot of time in here. These were Daddy's, his favourite place on earth. By now he's probably seen the world, though, and this greenhouse will seem small to him." Madeline's tone went a little meek, and it didn't go unnoticed.

"That's not true!" Ivory cried, and when Madeline blinked wide-eyed at her, she backtracked. "I mean . . . I don't pretend to know your father, but no matter how far he's travelled, there isn't any place like home. Or any place that has you. Or . . . your mother." The sentiment was honest, but thinking about two parents truly loving one another was a foreign concept in Ivory's mind, starved as she was for scenes of her parents' affections. Constance didn't seem to have much evidence that they loved each other either, let alone their daughters. Ivory wondered if it had been different in Knockum.

Madeline shrugged. "You're right. I just miss him." She traded the spray bottle for a tiny emerald watering can, the stream going into the bright red cup of a bromeliad. "How far have you travelled, Ivory?"

Ivory had been carefully spritzing, but her eyes darted from Madeline down to her shoes. "I travel only as far as the books that I can manage to sneak out of the Ferren City Library and past my governess's nose," she admitted. "I'd like to go to all the places I read about. But there's a very distinct *path* I'm being forced to walk. This is the farthest away I've ever been."

She expected Madeline, for all she was raised by a school-mistress, to look on her with pity, but instead, she sighed. "I know the feeling." She put the watering can down, lifting herself deftly onto a ledge and dangling her ballet slipper-shod feet. "Quixx is a nice enough town to grow up in. But I've grown out of it. I'd like to see the world . . . but my mother—"

"She's afraid of the world, I take it," Ivory finished for her, joining Madeline on the ledge.

Madeline nodded. "She thinks she can have it all here. And that the outside world gobbled up Daddy, and it'll do the same to me."

"Our parents can't wait to ship us off," Ivory countered. "We could switch places."

Madeline grinned, a mischievousness there that took Ivory by surprise. "Or we could run away together."

Ivory grinned back, heart pattering. "Run away to the finest university in Oiros. Or journey to Witching Cross Road, and the lost city of Connaught?"

"Let's say we go there someday. Together," Madeline said and clasped Ivory's hands so quickly she could only swallow in response. "Saying it can make it real. Like a druid's spell."

Ivory nodded, for this, too, was the soundest logic she'd yet heard. "We'll go. Of course we will! Society and proper hairstyles be damned!" She pumped their hands up and Madeline whooped, laughing to shake the greenery around them. She unclasped their hands and touched Ivory's hair.

"It's not so bad," she remarked to Ivory's self-conscious wince. "But I do all the girls' hair in my ballet class. I could try doing yours?"

Ivory knew in that instant she could trust Madeline Mott with practically anything. But her eye caught something shining and sharp by the beautifully trimmed bonsai at her hip, and scooping up the scissors, placed them smartly in Madeline's hand instead.

"I wouldn't want to cause any further hairbrush fatalities," Ivory said, nose in the air. "And I think I am due for an ecstatic transformation."

The song had not left Constance the whole walk to the canyon. She passed the line of cars, wind whistling through their hollow shells, the rain still pattering a quick drumbeat in time with her pulse. The strange things she'd heard, like that song, and the laughter in the Butterfly Room, belonging to shadows. Not to mention the things she'd seen, like the vision of a woman leading her around the town, the one who always vanished when Constance got too close. It all had to be due to stress, of course. Same with the dreams. The dreams that the mountain was speaking to her, the dreams that influenced her waking choices. *You must help him*, whispered a voice before she'd woken today. *You must stay. Only you can set him free.*

Stuff and nonsense, her logical mind countered, no matter that what she was doing now was strange, too. *Ivory is helping Derrek just fine; I'm barely doing anything for him. And he's saved me more times than is proper. What a lark.* She pushed her hood down as she rounded the corner to the current that would take her up the cliffside, but froze in her tracks.

A small floating tangle of tentacles and red eyes clucked at her, reaching.

"It's just you," she said, catching a hand to her breast. The creature went on clucking, an anxious tone that Constance herself recognized from personal use. "Are you all right? Where's your—"

A shadow fell over them both as the much, much larger tangle that Derrek had improbably called Maurice floated above them. "Erm," Constance said, still uncertain. "Hello."

The little one floated closer, a tentacle catching around her hand and guiding her forward.

"Ah!" Constance stepped to. "What's the matter?"

Maurice's eyes, while red, had yellow raindrop centres and were so glassy and numerous Constance could see many worried copies of herself in them. The eyes turned upward, to the mountain, pointing, then eight tentacles unfurled, miming a spider.

Constance's heart sped up. "Has something happened to Derrek?"

Maurice reached out then, grasping Constance tightly, and they floated up much faster, and more directly, than any current could have propelled them.

She felt the little one wrap itself around her arm, burying its warm, snakeskin body into her neck — a gesture that worried Constance even more. It was asking for comfort. It was afraid.

You are both afraid. The words were clear in her mind, though she was sure she hadn't thought them. They sped higher and higher, elegantly dodging trees and rocks, and Constance wasn't afraid. In fact she was calm, for once, and felt presciently that she needed to be for what was ahead. She knew they'd reach the observatory soon, but they took a turn, and went around. When they broke the fog bank, she saw what she'd seen yesterday — a charred scar gashed across the mountain face . . . but there was more to it, she discovered now. A chunk had been taken out of the rock. It put her in mind of the fire Derrek had mentioned, of the charred walls within the place he called home. From this vantage, Constance gasped at the full measure of the damage. It was a wonder that the observatory still stood. All she could feel, without reason, was a deep and heavy pain. She felt it through Maurice's tentacles, and she felt it now as they went down to an outcrop she didn't recognize, at the heart of where the blaze had raged.

And there was Derrek.

"Der—" Maurice's tentacles squeezed, pressing her close and stopping a fair distance from him. When she looked closer, she understood why.

Constance went numb. "What . . ." She swallowed. "What's happened to him?"

She didn't expect an answer, of course, so she tried to trust her eyes. For Derrek had changed, noticeably. He was not wearing his usual trim, fashionable suit. He was in a ripped undershirt; the teal hair that was always neatly kept now fell wild about his elongated neck and shoulders. His back was hunched, and he clutched himself tightly with all four arms, shaking violently. Something seemed to be moving beneath his skin, pushing outward, like spikes at his many, knotty joints.

"Derrek?" Constance peeped. She regretted it when he froze and turned, and she saw his eyes.

They were black.

Maurice chittered at Constance's back, and it sounded like a reassurance, though Constance didn't pretend she could parse tangle-speak. Derrek's eyes darted between them, his mouth a foul grimace. The corners of it were drawing back far across his sharp, cerulean cheekbones, revealing pincers at the corners.

"Derrek, it's me," Constance tried, though the breath was going out of her. "Maurice brought me to . . . to help you." For that much now had become obvious. "Will you let me do that? Please."

The mouth corners twitched. The four eyes did not blink, but shone inky and terrible in the sudden pattering rain, boring directly into her. His spider legs were raw with tension as they shifted him backward, like he was winding up to strike. She knew that breaking eye contact with a dangerous beast was ill-advised — but how could Derrek be dangerous? — and she was growing more frightened by the minute. *You must help him*, she remembered clearly. *You are* both *afraid.*

The shaking shoulders, the laboured breathing. Finally, Constance recognized this for what it was, a thing all too familiar to her: a panic attack.

"Derrek," she repeated, voice much clearer now as she mastered it. "I need you to breathe. I know you can hear me. Follow my count! Inhale. One one thousand, two one thousand, three one thousand. Exhale. One one thousand, two . . ."

She held on tight to Maurice, more for moral support than anything, as they dangled in the air just out of Derrek's reach. But as she directed him, his body began to even out. Their eyes did not break from one another's. In fact, as he breathed to her count, his eyes began to clear, to resolve into their yellow-amber hue. His shoulders eventually dropped, his skin growing still, his face clearing to its usual calm expression. The tension went out of his eight legs. Constance stopped counting, and Derrek blinked at her, looking at his hands in dismayed shock.

They began to shake again. "How did I—"

Constance twisted, nodding at Maurice, who floated towards Derrek calmly, with Constance in tow. The little one broke away from her neck, trilling excitedly around Derrek's face. He laughed weakly.

"I'm fine, Hilda," he croaked, wringing his hands. "It was just a bad one this time."

Maurice put Constance down next to Derrek on the sturdy ground, then floated off, nabbing little Hilda as they gave the two some space.

"Now it's my turn to ask if you're all right," Constance said, thumb at his chin. "What happened to you?"

Derrek seemed to be looking past her, staring at the blackened rocks. He was still shivering, still vulnerable, and Constance didn't want to take the chance he'd go back to what she'd seen him become, with nowhere for her to go but off the mountainside. So she took two of his hands in hers, which seemed to jerk him out of it.

"Let's go back together and get you tidied up, shall we?" she said, as less a suggestion and more a command. She led Derrek back to the observatory, countering his nervous silence with running commentary.

"I came to tell you that Ivory won't be coming in to help you on the machine today." *Serendipity at its finest,* Constance thought, though chilling given she'd almost predicted this with her odd dreams. "She was invited for tea at the Motts'. I figured she could use a break, and that you could, too." She'd led Derrek up to the attic, which was where he slept and kept his clothes, depositing him by the great web that was his bed as she sorted through his workbench's drawers. "Ah, here's the hairbrush." She went through the motions stiffly, trying to shake off her own state of upset.

Derrek rubbed each opposite forearm, a double-cross of waning shock over his chest. "Really, I can manage, Miss Constance."

"Ivory says that, too," Constance said, holding out the hairbrush to him. "She's rarely telling the truth."

He stared at it like it was a foreign object. She let her shoulders drop, trying to relax herself. "Would you . . . like me to?"

Derrek's mouth was hard while he deliberated. He nodded. Constance went around behind him, up onto the springy web that was, as usual, surprisingly comfortable. She hesitated at first, then pulled the brush gently through Derrek's long, seaglass-coloured hair, and felt him sigh throughout his entire thorax.

"I get the same thing, sometimes," she said quietly. "Panic attacks, the doctor calls them." His hair was silky and smooth in her hands as she glided the brush down. "They're not uncommon. It feels like the world is crashing around you when they happen."

Derrek turned his head. His eyes, which had all been shut as she brushed, opened slowly as if coming awake. "They come up out of nowhere, sometimes. They . . . change me."

Constance didn't dig further, just said, "I know the feeling."

But he grimaced. "I'm trying to get it under control."

That this conversation echoed their last one was not lost on either of them. "Fear is a monstrous thing," she answered. "It can control us. But there are ways to manage it."

She put the brush down, letting Derrek's hair cascade as she ran a finger through it one last time. "Can you tell me what upset you? You . . . don't have to."

A bead of silence. Derrek pulled away slowly, moving to a screen. Once he was behind, he began to remove his torn shirt to slip into a new one. Constance looked away quickly.

"There's a picture. On top of the trunk."

Constance scanned the room. Sure enough, nearby was an enormous steamer trunk, and inside were ties, suits older than her grandfather, and a round gold frame balanced on top. It was small in her hands when she picked it up, and even smaller in Derrek's when he came around and cupped a hand to it, but did not take it.

"This woman," Constance said, appraising the portrait. "I've seen her before." For once again it was the spectre she'd seen about Quixx, always leading her towards what she needed. In this photo she was bathed in sunlight, thin-rimmed glasses gleaming with her teeth.

Derrek nodded. "That's Camille. She was Klaus's wife." He pulled his hand away, and it brushed Constance's in the passing. Hair fell into his downcast eyes. "She had a way with the creatures here, with the mountain. You remind me of her."

"Really?" Constance could feel her colour piquing. "How so?"

Derrek buttoned up and smoothed his collar, considering his row of ties at the open trunk, but leaning against its brass-buttoned edge instead. "When I came in yesterday and you were singing . . ." Finally, his old smile returned. "Camille was very headstrong and passionate. Didn't care what other people thought of her. She knew the mountain best of all. Better than Klaus, even. She had grown up with it whispering to her, she said. It taught her how to sing."

Constance came closer as Derrek smoothed his hair back out of his face, and after putting the picture back she touched his arm, offering a hair clip she'd had in her pocket. He bent down and allowed her to braid it.

"Have you ever heard the mountain whisper?" she asked, hoping somewhere here she'd find an answer.

"Not me, I'm afraid," Derrek replied. "Too busy looking up to stay grounded." He stared at the picture again, and his voice broke. "I let her down. I let both of them down."

When Derrek buried his face in his hands, Constance's wavered above him, unsure, before finally coming back down and squeezing her arms around his shoulders. "It's all right," she said, though not certain it was. "Crying helps."

Derrek took a shaking breath — a broken laugh. "Not really. No tear ducts, remember?" But he still sobbed all the same. "You saw the black mark on the mountain. The damage to this place. I should've done more. But I was so scared, Constance. I— I had never seen fire. Not like that. It was *everywhere*. It seemed alive. And Klaus — it had happened at night. I don't know how. It wasn't the generator. A lamp, perhaps? It caught so quickly. Everything was so damaged in the aftermath it was difficult to tell."

Constance didn't move, knowing he could not see her nod, but she held fast to his shoulders as his gaze went deeper inward until his eyes closed: "The entire mountain roared. We all heard it. It felt like the world was splitting in two. Many hid — including me. It took me too long to remember Klaus, in the observatory, that he had a habit of staying up well past sundown to work. He had been spending weeks studying a heavenly phenomenon and had become wrapped up in it. Then the mountain shook.

"I raced to get to him. I could smell the smoke before I saw it. The observatory was a torch in the black. I was paralyzed. The other creatures of the mountain came to help before I could — they were loyal to Camille. Easier and less wild under her influence. They trusted Klaus, and me, because of the bond I had with both of them. The other creatures threw earth on the blaze, they worked together. Many were burned for their efforts. Maurice helped me inside to find Klaus, but the heat, the smoke . . ."

Constance shifted around Derrek. He had lowered himself, tucking his legs in close to his body, and so Constance perched beside him, sliding her own legs underneath her as she listened. His face was twisted in anguish, but he did not look at her.

"He was not burned, thankfully. But he was dying from the smoke. I begged him to hold on, promised I would find Camille, who would make it right. But it was too late. He said to me, 'Help Quixx. The stars, Derrek. The stars.' Then he said no more, and closed his eyes like he was only sleeping." His mouth made a weak frown. "He truly was devoted to his work. Even to the last. And that is why I must carry out his dying wish. To put Quixx on the map with this observatory, and to do that I must remove this fog so they can see the stars once more. I have to do everything he wasn't able to."

Constance considered Camille's smiling picture again, her mind aswirl with questions. "And Camille?"

Derrek exhaled a breath so large it could have powered his wind machine. "We grieved together. She still came to see me, to support me, for many years. She didn't blame me, but I still do. I can do so very much, but when it mattered, I could do nothing." He clenched and released his many hands. "She and Klaus were the closest thing I had to parents, although that could never be."

Now he glanced up at her, as if he were marvelling that she was there at all. "I suppose I should be grateful for the time we had together. But the fire took its toll on this mountain, and this mountain is all I've known. So it's difficult to simply . . . forget, when the past is cut into the very rock around me. I'm sorry if I frightened you. It seems to be getting harder, lately . . . but I suddenly feel like I have much more to lose."

Constance's face warmed, but she was only touched by his words, and not embarrassed. It had frightened her earlier, finding Derrek in such a state, but she realized that her feelings were similar to his: she was more afraid *for* Derrek than ever she would be *of* him.

"They must be very proud of you, wherever they are," Constance said finally. "Even though I didn't know him, I'm sure Klaus would never wish to see you so miserable about something you cannot change, or to put so much pressure on yourself as you are with all these *missions*. And don't apologize for what happened today! You can't change that, either. I understand it more than you know." She clasped his hand and held it firmly. "The reason Ivory and I are here. It wasn't for a vacation. It was a test."

Derrek held tight to her, his four eyes searching hers as he listened. "My parents were never going to join us. I should have realized it much sooner. I was just sent off to get used to my prospects, the ones they'd planned for all my life. And to straighten Ivory out to fit their expectations. I admit that I thought that part would be easy." They both smiled. "It's hard to admit that I don't even know myself. What I want. I suppose I wanted my parents' help. Or for them to listen to my concerns. But I'm learning far more about myself from you. Odd as it may seem."

Derrek looked dismayed and like he wanted to interrupt, but she went on: "People say the past can haunt you, but I disagree. The mistakes we make. The missteps and the fears. They can teach you so much. You are moving forward, Derrek. You've done many wonderful things, and not for your own benefit. You even managed to change *my* mind about quite a few things . . . and I am very stubborn, which is why I'm so anxious all the time. I'm as flexible as Cordova County steel."

The talking seemed to have calmed him, and he leaned his cheek on a folded fist. "But you strike me as someone who always has it together!" She snorted at that, and he smiled. "Aside from, well, the falling off things. And the tendency to exaggerate circumstances."

"Exactly," she agreed. "I've become very good at keeping up a face of togetherness and hiding behind manners. But here, on this mountain" — Constance turned towards the place in the attic where the wind crept in, and outside there was only crisp, clear sky — "I am undone. In a good way. Maybe my parents weren't so thick in sending me here after all. It hasn't been a cure-all for my worries, but it's shown me I can do things I otherwise never would have thought possible."

When she tipped her face back towards Derrek's, he was still smiling at her, and he tucked her hair familiarly behind her ear. She found she didn't mind.

"Miss—"

"No more formalities," she said. "Friends don't use them. 'Constance' is just fine."

And if anything, that seemed to gladden him most.

"You have taught me quite a lot about what it means to be brave," he answered. "Now, why don't we have some tea, as friends, and try to be brave together?"

9

WEAVE A CIRCLE
ROUND THEM THRICE

"**M**other?"

Victoria blinked and turned towards Madeline. "Yes, love?"

Madeline was dressed in her ballet slippers, tights, body-suit, and gauzy skirt. She held an emerald watering can close. "I did my exercises, and I went to the greenhouse but you weren't there. I took care of the orchids. You don't usually forget both those things, so I wanted to check on you."

Victoria stiffened, her jaw clamping. No, she did *not* usually forget these things. Or anything. But there were many other things crowding her disciplined mind, and being caught out in her slip was frustrating. "I was . . . ahem." She tightened her black kimono, the one with the huge flowers cascading down the back, which Victor had given her as a wedding gift. "And your advanced calculus? Have you done the chapters I marked?"

Madeline put down the watering can, frowning. Victoria watched her pull out a chair, climb onto it, and press a hand to her mother's forehead.

"Are you sure you're feeling all right?" Madeline asked again. "Today is Saturday. Maths are on Thursdays. Maybe we should go for a walk and get you some air."

If Victoria were prone to fits of emotion, she may have sniffled. Instead she kissed her daughter on the cheek. "You do remind me of your father," was all she said as she swept away to the stairs to get ready for the day.

"You're thinking about him, aren't you?"

Victoria stopped, her shoulders square. No, she would not cry. She had not, since Victor had gone.

"It's all right if you are," Madeline tried. "I think about him, too. And if he's in our thoughts then he is safe. I know it."

Victoria cupped her wrist with her thumb and forefinger, pressing into the pulse to force it to go still. "You're still too young to understand these things," she countered coolly. "Your father would not wish us to worry. Besides, you and I have work enough cut out for us here."

Madeline sighed, hopping gracefully down from the chair. "Mother, you can't still be thinking about the university—"

At this Victoria whirled, her hair and kimono swirling like the storm that welled inside her. "And why not? It is your education, and that of your peers, I am thinking of, Madeline. You have far outstripped Cardinal Quixx Hall and what the curriculum offers you there. I can hardly have you studying at the college level by correspondence."

"I don't have any peers, Mother. Barely any. Quixx is shrinking. Soon even Cardinal Quixx Hall will be empty. And besides I . . . I could study abroad." Madeline watched her mother's face darken. "Ivory and I—"

196

Her worst mistake. Victoria's hands were now tightly folded in front of her, bone-cracking hard. "Ivory Ivyweather?" One step. "And what ideas has she put into your head?"

Another step. Madeline backed up. "Nothing! Nothing that wasn't already in my head in the first place!" Victoria hadn't been expecting resistance, and she stopped at the sideboard. Her hand rested gently on it, but she was using it to support herself.

On it were pictures and medals and memories made. Before her, Madeline stood tall, though she wasn't done growing yet. Victoria was certain Madeline would do great things, but that she'd do them without her mother was a cruel reality she was not ready to face.

"Please, Mother," Madeline protested. "It would be good for you, too, if you dreamed beyond Quixx a little. Our world here is small. There's a much bigger one out there in Brindlewatch. For both of us. You're allowed to have dreams, too, even though you think they're on hold because of Daddy. He wouldn't want that."

Victoria forced a smile and took her hand away from the sideboard. "You're right." Madeline clearly hadn't been expecting that. "Dreams are quite important for moving forward into the future. I know that." The smile deepened. "I'll get changed, and we'll go on that walk, shall we?"

Madeline's smile was much slower, but Victoria knew it would be enough for now. "Okay," she said. "I'll get my coat."

When Madeline had left, Victoria's smile fell. *Everything was fine before those Ivyweathers showed up*, she sneered inside, turning brusquely for the stairs and taking them two at a time. *If they think they're going to take my little girl from me, they are sorely mistaken.*

But when Victoria reached her room, she stopped in front of the oval portrait Victor had had made, before he went off to be far braver than Victoria would have been. She reached out and stroked his cheek and felt his absence as heavily now as ever before.

"You would say I was too much in my own head, about all of this," Victoria whispered over it. "But where else am I to go?"

Victoria glanced out her window, towards the shape of the mountain up the hill road. She knew it wasn't *just* the Ivyweathers. It was the rest of Brindlewatch, invading Quixx, threatening everything she had built. They'd already lost so much — the Motts, and Quixx itself. Victoria knew she only had so much strength left to grandstand before she truly crumbled.

"Mother?" Madeline called from the bottom of the hall stairs. Victoria kissed her fingers and pressed them to the picture. Madeline needed her mother to have a clear head.

And there was no room in it for dreams.

"It's *fine*," Constance said through her teeth, and this time maybe a little forcefully. "I'm going to take this salt fish to Maurice and Hilda, you do your work, and I'll get over it in the fresh air."

Ivory stabbed her fists into her hips. "It's only hair, Connie."

But Constance's hands were flat in front of her in protest. "I don't want to talk about it anymore. It's not like Mother and Father weren't going to murder me anyway for wrecking their car. Or sneaking you around on a dangerous mountain. That you cut off all your hair is just icing on the cake." Her hands landed heavily on Ivory's shoulders, and she finally softened her eyes in defeat. "But you're right. It's your hair, not mine. And against my better judgment . . . I'd say it suits you."

Ivory's grin was huge. "So you'll be okay if I get a tattoo, right?"

Constance whirled out the door. "Good*bye*, Ivory." And she marched down the path. Ivory wasn't sure, but she thought Constance was humming.

So Ivory turned and climbed the great stairs, vaulting through the door in the floor into the attic, where Derrek was soldering wires together, the sparks bouncing off his mask. He flipped it up when she came round to inspect his handiwork.

"There," he said, holding the contraption up — a giant light behind movable metal flaps, which, with the flick of a lever, covered then exposed it. A signal lamp. "I'll install this later this evening and have it wired. And you take this one" — he passed the light's twin and its hardware to Ivory, who *oofed* with the weight of it — "and put it on the Happy Bell's dormer that faces northeast. Then, there you have it. I assume you're up to snuff on your Detalia Dots and Dashes."

Ivory saluted smartly and nearly dropped the light — Derrek swooped in and caught it with his lower hands. "Aye aye, Professor," she said as he placed it carefully back on the workbench with its mate.

Derrek laughed. "You're the one on the track for tenure here, especially after the past month and a half."

It was strange to think it had been that long already. Time moved more swiftly than the Volunteer Star Brigade launcher, and Ivory had seized every moment. Their work on Derrek's machine had changed it completely, but now it was nearly finished, and so too was the summer. The precious summer that kept them all safe from the future Constance that was always so afraid of.

Ivory picked up the remote with the improbably round red button — the one they'd taken apart so many times that it had to be glue-taped together, its antenna bent. At least now it was working as of the last time they'd tested it. There were still a few tweaks to make, true, but it was very close now. She smoothed a thumb over the star sticker that Constance had put on it when they'd celebrated the first successful test run.

"I'm worried about Constance," Ivory said suddenly. Derrek started.

"Why?"

Ivory carefully put down the remote and looked up into his four arresting eyes. She always said too much. "Never mind."

When she turned away, it only took a nimble manoeuvre of Derrek's eight legs to pop into her path, all arms folded and brow wrinkled. "It's not like you to bring something up and not elucida—"

"It's just that she still doesn't know what she wants, Derrek!" Ivory threw her arms up so violently that he jumped back. "Here we are, doing the work that drives us, but what about her? The summer's almost over, and she's going to walk back into the trap of society's expectations and be *eaten alive*." She snapped her arms closed then, like a jaw.

Derrek pulled on his tie. "I . . . see."

"Perhaps some might consider it a curse, but I've always known what I wanted." Now Ivory was pacing, hands tight behind her back. "Adventure! Discovery! Romance! These are the fundamentals of a well-led life. But Constance is lost. And I can't do a damn thing to help her."

"Language," Derrek said, though his mouth was crinkled in amusement. "What do you mean by lost? I know you hate to hear it, but you're still quite young. The person you are in ten years could be miles away from the person you are now. Constance is a grown woman."

"And you're likely a hundred years old and you probably haven't changed in all that time," Ivory countered.

Derrek scratched his cheek, glancing askance at the pile of romance novels on top of his steamer trunk that had only grown in the passing weeks. "You'd be surprised."

"Anyway." Ivory went to the observatory deck, marvelling at the glittering silk star map Derrek had made and remade over the years of his and Klaus's work. "Constance believes her only viable fate is to go off to college, meet her husband, get married, and have scads of babies. It's different for monsters. To me, that's a death wish."

Derrek joined her. "Is that so?" She blinked up at him, noting his disappointed tone. "Is all that such a bad thing?"

"I don't speak for everyone," Ivory backtracked. "It just isn't for me, so I can't fathom it. Especially the marriage and babies part. Too confining." She forced herself not to look back at the star map and wish on all the white pin dots. "Though I'd consider it . . . with a particular schoolmistress's daughter, maybe. Are you shocked?"

Derrek only smiled. "Thoroughly. So why are you so against marriage, then? I'm confused."

"Maybe marriage isn't the enemy. Just society's expectations. Anyway, love is different than marriage, you know. Surely you've gleaned that from that schlock you like to read." She elbowed him genially in the ribs. "But I don't think Constance understands the meaning of the word *love*. She's empty-headed when it comes to these kinds of things. What if she gets married to some bore just because of what they're like on paper, and it turns out her life is over? She has so much potential! What if she wastes it all just to please everyone else?"

Derrek was quiet for a while. Constance had told Ivory everything that Derrek had told her — about the cataclysmic fire, about the astronomer. About the solution to the mystery of Klaus Bedouin's fate, which was much sadder than the intrigue Ivory had been led to believe by the other Quixxians they'd met over the summer. And while she worried about her sister, this conversation was still sort of a test . . . because she'd clearly seen the change in Constance since meeting Derrek, and had seen the same in him.

"You must love your sister very much, to worry so," Derrek said finally.

Ivory shrugged. "It's what sisters do, I guess. Even when we both get on each other's nerves."

Derrek exhaled and paced back to the other side of the attic. Ivory followed. "I don't know much about your world other than what I've read. And not even all the theory in Brindlewatch could match practice." He leaned against the workbench, considering. "It sounds like you're concerned Constance doesn't know her own mind. I feel like a lot of the issues humans come up against — in novels, for example, however schlocky — could be solved just by having a frank, elementary discussion about it."

"You know Constance," Ivory retorted, feeling charitable and not making another dig about Derrek's choice of reading. "She doesn't do frank *anything*."

His smile betrayed him as he played with a curl of metal on the workbench. "That's what I like about her."

"Oh?"

Derrek snapped to, raising his hands flat in the air much the same way Constance just had on her earlier departure. "Err, I mean—" He backed up a step, clearing his throat. "I meant that Constance may *seem* like she doesn't know what she wants. But perhaps she does. Perhaps she just doesn't know how to express it quite yet. And I know that frustrates you, but just think of it scientifically: it's difficult to undo a lifetime of lived behaviour, or fears, in one summer. Yet your sister is here, on this mountain of all places, despite those fears. I think she wants to explore her options for the future . . . but no one should rush or badger her. Give her time." He patted Ivory's smooth, tangle-less head. "Whatever she chooses, you are her sister, and you must respect her decision. The only person you have control over is yourself."

"Hmph." Ivory fought to keep her grin down as she marched aside. "And what about you, Derrek? What about *your* future?"

He ran a finger across his mouth in thought, then closed an empty hand around the battered remote with the shining red button. "Do you know — I haven't really thought of much else these past decades except finishing the machine. Beyond that, beyond what will happen when we turn it on . . . is a dream the same as a plan? Sometimes I don't know."

"Well, you and my sister have a lot more in common than I already thought," she answered baldly. "Are you going to *tell* Constance, Derrek?"

He stiffened at her question.

"Tell me what?" And they both nearly leapt out of their skins as Constance struggled through the trap door. Derrek rushed to her, giving her a hand the rest of the way through. "Thank you," she huffed, dusting herself off. "What are you two doing, lazing about? If you're skipping brushing your teeth for the fact that you're a *very important scholar* now, Ivory, I'd like to at least see the proof of it."

Ivory grinned and they dove into their new norm of good-natured repartee, but Ivory watched Derrek during their exchange, how he straightened, adjusted his tie and coat, how his skin colour went through many flushing changes when Constance looked to him for mocking support.

Ivory knew it was already too late for the two of them, and that something must be done.

They all decided to walk down today together, to keep the conversation going with Derrek. The fog and the cloudiness hadn't changed, of course, but the longer they'd spent in Quixx, the easier it was to tell variable conditions, and the air was fine. Constance walked ahead, and when she'd paced far enough away, Derrek snagged Ivory, drawing her back a step.

"Ivory I just— I have a question—"

The uncertainty in his voice was new, and Ivory whipped towards him. "Yes?"

"Our conversation earlier, you mentioned, you know, marriage—"

She leaned in like a scenting Bawser terrier. "Yeeeeees?"

"No that's . . . I'm getting ahead of myself." He yanked on his stock, as he always did when agitated. "I just wanted to know — and you can give it some thought — but nowadays, what would constitute, you know, starting out . . . courting—"

"Courting!" Ivory cried. "That word's an antique. It's called dating now."

"Right. Yes. No, wait. I'm not . . . maybe I shouldn't have asked."

"No, no," Ivory said. She watched Constance weave through the cars, occasionally glancing back questioningly at them, but still giving them space. "Hmm. Well a date is basically a private meeting between you and the person you like. You can ask them, or they can ask you. I suppose you can wait around to see if the other person is going to make the first move, but it doesn't hurt to take initiative. The worst they can say is no."

"Right, right." From somewhere in Derrek's jacket he'd produced a pen and paper and was writing down everything Ivory said, while the other pair of hands clasped and unclasped.

"Then you sort of, I don't know, learn about each other. Likes and dislikes. Dreams and aspirations. See if you're compatible, like magnetic forces. Don't ask me about kissing and all that, you'd know more about it than me." Derrek stopped dead, and at that Ivory waved her hands. "Speaking of, in all seriousness, don't rely on those romance novels of yours for best practices. They're like candy — delightful but terrible for you."

"Sure. All right."

"Why?" Ivory stepped closer, flicking one of Derrek's eight knees as a little sister was wont to do. "Is there another arachnastronomer on Mount Quixx you've fixed your fancy on?"

The notepad went up to Derrek's mouth, doing an awful job of hiding his mottled-coloured face. "No, it's— just an anthropological curiosity—"

"Derrek, I'm fourteen. Not blind." Ivory sighed. "You should just tell her straight out. Remember the merit of the frank discussion you just tried to impart to me?"

And so Derrek was caught out. "You know her better than me!" he hissed. "What if she says— if she's—"

"Connie would have run for the hills ages ago if she didn't like coming to see you. Surely you know that by now." She thrust her hands into her pockets. "Is that really what's holding you back?"

Derrek let out a defeated groan through his flat nose, stepped back, and swept his hands over his arachnid body. "Isn't it obvious?"

"Not to me!" Ivory countered, grinning. "I just see an extremely canny scholar acting like a baby." Then she was back to business. "But I see your urgency, with the summer ending and all. So you'd better tell her. Tonight!"

"What?" Derrek was taken aback. "Tonight?"

"Yes!" Ivory cried, nearly dragging him down for leaping on him with an arm around his neck and a fist in the air. "Fortify your spirit, come to the Happy Bell, and proclaim your heart."

"*Gurk.*" Derrek pulled away. "My heart-tube is about to arrest, I think—"

"Ivory!" Constance called, presumably from the basket and finally impatient at their tête-à-tête. "Are coming or not?"

"In a minute!" she barked. "Debating socialist propaganda!" Then back to Derrek: "Well?"

"Ivory, I can't go to Quixx, to the Happy Bell." He looked utterly terrified, more so at the sound of Constance's voice. "It's too dangerous. What if someone sees me?"

But Ivory would brook no refusal. "Sometimes in life and in love, you take risks. Besides, you'll have to go to town sooner or later when you're a famous peer-recognized astronomer, which is just around the corner! Better get some practice in."

She dashed off, weaving through the cars that had lent themselves to Derrek's cause — a cause nearly come to its fruition. He followed, rubbing his forearms as he came upon both Ivyweathers waiting at the basket.

"Hoist us up, Cap'n." Ivory smirked, as if she'd won the argument.

"And what are you two scheming?" Constance asked Derrek, who was concentrating very hard on the task of grabbing the rope and pulling.

Ivory shrugged. "Just a proposal for a new project. Are you game, Derrek?"

His eyes darted between them as he cleared his throat. "I'll— err, think about it."

"You have a real good *think*." Ivory winked at Derrek, adjusting her pack. "I'll install this signal lamp, and we can chat later."

Constance elbowed Ivory, and the basket went up — and, perhaps, so had Ivory's spirits, just a little.

Derrek paced across the attic. He was accustomed to his tarsal claws making a staccato rhythm on the hardwood, but it was driving him mad. Madder than he had felt in some time. *What would Klaus or Camille do?* He'd observed, closely, their love for and devotion to one another, had carefully archived the story of how they'd met — he, a young man seeking knowledge from every hidden corner of Brindlewatch; she, a daring young woman looking for adventure beyond her mother's house. He'd begged them both for advice, and it always came with the same answer: *Trust yourself. Only you can make the decision that's best for you.*

It had sounded so easy, fated as they were like the lovers in his trashy books — which littered the attic floor now for how Derrek had torn through them today, searching for answers despite Ivory's warning not to trust them. But the real world was not so easy. He'd learned that very quickly.

He hadn't made up his mind tonight, of course not, but what was the harm in taking a walk down the mountain, to where he'd installed the signal lamp beneath the fog bank? He checked his pocket watch: 10 p.m. The sisters would be going to bed soon, presumably. He shuddered under the force of his heart thundering like an autumn storm cell beneath his waistcoat.

"Get a *hold* of yourself," he admonished and went out.

This was the mountain the girls hadn't learned of yet, and part of him was glad of it. The strange sounds that were a klaxon warning as the ridge came alive in the dark — the *others* were on their usual feeding hunt. The nocturnal creatures that eyed him now as he descended laterally, without thread to guide him, clinging to the rocks. Creatures big and small, with gnarled faces and bodies, slithering and chittering and moaning. They were, somehow, his brethren. He'd been one of them once, after all, a child of the mountain. Before he'd learned speech, or manners, or about fashion — the human things he so prized. Age was a strange thing to their kind. Some of them were easily a hundred or older, yet they were still developmentally adolescents. Derrek was partially the same; he hadn't "come of age" until his seventieth birthday, really. Humans aged much more quickly. How could he keep up with all the differences dividing them?

Once upon a time, he'd watched the loggers that came to the mountain with the same disdain he imagined the other creatures felt for him now, or at least the same wariness. He hadn't understood humans, yet part of him had become like them. And now he was caught between two worlds — and he didn't know if he could belong in either.

"Times do change," Camille had said long ago. "If you wait long enough, you'll see. Quixx can change. You can find places where you can belong amongst folk; the world can have an open heart." Even when she'd met Derrek for the first time, when he was a wild, curious thing, determined to follow her and Klaus around until they took him in, allowed him to help them make their dreams come alive . . . even then, she had believed in him, without knowing him.

He carried that with him always, even when he doubted. And Constance had changed just how much he doubted himself. Ivory, too, with her eyes that judged nothing and no one, not even her own reflection. Were there others out in Brindlewatch like them? Once the machine was turned on and the fog dispersed and all his grand intentions were laid bare, would the world accept him as he was?

Constance had. Somehow. He had to believe in that, and it buoyed him on past the shrieking night cries that may have scared anyone else, to the outcrop with the signal lamp.

He switched it on, and it tinkled to warm life behind the shutters. Yet in the distance, Derrek saw a blinking, and when he lifted his pocket binoculars, refurbished to satisfy four peepers, he saw, indeed, it was the light at the peak of the Happy Bell.

He scrutinized the flashing carefully: "Cinderella about to turn into a pumpkin. Speed it up."

Derrek grunted, grasping the lever on his own signal light and moving it accordingly. "Have not decided."

Ivory's responding flashes could only be described as furious. "Make decision before time does for you."

Derrek stayed frozen on the mountainside, his hand poised on the lever for a long while. The summer was two weeks from being over, and Constance would be gone forever. What on Earth would make her stay behind with him, in Quixx of all places, when the world was before her?

"Are we a go or not?" flashed Ivory.

The wind whistled through Derrek's hair and along the mountain face. He shut his eyes. Was it a message? An encouragement? He pressed his hand to the rock behind him, trying to hear the whisper that Camille had often told him of, the wisdom that the mountain had for them all.

But he heard nothing. Just the wind. And he knew that Constance would do nothing different if she *knew* nothing different. He had to tell her.

"En route," he flashed back and nearly threw himself down the mountain in his haste.

"You really have gone off your nut. Way more than usual," Leal said, flipping his collar up to his chin. "This is stupid, Slanner."

Slanner, on the other hand, was all business as he crept along the sidewalk, in the shadows, like a pointy-mustachioed cartoon villain. "You'll thank me when we finally have their number. Bartek told Sluggo told Avila from Hatch that he *saw* those two climbing out of that trench at the same time again today, right before supper. They've been going to that mountain, Leal my man, doing who knows what, and I needs to knows what."

Leal pressed his fingers hard into his throbbing eyeballs. "What the Ivyweathers do is their own business," he moaned for the eighty-sixth time. "If you'd put this much energy into our own stuff, we—"

Slanner clamped his hand over Leal's mouth, bringing his dangerously close. "For a guy who's back-up vocals, you seem like you wanna take lead."

Leal shrugged Slanner off, very much not in the mood. "What's that supposed to mean?"

But Slanner was turning on the charm that Leal seemed helpless against, despite his much better judgment. "Just trust me, Leal. Like you used to. I'm doing this for both of us, don't you see that?" He squeezed him in a hug, gave him a perfunctory smooch, and waited for Leal's usual dogged agreement.

Leal should've said *and the rest of the band?* but he was ashamed to admit he liked it when Slanner paid him more attention than barking orders. "Really?"

Slanner nodded, lips pursed, and hooked his arm with Leal's. "You'll see. Once those Ivyweathers throw us a bone, we'll be swimmin' in 'em."

Leal just sighed as they marched farther down the hill towards their spying destination, hoping that, for everyone's sake, they'd see nothing, and everything would be the same, no matter how much Leal wanted things to change.

Constance had gone downstairs to get a glass of water before bed, shooing away Ivory, who insisted she just *get on with sleeping*, and found, instead, Ms. Bougainvillea at the staircase landing . . . in a most compromising position.

Compromising because of the danger it could present, for she was perched on a rickety stepladder in front of the astronomer painting, dusting the frame, it had seemed at first.

But now Constance realized she wasn't dusting — she was still, touching the place where the face of the painting had been. She didn't want to scare the woman off her ladder, so she waited, still as a statue, at the bottom of the ladder as Ms. Bougainvillea completed her ritual, descending slowly.

"You're still up," Ms. Bougainvillea said in a tone that made Constance jump, for all she was trying to save the old woman the fright.

"What were you doing?" Constance countered, folding the ladder up and leaning it against the wall where it always rested. Ms. Bougainvillea took Constance's arm as she led her up the opposite stairs to the landlady's side of the boarding house.

"Listening to the Bell," she said. "It keeps time best, even when time slows down for some of us. So I was remembering the things, in time, it's kept."

Constance was sure, somewhere in Ms. Bougainvillea's mind, that this made sense. So she nodded, looking accusingly at Frederic perched in her hair. "You're supposed to be looking out for her," she hissed at the cranky bird, but only got a sharp *tweet* for her trouble.

"Never mind him, and never mind me," Ms. Bougainvillea said outside her room. She patted Constance's hands in both of hers, heavy and cool with age. Constance realized, then, that she wasn't wearing her huge spectacles; in the shadows of the hall lights, she tried to see what Ms. Bougainvillea might have looked like in her youth, but time had hidden all of that.

"Your summer is nearly over," the wizened landlady said, with that sudden tone of knowing that always threw Constance off. "Will you go home to your great sprawling city, and forget all about us, I wonder?"

Constance's chest caught. "I could never forget about you, Ms. Bougainvillea—"

"I meant less me, and more the dear friends you've made here in Quixx. And beyond it." Had her blind eyes sparkled just then? "You are dearly treasured, you know. You'll be missed."

Her pulse cooled. Surely she couldn't know . . . ? Several questions tumbled around in her head, and by the time Constance opened her mouth to allow them out, Ms. Bougainvillea had already turned and gone into her room.

"What tangled webs we weave," she said, as if she knew something Constance didn't, and shut the door in her face.

Bewildered, Constance tossed and turned. When she'd returned to the Butterfly Room, not even the wings stirred as they had in dream and vision. Nor Ivory, who was snoring like a tiny windstorm with her face down in the pillows. She must have worn herself out installing and playing with that signal lamp. Constance, on the other hand, was not so lucky, and when she finally rolled over, facing the window, she bit down on her pillow to stifle the yelp at what she saw.

Then she sprang up, launching herself at the window, which she hoisted open with all her might. "What in *bloody Brindlewatch* are you doing here?" she whispered, looking about wildly, for their window faced the mountain, and the street below, but as usual there was no one out this late. "Did anyone see you?"

Derrek was breathing heavily, something she'd only seen in his heightened state of panic earlier, since otherwise he was all grace and calculated steps. "I do hope not," he replied, helping her out the window and onto the dormer ledge he stood on. "I've got far too much work to do to get picked off tonight for my trouble. Besides, it's not that far from there to here, is it?" He jerked his head towards the mountain, dancing about with a tiny bit of mania. "You two are always coming to see me! I thought I'd go for it, for a change!"

His fists were up, coiled and ready, and Constance stepped forward when she should have stepped back. The dormer of their room had an overhang with a shadow that might offer some cover, for dark and foggy as it was, there were still street lamps.

"But what possessed you to take such a risk?" she scolded, then pre-emptively sniffed him. "You haven't been sampling that fungi we found last week, have you?"

"Madam!" Derrek cried, making the case that he probably had. "I am the picture of temperance and I am *affronted*." Constance let out a giggle, which seemed to only bolster him. "I just . . . wanted to see you. Is that so strange?"

The only strange thing was the silence that hung between them then, for Constance, clearly, was not expecting that to be his reason.

"But . . . you know I was planning on coming tomorrow. Like always."

Those last two words chilled her, because *like always* would soon be over, and it would be *as we once did*. But she held fast to the now.

"I know, I know," he said, rubbing the back of his neck. "I suppose I've been spoiled these past weeks. And the closer we get to completing the machine . . . I'm trying to make the most of the time we have left."

That definitely made it feel like someone was digging a hole in her heart. She tried to master her face, to hide that she had overheard his and Ivory's conversation earlier before bursting back into the attic. Ms. Bougainvillea's strange words, and now Derrek's appearance, electrified her nerves. Was he going to tell her, truly, that he had feelings for her? What scared her more was that she wasn't sure how she was going to respond if he did . . . but she was curiously excited for it to play out.

Derrek didn't seem like he wanted to discuss it further, just yet, because he turned away from her, moving to the scant roof rail and staring not out at the mountain as everyone else did — but at the town.

"Is this the first time you've . . . ever been here?" Constance asked as it dawned on her.

Derrek was reverent at the sight that Constance often ignored. "I suppose it is."

"And is it everything you imagined it would be?"

"Heavens yes," he said, looking at her askance and sheepish. "The company is a welcome surprise, too."

She tried to be forthright. "I have a feeling that something else is on your mind." *A feeling or a hope?*

Derrek cleared his throat, and Constance felt her whole body flushing. "I've been thinking. About . . . what comes after."

Oh no. "After?"

From his jacket, where he seemed to store and carry so many things, he produced the remote that he and Ivory had slaved over. Such a tiny thing, but it could change everything. "When we push this button, and there are stars once more, Quixx gets to meet me. What happens then?"

214

Constance chewed on the inside of her mouth. "I'm flattered that you think I have the answers. Maybe you'll find them up there." She indicated the stars they'd never had a chance to see from the boarding house's roof. Not yet.

It was meant as a joke, but he nodded seriously. "I always look to the stars for guidance. But I suppose I wanted to see if you were thinking the same thing I was." He stopped himself, obviously seeing the shock in her widening eyes. "I meant, err, maybe we could, you know, commiserate. In our shared unknowing."

Constance's stomach fell; not what she'd expected. "About the future, you mean."

"It's always on your mind, isn't it?"

Constance stared out into that dreary dark fog, wishing on the constellations she couldn't see. "I still can't see the future any clearer than I can see the sky right now."

Derrek sighed but smiled at the cosmic joke. "Then we're both doomed."

Constance shook her head. "I think I *have* learned a few things about the future, Derrek. You can search the sky and the stars for the answers all you want. But the solution is much closer to hand." She touched her heart beneath the frilly collar of her lace eyelet nightgown. "I wanted the hard decisions to be made for me, every time I shut down. Maybe that's why I fell back so often on what was expected of me. Then I felt trapped by that manufactured future." She turned to him. "But even though I'm not sure what will happen when the fog clears, at least now, after this summer, I feel a bit more in control of my fate than before. As in . . . I know what I *don't* want, at least. What about you?"

He had been staring at her, transfixed. She wasn't sure what he would do next, what she wanted him to do. All he did was blink each eye in succession, moving closer.

"Ah." He waved the moment away like an irritating fly. "I'll be far too busy being a famous astronomer. The galas. The conferences. Drowning in all those Penderton Peace Prizes."

Constance's smile was wan, but she played along. "You'll definitely need an assistant just to manage your bursting social calendar."

"Not an assistant," he said quickly, "but maybe a partner." His long legs glided another step closer. "Know anyone with a clear schedule this fall?"

That possibility made her chest thrill. To stay. For the spirit of this summer to become an every day. But she tucked her hair behind her ear and demurred. "Haven't you heard? I'll be on my world tour with the Kadaver's Soiree. I hear the lead singer is keen on me."

"Is that so?" Derrek made a show of flattening his hand over his eyes, leaning off the roof as he surveyed the town. "Point his house out to me so I can web the door shut."

They didn't have time to laugh as a pair of screech owls swooped out of the Happy Bell and on to their nightly patrols. Constance wheeled her arms as she stumbled into Derrek, but he caught her by the waist before she slid entirely off the roof.

"You could have a burgeoning career as a professional tripper-offer-of-dangerous-heights!" he said, backing them towards safety. "You really have to stop that."

When she giggled again, it was out of a sort of giddy terror, her hands over his. "Thanks. You can put me down now."

"Poor choice of words!" he scolded again and turned her around so she was facing him.

She put her hands on his shoulders. "You really are much stronger than you look. No offence, of course." Instead of a reply, he tossed her inches in the air, caught her as quickly, and she whooped. "I have to ask, though — what's it like having four arms?"

The upper pair bent back, hands laying firmly over hers on his shoulders. "I don't know," he said, sly mischief in his eyes. "What's it like only having two?"

"I don't get as much done," Constance answered, not sure where this was going.

He still held tight, examining her hands. "I suppose we're both anomalies to each other." Then he quickly squeezed her ribs and she squealed, wriggling.

"So sorry! The one hand doesn't keep track of what the third and fourth are doing!" But he wasn't cruel, and he tossed her into the air again, catching and spinning her about deftly, until she ended in a flourishing dip that would have left anyone in the dance halls of Ferren Academy in awe.

"I thought you said you couldn't dance," she said, breathless, her hands around his neck.

Derrek righted her, slowly lowering her feet back to the ground. "Let's just say I read about that in a book, and tell no one what kind."

She dimpled, and though he'd put her down, one pair of hands still held her waist, the others her hands.

"Constance, I . . ." He squeezed her tightly. "The real reason I came here tonight—"

"Yes?"

His eyes were earnest. "I just wanted to see you smile." He chucked a knuckle beneath her chin. "You carry the cares of the world. But the world is at your feet. Whatever the future holds, the opportunities will always be there, whenever you're ready. Just make sure you enjoy it. Whatever 'it' is."

Constance felt more weighed down now than she ever had before. They released hands. The moment to be true was well and clearly spent as she looked away. "Thank you, Derrek."

In the pause that followed, he tweaked her belly and she jerked away. "Sorry," he said, not meaning it in the slightest.

She pressed herself into the dormer over the window to the Butterfly Room, her cheeks still red but so many questions still unanswered. "I suppose I should go back to bed. I've got an arachnastronomer to see in the morning, so we can test their great machine at last."

Derrek nodded sagely. "And we can't disappoint them now, can we?"

Constance made one last attempt, suddenly worried. "You didn't really come here to tell me you're packing up and taking your marvellous show elsewhere, did you?"

"Of course not!" Derrek cried. "I'll see you tomorrow, as planned. Unless I've done that thing Ivory says all the time. Made it weird."

"Luckily you're already weird," Constance said, stepping towards the windowsill. "And so am I, it turns out."

"The weirdest," Derrek agreed.

She took his hand when he offered it to help her back into her room. But she pulled him down at the last, kissing him sweetly on the cheek. "Good night, Derrek."

His pupils were pin dots as she drew away, climbing back through the window. "Good night, Constance."

She went inside and he turned away as she climbed into bed. He touched his cheek, pressing himself against the dormer.

"Stupid," he muttered, going over the conversation again in his head as he slinked off the Happy Bell, dashed across the street, and scurried back into the mountain, where he would definitely not sleep for the shade of Constance's lips on his skin.

From the dead shrubbery they'd been hidden in this entire time, Slanner was shaking Leal hard enough to dislodge his brain. "I knew it I knew it *I knew it.*"

"And now the whole street's gonna know it, too!" Leal hissed. "Will you cool it?"

"Do you know what this means?" Slanner was basically spitting in Leal's face. "This is it. This is our big break. I knew those good-for-nothing sisters were good for something."

Leal watched Slanner throw himself into the road, almost running after the giant monster they'd seen skulk from the Happy Bell's roof and back towards its hellish mountain lair. Leal grabbed him by the jacket and yanked him back — along with the camera Slanner had been brandishing triumphantly, which was really Leal's, anyway.

"What are you thinking?" Leal snarled through his teeth. "You're going to go after that . . . that *thing*?"

"Not yet, I'm not," Slanner said, slapping Leal on the back. "And not alone. Call in the cavalry, send out a press release, and get the stage in tip-top shape. This town's gonna be bursting soon enough, once we wrangle that thing, and it's all hands on deck." He rattled the camera and the full film canister inside. "The proof's in the pudding, and Daddy's *ravenous.*"

Slanner raced back to the Expansive Manse, and Leal could easily see another wild, horrible idea blooming behind his cobalt eyes. All Leal could do was run after him — this time, knowing the worst was already coming.

10

The Platinum Plot

4:42 p.m.

Constance knelt in the street. The rain went on, even though the people had left the Happy Bell's sidewalk, rushing towards the show building in the town square. Crumpled and in the drain, stained with the dirt and the doubt she'd brought with her was the delicate blouse Derrek had woven from his own silken thread. A gift. For her. Ruined now, of course.

Just like everything else.

6:13 a.m.

Slanner leapt backward at the green-slathered, bloodshot eye pressed into the crack of the door.

"And what ungodly hour do you call this?" croaked the voice behind it, trying to muster patience against its storm-goddess fury.

"I beg your pardon." Leal mashed Slanner out of the way, hands pressed together in prayer at his nose. "We didn't mean to wake you so early, Mx. Mott—"

"Yet you did anyway," she snapped.

Slanner was the bolder, if not the dumber, of the two: "We've got an urgent matter to discuss, Mottie, one that affects us all, especially you and me, so if we could kindly take this proposition off the porch, that'd be por . . . tuitous."

Slanner played it cool but didn't bother hiding the fact that every inch of him was vibrating. He hadn't slept, which meant neither had Leal, who had been plying them both with coffee until the sun had risen on what might be the bleakest day in Quixx's history.

Mx. Mott had a curious mind above all else, which was both her strength and her weakness. So she pulled away from the door crack, undid the chain, and allowed them in. "I'd ask you to pardon my face," she said, meaning the bright green slime pasted against her black skin, "but I don't care what either of you think of me. Especially when I could harm you with less than a turn of phrase."

"Point taken," Leal said, steering Slanner in as the door closed behind them.

They all went to the sitting room, where Mx. Mott did just as the room intended, but the boys were either too terrified or too wired to take their seats. She crossed her long legs under her kimono. "Well?"

Slanner liked to make an entrance. So he paused, the anticipation — the *aggravation* — rising in the room like boiled mercury. Leal was about to start, but Slanner's voice boomed: "Everything is going to change, from this day forth."

Mx. Mott drummed her long nails on her armchair. "Why? Are you finally packing up and hitting the old dusty trail, as they say?"

"Even better." Slanner grinned, waving the fistful of pictures he held like he was fanning an emperor. "Ladies and gentlemen, boys and girls! It's the moment you've all been waiting for! Mount Quixx's star attraction is here! Come one, come all, we've got plenty of room, entertainment on deck, and more than one reason to stick around."

He spread the photos on Mx. Mott's coffee table like a Las Peleta blackjack dealer, and Mx. Mott's eyes went wide.

6:24 a.m.

Ivory turned over. A light was flashing in the distance. She checked her bedside clock — too early to even consider reasonable, but she dragged herself out of bed to the window, spreading her eyelids wide to get the air into them.

When she digested the message, she scoffed, looking over at Constance, who was dozing like the dead. She rolled her eyes, climbed out of the window, flicked on the signal lamp, and went to it.

"Calm down," she sniped to Derrek's light, which looked like it was strobing. "Repeat."

"What are Constance's measurements?"

So she hadn't been dreaming it after all. "No idea. Why?"

She barely got out her own message before he was flashing back. "Gift."

She blinked. Had last night worked? She'd, of course, been awake when Constance went out to see Derrek, but the walls were thin, and in order to avoid overhearing any awkward smooching, she'd stuffed cotton in her ears and wrapped her pillow around her head like a helmet. Still, she'd heard a lot of muffled giggling and chatter that went on and on . . . lovers! Sickening.

So Ivory went back into the room and went into Constance's suitcase, pulling out one of her dresses, which was twice Ivory's size for Constance's bustiness alone. From her own tool kit, she snatched a measuring tape, and laying the garment flat, she noted the size and went back to the lamp.

"42-32-46," she flashed.

The light was gone — she chuckled, imagining Derrek frantically writing it down. "Thank you," was his last message, and that was that.

Ivory sighed heavily as she threw herself back into bed. "Romance is gonna kill me."

6:24 a.m.

"You expect me to believe these are . . . real?" Mx. Mott pored over the pictures in her hands; some of them were blurry and taken in the dark, but many were in focus. If she believed them true then all that superstitious claptrap that people had said about the mountain was real after all, and the world was much wider than she wanted to accept.

And it was a golden opportunity.

"You know I ain't creative enough to come up with something like this!" Slanner exclaimed.

She sucked on her teeth. "Touché."

"Besides, what's there to gain in faking it? There's much more to gain in *this*." He pressed his finger into the photo that Mx. Mott had just scooped up, slipping her spectacles on to get a better look.

She blinked. "Is that—"

"I've made a study of *Ivyweather sapiens*," Slanner began, as he paced.

"Incorrect usage, but continue."

"And what I've found is that there's much more than meets the eye. Even if it's a good-looking one." Slanner elbowed Leal, who'd been falling asleep on his feet. "I cottoned on to it when she and that li'l punk sister of hers came back from the mountain with nary a hair astray. The nerve. And not just that! They kept going back for more! For what, do you think? Some hidden treasure? Spiritual knowledge? Thrill-seeking?"

The picture wasn't the clearest, but it was a full-figured girl with light hair, in the hands of the creature, and somewhere in the smudge of their faces was *delight*. Thrill-seeking might be a start.

Mx. Mott clenched the edges of the film paper. "She's going to bring these things into Quixx, isn't she?"

"Now we don't know that—" Leal tried, but Slanner only had to prod him with minimal force, and Leal crumpled into a chair.

"We don't know nothing. Which is even more dangerous . . . er," Slanner countered, "and that's why we need to get ahead of this. Maybe to our own advantage."

Mx. Mott turned a dipped brow up at Slanner. He couldn't plot his finger out of his own nose in her classroom. Still, she felt a chill creep across the back of her neck, and she turned in her chair to look up the stairs, hoping that Madeline hadn't woken to the sounds of their voices.

But the stairs were empty. And Mx. Mott turned back to Slanner, still thinking of her daughter. "And what do you propose?"

11:05 a.m.

"I guess it was going to happen sooner or later," Ivory sighed.

"It's just brunch," Constance said. "And it was Leal who invited us. We like Leal, don't we? Then as soon as we're done, we'll go to the mountain. 'Like always.'" Constance was still clinging to that phrase, the dwindling promise of it.

"Ohhh the *mountaaaain*," Ivory swooned as they left Farrowmarket, having picked up some dessert to take with them. If Constance wasn't so concerned about the tarts in the box on her wrist, she would've smacked her sister with it.

"I don't know what that tone is for," she huffed.

"You two really are the worst," Ivory groaned, head lolling back and tongue slavering out of her mouth.

Constance rolled her eyes, but she smiled all the same. Today felt different. Today it felt like everything was falling into place.

They started up the hill towards the Expansive Manse.

7:25 a.m.

Slanner leaned forward on the kitchen table since they'd moved there to brew coffee and get down to the plan.

"I dunno 'bout you," Slanner went on, "but I'd say this was a state of emergency. Especially if there's more of those *things* just at our doorstep, waiting to strike. We may be far away from that ol' war across Brindlewatch, but it's come to Quixx, and we've gotta fight back."

Mx. Mott had cleared off her face and was nodding as she stirred her hot water and lemon. Leal felt sicker and sicker. He didn't know what to think of this monster business, but he felt like maybe it was Constance's business, and not theirs. She and the creature had looked like a happy, normal couple. For a moment, Leal had even felt jealous, seeing them like that up there. Jealous that he and Slanner never talked that way anymore.

But if Mx. Mott was agreeing with *Slanner*, they were all doomed. Quixx, and Constance's rooftop friend.

"Those Ivyweathers have put us all in danger," Mx. Mott agreed. "I'll make a call to Ferren City. Send these photos over a wire, and they send the troopers. Then what?"

"Then we capture the thing and put it on display, of course." Slanner was about to raise himself onto the counter, but when Mx. Mott pierced him with her narrowed eyes, he went back down. "Listen, get the cops, sure, but it's the TV cameras and radio stations you want up here. Exposure means more people. Which means charging admission. Which means—"

Mx. Mott's teacup clattered as her mouth fell slightly open, the vision dancing clearly before her. "The university."

"Sure, sure." Slanner waved his hands. "Invite all those eggheads up here, too. Sure they'll want to dissect this thing and anything else we flush out. Then *badaboom* — everyone's happy, Quixx is back on the map, we're performing sold-out crowds every night, and everything's Platinum."

"Platinum." Mx. Mott's fists clenched the crockery.

Leal had to try, knowing it was too late to change their minds. "Maybe we should talk to the Ivyweathers first," he suggested. Slanner and Mx. Mott turned to look at him, pinning him to the greenhouse door with their fury. "I mean, Constance at least seemed familiar with him—"

"*Him?*" Mx. Mott exclaimed in surprise. "You mean *it*. Those girls have no idea what they've gotten into. What kind of danger they've put us all in. It isn't even troubling that the legends were true, but that the Ivyweathers ignored them and brought this on our heads. And for what? Frivolous frolicking!" But her next smile was worse than her protest. "Though you're right. We will need the Ivyweathers for this. If the older one is as close to this creature as you say, then she'll be the only one capable of luring him out. Makes things much less messy. Excellent idea, Mr. Synodite."

Leal's mouth went dry at her pointed spear of a finger.

"Invite them to brunch. Both of them. The younger one will be needed to persuade the older one. And I want to make a few things perfectly clear where my own daughter is concerned . . ."

Madeline, finally creeping out of hiding, steeled herself as she raced down the stairs with all the balletic grace she'd been trained with, and out the front door.

8:01 a.m.

"I'm very sorry, dear," Ms. Bougainvillea said, "but you just missed them."

Madeline hadn't had very many interactions with Ms. Bougainvillea — after all, her mother thought of her as a crackpot and an enemy since she wouldn't sell her the boarding house. But Madeline was never prone to judge and tried to get her mother to stop doing it so liberally, so in that moment, all she saw was a tired old woman at the door, who, even though she couldn't see Madeline very well, seemed very concerned.

"Do you know where they went?"

The bird in the old woman's hair trilled, and she seemed to be nodding along. "The market," Ms. Bougainvillea said. "Today is baking day. They do like to help."

Madeline glanced up the road and checked her watch. She would have to start home fast — her mother usually came in at 8:30 on weekends to wake her with tea. "I have to go," she said breathlessly. "I'll try again to warn them. But please, Ms. Bougainvillea. Do you know anything about . . . a friend of Constance's and Ivory's. Something — some*one* — from the mountain?"

Ms. Bougainvillea went very still, her bent back straightening to a point where Madeline figured that, maybe fifty years ago, she had been as formidable as her mother. "What's wrong?" the old lady asked.

"There's no time to explain," she said, backing down the steps. "Just please tell them to be careful. All of them. My mother and Slanner Dannen are planning something. Which can't be good."

Madeline nearly tripped into the gate when a large crow settled on Ms. Bougainvillea's shoulder, swooping down from the mountain. She ran a finger over its breast but did not look away. *She looks a proper witch*, Madeline thought.

"Thank you, love." She smiled, and for a moment Madeline felt at ease. "Take care of yourself, now."

And with that, Madeline was racing back towards the east end, trying to send her thoughts to Ivory as if there truly was magic in this world.

8:11 a.m.

"I'm just going to sit down for a moment." Ms. Bougainvillea waved Frederic and Mathias away. "I'll write to him. I'll warn him to stay put." She creaked slowly up the stairs, one at a time, clinging to the rail. "I am so tired, my loves, so very tired."

She took one last look at the great painting. "Keep watch on them, as I know you already do," she said, lingering there.

Frederic chirped, and she made the rest of the slow, painful climb to her bed. She sat on the edge. "Paper, Frederic. Paper and a pen. I'll write it now. I must."

Frederic paused before leaving the room, even though Ms. Bougainvillea waved him off, irritated. But the second he fluttered away, she clutched her head, suddenly dizzy.

"No," she said, quietly and to no one in particular. "Please... I must..."

But she said no more, and did no more, toppling to the side in an exhausted faint just as Frederic returned with the crow, Mathias, at his wing. They both squawked and trilled around her head, and though she was breathing, she did not move.

The birds agreed it was time to take matters into their own wings, and the crow went back to the mountain while the bullfinch kept his vigil.

11:20 a.m.

When they stood before the Expansive Manse, Constance flipped the note over, checking it again.

"It's the right time," she repeated. "Though Avila did seem in a hurry when he gave it to us—"

"Ivory!"

The sisters turned, finding the usually serene Madeline Mott in the path behind them, panting and pale. "Hello, Madeline..." Constance raised an eyebrow, more in Ivory's direction than anyone's.

"I looked for you earlier, then I couldn't leave again until now—" she panted, and Ivory started forward when she bent over, clasping her knees.

"Just breathe," Ivory said, patting Madeline's back. "What is it?"

229

Gasp. Gulp. "—warn you—"

But the three of them twisted around as the Manse door creaked open, and out walked—

"Leal?" Constance barked. It looked like he hadn't slept. In fact, he looked terrible. All the charm and joy in him had evacuated for higher ground. And they were on top of a hill.

His smile was like cough medicine: bitter and pointless. "Ladies." Even his bow was stiff. "Brunch is on." And then he turned, and the dark of the front hall swallowed him.

"It wasn't like this last time," Ivory warned. She meant the absolute maw of doom that was the doorway.

Constance should have felt it, should have known better, but the clock was ticking, and for once she didn't want to worry. On the other side of that darkness was the rest of the day, and in it was Derrek.

"Perhaps we'll just pop in and tell them we can't stay." She swallowed. "We'll be in and out quickly. Just stay close to me." *Just try to be brave*, she thought, and they all went inside.

The door slammed behind them.

8:25 a.m.

"I really don't understand, Mathias." Derrek shook his head, levelling the harried crow on his outstretched forearm with a glare. "You have no note from her. And I'm quite busy right now. Tell her I'm *fine*." He swept his arm up and the crow took flight, but even when Derrek sat down again at his spinning wheel, he was assaulted by black wings.

"Go on!" Derrek shouted, but crows rarely give a warning twice, and in a blustering fury, Mathias took wing back down the mountainside.

The mountain itself tried to shout, but Derrek only heard the wind.

11:33 a.m.

There were no lights in the hall. But they could all hear the music. Constance had heard something similar earlier that morning — a sort of music, when she'd left the market — and at first she'd thought it was nothing. But now she was certain it was some kind of warning.

"Leal!" Constance shouted into the black. Her arms were winged out, and Madeline and Ivory pressed into her as if she were a great shield.

"It's no use," Madeline whispered. "I saw Leal earlier. He was there in our sitting room — plotting with the rest of them!"

"Plotting what?" Ivory whispered back, but then a spotlight snapped on, fit to blind them.

"Come in, come in," boomed Slanner's ghoulish voice. "It's about to begin."

Then they heard the clicking and the whirring, felt the floorboards creaking and shifting. "It's just for show," Constance reassured the girls — reassured herself. "Just stay close together, it's harmless—"

The limelight snapped off. A scream. "Ivory?"

"No, Madeline!" her sister cried. When the light went back on, it was just the two sisters left, clinging tightly to one another.

"Sorry, folks, had to edit the crowd," Slanner sneered through tinny speakers.

"Stop this *right now*," Constance shouted through her tremors. "This isn't funny!"

"What's the matter?" The voice was mocking, and suddenly the hallway floor shuddered, the walls closing in. "You nervous, li'l Miss Con? Now, now. I thought we were friends. Friends *trust* each other."

"Give her back," Ivory snarled, "or I'll choke you with that gods-awful piano tie I *know* you're wearing."

The walls stopped moving. Silence. Then, much quieter, as if speaking to someone else, "But she harshed my mellow!"

And in that instant fumble, Ivory broke away from Constance and tore down the hall.

"No!" Constance cried, and unable to do much else, she ran blindly after Ivory. "Wait!"

One turn, another. Then the wall snapped up in front of Constance where Ivory had just been, and the floor went out from under her. She slid, screaming, into nothingness and landed with a hard *thump* on her rear, in the dark.

When the lights flashed on again, she got shakily to her feet. A hexagonal room — a lounge, with a bar, and the sickening glare of neon lights. A checkered polished dance floor. And the mirrors — the walls were made of mirrors, each cut like a diamond, reflecting back a hundred terrified Constances.

Until one of the mirrors flipped around and revealed Slanner Dannen.

He clapped, high-pitched laughter rising. "Entertainment at its finest. Must say, haven't had the opportunity to prank someone in this house in a long while who didn't already know my tricks. Thanks for that."

"Thanks for *nothing*," Constance said through her teeth, lips peeling back as her fists shook at her sides. "Where's my sister? And Madeline?"

Slanner strode forward, hands on his hips. "Wouldn't worry about them just now. Only about you, li'l Miss Con. Fitting name. For a con artist like you."

The way he circled her was hungry and mean, and the reflections dancing around her made her dizzy. Or was the floor moving? "What are you talking about?"

Click. *Shuck*. More mirrors like the one Slanner had emerged from flipped around, and with each successive turn came a member of the Kadaver's Soiree. They were all dressed in their finest, but their faces could have been painted on for their misery. Sluggo even seemed to have a nosebleed, staunched with cotton, but he was playing his sax despite it. The music came up slow and sad.

"I pride myself on being a showman. It's what got us the Platinum, isn't it, boys?" The band didn't answer, just played louder. "But you" — he jabbed a finger at Constance, and she backed up — "are the best showman I've ever seen. Especially last night's performance, on that rooftop. With that . . . *thing*."

If her heart had been made of plated mirrors, they would have all cracked, the shards burying deep into her shrinking resolve. "What?" Even her voice was small.

"You can't play dumb with me, sister, especially if you want yours back," Slanner sighed, and with a flourish and a clap, the trick door he'd appeared from swung open again, and this time framed in it was Leal, holding tight to a struggling Ivory.

And then the room truly began to spin.

11:34 a.m.

As soon as the hands had snatched Madeline and pulled her through a door, she did exactly as her father taught her: *If anyone ever grabs you, don't think. Use your head.* And she did just that, smashing her skull up and into something that crunched satisfyingly before the hands let her go.

"Sorry!" she called behind her as she fled, bumping into the walls. Beyond her heavy breathing, she heard no other sounds that told her she was pursued. She took one turn, then another, trying to master her terror. *Be brave like Father.*

She slammed into another body and went down in a tangle of flailing limbs, and when they both stopped screaming long enough, Madeline whispered, "Ivory?"

"Madeline!" They hugged in the dark. "Are you all right? I lost Constance—"

"Don't worry," came another voice, as the lights went on. "We're going to meet her now."

The girls stared up, but even Madeline knew there would be no reasoning with her, even when she said, "Mother, please—"

3:59 p.m.

Derrek had been waiting all day. The girls had not come. At first, he'd tried using the signal lamp, but Ivory had made no reply. Had something happened? He'd been so wrapped up in weaving Constance's gift, time had warped in on itself. The bundle was wrapped carefully under his arm, and when he checked his watch again, he knew he'd have to go and see for himself. What harm would it do? He'd been to Quixx just last night, after all. He'd been safe as houses! He'd resolved to wait until it was dark: he'd go to the Happy Bell, just to make sure they were all right. Maybe Mathias *was* trying to warn him, after all.

A flicker.

Derrek's head whipped up. The signal lamp at the Happy Bell was flashing.

"S-O-S."

Derrek swallowed, fearing the worst. "Repeat," he flashed back. But the message was the same. *Emergency. Help.*

There was still daylight left beneath the foggy curtain, but Derrek was lightning as he scrambled down to Quixx.

11:42 a.m.

Midway rides had always been Ivory's forte. The lounge room was a funhouse carousel, one in which Slanner seemed at home as the lights flickered like screaming devils over his cracking grin. All Constance could do was try to grab something and hold on as she watched Leal and Ivory disappear and reappear in random mirror doors when she tried to reach them.

Slanner seemed content to wax poetic from the sidelines as she struggled. "I well and truly thought all was lost till you girls came to Quixx. But then you wouldn't pay attention to me. Paying attention now?"

His voice seemed much too large, amplified, like he was stretching each word taffy-long. Constance had been within arm's reach of Ivory, but she stumbled, and Leal pulled her back, disappearing again.

"Just had to go poking round that mountain," Slanner went on, "making friends you ought not to have. But now I see how we can *all* benefit. You can make this Platinum shine again. Only you."

Only you can set him free. Constance squeezed her eyes shut, feeling so sick, so helpless. *You can't give Derrek away. You mustn't. But Ivory. The spinning. Just make it—*

"Stop!"

Constance was thrown onto the dance floor. Slanner whirled, the lights went up, and the band, pasty-faced and terrorized, scurried back into their holes. Leal stood out with Ivory, who threw up on his shoes, despite her love of midway rides.

"I deserved that," he muttered, and let her race to Constance's aid.

"What are you—" Slanner seethed, but from behind Leal came Mx. Mott, dragging Madeline along with her.

"Theatrics can only get you so far," Mx. Mott scowled. "You've done the job of scaring them. Now it's my turn to bring it home." One sharp look and Slanner backed up, folding his arms but keeping his sneer silent.

Ivory helped Constance to her shaking feet. Only when Ivory touched her cheek did Constance realize she'd been crying.

"I said enough of the theatrics," Mx. Mott clucked, letting go of Madeline. "It's no use. And there's no use denying it, either. This one may not be the sharpest brick in the yard, but he's good for sneaking around and gathering evidence."

The pictures she threw down at the Ivyweathers' feet had been blown up to enormity, and Constance felt the strong thing inside her that she'd built so carefully this summer crumble.

"As you can imagine, I am less than thrilled." Mx. Mott's impressive heels clicked harshly against the dance floor tiles. "I'm sure you think you're attached to this *thing*. But you've let something dangerous into this town. And I won't see you destroy everyone's lives here because of your carelessness."

Spots swam in Constance's vision.

"Mother!" Madeline cried. "Why are you doing this?"

When Mx. Mott turned to her daughter, there was only genuine concern. "I'm doing this for *us*, my darling. Don't you see? This is a disaster we must mitigate for the greater good." She rested her hands on her little one's shoulders.

"And, once it's been neutralized, and the rest of the world knows, we'll have everything we ever dreamed of."

Madeline was agog as Mx. Mott pulled away, facing Constance and Ivory.

"You can't." Constance had finally found her voice. "Please. Leave Derrek out of this. He hasn't done anything wrong, and he would never hurt anyone. I'll give you anything you want — just leave him alone."

Slanner laughed. "So *it* has a name now, does it?"

"Yes, *he* does!" Ivory cried. "Or *they*, as is his other preferred pronoun!"

"Tsk." Mx. Mott waved a hand. "Sentimentality. This thing is a monster, that much is clear. And besides, I don't wish to kill it. I think we can all find a much more genteel solution if we're all to come out of this with what we want."

"Why would we help you?" Constance sobbed. "You're both more monstrous than anything on that mountain!"

The room was still. Slanner glanced at Leal, who shook his head at first, but when Slanner snarled, Leal darted forward, yanked Ivory away from Constance, and brought her to Mx. Mott. Slanner stood between them.

"You Ivyweathers are a danger to us all. You don't see logic or reason." Mx. Mott's countenance was a thunderhead. "So I think we'll keep you two separated for now. Slanner has agreed to watch over Ivory, and of course, I'll be keeping Madeline as far away from your influence as possible." With that comment, she threw a dagger glare at Ivory. "When you've played your part to everyone's satisfaction, then you two can pack up and return to Ferren City to wreak whatever havoc you see fit."

Hatch and Sluggo took Ivory away, but before they could, she dug her heels in, her violet eyes straining on Constance. "Connie. Don't. You know me. I can take care of myself. Don't bargain on my behalf!"

But the mirror door clicked shut. Ivory was gone, and Constance was suddenly not as strong as she thought.

4:03 p.m.

"Well?"

Constance came down the stairs of the Happy Bell in a trance. At the bottom of them stood Slanner, Mx. Mott, and many judging birds that the latter scattered with a stomp. Ms. Bougainvillea was resting — sick, she finally admitted — and Constance was glad the old woman could be spared this macabre pageant. She doubted her heart could take its culmination.

"I told him to meet me. Using the signal lamp." Really, she'd sent out a desperate message of emergency. The only one she'd remembered from her survival training in grade school. She hoped Derrek would get the message to stay put. Another part of her desperately wished he'd bring back-up.

"Signal lamps." Mx. Mott shook her head. "It would be clever if it wasn't going to get us all killed."

"You don't know him." Constance tried to sue for peace again, as she had throughout the entire day. "You value logic and reason, Mx. Mott! Derrek is a creature of science. An astronomer, like—"

"Like the one who went up the mountain, was never heard from again, and most likely perished in the explosions he'd caused that made the crater round this mountain in the first place?"

Constance bit her tongue painfully, remembering the story that the junk shop clerk had regaled her with, seemingly so long ago, and Derrek's own tale of the fire. But Constance said nothing; Mx. Mott was happy to fill the silence.

"Failed to mention all that, did your little Derrek? People have always said that mountain was cursed; they weren't wrong." She turned to appraise it like a smudge on a fine tablecloth. "When anyone meddles with that mountain, the rest of us suffer. After the explosions, caused by Dinah-only-knows, the fog took hold of this town and has never loosened its grip. But now, the mountain can work *for* us, for a change. This is the start of a new era for this town. Quixx will be valuable to people again."

"It's valuable now! The things Derrek has been working towards — they'll help Quixx more than you know. If you just let him—"

Something changed on Mx. Mott's face; Constance thought, for a moment, she'd gotten through, maybe even just by an inch, but enough to continue to plead her case. Then Mx. Mott's eyes averted, and Slanner, seeing that control over their captive was slipping, took over.

"All right, all right." Slanner muscled up the stairs, grabbing Constance and practically shoving her out the door. "How's about you get out there, Missy, and wait for your big creepy crawlie paramour while the grown-ups wait inside?"

Then he slammed the door, clicked the lock over, and Constance was alone on the porch.

3:21 p.m.

Back at home on the east side, Mx. Mott had been all brutally efficient business once the Ivyweathers were separated and well-guarded — express-wiring the photos to the Ferren City Police Department, fielding the frantic phone calls that came in from the Brindlewatch Guard hours later, and handling all the press with aplomb. It was like track and field day all over again, the shotput landing home to first place.

"Daddy would be ashamed of you."

Mx. Mott was still, removing her plum gloves finger by finger at the sideboard. "I'd be careful, Madeline. You're in enough trouble as it is."

"And so are you, Mother. In your heart, how can you love me or anyone else if you'd do such a terrible thing?"

Mx. Mott absorbed the painful sting as she glanced at the photo of Victor, handsome and saluting in his uniform, but when she turned to look up the stairs, Madeline was gone, her bedroom door slammed shut.

4:10 p.m.

Please don't come. Please don't come. Constance sat on the edge of the trench, staring up and down its length, memorizing each jagged cut in the ground. In some parts of Quixx, there were high fences to keep people from driving off into the chasm. It had seemed odd, of course, when Constance first saw it, but what did she know about geology? *And what did Mx. Mott know?* The explosions, the fog appearing, the blame that seemed to rest on the astronomer's shoulders the more she heard tell of it. Did Derrek know the truth? Was he keeping something from her? Constance kept a vigilant watch for him, but also for the ghost of Camille, begging to be shown the way out of this.

But she was wide awake, listening hard for the mountain. Now it, too, was quiet. Any powers she'd had, or thought she'd had, were gone.

So she sang to herself when the mountain wouldn't, filling in the words for the melody that always seemed so familiar in her head.

My heart, my heart, is broken, my dear, for yours seems a fragile old thing.
And when I consider the stars, my dear, what tangled webs do they weave.
So when I come home to dark lonely peaks, to the place that I know is still mine,
I will return, my darling, my dear, and our fears will sparkle and shine.

Constance pulled her head up from her knees, for climbing out of the trench beside her, arms already encircling her, was Derrek.

"I still say you've a lovely voice." He smiled thinly. "Though the tears aren't my favourite part of this performance."

Constance held tightly to him, knowing that at her back Mx. Mott and Slanner Dannen were watching. Waiting. If only she could stop time.

"What's wrong?" he said, but he held on, stroking her hair. She only faintly noticed the package in one of his hands, which he placed on the ground behind her, but she refused to let go of him and see what it was.

"Are you all right? I came as quickly as I could. Please, you can tell me—"

She just wanted to look at him. She put her hands on either side of his face, saw herself in his eyes as she did in Slanner's carousel of mirrors. But this was different. *Sun-caught maple syrup*, she thought. Sweet and wonderful.

"Derrek," she said as bravely as she could. "*Run.*"

But there was shouting and clattering and the roar of engines, and suddenly the street in front of the Happy Bell was a battleground. Derrek leapt up, shielding Constance, as rifles and artillery and huge army autos blocked any means of escape.

Derrek's eyes darted. "What—"

She should have told him to go back to the mountain to hide. She should have said something else other than "I'm sorry— I didn't mean to—"

But the cavalry closed in, and they were too late.

4:12 p.m.

It was all much too fast. There was a lot of shouting, threats of force that suddenly became force. Weapons and people who would never understand. Blinding lights. Sirens. Derrek and Constance were separated immediately. All he could think was for her safety, but he should have been worrying about his own as he was slammed to the ground, unable and unwilling to fight back against these humans, those whose world he so desperately wanted to be a part of. And when they came at him with ropes, he let go. He let the darkness of his every fear take hold, and took on theirs, too, and he tried to fight his way back to Constance. Back to himself.

"Get the flypaper, lads, 'e's a wriggler!" someone shouted, and something hard came down on Derrek's head. Stars, so much angrier than the ones he knew and loved, appeared before his eyes, and in that instant, he picked Constance out of the crowd and held on to the sight of her even when he let go of everything else.

They bound his legs then, and his hands, and threw him into the cage.

5:00 p.m.

Camera bulbs flared and flashed, popping like candy corn underfoot at the Knockum pier. Townsfolk had gathered in droves and Constable Derraugh blustered through them all.

"'S the meanin' of this?" he shouted behind his bristling whiskers, his bathrobe looking a bit worse for wear as he joined the crowd.

A newscaster from the Cities, all towering bouffant and business as she dragged her cameraman into Derraugh's path, snagged the crimson-zoot-suited Slanner from an interview he was already giving.

"Yes, mucho scare," he said, yanking on his lapels and rocking on his saddle shoes. "But my humble band, the Platinum-selling Kadaver's Soiree, are sort of like, you know, neighbourhood watch round here. We had to do *something*..."

Meanwhile, a group of scholars in white lab coats, who had raced down to Quixx from their field station just a few towns over, were all furiously taking notes as Mx. Mott paced before a huge, sheet-covered obstruction now installed in the middle of Farrowmarket, replacing the headless fountain statue. It was illuminated with huge spotlights that the Brindlewatch Guard had set up, along with their extensively guarded perimeter.

"This, my friends," Mx. Mott said, her grin well pasted on as every camera turned to her. "This will change the course of history as we know it. For monsters do exist. And Mount Quixx has the honour of showing the first to you, and the world, this day."

She nodded. The sheet came down. The crowd gasped and the camera flashes strobed.

They had a hit.

11

THE MOST MONSTROUS
MONSTER OF MOUNT QUIXX

"Come one, come all! See the creature that has lurked on the shrouded mountain in secrecy — till now!"

The kid crying out scintillating cues from the edge of the cage had been Mx. Mott's idea, one of the many bored youths who took this entire monster spectacle in stride — and would do his job for extra school credit. And so many people had come to Quixx to observe, in person, what had only ever been seen in fiction.

But monsters were *real*. Monsters in Brindlewatch. What other fabulous secrets was the world hiding?

Mothers held tight to their children as they passed, unable to stop themselves from staring. The cage was open on all sides, and there was nowhere for the creature to hide. It stalked back and forth, agitated and fierce on eight terrifying legs. It was huge — at least seven feet tall, with four arms that could *snap two men in half at once*, the barker had sworn. Its skin was unnaturally blue, its hair dark and wild. And people swore, with each passing hour, that the creature was changing. There were fangs where there at first had not been: spikes rising and growing beneath its skin. And the eyes: unforgiving, black holes that surveyed and remembered them all.

A true horror show. And Quixx was the centrepiece!

The older locals scurried past, holding up warding signs with their hands. These locals, the ones who had lived here all their long lives, knew better, knew that this whole thing was a mistake. Why anger the mountain? It had already been angered, fifty years ago, and look what had happened, look at the fog choking their very humanity out of their bones.

But the television stations weren't interested in superstitious nonsense; they wanted the facts. And the fact was there were monsters on this mountain, and the world needed to know why.

"How long do you think these creatures have dwelled here, Mx. Mott?"

A much more serious news station, one interested in a full journalistic profile rather than feeding the tabloid claptrap, had Mx. Mott in one of the many small tents set up around the square, asking the hard-hitting questions, the morning after the creature had been captured.

"Who can say?" she said, sipping her tea. "Quixx has been here for hundreds of years, the mountain longer still. It will be interesting once Caden Morbatten, the famed naturalist, arrives with his star-spangled team to investigate. I'm sure they'll capture creatures even more fearsome than Quixx Case Zero."

For that's what the media was calling the nightmarish thing: a simple, sterile cataloguing title. "But it's clear these creatures have become much more clever as time has allowed them to thrive in safety. Cursory investigations have shown that Quixx's vehicle disappearances were *intentionally* caused by Case Zero. What it has been taking them apart and building them for . . . it's only a matter of time before we discover the purpose. Nefarious, I don't doubt."

Mx. Mott leaned in conspiratorially, as if this all wasn't being recorded. "Between you and me, I'm sure these creatures have been planning an attack of some kind. We're lucky we caught this one last night before anything dire transpired." Then she leaned back, satisfied with the interviewer's bulging eyes. "We've already learned so much in just a few hours. Imagine what the world can do once the proper resources start trickling in. I have had designs on a university here for many years, you know, and I believe that with this discovery, Quixx will soon be the place where top advances in many fields occur . . ."

Mx. Mott was a natural at this. Nothing would stop her now.

If there was anything in this whole situation that ranked as the most shameful, it was that Constance hid out in the Happy Bell of her own accord.

Of course, she'd been told to stay indoors overnight, as the rest of the town had been — *for their own safety*. Which meant she couldn't try to break into the Expansive Manse to get Ivory. Or seek help from anyone else in town. And truly, what could Quixx do now? Derrek, in the cage in the middle of town, blocked from Constance's view by the crowds, the tents, the military presence — evidence of the danger lurking on their doorstep. Who would help Constance free him? Her mind spun tighter, faster, than Slanner's indoor carousel. Her skull ached, trying to find the answer, or the bravery to damn the rules.

There wasn't anyone in the Happy Bell, either, who could help. Ms. Bougainvillea, who had gone to bed the previous afternoon, hadn't left it. She seemed to be getting worse. Constance sat at her bedside now, utterly numb with her tea untouched in her lap. At least watching over the landlady was something Constance could do, useless as she truly was.

Ms. Bougainvillea's breathing seemed to grow shallower, her nut-brown face chalky. The doctor, a man named Valentine, had been and gone.

"Rest is what's best for her." He'd appraised Constance's puffy eyes and startlingly white face with a frown. "And for you as well. For all of us. I'm not sure what to make about this spectacle outside, save that it's terrible for everyone's constitutions, I am sure of that."

Constance couldn't even bear to turn around and look out the window now, at the mountain, because she could feel its betrayal. All of this was her fault. She'd lured Derrek here. She hadn't been brave enough to stand up to anyone. She never would be now.

"You look like you ate a poisoned apple," came a small voice from the bed, and Constance jumped.

Her mood went back to sour. "I wish I had."

Ms. Bougainvillea's milky eyes squinted, offering the opposite of the doctor's advice. "A walk, my dear. A walk would do you good."

Constance's jaw tightened. "Not today, Ms. Bougainvillea. There are . . . too many visitors in town right now."

"Ah, visitors." She turned over, her eyes on the ceiling but memory elsewhere. "I remember when this boarding house was *full* of visitors. So many new friends to make, every week." She rolled her head back. "Perhaps you'll make one, if you go out. It will make you feel better."

Constance just stared straight ahead, her eyes dry and tone bitter. "There's only one friend out there that matters," she said. "And he wouldn't want to see me."

A cool hand on hers in her lap. She glanced down. "I think you're the one he wants to see most of all."

Constance stared at her. Her mouth twisted as she jerked her hand away. "But I can't. The brave one . . . it's not me. It never was *me*." She got to her feet, her exasperation the only thing keeping her up. "How can you *know*? Everyone is always hiding so much in this town! It would have been better if we'd never come here at all."

Ms. Bougainvillea only sighed again. "Go for a walk, dear. It will clear your head." And she rolled over, facing the wall, and said no more.

Constance's fists trembled, but she cleared her tea, left the room, and went down the foyer stairs. Where else could she go? The birds were gathered, staring at her.

"What?" she shouted, and some of their wings flickered. "What do *you* want from me? You think I have the answers? Well, I don't! No one does!"

Bernard honked at her, and she whirled on the goose. "Your mistress barely knows what she's saying half the time! Solve your own problems! It's none of my concern!"

The birds seemed to glance meaningfully at one another.

"Ugh!" Constance railed, and for the sake of departing the mass scrutiny of the Happy Bell's flock, she stormed out into the street.

Slanner had never been much of a babysitter. But Leal was practically a professional, with all the years he'd handled Slanner. Still, Ivory was *not* a baby and was smarter than all of them. It was only a matter of time.

She had been playing it cool ever since her fourth escape attempt had been thwarted by the extra tall sax player, Sluggo, who wasn't interested in having his nose broken again, and was, after all, twice Ivory's height. But Ivory was many things, and above all, engineering was her strong suit. She looked around the Manse and saw a machine that could be taken apart given the proper tools.

And when she looked at the Kadaver's Soiree, she saw much the same machine, and every moment afforded her a new view of their schematic.

They were coming apart, and they must have known it. They'd all taken turns watching over her, which wasn't too difficult since she was forced to follow them everywhere, regardless. She was press-ganged into service as a grunt, moving speakers, microphones, drums, and band equipment hither and yon across the massive stage she'd also helped build. This was the moment the Kadaver's Soiree had been preparing for the past ten years — their reunion with the stage, with attentive crowds they could play to every night of the week. So why did they all look so miserable?

Ivory hadn't *really* tried to escape. Not seriously. She found herself turning her naturalist's eye on these crooners as if they were a newly discovered species. She was testing them at every opportunity. Slanner berated the others constantly and it had only gotten worse. The crowds weren't here to be serenaded; they wanted to see the Monstrous Monster of Mount Quixx. They merely rolled their eyes on the way to the main attraction, the band worse than buskers in the background.

"The hot dog carts are getting more play than we are," Slanner growled, kicking over the amplifier that Ivory and Avila had just finished setting up. She observed how the others cowered, even huge Sluggo, passive Bartek, grim Hatch, and especially tiny Avila. They seemed more intent on diving in to clean up the mess that their diva leader had left than to try to upend his ridiculous rule. *Play louder! Play better!* he'd shouted till his singing voice was hoarse. They were all trying. But maybe ten years since they'd played a real show had been ten years too many.

And then there was Leal, the most loyal of them all. She'd watched him the closest, and realized that Slanner himself relied heavily on Leal — for comfort of all things — and Leal was willing to give it. Surely, out of all of them, Leal was the smartest, the most feeling. Surely he saw how twisted this all was. Ivory narrowed her leonine stare in on him. He was the lynchpin that'd undo this entire outfit.

Her usually calculating mind spun as she and the band righted the amplifier. It wasn't all the physical slave labour that had left her drained. Being kidnapped had been awful, and she shouldered the blame for it — blame she could talk to no one about. Her emotions tumbled in her stomach like clothes in a rusty electric dryer: shame for having talked Derrek into coming into Quixx the night he was discovered in the first place. Anger that she hadn't seen nor heard from Constance, who should be mobilizing someone, anyone, to fix this horrible disaster. Misery that she'd gotten Madeline in trouble, too.

Sorrow for her friend and mentor, whose shadow was crouched in the corner of the cage across the square, which she could see clearly from the stage. The cage may as well have been on the other side of the planet for all the good she could do its occupant right now. She counted the number of the Brindlewatch Guard until it went too high to even consider. Her bumbling captors were the least of their worries.

Avila sighed. "It's unnatural." Ivory looked up, noticed Avila, too, was staring at the cage. She frowned.

"What's unnatural is this whole thing," she snapped, grabbing a rag and wiping the grease off her hands. "The crowds. The circus. Derrek doesn't deserve any of it."

"That's what he means."

Leal had returned from trying to calm down Slanner, hands on his hips, kicking a stray soda can that had made its way onto the stage after their last set.

Ivory was perfectly still, but she tried to make her face bland. "So why don't you do something about it?"

The band all exchanged worried glances.

"What?" Ivory barked. "Too chicken to stand up to the man? Isn't that what today's music is supposed to be all about?"

Leal sighed heavily. "This is our life," he said, "our home. Stories from that mountain are what we grew up on. But we figured they were just stories. Maybe what you're saying is true, and your friend isn't dangerous at all." Leal seemed pained to look at her, so he looked away. "But we owe Slanner everything that we are. He gave us the music that makes us. We can't turn our backs on him."

"You think he's your friend?" Ivory flailed, unable to suppress her grimace. "Then you're all in a worse cage than Derrek is."

"Uh oh," Bartek grunted, pointing. "Better get Li'l Trouble backstage. Big Trouble's coming."

Ivory saw Constance before Constance saw her. She leapt up, waving her arms, but Sluggo grabbed her and dragged her away before she could get a signal across. Constance had been sneaking around behind the back of the cage.

"Well?" Hatch said to Leal. "Should we warn Slanner? The troopers? Mott?"

Leal looked like he'd had just about enough, especially of having to make tough decisions he probably didn't believe in.

251

"Warn them about what?" he said, and he turned the other direction. That was all Ivory saw before they took her away.

Constance hadn't necessarily wanted to come here, but giddy terror had seized her and taken control of her feet the second they'd hit the cobblestones. She darted through the swelling crowd, past the troopers, pulling her tweed jacket's hood close to her face as she checked out the crowd. So many rubberneckers and looky-loos; it really was a clown show. But still militarized. There was a cloud of fear hanging over everyone, thicker than the fog.

All she knew was that she had to see him. To talk to him. She'd caught snatches of the conversations of those coming away from Farrowmarket — *fearsome! Terrible!* — Derrek must be frightened out of his mind. What if, in his panic, he'd changed again, in the way Constance had witnessed? She was seized by the sudden, delirious hope that if she could just speak to him, calm him down like before, the town would see he wasn't dangerous and would let him go.

It was all very cinematic in her head. She'd gone behind the line of cameras, which were switched off, since the *star attraction* was in the back of the cage, in the dark, and not providing much entertainment for the prickly crowd.

So Constance managed to make her way around the back of the cage, which faced the perpetually closed flower shop. The only space behind it was the width of the sidewalk, and she squeezed in here where no one else had dared. The cage itself was raised high — even at five-foot-nine she couldn't see over the lip that was the floor of it. She certainly couldn't see Derrek, since on this side the street lamps were completely blocked, and it was always dark in Quixx, even at the best of times.

"Derrek?" she chanced. She waited, didn't breathe — nothing. So she climbed up on an empty stone planter, grabbing the bars for purchase, and tried to hoist herself up.

She swallowed a shriek as a hand snapped around her wrist, holding her in place, and a face she barely recognized, framed in wild, dark hair, was inches from hers.

Constance's vision swam. The four marks on Derrek's face she'd taken just as something like birthmarks seemed rounder, more pronounced. Then the marks lifted, and Constance realized they were eyes, black eyes, four now become eight, and if she hadn't already seen this before, she would have fainted dead away.

"Der . . . rek," she choked in a small, crushed voice. He pulled her up slowly, until her toes touched the edge of the cage, and he held her there, still staring, his face a cataract of fury.

And of fear.

"It's me," she said, every inch of her shaking. "You know it's me, don't you?"

There was a rumble so deep and terrible, Constance thought it was her own skeleton shuddering — but the noise came from Derrek, who drummed his eight legs on the floor of the cage like a stomping horse might. A huge hand, impatient.

"Constance," he hissed, sounding more like a snake than the gentle arachnastronomer she knew.

She nodded frantically. He hadn't let go of her wrist, and she was barely able to hold on to the slippery bars with her other hand for how her palms sweated. Then the tears came. "Derrek. I'm so sorry. I didn't mean for any of this to happen—"

"But it did," his dark voice replied. The voice of a stranger.

She shook her head. "I can help you. I can *make* them see you for what you are—"

"What I am?" He released her, but it was still a threat as he held out his four arms, long and spiked. "This is what I am. What I've always been. A *monster*."

"That's not true," she said, but her conviction was breaking. She held tighter to the cage bars. "You're a scientist. An astronomer." Then a gamble: "You're my friend."

He'd grabbed hold of her jacket as he slammed into the cage. He didn't want her to fall. Not yet. "You're afraid of me now, too," he said, his mouth so close that she could count the barbs at the corners of it, obstructing his speech and making his voice alien in her ears. "How can you help me?"

She blinked rapidly, the tears coming thick. "I don't know."

It was so quiet that she had to use every last bit of energy to keep looking up at him, to not let her vision close in and unconsciousness take her. All eight of those black eyes stared at her now not in rage, but in pain. Sorrow.

"It's too late," Derrek whispered, and Constance watched the long barbarous fangs lengthening, growing before her. "I can't control it anymore."

He was moving away from her. Against all reason, she thrust her hand into the cage, desperate, flailing, trying to reach him.

"Derrek, wait! Please — just give me your hand."

She pressed her face so hard into the iron bars that her teeth hurt. He stared at her. Once upon a time, all she could see when looking at Derrek was a monster that could swallow her whole. But now she didn't care. She just needed to reach him.

His hand rose—

Then he lurched, his body swaying and his legs skittering the whole of him back and forth like he was on a boat in the treacherous rocking sea. He let out a bone-cracking moan, his body stretching and crumpling, growing, arms akimbo, and when the thing that was no longer Derrek saw Constance, it charged for her, and she let go of the cage.

She pressed herself into the wall of the flower shop at her back, narrowly escaping eight legs, four arms, and a gnashing mouth as she scrambled to safety. She cried all the way back to the Happy Bell, almost suffocating by the time she threw herself over the threshold, shut and locked the door behind her, and slid down the other side, sobbing.

Derrek was gone.

Ms. Bougainvillea found her a short time later.

"It's all right," she said, helping the shaking mess of a girl to the wicker loveseat in the solarium. "There, now."

"It's *not* all right," Constance sobbed, burying her face in her hands. "I can't do anything. I can't help him. I can't help Ivory. I can't do this anymore."

Ms. Bougainvillea sat next to her, rubbed her shoulders. "I know," she said. "I know it's hard."

"Do you?" Constance asked. She looked like she was well and truly drowned. "How can you know?"

Ms. Bougainvillea's usually cheery mouth was a wry crinkle. "You don't live as long as I have without knowing a broken heart." She tried to soften her words. "I also know you'll get nothing done without rest."

"What about you?" Constance sniffed. "I thought you were . . ."

"Never you mind about me," Ms. Bougainvillea said, passing Constance a handkerchief from her pocket. "I've rested long enough."

Constance took the hankie and mopped her face. But her expression changed and she slowly pulled it away, seeing in the corner a monogram in a familiar script: C.B. She'd seen another one just like it.

"Sleep now," Ms. Bougainvillea said, steering Constance to lie down. "It will be better once you do."

Constance *was* tired. In every nerve. Every inch of her stricken heart. Perhaps if she slept, she'd wake back in Ferren City, and all of this would have been a strange dream.

"Just shut your eyes," she heard Ms. Bougainvillea say, and she did as she was told, and she found that sleep was a welcome reprieve from grief.

She waited, a hand on the girl's shoulder. Her breath was shaky, but that was the crying jag. Frederic twittered. She was asleep.

The old woman got to her feet, slowly, achingly. She shuffled to the solarium window, turning her face to the place where she knew the mountain loomed.

It is time, it whispered. *He needs you.*

She moved to the foyer, to the grand staircase. In the back of her mind, she heard laughter. Not the same laughter she listened to often, the memory of their past happiness echoing through the Butterfly Room, which had been Klaus's favourite. This was the laughter of the hundreds who had passed through these halls. The many friends she'd made and outlived. The lives that were merely ghosts now, perhaps only alive in her own memory. Not for much longer. Who would tend them when she was gone?

"You've all done me a great service." She nodded, for she knew that every bird of the Happy Bell was gathered here now, and she felt their eyes on her. Felt the sadness, too.

"Don't give me that," she scolded, raising a finger to her hair, and pulling Frederic down with it. "You knew this would happen eventually. None of us can stay forever."

Quiet cooing, quorking, even Bernard nudged her in the hip.

"It's all right." She'd been saying that too much lately. Nothing was all right as far as she was concerned, but that wasn't up to her now. It was up to the girls that the mountain had brought here. The girls she'd watched over. She'd done her part for the mountain and its children. This was the last verse to the song it had sung to her, all those years ago.

She placed Frederic carefully, lovingly, down on the card table by the front door. "Take care of the Bell, will you?" She smiled. She moved away, and Frederic did not follow.

Mathias flapped nearby, placing the purple scarf over her head as she grasped her cane, turned her face one last time to where she knew Klaus's portrait was, and left the Happy Bell for good.

It was dark. The crowds had thinned. She wondered where all of the people were staying. *Not the Happy Bell*, she mused. More than likely they were staying in nearby towns, too afraid to spend the night in a place where monsters dwelled. Perhaps the visitors were already tired of the monster they'd made. Perhaps they'd driven in and promptly left, once they'd had their fill. City folk had the appetites of spoiled children. It would take more to keep them here for good.

The mountain did what it could. It sent down an odd wind, and troopers and the guards on duty didn't see the old croggled woman make her slow progress to the back of the cage, pressed into the flower shop, the place Constance had stood an hour or so earlier.

She couldn't see, but she could hear the shuddering of a caged creature that had tired itself out with terror louder than any siren. She took her seat on the planter, leaning forward on her cane. This journey had taken the last of her strength. The night was cold for summer. It was about to get colder.

"I know you're there," she said. "It's fine. I intend to do most of the talking, and you were always a very good listener."

The shuddering snarl went still. She heard a clacking shuffle of two steps, and in the breath of silence, she nodded.

"I know you're afraid," she went on. "I am, too. All these years you always called me the brave one, but a mother's strength comes from knowing that the fear doesn't go away. So you do it afraid." She grinned ruefully at that. "Fear makes monsters of us all."

Her whole world had been darkness since her sight had failed her. But she held on to the light still inside her, though now it was dimming. "They all thought I was batty. That's fine. There are few people here who remember the night of the crater, the fire. They said it was my fault it happened, for meddling with the mountain. Or Klaus's fault. There's always someone else to blame. Let them say what they want. They've all said quite a few things about me since then. I preferred witch, most of all. Gave me some character." Her smile fell. "Sometimes I longed for them all to know the truth. That I continued to go up to the mountain until I was no longer able to. That I went up for you."

Her mouth twisted. "I wanted to protect you from this. I spent many years trying. The truth is that I hoped you'd never complete that blasted machine because I knew people far better than I wanted. I knew their fear would change you. Harm you. But the mountain seemed to know better, when it brought those girls to you. That's when I knew that, in the end, I couldn't protect you forever. Even with letters exchanged every single day, a mother has to let go, eventually."

She could feel him close now, even though he hadn't made a sound. She reached up and clasped his hand, which had become sharp. He did not pull away.

"I don't know how many times I've told you this. Klaus would have some ridiculous number to call up. But I'll say it again: Klaus's death was not your fault. It was not mine, either. Or the mountain's. It simply *was*. I should think that Klaus left the best parts of himself with you. And that I helped a little. You are and always have been my child. Our child. I have never lost sight of that, even after losing sight of everything else. Oh, Derrek" — she let a single tear fall — "I let them call me crazy for so long because I knew it was best for them. It is so much easier to be batty than to admit a broken heart."

The sharp hand squeezed hers.

"Take care, my darling," she said, for the night was growing far too cold to breathe. "Love is more powerful than fear. And it will save us all."

Derrek held on, long after that, and longer still after Camille Bedouin breathed her last.

12

SPLIT THE HEAVENS

A rabella waited for the sun to rise.

She'd heard the mournful moan in every fibre of her hairy legs. It carried from the Farrowmarket where it originated, through Quixx, and finally to her terrarium. She had spent too long now, waiting for things to right themselves. Sometimes, one had to take matters into their own eight hands, no matter how small they were.

So when the light crept into the Butterfly Room, Arabella gathered all her strength, wound up, sprang vertically, and scurried out of the Happy Bell to get help.

Constance dreamed.

More to the point, she fell deep into a dark sapphire sea, her hair a seaweed tangle about her face. She sank like a stone until she realized she was not in a sea at all, but in the sky, surrounded by stars. Stars that did not seem keen on remaining above her as they cascaded to the mountain below.

There were old paths, old ways, the mountain whispered, as Constance floated gently past it. *I have survived them all. There have been others who have heard my whispers, who have heeded my warnings. I did not expect the sky to fall, but it did. And it will again. And there will be newer paths to walk, should we survive to build them.*

Constance watched the flaring stars come down around her, as if they were harmless fireflies. They danced around her face, in the darkness, until they joined together, and she was somewhere wholly different, and yet the same, the lights leading her to a white-haired figure at a long desk, near an enormous telescope.

"The observatory?" Constance moved slowly, as though she were still surrounded by water, and when she came to the astronomer's shoulder, he looked right at her, right through her, blinked, then went back to his work.

"'A comet unlike anything I've yet observed . . .'" She read Klaus's notes aloud as his hand flew over a large journal, one Constance may have even moved amidst her many cleaning spells this summer, but never opened. "'It seems to grow nearer by the day, and by my calculations may be visible above this very mountain in a matter of days. It has never been catalogued. My colleagues think I'm seeing things. Am I?'"

Klaus cracked his knuckles, his writing feverish on the page. "'It will pass us by, it seems. Just by a hair. But comets always come back. And what if, next time, it comes back closer? I will wire this information when I go down the mountain next week. Surely this information can be corroborated, and Quixx must be warned ahead of time . . .'"

Klaus discarded his glasses, rubbed his eyes hard, and took a slug of cold tea. And while he took this moment to contemplate his next move, Constance shifted to the telescope, to try to see what he did, and what it revealed was far worse: the truth of it all, the one the town never had known, the one the mountain wanted her to see, and the one that had changed Derrek's life, and that of everyone in Quixx, forever.

I did not expect the sky to fall, but I could feel it falling before it did. If only, if only, a mountain had a true voice. But you do.

The comet had come like a rocket, passing over, yet its tail split, huge flaming hellish debris spiralling down, down, down. And Constance was viewing it from the mountain summit, then falling slowly with these celestial wreckers, as their streaking fire cut the face of the mountain, the observatory, too, in its wake, burning, burning, until their final rest came on the ground, and the crater she'd crossed was born in flame.

The scar still burns, the mountain whispered. *Will you use your voice? Will you help?*

"I can't help you," she said, voice slow with sleep. "I can't help anyone."

From the crater rose the fog, purling and weaving its threads tight around Quixx. Trapping even the arachnastronomer in its web, yet daring him still to dream. To wish to help.

You need help only one, the mountain replied. *But you need to ask for help.*

"So help me," Constance replied, but the mountain was gone from her head, and she had landed softly onto wooden planks. And as she spun, the Happy Bell resolved around her, but it was not as she knew it. The banisters gleamed bright, the crown moulding was fresh and clean. She stood on the landing of the great staircase, and saw the impressions of bustling men and women coming and going all around her.

There were no birds, only butterflies — a swarming cloud of living colour painting the boarding house in the hues it was meant to hold.

But she did not move farther, for at the bottom of the stairs, beneath the great ship's bell, the butterflies culminated in a swirling cascade. And when they parted, there stood the woman with the scarf over her head. The woman with the bright spectacles, the long black hair.

"Camille."

She smiled. "I don't think anyone has remembered to call me that in a long while." Her teeth were as large in her brown face as they were in Derrek's round-framed picture. "But you know me as—"

"Ms. Bougainvillea." Constance blinked, backing up into the wall behind her. Everything fell into place, much too late, she knew. Then she snapped her head up and saw the huge painting of the astronomer as if for the first time. He was climbing down out of it, his blank face resolving just as the warm mirage of the Happy Bell had.

"They were my favourite flowers." He, too, smiled, as he took Constance's hand in a firm, ghostly grip. "I'm glad I can finally meet the girl who has captured Derrek's heart." He winked. "He gets his charm from me."

Constance knew she was dreaming. But she felt him there beside her, holding her hand, and she knew that, somehow, this was really happening.

"Don't take all the credit," Camille said to Klaus as she came up the stairs, and if his smile for Constance had been warm, it was tender with affection now that he looked at Camille.

He released Constance's hand and took Camille in his arms. "You kept me waiting a long time," he scolded.

Camille shrugged. "Derrek needed me a little longer." Then the two of them looked to Constance. "But he has you now. And you must help him."

Constance clasped her hands tightly in front of her. "I can't," she said, sorrow rising, remembering what had happened in terrible waking. "He doesn't recognize me."

The Bedouins exchanged a look. "The fears of Quixx have changed him," Camille told Klaus, and he shook his head sadly.

"He has carried so much for so long." He turned to Constance. "You must ask the mountain for help."

"Help?" she repeated. "How can it help any of us? It's a pile of rocks! The Brindlewatch Guard is involved now. They have weapons. The world is watching. And Mx. Mott—"

"None of that matters," Klaus said, his eyes earnest beneath his white curls. "The stars, Constance. The sky is falling. They all must see before it's too late."

"The sky . . . you mean, your comet?" she stammered, but all around her, the Happy Bell was deteriorating, aging so rapidly that the floorboards split and cracked beneath her. "But you wrote that it would pass us by!"

The Bedouins held on to each other, but their eyes never let Constance go. "Not this time," Klaus said, his all-too-real face fading into the worn-down painting Constance had walked past so many times this whole summer. "This time, it will fall closer to home."

"But I don't know what to do!" Constance was chasing them, trying to outrun the decaying past, but the darkness was too pervasive.

"Just remember," the Bedouins said, as they, too, went into the dark. "Love is stronger than fear."

Constance wanted to ask them so much more, but the Happy Bell had split in half, and she was swallowed by the darkness below.

Constance was aware she was screaming only when she hit the solarium floor. She got to her hands and knees, shaking, trying to get control of her breathing, to summon Ivory's comforting count as she gripped the loveseat she'd rolled out of.

When she heard another scream that wasn't her own, she got stiffly to her feet to look out the window.

How long had she slept? People were running past the Happy Bell at breakneck speed. When she saw Doctor Valentine in his white coat trying to catch up, she feared the worst.

They were heading for Farrowmarket.

Constance was dishevelled and barely rested, and the warning words of Klaus and Camille rang in her head. She started. *Camille.* She spun and tripped up the stairs to Ms. Bougainvillea's bedroom. For the two had been one and the same all along, and when she burst into her room and found the bed empty, Constançe clasped her hands to her mouth.

She was not much of a runner, but she was now as she pounded the cobblestones for Farrowmarket. Had Ms. Bougainvillea gone to see Derrek? Had something happened? But no — Derrek wouldn't harm her. Not the woman he considered to be as close to a mother as ever he'd had. He was just afraid. He may look like a monster, but he wasn't one.

The crowd was too thick to barge through, and Constance didn't recognize Constable Derraugh until she caught sight of his whiskers beneath his police officer's helmet. He was dressed smartly in full retinue, and he'd mobilized the Quixx police to keep the crowd under control. He did not look like he wanted to be there.

"It killed a woman!" a man in the surging throng yelled. "Surely you lot are gonna do somethin' about this?"

Constance thought her heart had stopped. She tried desperately to get closer to Derraugh, who saw her and almost

265

winced. "What happened?" she asked, but the constable turned away, grimacing as he grabbed hold of her forearm and took her aside.

"I'm sorry, lassie. I know you had grown close to Mizz Bee. We all had. Grew up with her, most of us did." He doffed his hat in grief. Constance saw the cage in the far square behind him. Saw the ambulance door closing. Saw that the Brindlewatch Guard presence had tripled since yesterday. "It wrapped her in its webbing," the constable continued, looking pained to recount it. "She was stiff 'n' cold. She was old, true, but no one deserves to go bein' prepped to be snacked on."

Constance's head shook like it was on a spring. "No. Derrek was close to her. He would never. There has to be an explanation."

"I should have expected *you* would be here," came a voice that stabbed Constance right in the small of her back, forcing her to turn. "Constable Derraugh, were you about to arrest this disturber of the peace?"

Constance had spent all her sorrow. All she had left was anger as she rounded on Mx. Mott. "This is *your* fault!" she cried. "Derrek didn't do this, and you have no proof of it!"

"Proof?" Mx. Mott laughed. "What about the webbing covering her body? What more proof does the world need that this monster has killed, and will kill again?" She folded her arms, tipping her nose up in triumph. "Luckily for all of us, the exterminators are on their way."

All of Constance's conviction fled. "The . . . what?"

"Only the best, from Ferren City, it turns out." Mx. Mott planted her hands on her hips. "This situation needs to be controlled, after all. Besides, we'll need to rout out any others like your star-crossed monster here. Surely there are more like him that mean us harm. Really I should be thanking you. It's quite sad about Ms. Bougainvillea, true, but she had her time. Quixx University is closer than it's ever been before, and we will have our first specimen . . . once it's been dissected, at any rate."

Mx. Mott's eyes and mouth went wide as Constance launched herself at the woman. They fell to the ground, a thrashing of nails and fists. Mx. Mott was tall and strong, but Constance was a hurricane of sickened grief. Three police officers had to pull them apart, and it took two more to keep Constance back.

"Lock her up, now!" Mx. Mott screamed, cradling her face where Constance had got a hit in.

"You won't win!" Constance howled as the constable came towards her, reluctantly, with his handcuffs.

As she was taken away, Mx. Mott sneered, "I already have."

Ivory, on the other hand, was whooping and cheering as loudly as she could, though she knew the Expansive Manse was soundproofed, but she didn't care. She'd seen the entire fight from the top of the hill, since it gave a good view to Farrowmarket.

"She shouldn't have done that," Avila said, watching through the screen of his fingers.

"The game is on!" Ivory cried, and when she spun she bounced right off Sluggo, who barely moved.

"Slanner wants us on stage in five," Sluggo said, helping Ivory to her feet.

But she was wound too tight. She'd finally got her sign that things were looking up — Constance was a rebel now, but she needed Ivory, Slanner Dannen and his dysfunctional band be damned. She needed to get out.

She was about to spring into fight mode until she noticed that Sluggo had tears in his eyes.

"What's wrong?" she asked, against her better judgment. Then the sax player, usually either blank-faced or totally emotionless, broke down into a blubbering mess. For once, little Avila was the one giving the comfort.

"It's Miss Bee," he said. Even Bartek's cumulus cloud of hair was drooping. "She's gone."

"They say it was that *thing*," Sluggo whimpered, snorting into his forearm.

"No," Ivory said forcefully, and they all looked up at her. "Derrek would never. I've spent the last month and a half working with him. He'd never hurt anyone."

The band stared at her in awe. "Working with . . . them?" Avila asked.

Ivory nodded, though she, too, felt the keen sting of Ms. Bougainvillea's loss. She pinched her chin. "Derrek was in their cage, which meant she went to them. She'd been complaining of being tired the last while. I wouldn't be surprised if she were sick and was hiding it from everyone." She paced about the galleria, where they were all currently holed up. "She's lived here all her life. She's talked about the astronomer, who we know was Klaus Bedouin, who Derrek knew because Klaus taught Derrek everything he knew . . ."

The picture in the observatory — the man with the white curly hair. The woman next to him with the bright smile, the spectacles . . .

The faceless painting in the Happy Bell.

"Then . . ." Ivory stopped dead. "Ms. Bougainvillea . . . was she Camille Bedouin?"

"Of course she was," said a voice from the doorway. "She liked to change her name, remember?"

The band turned to face Leal, who looked like he'd shed his share of tears based on the red-rimmed circles beneath his usually bright eyes. "It was Quixx's greatest love story — the astronomer who came from afar. The girl who could charm the mysterious mountain. We all thought she was batty, but we didn't care. She was one of us. She told us so many stories. She taught us all how to dream."

The band nodded in their shared heartache. It was all quite obvious then, and yet Ivory, the curious one, the mystery-solver, had let it all slip past her until it was too late to do anything with the information. Had she really been so twisted up in her own plans, her desire to see Derrek's machine complete, to seize adventure, that she completely missed this?

"The band can't play in this state," Ivory said, ashamed at herself and angry at the demands of the world in the presence of Ms. Bougainvillea's loss. "Slanner can go stuff it."

"I know," Leal said, which took Ivory by surprise. "And I think, maybe, I believe you. Because I was the one who found Miss Bee this morning . . . and the creature? Derrek, you call him? He was holding her hand. He looked right at me. He wasn't going to eat her. The webbing . . ." His mouth pinched as he tried to express himself properly. "I think he wrapped her up to keep her warm. He knew her like we did."

The room was dead silent. Ivory took a step forward. "So what now?"

Leal sighed, his scarecrow shoulders drooping. "We do what we should have done from the start," he said. "We do what's right."

Ivory slammed her fist into her palm. "Righteous." Then she looked about. "We need to spring Madeline first. We'll need brains to make this work, and all the troops we can get for Operation Starscape." She darted about the room, and the rest of the band seemed like it was coming awake.

"But what about Slanner?" Hatch asked, drying his tears and replacing them with resolve.

Leal allowed a smile to creep up. "It's time to outplay the boss, boys. He won't like four more divas sharing the stage. Go find your inner Slanner. That'll buy us some time."

"So will this," Ivory said, reeling back and smashing the case that held their precious Platinum record. The glass rained down on the gaudy carpet, and when she plucked the record off of its frame, she bit into it.

"Sorry," she said at their horrified faces, "it's not really Platinum. But it'll do the trick." She tucked it into her pants and grabbed for Leal.

Arabella was much faster, though, and got to Madeline first.

Madeline had locked herself in her room since last night, offering little in the way of fodder for her mother. Instead, she'd fumed silently, fouettéing relentlessly to get her brain going. She'd also spent much of her time poring over her personal library on prison escape attempts, but she was coming up short.

Luckily, Arabella remembered her way to the Motts'. As spiders are wont to do, she found the easiest means of getting up to Madeline's room without being detected — through channels of cracks, between walls, and over ceilings — until she landed with a triumphant *plop* on Madeline's book in front of her.

She let out a shriek, then clapped her hand over her mouth, because her mother was downstairs — most likely at the sideboard, taking a draught of something strong after having dealt with the commotion in town today. Madeline had refused to speak to her, and instead got all her updates from her radio.

"Madeline?" she heard her mother call.

Madeline cleared her throat. "Nothing," she replied, then

quickly checked the lock on her bedroom door before she turned back to Arabella. "You are a different kind of spider, aren't you?"

Arabella just stared at her benignly — if spiders did such a thing — then started hopping frantically.

"What is it? Is it Ivory? Constance?" She cupped her face in her hands. "Heavens, it's probably all of them. I heard about Ms. Bougainvillea. But Ivory seems to trust that monster out there. Do you?"

Arabella chittered, waving her front forelegs. Madeline took that as a yes.

"I'm trapped here, I'm afraid." She hated to admit it, too, but she'd never get past her mother downstairs. "I could climb out the window, but she has a police officer watching our place. Then she'd probably tie me up and throw me in a closet." Madeline paced in her ballet slippers. "What would Ivory do?" A distraction. That's what she needed. She snapped her fingers and spun around. "Arabella, you seem forthright, and this is an old house. Can you gather any other vermin? My mother can't stand anything crawling underfoot." She smiled. "No offence to you. But we need all the help we can get."

The possibility that this spider understood Madeline seemed far-fetched, but so was this entire situation. So when Arabella scurried off into a dark corner of the room, and after many silent minutes passed, hearing her mother's panicked screams on the floor below left Madeline pleasantly surprised.

She darted to the window. The police officer had run into the house — she could hear him trying to find Mx. Mott to ask what had happened, until his screams joined hers, and Madeline thrust the window open, throwing down the bedsheet rope she'd made a few hours ago, and climbed down to freedom.

"I hope you have a plan," Leal mustered when he and Ivory stopped to catch their breath at the Motts' cul-de-sac.

Ivory checked to see if the coast was clear. "I like to improvise," she said as she dashed towards the red-and-white house.

Leal groaned. "I'm getting tired of hearing that," he said, but they both stopped dead and did a double-take as a pink streak went past them at full speed.

"Madeline!" Ivory cried, and Madeline Mott whirled, facing them in the street.

"Ivory?" she said. "What on Earth are you doing here?"

Ivory flailed. "Rescuing you, of course!" Then she noticed Arabella at Madeline's shoulder. "But it seems we're late."

"Not by much," Madeline said, and she grabbed Ivory's hands. "I was about to come rescue *you*, but this saves us time."

Ivory couldn't help her lopsided grin, but Leal grabbed them both and dragged them away. "Hate to break this up," he said, "but we've got another breakout to manage before this works out for anyone."

Constance had never been to a jail before. Considering such a thing was laughable social suicide. Only degenerates went to jail. And anti-capitalist activists. Yes. Laughable. And Constance was laughing now, hysterical and furious as she pounded her fists on the brick. Constance Ivyweather — scholarship blue-ribbon dancing panic attack princess in *prison*.

She looked at her clenched fist. Violence was a terrible thing. But so was fear. This is what it did. And deep in her heart was a coiled black kernel of dread due to what was to come. She'd been afraid of the future before, but this was bleak.

They were going to kill Derrek. She needed to get out of here. Of course she did. But what then?

Constance collapsed on the cot that was suspended by chains from the wall. She was the only occupant of the Quixx County Jail, which seemed like it hadn't seen a resident in decades. That offered some small pride, but barely.

Most of the modest force was out dealing with the crowds, the chaos in Quixx's usually untroubled streets; they were sorely out of practice, and so needed as many bodies as they could spare to talk empathetic sense into locals and visitors alike. But there were still officers just outside, and she'd never get past all of them.

She started when she'd heard the screams. They came in waves. Then silence. Then the door opened, and in strode three people she never dreamed she'd see on the lam together.

"You know, I always pictured you rescuing *me* from jail for some protest or another." Ivory grinned, and they hugged through the bars.

"Oh Ivory . . ." Constance felt the tears welling up again, but Ivory pulled away.

"Don't," she said. "We're both to blame. Well — all of us played our part. Which is why we have to work together to make it right." She let go of Constance and spun to face Madeline and Leal. "Where's the key?"

Constance raised an eyebrow. "The officer outside that door had it." She jerked her chin. "What'd you do with him?"

Leal pulled on his collar. "I mean . . . he sort of scattered when all those spiders swarmed in . . . it happened so fast." And he thumbed to the bristly figure perched on Madeline's shoulder, which would have shrugged, Constance knew, if it could.

Constance shook her head. "Whatever that means," she said. "I can't do much from in here. Or out of here."

"Don't quit before we even get you out," Ivory exclaimed. Then she yanked something bright and shining from her back pocket. "I hope you don't mind, Leal, but it's an emergency."

Leal nodded. "It never was the most important part of being in the Kadaver's Soiree, anyway," he said. "I used to think it was singing with Slanner. But now I'm not sure."

The girls all cocked an eyebrow at him, but Ivory just shrugged, and snapped the record into manageable pieces, and went to work picking the lock.

"But what can I do, Ivory?" Constance tried again. "You've been lucky so far, but there are Brindlewatch Guard patrols everywhere. And now that these exterminators from Ferren City are coming, security will be harder to get through. I'm sure Mx. Mott is expecting something like this."

Madeline pursed her lips. "I'll worry about Mother. Leal will handle Slanner. Ivory will handle the Guard. But we all agreed. You have to be the one to go to the mountain."

Constance froze. "What?"

"The remote, Connie!" Ivory cried, and the lock sprang free, the door creaking open on its rusty hinges. She stretched her hand towards her. "C'mon!"

But Constance couldn't move. She shrank deeper into the cell. "Ivory I . . . I can't do it. I'll fail."

"You've failed if you won't even try!" Ivory was getting angry, familiar irritation at her older sibling flaring. "Connie, don't be such a—"

"I'm scared, Ivory!" Constance lunged forward, frightening her sister back. "You've always been the brave one, even though I'm older, I know that! I can't just be the hero you want me to be!"

Ivory had no witty retort to that. Leal was the one who broke the stalemate: "But you were brave, yesterday. We saw you sneak over to the cage. You tried to talk to him."

Constance folded her arms. "A lot of good it did me. I don't know if you've seen Derrek lately, but, well, it's fairly awful." Her arms tightened around herself, trying to remember the feel of his arms gently around her the night he'd been discovered. "He doesn't recognize me at all."

"Maybe not now," Madeline said. "But Ivory told us of the machine Derrek built. If we turn it on, and people *see* what Derrek did for them, maybe their fear will turn to understanding."

Constance raised her head. *The fears of Quixx have changed him*, Camille had said. Constance was willing now to take advice from ghosts and dreams, for it was all she had.

"Fear," she said slowly, thinking it through. "It's what makes him change. I saw it before, on the mountain. He was reliving his fears from the night of the fire on the mountain fifty years ago."

"And you managed to calm him then, didn't you?" Ivory prompted.

Constance shook her head. "It didn't work when I tried yesterday."

"But if fear has changed him," Madeline added, "then perhaps removing it — or transforming it — might change him back?"

They all looked to Leal, who hadn't yet made a contribution, as he'd been checking the windows and the door. He blinked round at them, shrugging. "It's worth a shot," and he turned away again. "But we better make up our minds. That spider trick can only work so many times, and those officers are coming back with a lot of rolled-up newspapers."

Ivory and Madeline turned back to Constance, who still stood at the threshold of her cell. She shut her eyes and tried to listen for something, anything, to push her over.

Love is stronger than fear, her memory whispered, and she nodded.

"Okay." She took one step. Then another. "It's not a guarantee. But you're right, Ivory. We have to try."

Leal flung open the door to the station and they all burst through, but when they got out to the street, Mx. Mott and a sizable force were waiting for them.

"Madeline," she said through tight-to-cracking teeth. "Get over here at *once.*"

Ivory and Madeline clasped hands, and when Ivory nodded at her, Madeline's resolve steeled.

"No, Mother," she replied. "I'm right where I belong."

Mx. Mott looked apoplectic with rage and indecision. "Very well," she said. "We'll lock them all up in the school, I think, until this is all over." She turned her stabbing glare at Leal. "As for you, I think I'll return you to Slanner, who is as useless as you are."

Ivory turned to Constance. "This is where we part ways," she said, and she shook her sister's hand. "Good luck."

Constance blinked. "What—"

But Ivory had already broken from Madeline, launching herself from the station steps and into the tight throng of Quixx's finest. The officers were ill-prepared for Ivory Ivyweather. Madeline followed suit, howling to beat heck, and while everyone scrambled, Constance dashed off towards the Farrowmarket junk shop and what awaited her in the trench across the road.

"After the blond!" she heard Mx. Mott scream, and Constance dashed and darted out of the way of reaching hands that grabbed for her, as any blue-ribbon multi-partner Fandango champion could have.

She took a corner and an officer grabbed her jacket, but she twirled her way out of it. The junk shop was in view — she zigzagged, made it across the street, and nearly slid past the platform, but leapt around so she could get a clear look at them as she stepped to her mark.

She had no time to even consider the terror nipping at her heels, so she pulled the lever on the Volunteer Star Brigade launcher, thinking only of Derrek as she took to the air, screaming.

The skirmish at the station had only lasted as long as it needed to. Victoria dragged Ivory and Madeline back to Farrowmarket, becoming more unhinged the closer they got. How could this be happening? Perhaps it was the lack of sleep catching up with her, but Victoria felt . . . odd. She rubbed her sore cheek, wondering what had been knocked loose by that brazen elder Ivyweather. She seemed to be both sleepwalking and too awake for words.

"The school," she was muttering, "Yes, the school will still be the safest place for both of you, until this is over and I decide how to deal with you."

Madeline rolled her eyes. "We'll just escape again. I am Daddy's daughter, after all. I'm tenacious."

Victoria felt her tough exterior cracking like an eggshell, imagining what Victor might say about all this. *How could you fail your daughter so utterly?* he'd say. Or perhaps he wouldn't. Victoria swallowed hard. "Please, Madeline, don't mention—"

"It's not too late to stop this," Ivory tried. "You must know, deep down, that this is wrong."

But it wasn't Ivory's voice that Victoria heard these words in; it was Victor's. *You wanted to protect our little girl,* he reminded her, as if his picture had been listening. *How is this protecting her? Protecting Quixx?*

"Quiet, *both* of you!" Victoria howled. "I can't hear myself *think*."

Her daughter's eyes were full of pity. And disappointment, still. Victoria couldn't take it any longer.

They'd made it to the square, but it was packed with spectators. Word had spread quickly about the tragedy and the coming great spectacle. Slanner's stage was nearby, too, and it was currently being commandeered as men and women in hazmat suits swarmed it and covered it in plastic sheeting.

"The exterminators," Victoria muttered, but it was not with the glee she'd had earlier. Somehow, then, it had felt unreal. Something had unwound a very important spring inside her, and everything attached to it was uncoiling, too. Now that they were here, now that she saw what it meant. Death. The death of something — someone . . .

"Please!" She looked down at Madeline, shaking her hand frantically, and all she saw was her frightened little girl. Except the thing scaring Victoria was not the monster that was about to be publicly executed. It was Victoria herself.

Victoria looked back up to the cage, which was surrounded now by troopers and handlers alike, about to open the door, cuff the poor devil, and drag it to its untimely end.

"Wait," she said, too quietly, then she scrambled to push her way to the crowd, towards a trooper, to explain with reason. Something she was only seeing now. "Wait, stop this! Right this instant!"

The troopers looked down at her, their human faces completely blocked out by soulless helmets as they shoved Victoria back. The crowd shuffled, grew louder, and panic wreathed Victoria's very steps.

For the barest moment, she did not recognize the town she loved and prized, the one she'd only ever wanted to improve. But she had made it this way, and now there was no turning back. There were so many people, and cameras, bulbs flashing, live feeds recording.

"It's too late," Victoria said, and not knowing what else to do, she fled from her daughter's pleading eyes and into the crowd.

"But this is *my stage!*" Slanner screamed, unable to stop the faceless goons from stripping all their instruments and equipment, save a few microphones and amplifiers. "I had to deal with a bunch of crybaby Slanner wannabes all day, and now this?" Slanner himself was about to become a crybaby. Why was this happening now, after everything? After all the waiting? He whirled, panicking, searching for Leal. For comfort, at first, and then, somewhere to point his rage.

"And you! You, you . . . traitor to the cause! Springing those girls, going behind my back! You—!"

"Cram it, would you?" Leal said, and Slanner stopped dead.

"What?" he croaked. And what was this? He was used to the spinning basement of the Expansive Manse, but this was far more unnerving. It was stillness. It was nothing.

"Look around you!" Leal waved. "These crowds don't care about us! They never did! And neither did you. All you cared about was fame and attention, on your own terms, so much you'd do anything for it. You'd even *kill* for it." He stalked up to Slanner and stood up to his full height, and for once, Slanner shrank away. "This is not the band any of us signed up for. I dunno about everyone else, but *I quit.*"

Slanner shook, temper entirely replaced by terror. Everything was moving, but this time he wasn't. "You . . . no. No, wait, Leal—"

"Me, too," said Sluggo, throwing down his sax. Bartek, Hatch, Vatos, and Avila followed suit, and they all filed off the stage, Leal bringing up the rear.

"Leal?" Slanner begged, all oozing charm evaporated. But he still wouldn't say he was sorry. Leal scoffed.

"Enjoy the limelight, Slanner. You earned it." And Leal left with the rest of them. Slanner himself didn't get off the stage until the hazmat-suited goons carried him off, depositing him on the sidewalk, where he crumpled and stayed for a long time.

"I didn't do it for me," he said, but for once there was no one there to listen.

Constance was not faring any better than Slanner, even though she'd landed on Derrek's spider net safely. She was still trying to get the feeling back in her extremities, and once she did, it still didn't matter. She'd heard so many sounds in the last few moments she had never heard before, and her heart was in her throat.

It was getting dark. She had no light with her, no way to navigate. And the first night they'd met Derrek, he'd warned them that things only got more dangerous on Mount Quixx when the sun set.

Which it just had.

Constance picked her way to the rock ledge that she knew was there. She could sort of make it out in the bleakness. Nearby was the ascending current. All she had to do was reach it, then another short climb, then get to the observatory. The remote had to be there. It *must*.

Or she could misstep and fall to her death, and her ghost could haunt the mountain forever along with Camille's, Klaus's, and soon, Derrek's.

"Get a hold of yourself," Constance scolded herself. "Everyone else thinks you can do this, so you might as well start believing it, too."

Talking to herself was a new tactic, but she was willing to try anything. She pressed into the rock face. One step. One more . . .

A blood-curdling howl broke the quiet, and she nearly lost her grip.

She turned her head towards the noise. The fog and the darkness only made it worse, but were there glowing lights just nearby? Fireflies? Or eyes? Perhaps it was Maurice and Hilda, and they would rescue her, as they had before.

A warm gust of air blew across her cheek and into her hair. Not air. Breath. She looked up, and there it was, a monster she had only become close and personal with once before.

Derrek had called them Arnold. She remembered all those weeks ago, their head swivelling, their spine-covered arms chopping, as they'd come down the mountain, a terrifying, hungry menace like every Quixxian had warned of.

Arnold grabbed her then, and she kicked at the mountain face, desperate to keep her footing. The knee of her trousers tore, skinning the flesh beneath, but she had other things to worry about as she was torn through trees and skimmed sharp rocks. Arnold was dragging her away, most likely to their lair.

Constance screamed, "Help me!" directing her desperation to the mountain, but there was no answer. When Arnold finally let her go, she went crashing backward into the open air.

Derrek was pressed into the back of his cage, which he'd filled with a complex tunnel web. But that didn't stop the troopers — they came in with guns that had flickering torches on the end, and when Derrek saw them, he shrank into himself and went willingly.

They bound him well but still had a time manoeuvring him where they wanted. He was enormous, after all, and they were small and fragile. He didn't want to hurt them. Not really. But he snapped and snarled as a reflex. When they brought him out into view, the crowd jeered.

He cowered, but they thought he was rearing back to strike. People gasped. His eyes darted wildly as if searching for someone, someone he didn't quite remember but who he couldn't quite forget.

All of his senses had been made maddeningly stronger, too, and he whipped his head in the direction of a scream that echoed off the mountain. No one else seemed to hear it. But he didn't turn away from the sound, because he recognized it. Deep down, somewhere, a small part of him still flickered.

Constance.

They dragged Derrek from the cage across the square, towards a stage, and he heard no more.

Constance's eyes were squeezed shut against the pain. When she opened them, it was to find herself in a place she'd never been, a place aglow with bulbs of light. No, not bulbs. Eyes. Many eyes. Red and yellow and blue. And they were all turned on her.

She was in a grove of trees so twisted and hugely overgrown that the branches twined together, and she couldn't tell where one tree ended and the next began. She sat up. Was this the other side of the mountain?

It didn't matter now, though. She was surrounded by monsters.

She shook her head. She knew better. They were simply creatures she couldn't identify. Tall things with two heads and feet like an elephant. Something that may have been a spindly crab with trailing eyes and giant tusks. Tiny chattering blobs, the size of children, with single white horns capering around her frantically.

Maurice and Hilda floated into view, with still more of their kin in the air behind them. And suddenly the crowd parted, and Arnold, the thing that had dragged her down here, came forward.

Constance may have hit her head, but she still had the presence of mind to scurry backward. The only thing behind her was hard rock. The spine of Mount Quixx. *You must ask the mountain for help*, the Bedouins had begged. So she shut her eyes, steeled her heart, and asked — but not for herself.

Please, she thought. *I need to help him.*

A great wind rose, and on it, an answering whisper. *Listen to my children, then, for you can hear them now.*

"What?" Constance squawked, and Arnold stopped dead in front of her.

Arnold did not have eyes, but they had a mouth — a mouth that opened, and closed, and issued what might have been words.

"I'm sorry?" she tried again.

"You can understand us?" Arnold asked, in a voice that was soft and not at all patient.

Constance blinked. "I— yes?"

She heard murmuring amongst the gathering, sounds that may have, before, only sounded like howls and yelps in the night. "The mountain must have intervened . . ." someone posited.

"Human," Arnold raised their voice. "You have walked this mountain many a time with the one we call Derrek. But we know he is in danger. You will tell us what you have done to him."

Constance swallowed, not having prepared herself, at all, for this tribunal. "Derrek has been building a machine. One that will rid Quixx of the comet's fog and return the sky to the townsfolk. But they think he's done something terrible, which I *know* he hasn't, and they're going to punish him for it." She peered round in the dim glow at these creatures as they exchanged confused glances. "With his life."

Maurice lifted their tentacles to cover their eyes. "We have to help him!" cried a little voice close by, which must have been Hilda's.

"How can we?" Arnold countered. "If this is true, then the humans will come after us, too. It is only a matter of time." They appraised Constance then with a snarl. "Humans are all the same."

"We're not!" she protested. "Please. I need your help. I came here to get the remote for the machine Derrek was working on, to show the town his true intentions. If I can do that, they might change their minds."

"Might," Arnold stressed. "Humans rarely change anything. They are stubborn."

"And so are you, apparently." Constance clapped her hand over her mouth, but she couldn't take the barb back.

Arnold sat back on their haunches, jerking their head towards the giant tusked crab. "Bring it forward, Agatha," they said, and when the crab came nearer, they spat out what was in their mouth on the ground between Constance and Arnold.

The remote. Constance had last seen it on the Happy Bell rooftop. He must have been carrying it, before—

"We planned on returning it to him. Now I think it is better off destroyed." With that Arnold stood and pressed a hard knuckle into the device.

"Don't!" Constance dove forward and laid her hand over Arnold's. The grove was still.

"Please," she said again. "I have to save him." She swallowed. "I *love* him."

Something let out a dove-like coo, and everyone looked up at Maurice.

"Like Camille," they said.

The monsters were easier when she was around. Less wild. Derrek himself had told her that. She looked at Arnold with renewed confidence. "Camille told me I had to ask for help. I thought she meant the mountain. But now I know what she meant. She wanted me to ask you. Ask you all. Together we can show Quixx that they have nothing to fear. We can stop all of this before it starts."

Arnold could have snapped Constance's nose off for how close their mouth was. Could have crushed her, too, for just feeling their powerful hand under hers made her think they had been carved from the mountain itself.

But Arnold stepped back, moving their hand off the remote.

"Love," they repeated.

Constance nodded. "It's stronger than fear."

It was too dark to tell, but Constance thought she saw Arnold smile. "Camille did say that often." They turned to the others. "Well? How about it? We've all wondered what that village is like for hundreds of years. We may as well find out now."

"But the risks!" a creature cried.

"We will face them together, as we always have," answered another.

And that is how Constance Ivyweather, remote control in hand, went careening down Mount Quixx in Maurice's arms, heading towards the town with an army of monsters at her back, praying she wasn't too late.

Victoria had tried to pull herself together. She couldn't go home. She'd be confronted with silence for company; Victor's judging eyes. And Madeline's, too, from their family portraits. She'd paced around the square a few times, but even though she was free, she may as well be in her own cage. The bars were her mind, closing in tighter, for the first time uncertain what the correct course was.

So by the time she climbed up the stage to the microphone, she was glad it was evening and that she couldn't see Madeline in the crowd. She felt utterly sick.

She wrung her hands, praying, suddenly, for a miracle to undo every giddy misstep she'd made up to this point.

"Ladies and gentlemen of Quixx," Victoria began. The microphone rang out, and both she and the crowd shied. In that instant, Victoria turned and caught sight of, in her periphery, the monster sharing the stage with her. Proud and tall, it did not fight its fate. It seemed resigned to it now.

The only monster here is you! Constance Ivyweather's words rang louder than the feedback from the speakers.

She lowered the microphone, looked from the crowd to the creature, and muttered, "Why don't you fight back?"

No response. She stared into those black, expressionless eyes. It seemed to see itself in her eyes, too, and cowered at what it — he, they — saw.

"Ahem." Victoria turned away, tried again, as the group of exterminators shifted from foot to foot, anxious as anyone to get this over with. "I . . . I—"

There had been so many screams today that when more of them sounded from the edge of the crowd, Victoria was quickly weary. "Oh, what is it now?" But the screams grew manifold, and she gasped and backed away from the microphone as the Brindlewatch Guard fell one by one to the quickly amassing force now in their midst.

The crowd scattered, but most had come for a show so they didn't disperse altogether. For now there were too many monsters to count in Farrowmarket Square, and leading them in the arms — tentacles? — of a huge floating mass with infinite red eyes, was Constance Ivyweather.

Victoria didn't know if she should cheer or call for more brute force, but she did neither as Constance stepped up onto the stage. The girl was shaking all over.

Victoria looked her up and down. In the huge stage lights, she was a sight — her hair was a wild golden mane, her clothes tattered and torn. Her chest heaved with determination, and her fists were clenched at her sides.

"Well?" Victoria asked, but there was no sneer. An edge of a plea, perhaps. "What are you going to do? Kiss the frog and turn him into a prince?"

Constance bit the inside of her cheek. "I'd like to prove you wrong, first," she said, and stepped up to the microphone.

Constance stared out into the crowd. She was not a person of Quixx. She was a stranger, a foreigner. It was a sleepy town with strange quirks that had nearly gotten her killed more than once. If she ever got the chance to recount every odd thing that had led her to this moment, on this stage, in a foggy valley village the world had forgotten, even she could barely believe it.

But she had to believe in something. Out in the crowd were faces she recognized. The Kadaver's Soiree. Madeline Mott, Ivory at her side, giving Constance a double thumbs-up. Slanner Dannen, who seemed like he'd had his Platinum handed to him. Leal. The constable. All the neighbours who had offered her advice and scones and warm thoughts for an odd old landlady that Constance wished, desperately, was out there amongst them now, smiling and nodding for her to go on. Maybe even hidden in the eaves were the birds of the Happy Bell, carrying Ms. Bee's memory with them.

And past the human townsfolk, she saw the monsters, the shadow of the town, now finally come to light.

But Constance was not here for the crowd. So she turned to the person that needed her most to face up to what she was afraid of. And what *he* was afraid of. She needed to be strong for both of them. Derrek regarded her dully but did not look away.

"Monsters are a funny thing," Constance said, not sure where this would take her, as she looked back out at the gathering, human and creature alike. "We think we know what they are. We hear stories of them and we learn to be afraid. But a monster can be anything — the unknown future. The things we can't see or understand. What it comes down to is fear." She glanced at Mx. Mott. "Fear makes monsters of us all, no matter our biology. I haven't been here long, but that is what Mount Quixx has taught me. Maybe . . . maybe some of you know what I mean by that."

Her words dried up then. What else could she say? But a warm comforting wind came down from the mountain, and on it drifted a melody, and she cleared her throat, eyes locked with Derrek's as she turned to him again, and she did what she had to, even though she was afraid.

She sang.

> Oh I have seen sights that are wonders, my dear.
> Sights like the stars and the sea,
> But never a sight like the one that I've seen, when I look upon you seeing me.
> Oh the stars are fine, and the mountain is clear, yet there's one thing I've always known:
> A heart that feels fear is a dark one, my dear,
> And will be when the birdies have flown.

Constance was surprised to hear that the crowd had taken up a clapping rhythm to match hers and that some voices, old and croaking, but true, were joining along at the chorus. Someone had picked up instruments — maybe even a bass — and she trusted the Kadaver's Soiree to bring her home:

> My heart, my heart, was broken, my dear, but ne'er again will I grieve.
> And when I consider the stars, my dear, what tangled webs do they weave.
> So when I come home to dark lonely peaks, to the place that I know is still mine,
> I will return, my darling, my dear, and our fears will sparkle and shine.

When the song ended, the spell still hung over the crowd, even though it was silent. But someone gasped, and Constance turned, and she let out a sob that bubbled up without warning.

Derrek was themself again, his golden eyes gleaming. They looked out on to the town, first squinting, then admiring.

"What's 'e lookin' at?" someone muttered from the crowd. And Derrek smiled.

"All of you," he replied. "I'm so happy to see you. To see Quixx."

Mx. Mott, though, was a wreck, trying desperately to mop up her mascara-streaked face. She was surprised when Madeline appeared at her side with a hanky. Madeline jerked her head, suggesting something else.

"Well . . ." Mx. Mott replied, looking helplessly at the guards holding Derrek back. "But . . . the accident, this morning . . ."

"Camille Bedouin was my mother," Derrek said, his voice clear. "I would never hurt her. And I wouldn't have become what I did if you hadn't have done what *you* did."

Mx. Mott looked out at the crowd, the cameras. Then she let sentimentality override her crumbling resolve. "Just release him, already."

The guards, though, didn't respond. It couldn't be that simple, could it?

"I could do it for you," Derrek offered, holding up both sets of hands and rattling the double handcuffs, "but I, too, adhere to order and decorum." He smiled at Constance. "Most of the time."

But after some hushed protests, the order went through, and the guards undid the bonds on his wrists and his spider legs, and everyone gave Derrek a wide berth as he approached Constance.

"So you're the hero of this romance," Derrek said, parting Constance's hair out of her face.

"We can both share the title," Constance smiled shyly, handing him the worse-for-wear remote control with its gleaming red button. "You do the honours."

Ivory had sprung onto the stage at some point during these proceedings, and she took it upon herself to grab the microphone. "Folks of all stripes and stirrings!" she boomed in a voice that rivalled Slanner Dannen's. "You came for a show, and you're about to get one. Presenting the culmination of the life's work of Professors Klaus and Derrek Bedouin — made possible with you in mind — the Marvellous Mount Quixx Wind Machine!"

And with that, Derrek pressed the button.

Of course, down below, nothing happened right away. And Ivory, Constance, and even Derrek were suddenly worried that the range on it wasn't calibrated properly . . . but just then the gauzy dark that everyone in Quixx had adjusted to or grown up in was, miraculously, parting. And no small wonder; Derrek and Ivory had installed *four* new airfields to rival the first, and so the mountain coverage was total, creating a gust that acted like a broom. Even though it was the dead of night, the fog lifted at last, and for the first time in too many years to count, the people of Quixx looked up and saw the stars.

"Beautiful," someone exclaimed. It was Mx. Mott.

"Wait . . ." said someone else in the crowd. "They're—"

"Falling?" Leal answered.

"Quick, make a wish!"

Derrek's eyes were enormous. "Oh. Oh no."

The stars *were* falling — or, at least, *something* was. And it was hurtling towards them at too incredible a speed.

"Oh," Constance muttered, grabbing Derrek's hand. "There was so much going on that I—"

Derrek's eyes were darting across the sky, as if they were reading some hidden message in the heavens.

"This is how the sky looked the night when . . . when—"

"Incoming!" Ivory cried, and the crowd scattered as the sky fell on their heads.

13

A METEORIC BRIDGE TO THE
BLESSED UNKNOWN

Fifty years ago, the first asteroid, meteorite, comet-tail remnant — whatever it was — struck the mountain. This first one had just skated by, leaving a scar on the mountain. But now, this second time, it was a wrecking ball. They all watched it happen — as if the mountain itself had always been there to shield them from this, and maybe the fog had been sent to get the people out of the town to save them, something collided with the peak and sheared it clean off into oblivion.

Everyone took cover together — humans and monsters both.

"It's a good thing you brought all the other creatures into town," Derrek told Constance from their own hiding place. "It's like the mountain was protecting us all along."

But Constance's hands were clutching her throat. "Oh, Derrek," she moaned. "The observatory." For the last meteorite crashed into the place where surely the observatory had been. Which meant that the next thing to come down would be the wind machine network.

All Derrek could do was grimace and try to be a good sport. "We can always rebuild." He clutched Constance closer. "I have a terrible feeling Klaus saw this coming, too—"

"He did!" Constance cried over the screams of the fleeing Quixxians. "I'm sorry, Derrek. He didn't want you to give Quixx back its stars. He wanted you to save Quixx *from* the stars. It happened fifty years ago, and now—"

Ivory was not cowering like everyone else, of course, but watching with binoculars from the stage above them. "A recurring close-shave meteor shower!" For now the raining debris was expanding the trench, scorching it bright red in the dark. Houses, all likely empty for the crowd in Farrowmarket, fell into the expanding chasm. The Happy Bell, nearly on the chasm's edge, shivered but held. The world shook as half the mountain came down before them.

After the worst of the tremors subsided, all went still. "Is it over?" Constance asked, looking up at Ivory, who was slowly tipping backward with her binoculars.

"Criminy," Ivory peeped.

Then she dove onto the stage and grabbed the microphone. "Everybody! Duck and hold on!"

But they'd all seen it coming — one last rogue boulder streaking past the first two that punched through Mount Quixx. And it was heading straight for town.

The streets were chaos as people tried to make for better cover. Derrek held Constance close and snatched up Ivory, galloping away at top speed, but he stumbled and they all went flying when the meteor made impact just beyond the hill behind them.

"Nooooo!"

Constance's ears were ringing, but she could hear the painful howl over even the earthly percussion, past the ashes and wailing crowd. The meteor had missed the town, at least, but it had spread its flaming tail in its wake. Debris had landed on a few roofs and in the street. Fires sprang up, and townsfolk sprang into action to put them out.

But one huge flaming rock had torn right through the roof of the Expansive Manse, sending it up in flames almost instantly.

That didn't stop Slanner, still howling, from running right for it.

"What is he doing?" Ivory shouted when she scrambled to her feet, Derrek joining her and Constance in the cobblestone road.

They watched as a tall and gangly figure broke from the crowd and streaked after him.

"Dammit, Leal!" Ivory cried, and she started towards the hill herself. "C'mon! We have to help them!"

Derrek and Constance sprinted ahead. A bell was ringing somewhere; the Quixx Fire Brigade was mobilizing.

They made it to the bottom of the hill below the Expansive Manse, but a huge flare went up just as Leal disappeared inside.

"Ivory, no!" Constance grabbed her sister, pulling her back. "It's too dangerous!"

They turned towards the sound of the ringing bell. The fire brigade was too far away, trying to fight more immediate blazes in its path. "We have to do *something*," Ivory pleaded.

Derrek flashed and past them before Constance could stop him, too. This time it was Ivory holding Constance back.

Derrek leapt and spun mid-air, sending out huge gobs of webbing onto the immediate flames within his reach. Then he tucked and rolled his enormous body through a window he'd blasted a path into, and was gone.

Constance was the one howling now, holding on to Ivory for dear life. Derrek's greatest fear was fire, and no amount of well-intentioned singing could save him now.

The whole town was holding its collective breath. Monsters and townsfolk had come with water and handfuls of earth, creating a great chain and trying to extinguish the flames. Constance saw Maurice snatching buckets from outstretched human hands and dumping them on the blazing house, but it was no use. Suddenly the front of the Manse collapsed, and Maurice barely made it away in time.

Please! Constance begged anyone who would listen. Given the blow it had just taken, it was unlikely the mountain could do anything more for them now.

Then suddenly, improbably, the collapsing doorway rose up, seemingly bolstered by something it had just spat out. Then, from the tiny corridor came a tall crooked figure, carrying a smaller one in his arms, and behind them a much larger figure on skittering legs, which scooped up the other two and made a run for it just as the rest of the house collapsed.

Derrek came to a halt at the bottom of the hill, coughing and shaking. He deposited Leal, a soot-stained mess who, in turn, held tight to another slightly charred man whose red zoot suit had seen better days.

"C'mon, Slanner." Leal shook him, clapping his cheeks and trying to rouse him. "You stubborn idiot, you can't just go dying without me!"

Desperate, Leal pinched Slanner in the ribs, under the arms, and suddenly he spluttered to life, squirming.

"Agh, all right, geez! My cred!" Slanner rolled over, coughing his guts out, but he was alive.

Derrek patted Leal on the back. He looked up at Derrek with grateful, glassy eyes. "Thank you."

"Oh," Derrek said, rubbing his neck. "Of course." Then he got to his eight shaking feet, barely composing himself before Constance threw herself into his four arms.

"You weird ridiculous *scientist*," she cried over him, holding tight to his neck with her feet dangling off the ground. "I swear my hair is going white."

"It would suit you." Derrek grinned. "Sorry if I frightened you. Old habits." And he squeezed her ribs playfully, which she allowed without repercussions.

Meanwhile, on the ground, Leal was scolding Slanner in the same manner.

"What the Helena were you thinking?" he practically shouted in Slanner's face, which was turned aside, ashamed.

"I was . . . I was trying to get the Platinum . . ." he said in a voice that didn't sound at all like the brazen one everyone was used to hearing; instead, it was meek and small and afraid.

Leal jerked in surprise, remembering that he'd given it to Ivory to use as a glorified lockpick, but Slanner had no idea about that. Instead he asked, "But why?"

"I just wanted . . . I needed to have some proof. That the band that you and I had built together was real. And still worth something." Slanner's eyes were swimming with tears when he met Leal's. "Since you're leaving me and all."

Leal's hands on Slanner's shoulders were shaking. "You are impressively, lovingly stupid," he said. "I'm not leaving *you*."

Slanner blinked. "But I . . . I messed everything up. I'm no good for anyone. I couldn't even buy that stupid boarding house for you—"

"I thought *you* were gonna leave *me*!" Then, comprehending another surprise that was a punch to the gut, "Wait. *That's* why you wanted to buy the Happy Bell? For me?"

"Well!" Slanner threw up his arms. "I figured that, like, it was time to move on, maybe, even if it was just down the street! Start a new kinda life. You know. Maybe a normal one?" The flush on Slanner's face had nothing to do with the fire. "I couldn't think beyond Quixx. Because you're Quixx, to me. I'm sorry I held you back."

"So incredibly, awfully, *majestically* stupid," Leal said, and he grasped Slanner by the face and kissed him.

"Ohhh," Constance and Ivory said in unison. But they decided it was best to turn away and let the boys have their moment.

It was a long night. Mountain creatures worked shoulder to shoulder with the Quixx Fire Brigade, the Brindlewatch Guard, and Constable Derraugh's police force to bring some semblance of order back to town by the time the sun had risen. The fire damage had been minimal compared to that from the asteroids that had hit the mountain, but it was managed now — save for the Manse, of course, which was just a pile of smoking ash. Damocles Dannen, still on the road buying replacement parts for the marvel that was no longer there, would have quite a surprise to come home to, once he did.

There were more than enough rooms at the Happy Bell for the Kadaver's Soiree, though, to rest in while they recovered. It appeared that Derrek was as close as anyone got to next of kin when it came to Camille Bedouin "Bougainvillea." So he told them to make themselves at home, and that was that.

The mountain creatures, too, seemed to be a bit dazed and dispossessed. Everything looked different in the dawn: the falling stars had taken out a chunk of the mountain, leaving a perfect crescent like a chomped-off bit of melon, but part of the wind machine was still functioning — no one knew for how long — and the fog stayed at bay.

But the world had seen into Quixx already. The cameras had been rolling throughout the entire ordeal — the revelation of Derrek's work, the meteor shower, the daring rescue. Constance beamed from a weary distance across Farrowmarket Square — which had become recovery ground zero for the town and its sudden influx of curiosity seekers — watching Derrek surrounded by all the visiting scholars, asking him probing questions about all his engineering and astronomical work over the past fifty years.

Constance watched as Mx. Mott approached, looking sheepish with Madeline at her side. Madeline promptly ran off. The schoolmistress took Derrek aside, and they spoke openly. There was no animosity there — simply two reasonable people trying to make and accept amends.

Ivory joined Constance, passing her a paper cup of what she thought was tea, but was actually something much stronger. Constance sputtered. "Where did you get this?"

"Derraugh's handing them out. He seems to have forgotten I'm only fourteen." Ivory took hers in one shot, and was, of course, not fazed at all. "What a night."

Constance let out every breath she'd been holding throughout it all. "Everything is going to change."

Ivory nodded. "It had to eventually."

More and more cars were arriving as the morning went on. Constance went on handing out blankets and tea and helping where she could, putting her organized mind to work. But she couldn't help feeling that familiar buzz of worry in her chest, even though it was technically over.

Derrek, too, was busy, speaking with the mountain creatures, trying to find a resolution among them. They couldn't go back to the mountain just yet; Maurice had gone on reconnaissance, and many of their homes had been damaged.

So they'd have to be billeted in Quixx, and he'd been liaising with Mx. Mott to set them up in the vacant school, for now, until a more permanent solution could be reached.

Constance didn't want to admit it, but she and Derrek had been avoiding one another.

Ivory had gone back to the Happy Bell with the rest of the Kadaver's Soirée to try to get some sleep, on Constance's insistence. But now, she needed to get away from the crowd, just for a moment to herself. So after another hour, she, too, went to the only place she could rightly consider home, now that the mountain was closed off.

She went inside the Happy Bell and shut the heavy doors, pressing herself against it as she had after she'd seen Derrek in his cage. What was she still so afraid of, even now? When she went into the foyer, the room was a scatter of fluttering wings, all led, she assumed, by one little bullfinch trying to get the place in order for the sudden pile of guests prevailing upon his patience.

Constance stopped when she saw the figure standing on the staircase landing, considering the painting that hung there.

"She would get up on that ladder, there," Constance said, indicating the stepladder on Derrek's left side, "and touch the face, to try to see it with her hands. When her eyesight started going. That's why it's so faded, I think."

Derrek just nodded, his hands clasped behind him. He was wearing a jumper, slightly too big for him, and with only two arms. Constance was sure some well-meaning Quixxian had given it to him, and that he hadn't hesitated to put it on.

"They loved each other dearly," Derrek said, still staring upwards.

"I know," Constance said, and that made Derrek turn to face her, quizzical. "They visited me in a dream, the night she . . ."

Constance looked down at her beyond-repair borrowed tennis shoes. "They loved you, most of all."

Derrek's mouth puckered, but he tried to smile for all that. "I'm glad, at least, that they're together now. Causing mischief somewhere beyond."

"In the stars, most likely." Constance moved towards the solarium, which was quiet and empty. She wanted to take their conversation away from where the other guests, asleep or otherwise, might hear them. Derrek followed and joined her at the bright windows, filled now with miraculous sunlight.

He reached for her hand, but pulled away. "I'm ashamed," he said, "of what happened between us when you came to me. In the cage."

Constance looked up at him. "I'm ashamed, too. We were both very afraid. You weren't the only one who was changed by it."

Derrek risked an upturned corner of his mouth. "I hear you gave Mx. Mott quite a smack."

Constance did not smile. "Violence is never funny." She looked back out the window, biting her lip as she recalled Mx. Mott pulling Constance into a stiff, silent, but meaningful embrace, before stalking off to bark orders about organizing the school. Constance huffed. "I'm just glad our argument forced us both to do the right thing. Silver linings."

She let her hand rest at her side, then felt a finger curl around her pinky, pulling on it gently.

"Constance."

They stood side by side in the sunlight of a new day, connected tenderly by a silken thread of trust.

"You are the only fixed star I'll ever need to follow," he said. "And wherever your light goes, I'd like to follow. I know I would be lost without it."

Constance felt her chest expand. "Derrek—"

They both started at the sound of car doors slamming, of hurried footsteps coming up the porch. Of an insistent knock on the heavy wooden doors.

Both Constance and Derrek pressed their faces into the window, trying to see the street beyond. She didn't recognize the car, but the licence plate read IVYWTHR.

"Oh no."

Constance poked her head out the door. She never imagined she'd see the sight of her parents standing on the porch of the Happy Bell, staring back at her, but there they were. She'd almost entirely forgotten about them.

Constance did not blink. "Mother. Father."

They looked her up and down, probably equally unsure who it was, exactly, standing before them in torn trousers, no jacket, her hair a tangled mess, and probably more than one bruise or scrape Constance hadn't accounted for. After all, she hadn't seen a mirror in days.

But it was her father who started forward, hugging her gruffly. That was even more shocking than their presence.

"We've been watching the whole thing from home," her mother interrupted with a *hem hem*. "Edward thought it was a hoax, of course. Many people did. But then, there you were, singing!"

Constance's tone was dry. "I'm sure you thought that was a hoax as well."

Her mother, Constance's spitting image save for her fur coat, red dress, and turban-style hat wrapped around dark curls, adjusted herself. "This has all been a very odd week," she said, looking like she'd eaten a soiled pear. "We've come to collect you. Where is Ivory?"

Constance didn't move. "Collect us?"

"Of course," her father said, as if it was the most obvious thing in the world. "Your life isn't here in this backwater nuthouse we've all seen on the telly. It's in Ferren City, among the civilized."

Constance narrowed her eyes, that strange mixture of anger and giddiness rising. "The same civilized people who descended on this town to murder what was very quickly proven to be an innocent creature, yes?"

Her mother was idly playing with the large pearl necklace at her throat. "Well . . . we don't know anything about *that*—"

"What else don't you know?" Constance pressed, folding her arms. "How long did it take you to even remember you'd *sent* us here at all? Before or after the news reports? Or were you both too busy gallivanting about your narrowminded circles of friends and business associates to recall you had daughters in the first place?"

Her father's moustache fell and his eyebrows shot high above his violet eyes. "Constance Aberdeen Ivyweather—"

"Oh spare me the use of all my ridiculous names, Father; you don't get points for reciting them." Constance was exhausted, famished, and tired of being worried about nothing. "I have a better notion. You two get back in your car, drive back to Ferren City, and go on enjoying yourselves. Ivory and I are quite capable of handling things on our own right here, thank you kindly."

Her mother, most of all, seemed like she was going to burst more than one seam. "But what about your future! Everything we worked so hard to give you, to plan for! You're going to throw it all away for — for what? Some hideous monster and a town about to fall back into obscurity?"

Constance moved towards her mother and planted her hands firmly on her shoulders. She made sure to look her square in the eye. "We are grateful for everything you gave us, Mother. It has made us into what we are today." Even though Constance's mouth smiled, her eyes were fierce. "But you'd do well to remember that we were happy, once, in a town not unlike Quixx, by the beach where you used to tell me stories about mermaids. Before all the money and social climbing took precedence over your own children's dreams and fears." Then she steered the stunned woman down the stairs and back to their shiny car. "You can think more on what I said on the drive home. We'll write to you soon."

As if she'd been slipped a paralytic, Constance's mother allowed her to tuck her safely into her seat and shut the door. She met her father on the driver's side.

"We came because we were worried, you know," he said. "We did think the worst."

"The worst came and went," Constance found herself saying. "That I'm still standing surprises me more than it does you, I'm sure."

"So." He patted her on the shoulder. "You have changed your mind, then. Probably for the best. Do you know what you're going to do with your life, at least?"

Constance looked back up at the Happy Bell, towards the solarium windows where Derrek waved awkwardly at her father, with his bug-eyed expression. She gently guided him, too, into his seat. She shut the door behind him.

"Not at all," she answered cheerily through his rolled-down window. "But at least I'm not alone in that."

And she watched her parents drive back to Ferren City without her, as she stood on that cobblestone road between the boarding house and the trench to the mountain that had changed everything. And for today, that was enough.

EPILOGUE

The Quixx More-Than Quarterly News

A Special Feature on the First Semester of Quixx County University

Editor: Max Avila

Our fair town has certainly seen its fair share of fair weather these past two years since the sky itself fell on everything we knew. Back then it was a simpler time, before the creatures now known as Camillites took up residence amongst us — though by now, of course, we've all grown quite accustomed to each other, as if it's always been this way.

A sleepy hamlet of a hundred or more years and just as many people, Quixx needed a reawakening, and we got it in spades with arachnastronomer Derrek Bedouin, who not only cleared Quixx's perpetual foggy cough, but taught us more about ourselves than we care to admit. His first program, approved by the mayor's office, to install a windmill on every home, has been fully implemented as of this spring, just in time to see the flock of new students grace the freshly minted halls of Quixx County University, a sorely needed institution for the small towns in the surrounding area to partake in higher education, thanks to a partnership between Bedouin and Victoria Mott, recently of Cardinal Quixx Hall.

A shake-up in that family, too, saw the return of Captain Mott, decorated war pilot, just in time to bid their only daughter adieu as she went off with girlfriend and fellow scholar Ivory Ivyweather to take their own advanced studies abroad.

Change seems to be in every corner we turn here in Quixx, and believe you me, we have been gobbling it up every chance we get. The Bedouin Grand Observatory on the new promontory of Klaus Peak has been unveiled, so many of Brindlewatch's brightest minds are on hand this weekend for its prestigious ribbon-cutting. Watch your language in all those fancy new cafes and pubs our Camillite friends are running with aplomb — it's best behaviour on this new day, for the world is watching Quixx, as usual, with bated breath.

Constance folded the newspaper, shaking her head as she rose from her morning tea. Avila had always been so quiet, but he really did have a way with words.

She passed a mirror in the hall on the way out the door, adjusting her hair and the fashionable bow at her throat. She had promised to meet Derrek bright and early, to calm any pre-ceremony nerves. For both of them.

Some things never changed.

"Thank you, Mathias." Constance smiled as the crow passed her the purple scarf, which she fixed over her hair. As she passed the new parlour, she said hello to Dr. Garnet, the physicist all the way from Kembra who had let his room the week prior to discuss new research with Derrek.

The Happy Bell's heavy expansion and repair was owed to a generous donation from Edward and Estella Ivyweather (on gentle insistence), and it had gone over well. Isolde, the Camillite with the single bright shining gem in the centre of her head, continued chatting mildly with her snake-tailed daughter Sable, after complimenting Constance on the new wallpaper with one mouth, while daintily tucking into a tart into the second.

Constance left the Happy Bell and wandered down the road to Farrowmarket, to what had once been the junk shop but was now the Quixx Historical Society, run by a representational board of Quixxians (including the ever-dramatic, triplet-mothering Letitia Cord) and equally mouthy mountainfolk, who were determined to get the story right since many more people than expected had been asking. Constance waved as she caught sight of Slanner and Leal, back in town for the festivities, too, all the way from Oiros City, where it turned out Leal "knew a few guys" after all. They didn't stop to visit with Constance, though, since they'd been accosted by a group of young swooning fangirls demanding autographs.

Constance stopped by the Volunteer Star Brigade launcher, patting the rusted levers, the machine long since decommissioned. It was an act of nostalgia more than anything, and another old good luck trick to keep her anxiety down. It still flared up; that would probably never go away. But she had done many things as bravely as possible these past two years. And she would have to keep doing them — even if it meant doing them while afraid.

Instead, she continued down the road, past the market, to the bridge that had since been built to take people safely to and from the mountain. A much better idea than a basket-and-pulley or a haphazard daredevil launcher. Not as thrilling, but practical. Students in white coats milled in groups near the bridge, likely waiting for the ceremony. The air was kinetic with excitement, and Constance smiled and waved back at them.

But there were some things that never got old — like the air current Constance stepped into when she got off the bridge, whooping as she pushed her skirts down and ascended. Or the series of elevators Ivory and Derrek had built before her tearful departure to the other side of the split continent, finally ready to seize the adventures she'd planned so meticulously. At least she had Madeline at her side. Those two would conquer the world.

The lift came to a stop, and Constance stepped out onto the quarried stone pathway to the new observatory. It was a shame the old one was destroyed; a few trinkets had been saved during the great clean-up that seemed to take eons, but it would never be the same. Constance tried to imagine how she'd felt her first night there, terrified and unsure of the creature that had saved her life. The person she was then was miles away from who she was now.

She let herself in, calling out, "Hello?"

It was stark white and all windows, clean and crisp (so long as Constance came up to tidy every now and again), but she seemed alone. She approached the brand new viewing deck. Derrek had received quite a lot of help, and grant money, to build it using the latest technology and devices. There had been many new celestial phenomena lately — and a lakebed sample from Knockum still left Derrek and his colleagues baffled . . . but best to focus on today.

Once they cut the ribbon, anyone could come here and study the stars. Just as Klaus Bedouin had always wanted.

The ribbon itself, the colour of fresh bougainvilleas, was strung across the room. Constance ran her hand over it thoughtfully. Then she turned around, letting out a gasp of surprise as she nearly tripped over Derrek, who snatched her up and spun her around straight away, laughing.

"Now, miss," he said, all serious aplomb, "who let you in here before the ceremony?"

She grinned. "A world famous arachnastronomer who shall remain nameless left the door open. *Again*."

"Ah," said he, "then I suppose you can stay."

They walked hand in hand to the walls of glass overlooking absolutely everything, unhindered by fog or hesitation or fear. They could see well to the bridge below them filling with people who would soon be filling this very room, with every curiosity it offered. *There were old paths, old ways*, the mountain had said. But here was a brand new one, walked by many now, and many more to come.

"I sometimes wonder," Constance said, "if this is what the mountain meant to happen, for all its whisperings."

Derrek glanced down at her, his eyes brimming with deep affection, as if he were seeing her for the first time all over again. "No one can say, that's for certain. But whatever it meant, I'm glad we're here together, on the bridge to the blessed unknown, both of us without a clue."

Constance smiled as he brought one hand around her waist, drawing her close, another squeezing her shoulder. He asked, "Does the mountain whisper to you anymore?"

"No," Constance answered. But she didn't need it to. It had said its piece. It was their turn to speak theirs.

ACKNOWLEDGEMENTS

Time is a funny thing. I wrote Quixx right after *The Lake and the Library* (high school!) then abandoned it, then finished the final draft in 2018. It's a story that's been on quite the ride (and it's only just begun!), which means that along the ten-year path there are many people to thank.

My editors at ECW, Jen Hale and Jen Albert; this book has once again come leaps and bounds with your helpful insight and guidance. And patience. And open-mindedness. And I always appreciated the "lols" in the margins.

My husband, Peter, a.k.a. Dr. Hubs, who read the long-ago-embarrassing-first-100-pages-of-Quixx and, bless his heart, praised it. This was during our courtship phase where he was very excited in general, bless him. But thank you anyway, Bear. You're always my first champion and chief consoler and no matter what, you always believe in my stories.

To my readers! Gosh, you're really the big reason I keep writing. I love meeting you all at conventions and events and reading your reviews. I hope this story fills your heart as much as spending time with you does mine.

And, finally, to Wes. What will you think when you can finally read this book (which you can't for another ten years, probably)? Just know that Mummy loves you very much, and I'm so grateful for how much time you let me stare into the distance while I push you on the swing; it's vital to my developmental process.

S.M. Beiko is a Winnipeg-based fantasy author and an award-winning graphic novelist. Her work includes *The Lake and the Library*, the Realms of Ancient trilogy, and the webcomic *Krampus Is My Boyfriend!* Beiko won the 2020 Best Graphic Novel Aurora Award and was nominated for the 2020 Joe Shuster Award.

This book is also available as a Global Certified Accessible™ (GCA) ebook. ECW Press's ebooks are screen reader friendly and are built to meet the needs of those who are unable to read standard print due to blindness, low vision, dyslexia or a physical disability.

Get the ebook free!*
*proof of purchase required

At ECW Press, we want you to enjoy our books in whatever format you like. If you've bought a print copy, just send an email to ebook@ecwpress.com and include:

- the book title
- the name of the store where you purchased it
- a screenshot or picture of your order/receipt number and your name
- your preference of file type: PDF (for desktop reading), ePub (for a phone/tablet, Kobo, or Nook), mobi (for Kindle)

A real person will respond to your email with your ebook attached. Please note this offer is only for copies bought for personal use and does not apply to school or library copies.

Thank you for supporting an independently owned Canadian publisher with your purchase!